I REALLY NEED
A BETTER CAREER PLAN...

...That's when the screaming started.

I will admit to a certain amount of *schadenfreude* there, as much as I was capable of while still chained to an altar. But watching a bunch of people who until five seconds before had thought of themselves as the black-clad army of the apocalypse start screaming like terrified kids and flinging themselves under pews to hide is *hilarious*.

PRAISE FOR MR BLANK

"To read Justin Robinson's *Mr Blank* is like following some self-deprecating, white rabbit into a sprawling, L.A. noir wonderland on a 100-MPH, nerd culture-fueled rollick."

—*Fanboy Comics*

FILL IN THE _____:

Mr. Blank

Get Blank

OTHER CANDLEMARK & GLEAM BOOKS BY JUSTIN ROBINSON:

City of Devils

GET BLANK

JUSTIN ROBINSON

Candlemark & Gleam

First edition published 2014.

For information, address
Candlemark & Gleam LLC,
104 Morgan Street, Bennington, VT 05201
info@candlemarkandgleam.com

Library of Congress Cataloging-in-Publication Data
In Progress

ISBN: 978-1-936460-57-1
eBook ISBN: 978-1-936460-58-8

Cover art and design by Kate Sullivan

Book design and composition by Kate Sullivan
Typeface: Droid Serif

Editor: Kate Sullivan

www.candlemarkandgleam.com

For Lauri,
you are pot roast

I'M RETIRED.

Not sure how many times I have to say that. And it's not like I'm saying it to anyone else. Who would even believe me? At my age, there's no way I'm rich enough to retire unless I'm some kind of internet billionaire. I'm not. I've checked. And there's the fact that I still have a job, actually, just not the completely insane plethora of jobs I used to have. Only a few people know about that, and they know all about the retirement thing, too. So really, I shouldn't have to keep saying it. But there it is, all part of the internal monologue, delivered in a weary fisherman's cadence like so much Morgan Freeman narration. It plays in my mind every time something weird comes a-knocking at my door.

So, pretty much every other day.

I always thought my old life was all my fault. Like if I'd never answered that ad on Craigslist asking for security guards, I might have a normal life. I wouldn't know all the things I know or have seen all the things I've seen. I'd live one of those lives of quiet desperation I've heard such good things about. I'd be married to a hot woman who hated me,

I'd have two kids who hated me, and I'd have a dog who... well, he wouldn't hate me, but he'd suspect, somewhere in the back of his canine cranium, that he could do a little better. I'd work in an office, I'd have high cholesterol, and I could die in a workplace shooting. You know, the American Dream.

Nope. Turns out I have a giant "kick me" sign on my back only legible to the homicidal, desperate, and whatever Cosmic Tricksters are manifesting themselves these days as digital deities. They can read it—hell, they can sniff it out for miles and miles—and they come to me like I'm the only Maglite blazing in an endless field of moths.

Oh, god. Why did I have to say moths? Okay, I'll get to that, too.

I left town. Took to the roads. Pulled up stakes and cut all ties. I got the fuck out while the getting was more or less good. And it hasn't helped. It's like anyone who has an insurance scam on their minds, lost a piece of Templar treasure, or just had a good old-fashioned dimensional rift manifest in their backyard somehow finds me and wants to hire me to be a fall guy/track down the gold falcon/ask those tentacled abominations to keep it down because some people have work in the morning. It's like the Collective Unconscious knows—and yeah, not only is that a real thing, it's one of the more powerful Communist groups out there—where I am, what I'm doing, and I'm the only one who can help.

When I made a break for it, I thought the groups I'd stabbed in the back most dramatically would come looking for some payback. I could at least plan for a revenge scenario. I knew my Rogue's Gallery. I had their numbers. I was more or less ready for one of them to say howdy. But no, it couldn't possibly be something that straightforward. There were entirely new faces trying to draw me into some byzantine plot that no one really understands.

But it's like I said. I'm retired.

You misplaced the Koh-i-Noor Diamond? That's your problem, and I will not find it for ten percent of the market price or its equivalent in lead. You need someone to ambush your husband on his way home from work and make it look like an accident? I don't care how that anklet looks on you, find a different patsy. Oh, your insurance pays double if you get eaten by an orca while on fire? I will not help you make that happen. You got a rogue Merovingian who needs drying out? I've got an ass that needs kissing.

It's like I'm the Make a Wish Foundation for sociopaths.

That's why I moved away, goddamn it. That's my I left my city behind. Get a little peace and quiet. Stop dealing with the insanity of the true masters of the world. Unplug from the Information Underground. Stop with the errands, stop being an accessory to terrible things, stop helping horrible people run the world from the shadows. Live a life I could live with.

I tried. I really did. But the universe wasn't done with me. Take last Tuesday. Please. (Sorry, but Tuesday really was a lousy day.) The funny—not funny ha ha, more funny uh oh, as the man said—thing about it, was I could pick almost any day. Every other day I was getting propositioned. I was like a hooker whose only clientele consisted of the criminally insane. I was at the local train station—all right, yeah, first mistake, you don't hang out in a train station unless you want to get involved in a shootout, a fatal misunderstanding, or some light espionage. But there's this taco stand right outside, and they do their carne asada Baja style, by which I mean it tastes like everything has been soaked in lime, and if I don't eat there once a week, I begin to question the entire purpose of my existence. So I'm sitting on one of the benches in this tiled Spanish station, eating tacos, and listening to the tap-tap-tapping of the juice falling into the butcher paper on my lap and thinking that this was the sort of situation when someone would proclaim, "This is the life."

Which, of course, is right when the man with the drooping eye and slouching fedora slid onto the bench next to me. He was dressed like a colorized photo of Jay Gatsby's creepy uncle. The pencil-thin mustache alone would have prevented him from coming within a hundred yards of a school. The suit looked brand new, even though it hadn't been in style since booze was illegal. He dropped a broken-in paper sack, really more wrinkle than bag at that point, the kind that has never once contained something wholesome, onto the bench beside us.

"Deliver it to the Pea Soup Anderson's in Solvang. Payment is..."

"Nope," I said.

"Huh?"

"You clearly think I'm going to take that bag to someone. Why? Did you hear that your contact would be wearing black Chuck Taylors and dripping taco juice all over the place?"

"Um... well..."

"Yeah, right. Not me. Now fuck off."

"Look here, friend, I've..."

"...got a gun? That's adorable. I'm betting whoever needs what's in that bag—and notice how I've not asked what's in there, thus demonstrating the depths of my not-giving-a-fuck?—really wants it. Enough to hire a guy who looks like he molested Al Capone to deliver it to a train station on the last stop before the Central Coast. Well, if you give it to me, I'm caught in a whole mistaken identity plot, I'll find your body with a bullet to the head right at the end of the second act—you know, to show me how deep I'm in it—and I'll have to come up with some kind of eleventh-hour save that puts the bad guys in prison and keeps my blood on the inside of my skin. Well, I'm not interested. Sounds like fun and all, but no thanks. I'm going to eat my taco, and then I'm getting back to work."

"Are you..."

"Yeah, I'm sure." I took a bite of taco. "Also, there's a guy at the other side of the terminal who kind of looks like me if you squint really hard and maybe suffer from fetal alcohol syndrome. And he's waving at you."

I pointed. The other guy held out his arms with a semi-panicked, "What the hell, man?" look on his face. The guy with the mustache picked up the bag.

"If you tell anyone about this..."

"You think I want it getting out that I look like that guy?"

Pencil-Thin Mustache left me alone after that, and I went back to work, and tried not to think about whatever illicit rendezvous had gone down at lunch.

Or take the very next day when I was trying close up shop, when a woman—the kind who might as well be wearing a t-shirt proclaiming GENTLEMEN LOCK UP YOUR PENISES—slithered into my store with the kind of skill it usually takes several years of training in a monastery with a ninja master to accomplish. I swear to god, she got through a closed door. She was some kind of rockabilly goddess, with a halter top showing off an uneasy detente between cleavage and tattoos. She smelled like cinnamon, and wanted me to be damn sure of that fact as she leaned to tickle my ears with her breath.

"Do you know about the Hentai Am?" she whispered.

Of course I did. The pornographic anime in which the chief animator supposedly attained perfect enlightenment halfway through and now had the habit of reducing unsuspecting masturbators to gibbering madness.

"Never heard of it."

"It's in town... and all I need is... help obtaining it." She somehow discovered a way to close even more distance with me. If she got any closer, we were going to discover some new kind of fusion bomb fueled entirely by hormonal flesh and whispered entendres.

"You've got the wrong guy, lady. I'm closed."

"I'm not."

"Yeah, I'm getting that, and the last person who touched me like that was testing for a hernia."

She blinked. "What?"

"Shop's closed, sister. Now get the hell out before I have you busted for trespassing."

She slapped me, but I don't think her heart was really in it.

Two days later, right before the Cosmic Trickster decided to really wind up and punt my crotch into orbit, I had another one. It was a Friday evening and I was getting ready for my girlfriend to arrive. I was at the local market trying to decide on wines, which mostly consisted of me squinting at the labels and pretending I knew what they meant. "The Safety Dance" echoed over the PA while outside the rain clattered off cars and pavement. Now, I've got nothing against Men Without Hats and I've worked for their one-world agenda in the past, but it did cut into the ambience of the rainstorm.

Anyway, I reached into a gap between bottles, positive I was going to bring out something with a label that said, "Perfect Romantic Wine; Not Too Heavy or Pretentious; And Tell Me All About Your Day." Instead I got a dusty bottle in one of those woven casks with a melted candle cork. It looked like the kind of thing Kiefer Sutherland would have given me to drink in an abandoned hotel while mulleted vampires girlishly skipped around me. While I was staring at it and wondering how the thing had found its way into a Vons, a grinding sound came from the shelves and they retracted to reveal a staircase down.

The aisle was empty. Just this yawning darkness, barely

lit with guttering candles. Chanting sounds snaked up to me. The smells were just as culty, and I swear I could see cloaked and hooded figures moving through the firelight.

I put the wine back and picked up a local merlot.

Like I said, retired. I wasn't going to get involved in a goddamn thing, no matter how much the universe seemed to want me to. I was going to hunker down and live a life I could describe to someone without a security clearance. But no. The Cosmic Trickster had other ideas.

God, he's a dick.

It started the very next Tuesday, right as I was in the middle delivering of a civics lecture.

"There are actually four branches of government," I said from my position on the step stool where I was alphabetizing the witchcraft section of my bookstore. "The executive, the legislative, the judicial, and the prejudicial."

"Are you certain?" Khaali asked, her Somali accent making her sound so earnest.

"Only four they're going to test you on," I said. "The legislative makes the laws, the executive enacts the laws, the judicial interprets the laws, and the prejudicial ignores the laws. It's a delicate system." I peered at the shelf. "Are we out of the *De Vermis Mysteriis* again?"

Khaali leafed through her textbook. "I sold one to a man the other day."

Couldn't keep that one on the shelves. If I didn't know better, I'd think there was a whole coven of witches in the area, but that was silly. They were out near Bakersfield. Good thing, too, since my store had the largest occult, history, and occult history section in the continental United States, not including Alaska (thanks a lot, Books, Sects, and Secret Masters of Anchorage).

"Prejudicial?" she asked again.

"Arguably the most important branch."

Khaali looked up from her citizenship exam like I was the crazy one here. "I don't think that's right," she said.

"What do you mean?"

"There's no mention of a prejudicial branch anywhere." She paged through her book as though to check one last time, just to be certain.

"They're not going to come right out and say it. Defeats the whole purpose."

She shook her head. "All right. What does the Constitution do?"

"Uh... let's see. Defines the government and our basic rights as Americans. Provides loopholes for the Secret Masters. Oh, and determines hit point bonus per level."

"That can't be right."

"Trust me. Come on, give me another."

"How many Constitutional amendments are there?"

"Sixty-five."

"It says twenty-seven here."

I laughed. It came out a little nasally what with the bandage over my nose. Don't worry—I had been beaten up by a book. "Right. Pull the other one."

"Do you know *anything* about your country, Mr. Blank?"

That's what she thought my name was. Robert Blank. It might as well be, legally speaking. I have a driver's license under that name. A birth certificate and a library card, too. A membership to the local Elk's Lodge and a card that says if I eat three more subs at Gaetano's, I get the next one free. Amazon, Netflix, and Hotmail all know me by that name. Yeah, I even have an email that goes right to me, and it's pretty easy to guess the username once you realize that I'd have to add numbers to the back half since just about everything is taken at this point. Besides, if I didn't have one, how would I know about all these exciting new ways to increase my sexual potency?

Is it the name I was born with? Oh, hell no. I can barely remember that, and it's not like anyone else is using it. My mother doesn't talk so well anymore and who the hell knows where my father is. But for all intents and purposes it's mine, and it's the only name I use these days. And honestly, the only thing that made it truly part of me was having someone important to call me by it.

I used to have more names than anyone really needs. So many I lost track of them. Ask a Freemason and he'll tell you I'm Colin Reznick. One of the ladies of V.E.N.U.S. would say Jonah Bailey. A Satanist would call me Sam Smiley, unless he's the other kind of Satanist, in which case I'm Eli Simms. The ascetorexics over at the Anamadim Temple think I'm Ivan Cohen, and the Illuminati call me Daniel Isringhausen. They're all real in that they each correspond to a flesh-and-blood person with a digital footprint and a paper spine. Each name has favorite haunts and Facebook accounts and a favorite video on YouTube of a puppy. They each have acquaintances, cronies, well-wishers, and contemporaries. They were as real as anyone else is in this world, and about a year ago they all died.

It was an unceremonious death, and there were no bodies. They joined that terrifyingly large number of people in the world who just up and vanish. Probably around six months ago, people who knew them began to realize the poor bastards weren't coming back.

I left Los Angeles a year ago, leaving the names in a shallow grave. A figurative one, mind; the IDs were still as valid as they ever were. I didn't update their various social networking pages, I stopped using their phones and their credit cards, and I abandoned the champion bar trivia team Hyperactive Crime Scene. I introduced myself as "Call me Bob," and I cultivated a handshake that would make Roger Sterling proud.

I stepped down from the ladder. "Way too goddamn much, Miss Barre."

Khaali Barre was a pleasant woman, and had been in the country for a little over five years. She didn't opt for the easy green card marriage, which I admired. Instead, she decided to do things the hard way, by navigating American bureaucracy, which I didn't admire. She was a good employee, though, and had driven me to the hospital when the *Necronomicon* decided to get revenge for all those midnight screenings of *Army of Darkness* I'd gone to. Had I known the actual hardcover book was directed by Sam Raimi, I might not have stocked it. I certainly wouldn't have put it on the top shelf.

Mina had seen the falling book's handiwork late Friday night when she finally got here. The actual accident had happened Thursday morning when some asshole from UCSB wanted to have a look at the thing. He must have gotten to the Lovecraft section in his 20th Century Lit class or, more likely, someone was running a *Cthulhu* LARP on campus and they'd heard about the local occult bookstore and its cranky proprietor.

The nice part of having a girlfriend—okay, not *the* nice part, because there are a ton of nice parts, and I'm enough of a grownup not to make a smutty joke here—is that when you hurt yourself, you get the sympathy affection. And Mina, even though she had just suffered through literally hours of bumper-to-bumper traffic on the 101, made the ouchy face and gave me a hug that turned into a kiss. And believe me, that was worth her hitting the bandage accidentally.

So yeah, a year later and Mina Duplessis and I are together. I'm still puzzling over that one. I've pointed out that she can do better, but she never takes me seriously. There's the obvious: she's a beautiful woman, and I mean professionally so. She's a model, a plus-sized one, who generally gets the call whenever a designer wants a classic old-Hollywood look. More importantly, she's smart as a whip and funny as hell when she wants to be. I'm just in the business of making sure that whatever reasons she had for hooking up with me remain true. She tells me I have nothing to worry about, but I didn't spend a decade being paranoid for nothing. No thanks, I'll keep making date night something fun.

Granted, there have been a few changes here and there, and if you ask me, for the better. Mina has me dressing a little better. The woman knows clothes. She knows a lot of things in point of fact, but like I said, she's a model, so the clothes part makes sense. And because she's a plus-sized model, she's also used to working with what someone's got rather than trying to simulate something they don't. She's got me in guayaberas and the occasional bowling shirt. Slacks, too, although she's nice enough to get me the ones that don't need to be ironed. She briefly tried to get me in something other than my Chuck Taylors, but I put the brakes on that right quick. Still, she says it gives me a laid-back island look. I have to be attractive to exactly one person in the world, so as long as Mina likes it, so do I.

The biggest hit to my identity, the part separating He-of-a-Thousand-Names and Robert Blank of the California central coast, was when she made me cut the Reagan hair. The haircut that had been my unofficial trademark, the 'do that ushered me into countless ultra-right wing hearts is gone. It's not like I need it anymore. I don't need to get the masters of the world to trust me, so there's no real point in looking like a repurposed Big Boy anymore. Occasionally I miss it, since there really was an art to getting the swirl exactly right, and doing so was the closest I ever got to meditation. But truth be told, I look better now.

The giant duckbilled bandage on my face wasn't part of the fashion makeover, but it'd be gone in a little bit and

I could go back to smelling something that wasn't my own dried blood. Kind of funny that I'd made it through an entire noir murder mystery with my sniffer intact, only to take a book to the face during my premature retirement. Somewhere, the Cosmic Trickster is laughing.

"I don't want to offend you," Khaali said from her place behind the counter, civics book in her lap, "but I think I should probably study on my own."

I shrugged. "If you want. I think we have a couple good civics texts in the back."

"In the Conspiracies section?"

"Yep, those are them."

She chewed her lip. "I think I'll keep with the one Immigration recommended."

"Your lo—" My ringtone cut me off. It was the riff from Boston's "Peace of Mind," the only Boston I was getting these days. I checked it. Mina Duplessis calling.

I answered it. "Sheinhardt Wig Comp—"

"Rabbit." That was Mina's nickname for me, something she picked even before I had a "real" name. ."I need your help." Her voice was tense, scared. Normally it's incongruously soft, probably something she affected around the time genetics turned her into the avalanche of beauty she had become. Now, the blade in her words cut through any joke I might have made.

"What's going on?"

"I've been arrested. They say I killed somebody!"

Goddamn it. I guess I'm not retired after all.

TOOK ME A SECOND TO RECOVER MY POWER OF speech. Mina was no shrinking violet and, sure, she'd been known to counter even casual sexism with a bit of light crotch soccer, but she'd never kill anyone.

"What?"

"The cops. They have evidence. They didn't even bother to question me, not really. They just arrested me as soon as I got home from your place. They're holding me without bail, they said."

"Don't worry, Mina. I'll be right there."

"What should I do? I've never been arrested before."

"Just sit tight and don't say anything. I'll get you a lawyer. He's a little weird, but trust me, he's gotten me out of some shit before."

I could tell she was trying not to cry, and I really wished there was some hugging technology I could deploy through the phone that wouldn't be terrifying. "I don't know what's happening. I don't even know this guy, and they're saying we were sleeping together."

"I know. It's probably just a misunderstanding," I said, trying to speak in the soothing tones of late night call-in radio. I was really thinking that this sounded like a frame job, but I wasn't going to say that. Not making Mina cry was one of my primary purposes on this earth. "Did they give you a name? The guy they think you killed?"

"Um... Neil Greene, I think? I've never heard of him before."

I had. Neil Greene was a Seventeenth Degree Freemason, a government bureaucrat for the city of Los Angeles who controlled roughly 1/17th of the flow of paperwork that kept the city running, and through that, about the same fraction of the city itself. Plus he was a member in good standing of the First Reformed Church of the Antichrist. He was also a friend of mine, or as close to those as I got. Literally the last thing I had ever seen him do was attempt to save my life. In my head, I briefly went over the pros and cons of telling Mina.

"I know him," I said. "Knew him, I mean. Look, this changes nothing. *You* didn't know him and you sure as hell didn't kill him. I'm driving down now, all right? We'll have this all straightened out before dinner."

She exhaled and I pictured her gathering herself. She was a strong person, and like most strong people, she was not a fan of being in situations that were out of control. "Okay," she said, then repeated it. "Okay. I'll see you soon."

I was on the road pretty much immediately. I told Khaali that I had to go, glossing over exactly why, and asked her to close. She wanted to know what was wrong, but it would probably take too long to explain. I almost headed out with nothing but the shirt on my back, but something made me hold off. A little voice whispering that maybe, just maybe, this was a little more sinister than it appeared—and it already looked sinister enough to be twirling a mustache while it tied Mina to some train tracks. That I should be prepared for another bout of insanity courtesy of my long association with the Information Underground.

I was retired, right, but I could unretire for a day. This could be like Michael Jordan with the Wizards, if Michael Jordan had never been very good at basketball. No, no problem, this was even less than that. I wasn't deluding myself. I wasn't trying to come back for good. I was going to do one thing and get out before anyone knew I was there. Get back to the City of Angels, Casablanca for the Secret Masters of the world, the city where shit gets done, where shadow governments can meet and hash out their differences over sushi and cocaine. And here comes Peter Lorre, the Boy Friday for every last one of these groups.

But Peter Lorre wasn't looking to get any of his timecards stamped.

This wasn't a job. Not a breach of the retirement thing. This was personal. One of my contacts, a contact I later found had himself been double-dipping, had showed up dead and my girlfriend was being framed for it. It didn't just stink; it reeked like a whorehouse after fleet week. And that internal monologue—you know, the one trying to soothe me with Morgan Freeman's stentorian tones—was telling me, "Make sure you have your operative kit. Get busy livin', or get busy dyin'. We will prevail and the world is a fine place and worth fighting for."

My internal monologue doesn't always differentiate between Freeman movies very well.

So I stopped by the homestead. Mina had been here the day before, leaving early Monday morning, and I swear I could still smell her. Evidence of our weekend was still around. Her bathing suit hung in the bathroom. There were Thai takeout leftovers in the fridge, the two DVDs we compromised on still sitting on the coffee table (*The Day the Earth Stood Still* and *Music and Lyrics*, for any who care). The empty bottle of merlot, which had turned out to be a good choice.

Bathroom first. I tried not to focus too hard on her things in there, the various lotions, cleansers, unguents, and oils scattered around that I'd never heard of in my single days. Her toothbrush, her makeup, the bandanna she used to keep her hair out of her eyes when she washed her face. I kept my attention on what I was there to do, grabbing my scant handful of toiletries (with a few additions from Mina. Who knew what a difference moisturizer makes?) and shoving them into a didi bag. Then the good stuff.

I opened up my closet. Lockpicks, because you never know when a little light breaking and entering will help out. My case of fake IDs. With no recent credit card purchases to establish them as real, eating, sleeping, cable-watching humans, they wouldn't past close inspection like they used to. They'd do, though. My police badge, and yes, it's real, though Detective Saroyan, who had the name associated with it, had vanished into the Bermuda Triangle for all anyone knew.

Those were easy. The last thing I wasn't so sure about. I stared at my aquarium for a good five minutes or so, weighing my options.

I have a rectangular seventy-gallon tank in my living room about three-quarters full of water. There are a few fish squirming around in the depths, a couple catfish and algae-eaters employed to keep the whole thing relatively clean. The marquee inhabitants are my three axolotls—salamanders to you and me—two of which were resting lightly on the gravel floor while one had crawled partway out to sun himself on a smooth section of lava rock. I've kept three of them as pets since the old days, Normally neotenic—that is, they stay in an aquatic larval form into adulthood—mine had metamorphosed in a misguided bid for symbolic relevance. Now they looked like grumpy pink tiger salamanders.

I wasn't looking at them, but rather the largest rock in the tank, nestled in the corner, and contemplating whether it was coming with me. Taking it was an admission that this was probably going to be pretty bad. Not taking it could be the last mistake I ever made.

To the untrained eye, it looked like a faintly glowing gray rock, pitted and rough. A rusted and sooty chain was bolted into the side, making it look like an artist's conception of Lemmy's sperm. The area of the tank where it sat was crusted in more of the same glowing rock, heaviest in the places where the stone sat and stretching outward like silicon algae. Only the chain was completely clean, though with the fire damage, it looked like something from a shipwreck. The axolotls often crawled on the rock, and though I might have been imagining it, I think they had started glowing slightly.

To an illuminated eye, it was blasphemy. The rock was the Genesis Stone, coming straight from the moon to my aquarium. It was one of the more powerful objects in existence, and responsible for at least one apocalypse back in '69. It had been bolted to the Chain of the Heretic Martyr, the same thing that had bound Joan of Arc, Maid of Orleans, schizophrenic and saint, to the stake. Sticking these objects together was pretty much sacrilege to any number of mystery cults. Since it had been done as a deliberate act of heresy by the head of a Discordian splinter sect, it sort of fit.

To my eye, it was the thing I had attempted suicide with. Of course, I couldn't even do *that* in a relatively normal way. The most insulting part was that I never even left a note, not that I had anyone who would've read it back then. I did now, and she was scared and in jail. And she needed me.

I could do this for her. One last thing.

I grabbed the chain and hauled the Genesis Flail (as the unrepentant D&D player in me had named it) out, mopping up the stinking salamander water with a towel. The axolotls watched me with Permian hunger. The stone was lighter than it should have been, something to do with the moon's gravity, but then it was pretty much all magic at that point and could be safely ignored. Sticking all my supplies in the trunk and resigning myself to having some moon rock start growing back there, I got behind the wheel and drove down Pacific Coast Highway toward Los Angeles.

On the stereo: "Local Boy" by the Rifles.

I should probably explain. If you know me, you know I can't stand most music because it's pretty much just occult viewpoints with guitar solos. The only band this isn't true for is Boston, because Boston's music somehow manages to be shallower than one of those plastic wading pools with Spongebob on it. The problem is, music is one of those things Mina knows about. A *lot* about. And she's a total snob to boot. Can't stand Boston for the exact reason I like them so much. So every time she comes up to see me or I go down to see her, she filches my iPod and packs it full of what she calls good music.

Only I can't turn off my brain, even when I'm supposed to be retired. So I'm trying to listen to this stuff and all I can think is, "Oh, these guys are just mouthpieces for the Flat Earth Society, or the Merovingians, or the Ordo Templi Orientis." So where she listens to "Local Boy" and hears a poppy punky tune about a veteran returning home and finding it's not the same place he left, I hear a song about the hashish trade as related to the Assassins, a thousand-year-old Islamic death cult. It's exhausting.

I'd go point by point on the lyrics, but I can't, since the record companies will sue at even the slightest hint of unfair use. I'd probably be in the clear if not for *Geffen v. Spade*, where a guy was actually sued over his internal monologue. And the record company won! Garnished his dreams for the rest of his life.

The Rifles are all about the Assassins and once you know that, their song "Peace and Quiet" becomes downright threatening.

So there I was on PCH, which, at the risk of hyperbole, is the most beautiful stretch of anything in the galaxy. To the east, you have the greens and golds of the California coast. As you go north, you start with Southwestern desert, which fades into something almost Mediterranean, going up into full *Twin Peaks* pine forest. To the west you have the endless blue of the Pacific, with alternating sandy beaches and rocky cliffs. Because of the storm on Friday California was still in the middle of a rain hangover, which is the exact opposite of what it sounds like. Meant the sky had been scrubbed and the cool wind blowing inland kept the shine.

Meant that when PCH turned into the 101 and I pulled into Los Angeles, the skyscrapers downtown were glittering in the sun and the snowcapped peaks of the San Gabriels made the whole thing look like a tourism ad. Made me wonder why I had ever left.

Oh, right. All those really dangerous people I stabbed in the back for about ten years while I was making a living. Thanks for the reminder, Morgan Freeman. "You're welcome, and I hope I can see my friend and shake his hand."

I took the 134 over into Glendale, a neighborhood chiefly known for having a mall, which I'll probably have to explain to children someday as being a lot like the internet, but minus the porn and cat pictures. I wasn't after the mall, mostly because I knew about the internet. I'm savvy that way. No, my destination was a little restaurant on a quiet street several blocks north. Glendale was mostly a grid, but lots of trees were planted around to make it feel like Mayberry or something. Now they were rattling in the wind.

The restaurant was nothing special from the outside. The sign said Sevan, and most people would have thought that was a typo; it was actually the name of a lake in the old Armenian Empire, back when that was more than a cruel joke at a Kardashian's expense. I headed inside, passing the mixture of balding Armenian men and younger hipsters there for lunch. The dining room was wide and pleasant, carpeted in blue with tables lined up in a grid pattern just like the streets outside. I went to the register, where a bored and impeccably groomed teenager was sullenly waiting. Two older men chatted over the grill, searing a variety of garlicky meats.

"What can I get you?" she asked me, barely looking up.

I felt like an asshole. I always did. "I have a problem with the Reptilians."

She jumped, focusing her big brown eyes on me with a mixture of pity and wonder. "What?"

"I need to see Dan. That's the code, right? It hasn't changed?"

The two older men had turned from the grill and one was staring at me. They were familiar, and were probably trying to place me. Problem was, I was in a big duckbill bandage and the Reagan hair was gone. I looked like any other schmuck. Well, not *any* other schmuck, but I didn't look like me, or the me they knew.

One of them said something in Armenian to the girl. She nodded, still nervous, and said, "Come with me."

I went around the side of the counter, past the grill, and followed the girl. The door was nearly hidden by a pantry of ingredients and a bulletin board covered in flyers and pushpins. She opened it to reveal an office that was almost big enough for half of me.

The impressive thing was that it held a man who was easily three of me, all crammed behind his desk. I never figured out how he managed to get in and out of that office. I imagined it had something to do with wormholes.

Dan Onanian was my lawyer. He had been since my first arrest about seven years back on a B&E gone wrong. I don't think it helped that the whole operation was an attempt to give all the chimpanzees at the LA Zoo Brazilian waxes. The Knights of the Sacred Chao can be a little odd. Anyway, I was the one in charge of actually breaking the locks on the side entrance and the cages. I was also the one left holding the bag when that little errand predictably went down the tubes. I mean, who could have foreseen that attempting to conduct painful grooming procedures on murder machines with seven times the strength of your average high school linebacker would be a terrible idea?

I got his name from another contact. Dan came down to the lockup and had me out on bail in two hours. Made sure everyone knew it was my first offense, and I was out with a small fine and time served.

Granted, our second meeting was a little awkward, since I got caught with stolen goods under a different identity. It was just a shipment of Hello Kitty heads I was delivering to the Order of the Morning Star, but that meant that this time I was arrested as Eli Simms. Dan blinked a couple times when he saw me, then rolled with it, introducing himself and pulling my ass out of trouble yet again.

Dan wasn't exactly clued-in. He knew there was something big out there—well, bigger than him, anyway—and he was friendly to folks like me. He was discreet, affordable, and best of all, good at what he did—so pretty much the perfect lawyer for my purposes.

He did have some weird beliefs, though.

Dan's face split into a huge grin when I came through the

door. "Mike! Or is it Ivan this time?"

"It's Bob now, actually," I said, reaching across his desk and shaking his pillow-like hand as I got hit in the face with a solid wall of cologne. "Bob all the time."

"Bob. I like it. What happened to your face?"

I touched the bandage like I had to be reminded it was there. "Prizefighting."

"Sure, sure it was. You look thin. Much too thin. I'll get you some chicken."

Before I could stop him, he shouted something in Armenian through the closed door. Oh well. I was a little hungry anyway. I sat down in a slumping wooden chair across from his cluttered desk.

Dan rubbed his bristly goatee. "What can I do for you today, Bob? You're not calling me from the county jail, so you're better off than you are normally."

I tried to focus. Behind Dan was an impressive psycho wall setup. Pictures of people, some connected to one conspiracy or another, some just weirdos he was fixated on, were linked with lines of colored string and annotated with brightly colored sticky notes and articles from various news sources, some clipped from the paper, others printed out from one of his wingnut websites. Some of which, to my embarrassment, I'd made up.

"I'm retired."

"Are you an internet billionaire? Did you make an app?"

"No, I'm just not doing... what I used to do."

"That's good, because that was crazy. Really crazy. What are you doing here? Seems like it's not just to catch up?"

"A friend of mine was arrested."

"Breaking and entering? Malicious mischief? I love the cases you used to bring me, Bob. Always so interesting."

"Murder."

Dan's jaw dropped, making his jowls wobble. The door opened and the girl who had led me back leaned in with a styrofoam plate covered with rice, several generous chunks of chicken breast, a little hummus, pita, and tabbouleh. I thanked her and tore into it. "You going to say anything else there, Dan? Or just stare at me?"

"I'm sorry, it's just... murder. That's more than you usually come in here with."

"Yes, but you *are* a criminal defense attorney. You've dealt with that kind of thing."

"Of course." He watched me eat, making up his mind up. "Who killed who?"

"Not who they're saying. They arrested my girlfriend."

Dan laughed. "You have a girlfriend? Come on, Bob. You don't have to front here."

"I have a girlfriend." I thought some detail might help convince him, but didn't think about how it would sound until it was too late. "She's a model."

Dan laughed louder. "It's all right. You like her. I get it. You know, you should date my cousin. She's about your age. Very pretty. She has never killed anyone, and has never even been arrested. Are you Armenian? Doesn't matter, you can fake it well enough to fool my grandmother."

"Dan, seriously. My girlfriend, who is a breathing carbon-based lifeform, was arrested for a murder she—and I cannot possibly stress this enough—did not commit."

He stopped laughing, which was good because his chins were wiggling around in a very distressing way. The twinkle in his eye said he didn't believe me entirely, but did believe there was a living woman arrested for a murder she might not have done. "All right. What happened? Do you know the specifics?"

"I know a little. The victim's name is Neil Greene, who

she doesn't know, but I do. Did." I tried to explain Neil as best I could in between minty bites of tabbouleh. Just the highlights: powerful bureaucrat, religious Satanist, high-ranking Freemason.

"I see."

The gears were whirring behind his shiny forehead. I knew what he was going to ask before he said it, so I figured I'd just cut it off at the pass. "The Reptilians are not involved."

"You're certain?"

"Well, no. Not a hundred percent. But I'd look at a lot of other groups before them."

He nodded thoughtfully. "Those masks are very convincing."

"And there's that."

Dan was obsessed with Reptilians, and had been since before I had met him. It's probably not the most normal thing to be obsessed with, but then, my frame of reference is a little off. Reptilians, for those who might have slept through that portion of the crazy homeless subway guy's rant, are a kind of alien. Well, they might actually be highly evolved dinosaurs, but that hypothesis was advanced before we knew that *T. rex* basically looked like a giant angry chicken. So they're featherless, but hey, maybe they shave all over. You don't know.

They were first sighted during alien abductions. While the little Grays—the ones you're familiar with, who've been guest-starring in *Close Encounters of the Third Kind*, *X-Files*, and those talking-baby commercials—are working the anal probe like Daniel Plainview in a virgin field, the Reptilians are standing in back observing and issuing the occasional order. I always wondered what the hell they could be saying back there. "He's not really wincing enough. Did you use too much lube?" or "Jesus, Gary, turn left at the colon or you're going to rupture something!"

After these initial sightings (which someone noticed

looked a lot like hypothetical models of a humanoid dinosaur descendent, again, minus the feathers which we now know would probably be there like New Wave body hair), the Reptilians developed a life of their own. They branched out from merely being the shadowy overlords of the Grays to appearing in conspiracies in their own right. It was like a paranormal bar mitzvah, minus the awkward reading of the Torah and the terrible DJ. Pretty soon they had basically become the bad guys in *V*, wearing human masks and infiltrating various world governments for nefarious-yet-murky purposes.

And yes, I know dinosaurs were not reptiles, but that's what they're called and it's a little late to go back now. So until they appear on the scene and tell us what their equivalent of "Native American" is, they're going to be called Reptilians. They're distinct from the lizard people who supposedly live under Fort Moore Hill downtown. Probably. I don't know. I've never seen a family tree.

The point of all this is that Dan Onanian firmly believes in Reptilians, blaming them for everything from the tax code to the time he left the driver's side window of his BMW down before LA's one rainstorm of the year. He was monitoring several people in the city he was convinced were wearing high-quality latex masks. He was correct in several instances, although two of them were wearing masks for totally unrelated reasons.

Dan probably would have been horrified to learn that I had worked for three different Reptilian splinter groups in addition to the Little Green Men, who had been Reptilian-free since 2003 (slogan pending). I never brought it up and lied whenever he asked me point blank. Dan was too good a lawyer to lose over something as silly as totally justified feelings of betrayal.

"All right. You know my usual retainer," he said.

I already had his money stuffed in an envelope and put that on the desk.

"I have to ask the obvious question here. You're certain that she didn't know this man?"

"She said the cops claimed to have evidence that they knew each other. That they were sleeping together."

"Were they?"

"Of course not."

"You're certain?"

"I know her."

"You can know someone and not know someone. You of all people should know that."

"Believe me, I can spot a phony from a mile off. Mina is exactly what she appears to be. Once you meet her, you'll understand."

He took the envelope off the desk and put it in the top drawer. He didn't bother counting it, such was the trust between us. "On that subject, I should go meet my new client. You included money for her bail?"

"There's no bail. I guess because it's a murder."

Dan shook his head. "It might be high, but there should still be a number. Is this her first offense?"

I nodded. "I mean, it wouldn't shock me if there was something on her record, like getting arrested at a demonstration or something."

He waved that off. "She's never been arrested for any felonies?"

She could still vote. Somewhere else that might have meant no felonies, but in California, as long as you weren't actually in prison or on parole, you were good to go. Since most politicians are criminals, it cuts down a bit on the hypocrisy of the whole affair. I knew she could vote because she treated it like an important thing and had been horrified when she found out I didn't. I tried to tell her that it didn't matter who was actually in office, since it wasn't like there were term limits for Secret Masters. She made certain to note that men who didn't vote had much less sex than men who did, and after that I boldly cast a write-in vote for C. Montgomery Burns in the next election. I figured if I was going to be ruled by a terrifying plutocrat, it might as well be the most terrifying one of all.

She probably would have mentioned if she had been arrested for any felonies. Or had a parole officer. Or time spent in the joint. She didn't have any tattoos, let alone a badass spiderweb on her elbow. Mina wasn't the felonious type. "Never."

"That is a little odd. You're certain she hasn't angered the Reptilians?"

The Guardian Servitors of the Anorectic Praxis, sure. Possibly the Kosher Nostra, Freemasons, and the Knights Templar, but... "Nope."

Dan began the geologic process of getting to his feet.

"Wait, Dan. I want to see her first, and it's probably best if we go separately, you know? Can you give me like an hour's head start here?"

"Certainly. I should look into things a bit before I head over anyway."

I stood up, still holding my plate, which, by now, was as clean as I was going to make it. "Thanks." I took his hand, and knew I would be smelling his cologne on it for the rest of the day.

He smiled at me. "Don't worry. I've gotten guilty men out of murder raps. An innocent woman should be cake."

"Famous last words, Danny. Thanks for the chicken."

I went out the door, where the teenaged girl was staring at me in concern. "You're not his cousin, are you?" I asked her.

She jumped a little. "Uh, no. Niece."

"Okay, good. Stay in school."

The two men at the grill ignored me. They were probably used to the drill, knowing the kinds of people Dan brought into the restaurant. Kind of made me proud, that I was the riffraff here. I almost wished one of them would adopt a '50s Dad voice and tell me to "Get out of here, you hooligan." That's right. I'm teaching your town to dance, old man, and I'm romancing your daughter while I'm at it. And we're going to save the community center, defeat the bullies, and help that friendly alien make it home.

I got back in my car and drove down to the county jail, a building just as squat and ugly as it sounds. I didn't know much about women's incarceration, apart from what I had learned in academic treatises like *Caged Heat*. I was fairly certain that the pillow fights would be kept to the bare minimum and the showers were probably not as soft-focusy. I didn't want to think about what jail was really like, so I had to try to drown out the worry for Mina. I'd get her out of there. Fast as I could.

On the stereo: "What's My Scene" by the Hoodoo Gurus.

A little on the nose, if you ask me, since it was the lament of a double agent working for the Office of Naval Intelligence. Sorry, ONI, no one is buying what you're selling.

Bordered by the 101 freeway to the south and railroad tracks to the east, the county lockup was the kind of place where hope was shot in the back of the head and buried in an unmarked grave. It almost could have been an office park, if not for the larger, intimidating structure with barred windows growing behind it, like the big scary goon looming behind the little mastermind. I parked a block away, because I'm not a total idiot. No reason to lock your car behind another layer of security when you can just have it on the street.

I popped the trunk and opened up my bag, sifting through the IDs. Who was I today? I squinted over at the jail like it would tell me something. Who ran the jails these days? It was one of those institutions that passed through a lot of hands because there was a lot of really obvious power in controlling how people were incarcerated. Before I left, LA's jails were squarely in New Camelot hands, but I'd been gone for a year. No telling who ran the place now, or how happy they'd be to find an errand boy suddenly back from the dead.

I decided to play it more or less safe and grabbed my LAPD ID, slipping it into my wallet and putting the badge wallet in my other pocket. I approached the jail confidently. A lot can be said for simple confidence, and I'd gotten into a ton of places just by playing it Bogart. Most people don't want trouble, and if you look like you belong, they're not going to challenge you.

The front of the jail was almost the exact foyer you'd see in an office. Floor-to-ceiling windows with some stencils on the glass. But just inside, instead of a pretty receptionist, there was a metal detector and large men with guns on their hips. The glass was probably bulletproof, but that wasn't something I planned on testing. I went up to the detector, emptied my pockets into the plastic tray, and went right through.

It's times like this I'm glad I don't have a plate in my head or an adamantium-laced skeleton. The guard gave me a look, but I could tell he couldn't see much past the white duckbill on my face.

"Boating accident," I said to him.

"Uh-huh."

As I gathered my stuff up from the tray and put it back in my pockets, I glanced around and met the eyes of another guard. She was staring at me hard and speaking into a walkie-talkie. Probably a coincidence. Could have been talking about anything, right? I gave her a thin smile and started down the hallway, fighting the urge to walk too fast.

The hallway took a turn up ahead. I figured I could get my bearings in a little while. My steps echoed off the sterile walls and floors and I tried to pretend that this was just another day in my life as an LAPD officer. I had been here lots of times before, and not as a prisoner. I fit in here. I belong here, on this side of the cage.

Two guards came around the corner ahead of me, looking like they were trying to stare me down into the floor. One said something into his radio, but all I could hear was a mutter and a click. Maybe I should leave talking to Mina to her lawyer and get the hell out. I turned, only to find two more of the guards from the security checkpoint coming up quick, blocking the path to the exit. I was trapped in the hall. There were a few doors around, but it wasn't like they wouldn't see me go in one of them.

"Nicholas Zorotovich?" one of the guards said, using the name I employed in my association with the Russian Mob.

And that's when my reflexes screwed me over. "Huh?" I answered.

"Nicholas Zorotovich? You're under arrest for bookmaking and racketeering," said the lead one, who looked a little like what would happen if Patrick Wilson really got into steroids and angrily denying homoerotic impulses. He had a hand on my shoulder and was already turning me to kiss the wall. I had the feeling that if they slapped the cuffs on, I was going to have much more trouble talking myself out of them. I didn't think the whole "I'm retired" thing would fly here.

So I just blurted out the first thing that came to mind. "How the hell do you know my CI?"

CI meant Confidential Informant, which is a nice way of saying rat, snitch, or stool pigeon if you find yourself stuck in a Raymond Chandler novel. They're low-level crooks who stay on the streets doing their relatively harmless criminal activities while feeding information on the big fish to the police. Nicky Zorotovich didn't have a snitch jacket, but he was exactly the kind of guy who *would* have one. When I created the alias to go work for the Kosher Nostra, I had to make sure he looked legit, and that meant giving him a record. Nothing too bad, but I implied worse by including a couple arrests for code-type offenses, where cops book you on something unrelated that won't stick, but that *will* get you off the streets for a night. I managed it through a combination of my police identity and Joel Hernandez, an acquaintance who worked in the evidence room at Hollywood Division.

On the upside, it meant I had a workable identity as exactly the kind of scumbag Vassily "the Whale" Zhukovsky was comfortable enough in trusting with the bullshit that kept the Russian Mob shaking down hockey players. On the downside, there was a hypothetical asshole running around Los Angeles with my face doing just enough to ensure a short stay in San Quentin should any cop actually have that name and face at his fingertips.

"CI?" asked Not Patrick Wilson.

I shook the man off and turned my back to the wall, affecting a calm I didn't feel. "Nicky Zorotovich is my CI. Why'd you grab me?"

They looked at each other, momentarily unsure. I jumped on that, knowing if I could keep talking, I could keep them from thinking, which was the key to making it out of this situation intact.

"Eh, it's okay. We look a little alike, I guess. Well, apart from the nose." I laughed, gesturing at the big bandage that was keeping the middle third of my face from being seen. Never felt so lucky about getting hit in the face with an ancient book of devil magic. "And the hair. I mean, you've read the descriptions. Do I look like Bob's Big Boy to you?"

"Uh... can we see some identification, officer..."

"Detective," I snapped. "Detective Art Saroyan. I have my badge right here."

A badge that would say I had abandoned my job at Hollywood Division a year ago, if they bothered to check it. I flipped it open and showed it to Not Patrick Wilson.

I saw him reading my badge number, mostly because he had to move his lips to do so. No matter how much I wanted to mock him, there were still three more uniforms all around me. Granted, they were confused for the time being, but nothing clears the cobwebs in a cop's head like getting to hit something with a nightstick.

"I'm going to call this in," Not Patrick Wilson told me.

"You do that. And make sure you mention how you wasted my goddamn time while thinking I was my own fucking snitch." I shook my head like it was really an imposition.

The guards had a bit of a confab and two returned to their posts, leaving me with a young guy whose nametag said Gutierrez. He was the smallest guy there, and from the looks of him, couldn't grow a full beard. "He always such a hardass?"

Gutierrez snorted. "He's being easy on you."

The way he said it made me think that if my skin had been a shade darker, I'd be in cuffs and then some. "It's my lucky day."

Not Patrick Wilson had made it back to the guard station and was on the phone. He wasn't going to like what he found and I had to make tracks.

"Hey, Gutierrez? You mind if I take a piss?"

"What, here?"

"Yeah. I was thinking right up against this wall, so that when the K-9 units come through, they know it's mine. No, I was more considering heading to the bathroom over there," and I nodded at the men's room on the other side of the hall, "and seeing if I could figure out what those porcelain cup things on the wall are for."

"Yeah, go ahead," he said, trying not to smirk.

I forced myself to stroll over slowly, pushing the door

open into a tile room permeated with enough industrial cleanser that I was pretty sure the soles of my shoes were being eaten away. I could see why Gutierrez wasn't concerned about my running. There was a window, but it was closed, with chicken wire crisscrossing through the opaque glass. Fortunately, this wasn't my first rodeo.

Look, I'm not proud of how many buildings I've broken into and out of. I'd like to list them off, but the sad fact is I've lost count. I'd never actually broken into or out of this particular building, and I was going to have to do it on the fly while three armed men and one armed woman tracked me down, which would make things difficult. But suffice to say that if I were applying for a job, in the "special skills" section, I'd be totally justified in describing some form of what I was about to do.

I went to the last stall and stood on the toilet tank. Any minute now, Not Patrick Wilson would get the word that Detective Art Saroyan was missing, even if barely anyone could remember ever seeing him, let alone working a case with him, and he'd try to figure out why he or possibly Nick Zorotovich had shown up claiming to be the other. I would have to work quickly.

I pushed up the false ceiling and shoved the panel to the side. An amateur might have gone right for the air ducts, but it takes a special kind of person to go through those: namely children, contortionists, and Olympic gymnasts. I had lost a few pounds since I stopped stress eating on the job, but it wasn't like I had suddenly turned into Bishop the android. I grabbed the supports in the ceiling, jumped off the toilet tank, and hauled myself up.

The smell of ammonia had been replaced by the stench of ammonia. Down there it had been produced by Dow; up here, rats. And it was everywhere. I was hoping they were nice and small, none bigger than a housecat, but I didn't plan to stay and measure them. The turds were all around, along with chewed-up insulation, warnings to trespassers like myself: "Okay, human, this place is ours and you're here because we let you."

I replaced the panel in the ceiling and started moving. It got pretty dark, but with the light bleeding up through the minute holes in the acoustic tile, I could see a little. I fished my phone out of my pocket and turned on the flashlight app. Amazing what they can do with technology nowadays.

Up here, the false ceiling stretched over most of the expanse, though it ended in solid blockhouse, which was probably where the jail started. There were ducts and pipes and tubes leading into the ceiling below. I went on hands and knees, keeping to the splinter-iffic beams crisscrossing my new floor. With the silvery tubes snaking every which way, I felt like I was performing a colonoscopy on Robbie the Robot. I could hear the noise of the building below me, but the barrier had turned it into a muted slurry. If Not Patrick Wilson was shouting at Gutierrez and the other guards as I assumed he was, it was just another "Wub wub waaaaanh," like Charlie Brown's teacher.

Still, I knew odds were at least one of them wasn't a total idiot. They might guess what I did and it would be hard to protest my innocence with my knees covered in rat piss. I crawled quickly toward a nice tangle of silvery tubes that should hide me from the spot where I came in.

I skirted around it, finding what looked like the abandoned nest of an especially large rat, and paused, turning off my light.

Not a second later, I heard a thump. "You see anything?" Not Patrick Wilson's voice, complete with a hollow echo from the men's room.

"He's not up here," Gutierrez said. Just to really complete

the heart attack for me, the beam of a flashlight splashed underneath the tubes, trying to halo my foot. I shifted, and the light followed my motion. "Wait."

"You see him?"

The light twitched again, trying to draw out the movement. "It's just a rat."

The light was on the far wall now, a series of concentric circles fading away. I turned around. I was about halfway to the front of the building and still hugging the wall for the most part. If memory served, I was over some offices.

"Can I come down now?" Gutierrez asked.

"Yeah, there's—" And the rest of what he said was cut off by the thump of the panel going back in place. I turned my light back on and crept along a few more feet, then figured, what the hell. I was going to have to do this eventually. I lifted the panel and peeked underneath. It was a large, open office with several desks and, more importantly, several people. It wasn't the kind of place I could just jump down into, tell them I was Harry Tuttle, here to repair their air conditioning, and leave.

With the side of my head pressed into the ceiling, peeking out of the smallest possible crack in the panel, I considered my options. That's when I heard a door open.

Not Patrick Wilson said, "I need everyone to stay in their offices for the time being. It's nothing to worry about, but we've lost track of a visitor."

Then came the sweetest words I'd ever heard. Well, okay, not the sweetest, but certainly welcoming ones for my present situation.

"Mr. Harris is at lunch," said one of the clerks. "Is he going to be able to get back in?"

"We'll have the situation cleared up before that. Don't worry."

I mashed my cheek into the floor, wincing as that bit into my tender nose, trying to see what I hoped that exchange implied. There it was: right at the end of the larger office zone was a smaller, single office. Sure, there were windows looking out into the common room, but I could work with that. Kind of. Or at least for as long as this would take.

I crept along the beams, my legs burning the whole way, until I judged I was above Harris's office. I checked from the panel and saw that my estimate was good. Just beneath me was a good, old, city-issued desk, with an outdated PC riding it. There was a chair that had dished out more lower back pain than most football players and a cluttered couple of filing cabinets.

I lowered my head into the room upside-down. Through the glass window looking into the larger room, I could see three clerks going about the business of the office, all of them with one eye on the clock. It was one of those large ones that reminded me of the clocks in school marking the cursed minutes until Mrs. Dugan's math class was over. None were really looking at Harris's office, but then, why bother looking at the boss's office when you know he's not there?

There really wasn't going to be a good time to do it, so I just went for it, slowly lowering myself into the room, watching the clerks on the other side of the glass. They went about their work, and the whole time I was willing them not to look at me. I hoped for the sudden development of mutant powers. Wouldn't be the first time I'd tried that—it pretty much summed up my entire adolescence. Then, as now, it didn't work, or there would have been a lot more of my teachers bursting into flames and girls' tops falling off. In retrospect, I'm glad I'm not a mutant.

I didn't hear any shouting as my shoes made their gradual way into the room, nor when my legs followed. I eased myself in, watching the office drones, thinking that as long as I didn't move quickly, I wouldn't trip that part of the brain that associates movement with predator or prey. Either one would get me a date with Not Patrick Wilson's nightstick. I landed on the desk and stayed frozen. That would be fun to explain should anyone glance over.

The clerks kept right on doing clerk things. I carefully stepped off the desk and dropped below the line of the window into the office. Harris also had a window looking onto the lawn and the parking lot. It was reinforced exactly like in the bathroom, but unlike that one, this was not a window intended for just *anyone*. This was for Mr. Harris, who was the... I picked up the nameplate on his desk. Head Administrator. There you go. The picture of him with his family at Disneyland said he was a big, heavyset guy who looked like a more mobile Baron Harkonnen. Even better, there was an ashtray next to it with the caked black ash that said someone used it. All city buildings in LA are non-smoking. So if Harris wanted to enjoy a smoke, he had two options. One, go through security, which would be a hassle, or two, crack a window. I was betting a big guy like Harris had chosen two.

I worked my fingers between the sill and the frame, really hoping Harris kept the whole thing nice and oiled so the rest of the office wouldn't know about his shameful secret. I was terrified, of course. Jail was literally right around the corner and if I slipped up, I could be condemning Mina to a fate she didn't deserve.

I was also having a hell of a lot of fun. I couldn't deny it.

The sill jerked up all of a sudden, like it had realized what I wanted. "Oh, time for a smoke? Hell yeah, H-Dawg!" I had a minor cardiac event while my brain supplied the ear-splitting protest of the frame. Only there wasn't one. Harris wasn't an idiot, apparently, no matter what the picture on his desk of him in a Goofy hat might have implied. The window opened about eight inches and stopped.

Right. Because it's not like Harris was leaving his office like this every day. I pictured the red-faced balding man slithering through the crack like that bad guy on the *X-Files* and had to accept that stranger things happened all the time and I used to be responsible for a lot of them.

I was measuring the gap, wondering what would happen if I sucked in the belly and collapsed the old ribcage, when I heard the door to the hallway open.

"What's going on out there?" The voice was thick and gravelly. I'd never heard it before but Murphy's Law supplied who it belonged to.

"Some kind of security thing, Mr. Harris. They said it's nothing to worry about."

"All right. I'll be in my office."

Harris, you asshole.

Time was in short supply and I was going to get caught anyway, so I stood up and really put my shoulders into it.

"Hey! Hey, you!" Harris's voice in the main hall.

The window didn't budge. I put my legs and ass into it.

"He's in here! Help!"

The window jerked up another six inches. The door into the hall slammed open. No time like the present, right? I stuck my head through the opening and pulled, spilling out onto the little patch of dying grass they probably called a lawn. I hit the ground on my hands and knees, pushed myself vertical, and sprinted. Cops were being called, but I'd be long gone by then.

Great start to this caper. Already wanted by the police. I kicked myself the whole way back to my car. I pulled the door open and was driving before I even picked a destination.

On the stereo: "Behind the Wall of Sleep" by the Smithereens.

Yeah, it's not actually about a guy who loves a sexy bass player. Not that there isn't something to be said for sexy bass players. No, listen to what he's actually saying. Read the goddamn title. This is Ordo Templi Orientis all over. What's behind the wall of sleep? Oh, that would be the devils in our minds and out of space, looking to corrupt us little fleshbags. Possibly with the aid of sexy bassists.

Already wanted by the police. That's not quite right. Those fuckers were *waiting* for me. Like they knew a small-timer named Nicky Zorotovich would be showing up there and could be brought in.

Mina would still be waiting on me, and she'd probably be a little confused when Dan showed up saying he was her lawyer. More to the point, Mina might still be in danger. Locking her up seemed like an opening gambit, and it's not like there wasn't someone who had tried to kill her recently and, in fact, had once tried to hire me to do the deed: Vassily "the Whale" Zhukovsky, local boss of the Russian Mob.

Nicky's boss. Another coincidence.

My connections were a year out of date, but there was still someone who might try to help me. She had put herself on the line before, trying to keep Mina safe, and owed allegiance to the same cult Mina had once called home—before they had tried to betray her, of course. V.E.N.U.S., a feminist conspiracy that was pretty all right as these things went, final betrayal notwithstanding. I didn't get along with the leadership, but Oana was okay. Even if her Romanian accent made her sound like Dracula's petulant kid sister.

Oana Constantinescu was the winner of the bronze medal at the Women's Individual All-Around in Gymnastics in Sydney. She was also a master of hand-to-hand combat and just crazy strong for a hobbit. Last I heard, she was coaching a team of gymnasts, trying to be Bela Karolyi minus the focus on eating disorders and plus a little ninja action. I'm not big into black-and-white morality, but within the shades of gray in the Information Underground, Oana Constantinescu was one of the good guys.

I pulled over a couple miles from the jail and called her. Her phone rang a few times and went right to voicemail. "Oana, it's..." Who was it? Oh yeah. "Jonah. Call me. Number's on your phone."

She might be with her team and not taking calls, so I tracked the team down on my phone. They had a website, a Facebook page, and a Twitter account that, judging by the tweeter's stern command of the English language, there was no way Oana ran. They operated out of a gym in Santa Monica, which was a short trip over off the 10 freeway, and it looked like they were in the midst of practice, based on the Instagrams one of the girls was compulsively uploading. Maybe their fans were really into sepia-toned pictures of muscular girls flipping around or practicing painful jiu-jitsu holds.

On the drive over, I had a lot of time to brood on this thing I'd found myself in the middle of. It was a lot bigger than it looked, and right now I was at the beginning. I could only see a single corner of it, and it would be hell trying to see the rest. But I had no choice in the matter, and with any luck I would shortly have help getting Mina and me extricated from the whole thing.

The gym was a white boxy building with blue trim and a variety of signs and flyers stuck on the wall, like the uniform of a fat and overfunded NASCAR driver, located a couple blocks from the beach. A stiff salt breeze was blowing inland when I got out of my car.

The inside of the gym was basically one large room filled with the smell of sweat sunk into canvas pads. In one corner, there was a raised boxing ring where two girls were drilling jiu-jitsu, which to the untrained eye looks like an exceptionally angry game of Twister. Another girl was flipping along a balance beam while two more were taking turns tumbling across a mat. Even though they were black, white, Latina, Asian, and someone who looked like a mix of all of the above, they were all of a type. None of them was over five feet tall, and while they had more curves than your standard gymnast, they were solid blocks of muscle with necks like my thigh. They wore their hair in perky ponytails and for some reason I will never understand, they were working out in full make-up. They wore shorts over their leotards, and almost all had a wrist, a knuckle, or an ankle wrapped in graying athletic tape. Chalk dust coated their hands and feet.

One by one their eyes went to me. I realized that a man my age wandering in and staring at them—and none of them was over seventeen—was probably an automatic pervert. They didn't look particularly scared, though. The girl on the balance beam dismounted with a flip and cracked her knuckles like she was the bouncer at the Green Dragon.

"I'm looking for Oana Constantinescu?" I said.

"And who are you?" asked the girl from the balance beam. The two jiu-jitsu girls were leaning against the ropes. The tumblers had their veiny hands resting on very muscular hips.

"I'm a friend of hers. Jonah Bailey?"

I doubted they'd look into that name, but it was a work of art, if I do say so myself. I put a lot of thought into that one. See, I was looking at V.E.N.U.S. as a possible employer, so I wanted a name that sounded just a little feminine. Kind of a subconscious sort of deal. Also, the leadership of V.E.N.U.S. is extremely... zaftig. Actually make that zeppelaftig. They're huge. And I say that as someone who finds the skin-and-bones look disturbing. So I figured if I was going into the belly of a whale, I might as well be named Jonah.

More than just the name, though. I made sure Jonah Bailey had the feminist bona fides. Registered member of the Peace and Freedom Party, a blog that mostly mined and reposted stuff from Jezebel and similar sites, and even a dummy piece from the Vassar College newspaper about how Jonah organized a march against sexual harassment amongst the dining hall employees. Jonah Bailey looked like the perfect well-meaning stooge for V.E.N.U.S.

Problem was, while I personally hold the opinion that women are pretty fantastic, I'm also an unrepentant asshole who has no filter on the jokes he makes in mixed company. Didn't make me terribly popular with V.E.N.U.S. leadership. Still, the Jonah Bailey name would probably hold up if I claimed I had spent the last year working on an organic kale farm.

"Never heard of you," said Balance Beam.

"You know all of Oana's friends, then?"

Balance Beam was not amused. "Why didn't you call her?"

"I did. No answer. I haven't seen her in a while, and I was wondering if she had changed phones or something."

"I'm not giving some creep off the street her number."

I let the creep thing slide. "How about you call her and tell her Jonah Bailey is here to see her?"

They all exchanged looks. Finally, Balance Beam, who appeared to be the leader, said, "All right. Emma W., could you do it?"

One of the tumblers, a tiny Asian girl who might have been some kind of elf, nodded and zipped off to the office. Even running casually, she did the light-footed and stiff-armed run gymnasts use in competition. I turned a chuckle into a cough when I saw the others staring at me.

"So... how are you ladies doing?"

The gymnasts just stared me down. It was rather disconcerting. I had no idea how clued in they were, so it wasn't like

I could just start throwing around conspiracies and make any headway. I had no idea if Oana was still with V.E.N.U.S., especially considering how they tried to sell Mina out while Oana had put a lot on the line trying to keep her safe. I sighed. Somehow I had managed to make my dizzying array of loyalties even more complex.

Emma W. emerged from the office. "She's not answering her phone."

"Did you try her house?" Balance Beam asked.

"I tried home and cell."

Now I was worried. "Guys, look. I swear to the goddess or Nadia Comaneci or whoever that I am Oana's friend. I owe her a lot. I need to see her, so if one of you could tell me where she lives, I'd be grateful."

Balance Beam shook her head. "I don't think so."

"Then one of you can come with me!"

"Get into a car with a strange man?"

"If Oana taught you *anything* she knows about jiu-jitsu, I'm about as dangerous to you as a corgi with pillows for teeth."

Balance Beam smiled at a memory. Pretty sure it involved her breaking someone in half with her shins. "You have a car, right?"

I nodded.

"Three of us will go with you."

"Fine. Let's just go now, please?"

"Emma K. and Emma R. Let's go." The two jiu-jitsu girls hopped out of the ring with disconcerting grace.

"Wait. All your names are Emma?"

"My name is Emily," said Balance Beam.

"Right. Totally different." I shook my head and Emily and the two Emmas followed me out the door. Emily got in shotgun, leaving chalky handprints on my door handle. The Emmas were in the back. I felt like the oddest combination of hostage and sex criminal.

"Where am I going?"

"Near Dodger Stadium," Emily said.

I nodded and got back on the freeway, grateful I wouldn't be transporting any minors over state lines. "What happened to your nose?" asked one of the Emmas.

"Headbutted an orc."

On the stereo: "I Am the Resurrection" by the Stone Roses.

Pretty tempting to call it Christian claptrap with a title like that. It sort of is, but the first clue is in the name of the band. See, the term "sub rosa" originally came from the Knights Templar, who would hold their meetings under a stone carving of a rose. When you realize that, it's a short road to determining the purpose of the song as a not-so-subtle threat to those who thought the Knights Templar were dead and gone.

I got off the freeway and drove east of downtown up into the short hills at the edge of Chavez Ravine. The houses had a pleasantly ramshackle look to them and apart from the cars on the street, the neighborhood had probably not changed much since the '40s. Large berms rose on either side of the road and palm trees and cactus sprouted from the yellow dirt. Emily guided me through the winding streets to a modest one-story house poised at the end of a street.

Right away, it was obvious there was something wrong. The front picture window was shattered, glass in the dirt and stuck amongst the needles of a barrel cactus beneath it. The house was on a small rise, with a decent amount of distance between it and the neighbors. Probably one of the selling points to someone like Oana.

One of the Emmas gasped and all three were scrabbling at the doors as soon as I stopped. I was a little slower out of the car, trying to take the scene in. Unlikely Oana would still be there in light of that window. There was no police tape, either.

Emily was one step into a gymnast's run for the front door when I grabbed her shoulder and said, "Wait." I'm not sure exactly what she did next, but as soon as conscious thought returned, I found I was on my knees wondering how one finger could cause me so much pain. "Don't... don't run in there," I gasped. "We don't know what... could you stop hurting me now, please?"

"Sorry," Emily said, but I don't think she was. She let me go and I got to my feet, massaging my finger. "You shouldn't grab people."

"I didn't want you running in there into who knows what. Just do me a favor and hang back. If someone my age dies, it's not quite as much of a tragedy."

The gymnasts exchanged a look and Emily nodded.

"One thing," I said. "When was the last time any of you talked to Oana?"

"Practice yesterday," one of the Emmas said. "She was helping me with my leglocks."

That was Monday, the same day Mina had been arrested. I looked back at the house. No tape. Nothing over the window. That meant no one had called the police. This wasn't the best neighborhood in the world, but you'd think an altercation would have at least triggered a 911. I went to the door and listened. Nothing inside that I could hear. I tried the door. It opened.

Into chaos. Oana's house was trashed. Whatever had happened in here was brutal. Furniture was smashed, shelves toppled, her chess set had its marble board broken in half. In the opposite wall, I spotted a bullet hole. That made the lack of police even more suspect, unless the attackers had silencers on their guns. I liked that idea even less. I stepped inside, shoes crunching on glass from shattered picture frames. I tried to keep the emotion out of it, to just take in facts, but it was difficult. Oana had gotten her ass royally kicked saving Mina one time, and as far as it went, that meant I owed the little gymnast. And it looked like I was too late to repay her.

In the wreckage on the floor, Oana's medals from the Sydney games glinted up at me, as if to say, "She'd have taken us if she got away!" There was the gold, which she'd won as part of that unstoppable Romanian women's team, her silver for the vault, and the big one, the bronze in the women's all-around that said in 2000, she was the third best in her sport on the planet.

My mind ran through a hundred conspiracies, trying to figure out who had a beef with Oana and V.E.N.U.S. There were the Guardian Servitors of the Anorectic Praxis, of course. The Knights Templar. New Camelot. The list went on and on, and I still didn't know who might want Oana dead. Who knew what she had been up to in the year I'd been gone? And even before then, it wasn't like we were confidants. Truth be told, *I* thought she was an annoyance right up until she proved to be the best ally I'd ever had.

I went deeper into the house, seeing the same story throughout. It got a hell of a lot worse in the kitchen. On the white wall, over a calendar of puppies, was a spray of blood followed by a messy streak. It went from the doorway into the kitchen on a downward stroke, like someone had been shot, hit the wall, and had fallen.

A strangled sob came from behind me. All three girls were in the little breakfast nook leading into the kitchen, tearing up as they stared in horror at the blood.

"This isn't a lot of blood. Nobody's dead from this." I tried to sound authoritative. It wasn't too hard; I had a little experience, not in the investigation of murder, but certainly in the covering up and in the faking thereof. I was pretty good at those.

I walked into the kitchen, the linoleum creaking with

my steps. A wooden door with a broken window looked out into Oana's backyard, a nice open area that ended when the ground dropped away. It was a pretty view of a hilly area of Echo Park. I thought maybe I should have a closer look.

My foot creaked again. I looked down. Stepped. Stepped again. Frowned. I knelt and moved the knit rug away from the side of cabinets. There was a trapdoor beneath it, blood smeared on the handle. I allowed myself a smile. Oana had a way out. Of course she did. She was smart.

The girls were comforting each other. One of the Emmas was going to pieces. I opened the trapdoor and poked my head in, shining the light from my phone inside. There was a cramped tunnel burrowing away into the earth, way too small for me or any other grown human being. For a tiny person like Oana, it was the perfect escape hatch: a place where the vast majority of pursuers could not follow. To confirm it, a few drops of blood shone on one of the wooden supports. In the business, places to hide small things like documents and Romanian bronze medalists are known as slicks, and that's what this was.

I closed the trapdoor and replaced the rug, heading for the back door. I went outside, where Oana had a comfortable porch set up in front of a cactus garden and her view. I went to the edge of the little cliff and looked down. About fifteen feet below, there was a shack with a dirt road tracing the side of the slope and ending at a side road. I knew just looking that Oana's slick led into that shack and that was where she had kept her car. It looked about big enough for a Mini Cooper, which would have been a luxury sedan to her.

I turned around. The girls were on the back porch, looking at me with the same fear as someone waiting for a doctor to dispense the bad news. "I think Oana made it out of here," I said. "I need to check something."

The slope was steep, and what started as careful steps turned into an out-of-control dusty slide. The little garage was made of sagging water-damaged wood, and there was so much paint chipped off I couldn't even tell what color it had been back when the earth was young. The door was open and in the cool shadows beyond, the shed was empty.

Tire tracks, still intact on the dirt just outside, said what I had thought: Oana had a car in there at one time. The slick emerged from the wall, some dried blood on the wooden door leading into it. Oana was alive. Now the question was: where was she? I thought back to the house, trying to find that one clue that would lead me right to her hiding spot. There was always one of those on TV. The picture on the mantel would have something distinctive in the background, or those cacti in her backyard could only be bought in one nursery.

I chewed it over as I made my way down the dirt road onto the street. This street wasn't even connected to Oana's; to get to that, there was a concrete staircase up a berm, which spat me out right next to the Dead End sign on Oana's street. I went back to the house to fetch Emily and the Emmas.

Where would Oana go? Where would she feel safe? Maybe where she learned gymnastics? Where she was recruited? But those places could be found by the same people she was hiding from. I missed Mina. She had a way of cutting through the bullshit while my mind was spinning on an overload of speculation. Oana was in the wind and she was much too smart to leave clues lying around as to where.

I went back into the house; the girls were still on the porch. One of the Emmas was crying and the other one was heroically trying not to join in. Emily just looked angry.

"She was alive when she left here," I said.

"How about now?" Emily asked.

"No idea. But if she got away, my guess is she's holed up

somewhere and is gonna stay that way."

"Who did this?" asked the crying Emma.

"Wish I knew." She almost dissolved into a fresh bout of tears when I added, "But I'm going to find her. You have my word on that."

"Who are you?" Emily asked, and now I had three upset teenaged girls looking to me for some hope. I really wished I could grunt, "I'm Batman," but that didn't seem like it would be helpful.

"It's like I said: I'm a friend." A friend who is finding more and more that "retired" is a word that, to paraphrase a certain Spaniard, does not mean what I thought it meant.

I picked up Oana's medals. I didn't want them just lying there, probably because I'm a total sucker. I handed them to Emily and asked her to look after it. The girl nodded, folding the ribbons carefully and cradling the clinking discs with the respect due religious relics. I drove the three girls back to their gym and dropped them off.

"You promise?" Emily said from the curb.

"I promise," I said, feeling stupid for promising the impossible.

She nodded and the gymnasts disappeared back into the building.

Mina arrested and Oana attacked. Both were or had been members of V.E.N.U.S., a feminist conspiracy dedicated to the advancement of a positive image for women, so it was entirely possible someone was targeting the oldest secret society there was by framing a rising star and taking out their dirty tricks specialist. I might not like management, but that didn't mean I wanted to see them all dead. Add in the fact that the first two people targeted were important to me, and it was time to get a little more hands- on.

I drove back across town to V.E.N.U.S. headquarters, a

big Craftsman mansion on Mount Washington, to warn them about what might be coming their way. Memories being what they are, it was tough not to smile a little, since that's where Mina first realized I was something more than just a creep hitting on her. Of course, it caused her to beat me up, but what are you going to do?

I pulled up at the gate and the grin vanished. Out front was a Realtor's sign. V.E.N.U.S. headquarters was abandoned.

$$\bullet$$
$$\bullet \ \bullet \ \bullet$$

NOT CONTENT TO JUST ACCEPT MY DEFEAT,
I actually looked around a little, wandering around property I had once broken into. Gone. Even the garden, which had once been a series of terraces mimicking different environments, had been torn up and replaced with local plants. The concrete porch where the leaders had once lounged was bare. The house was cool, dark, and echoey. I kept thinking if I walked around the whole place, the command structure of V.E.N.U.S. would emerge from hiding, although having a hiding spot large enough for all of them seemed a bit of a stretch.

Served me right. I had been retired for a full year. Not exactly shocking that a secret society might pull up stakes and move after the place had been turned into a shooting gallery, even if it was hard to picture one of those terrestrial cetaceans V.E.N.U.S. called leaders actually moving. I got back in my car and stared at the gate, trying to will a conspiracy into existence.

I had been trying to ignore what the evidence was saying, mostly because it was too scary to really entertain, but

I'd foolishly thought of V.E.N.U.S. as a bunch of whales, opening up the free association floodgate. There was another connection between the name "Nicky Zorotovich," Neil Greene, Mina, Oana, and this place: Russian Mob boss Vassily "the Whale" Zhukovsky. Other than once trying to hire me to kill Mina, he also knew Neil and Oana from their time in a short-lived cabal whose purpose seemed primarily to betray one another. Vassily didn't like me much after I tricked him into getting ruthlessly probed by the Little Green Men, and he hated Mina just as much after she led him to this place and a date with a firing squad.

Even though he must have eaten sixty bullets from V.E.N.U.S. guards, he didn't go down. The guy was plain impossible to kill. There were legends throughout the Information Underground about his resilience. The bear-punching incident. The atomic wrestling match. The bomb-eating contest. I was there for the raygun shootout. Half of them had to be made up, but from the sheer size of the guy, you believed the stories. No one had yet figured out the way to kill Vassily, and personally I suspected it would have something to do with Mecha-Vassily.

Mina's frame-up and Neil's murder seemed a little too subtle to be one of Vassily's plans, but maybe he'd turned over a new leaf. The fact is, I didn't know enough about Mina's case to make a determination. That was a situation I had to rectify and I hoped I knew how.

I dialed a number. "Hey, it's me. I need a favor. A couple police reports." Joel's voice was quiet and a little surprised, but she was as helpful as ever. We arranged to meet at a bar not far from where I was. It was getting on toward the evening, so the regulars would give me a little protective coloration.

On the stereo: "Strychnine" by the Sonics.

Considering the name, you might think it's all about the

Assassins, or with the "water, wine" rhyme scheme, maybe the Merovingians. Nope. They're talking about a crew of narchemists from down south who were big shit in the early '90s. They were a combination of CIA psych-ops, turncoat DEA, corrupt local Mexican law enforcement, and cartel chemists. If there was a designer drug you heard about messing up heads, they were ultimately behind it, all for some weird claptrap about enlightenment and a buck.

The bar was chintzy wood, scratched and dented, with red plastic seat covers on the stools. It was a dive that earned its status mostly honestly, and it was a good enough place to wait it out where the cops wouldn't bother me. Sort of ironic considering who I'd called.

Joel wasn't a cop. She worked as a records keeper, keeping an eye on the LAPD for the Hermetic Order of the Golden Dawn. She wasn't what you'd call inconspicuous, but because of diversity requirements and the fact that she did her job well, she was practically impossible to fire. She was impossible to promote, too, but considering the Golden Dawn wanted her exactly where she was, that wasn't a problem.

We knew each other from way back and were pretty friendly. After one job where we had to stay up all night calling this one whistleblower every twenty minutes, she had come out to me. My response was something along the lines of, "Yeah, and...?" I came out that night as a *Farscape* fan, which actually *is* a lifestyle choice.

Joel knew me as Jack Rizzo, a philosophy dropout whose choice of reading material had been deemed questionable by NYU. A seeker of truth, Rizzo had later been fired by the *LA Times* for a series of pieces on the mystical roots of Boy Scout merit badges. He was a man in need of direction, which the Hermetic Order of the Golden Dawn was only too happy to provide, in exchange for running some errands.

I drank cheap whiskey and waited. Halfway into my first, I realized this thing was going to take longer than I wanted it to, so I made a phone call.

"Blank Books," Khaali said.

"I really should have thought that name through. It's Bob."

"Are you all right?"

"I'm fine, but this is going to take a little longer than I thought. Could you do me a favor? I need you to feed my salamanders."

"Those horrible creatures?"

"Yeah. There's frozen bloodworms in the fridge. If you could just give them two cubes a day..."

"Bloodworms?" She was horrified.

"Yeah. Don't worry, it's mosquito larvae. You're doing the world a favor."

"Okay. Where is your spare key?"

"Look in the turtle out front. Thanks, Khaali. If I don't see you, good luck on the exam."

"Thank you. I hope this turns out well."

"Me too."

I hung up the phone right as Joel came in out of the windy night, fixing her hair. I got up from the table, grinning. She'd finally done it. She was a little taller than me, with broad shoulders and big hands. The hormones and surgery had softened her face, and the modest skirt and blouse suited her. She looked comfortable for the first time since I'd known her.

"Joel," I said. She came over and hugged me. "You look fantastic."

"Actually, it's Lara now," she said.

"Lara, you look fantastic."

She appraised me. "So you do, Jack. Apart from the nose."

"Actually, it's Bob now," I said.

"When did that happen?" she asked, sitting down at the

table and putting her briefcase on the chair next to her. She raised a hand to signal the waitress.

"Turns out I had a more complicated professional life than I might have let on in our previous association."

She raised an eyebrow. The waitress stopped by our table and, without turning, Lara said, "Seven and seven. And get him another round on me." When the waitress scampered off, Lara said, "More complicated, hmm? I go away for a little while, and when I come back, you've vanished. Word around the campfire is there was some big shit going down right around that time."

I nodded.

The waitress was approaching the table, and though I was positive there was no way Lara could see the woman from her angle, she opened her purse, set a couple bills on the table, and kept talking. "And then you call me out of the clear blue asking for a couple files."

"Could you get them?"

"Who are you asking?"

"Right, sorry."

"What happened to you?" she asked, gesturing at the duckbill.

"Filing mishap."

She snorted into her drink. "I wasn't just blowing smoke up your ass. Other than the nose, you do look good."

"You too."

"What's this about?"

"My girlfriend was—"

"You do not have a girlfriend."

"I do! That's what that file was about!"

"Oh yeah? What does she do? Or do you even know, since you obviously met her in Niagara Falls on a class trip."

"She's a model."

Lara snickered.

"I'm serious! She's the hot redhead who was in that casserole commercial!"

Now Lara was really laughing. I swallowed the last of the whiskey in my glass and switched over to the one she got me. I had earned it.

Finally, she got herself under control. "Okay, I don't know what this is about, but that's the most I've laughed in a long time, so I guess you earned your files." She dug into her briefcase and put a pair of files in front of me. "So, you dating Vassily Zhukovsky, too?"

"Yeah, we met at Niagara Falls."

I opened the top one. It was a collection of Vassily's greatest hits, and I could tell Lara had chopped it down for my benefit. There were his earlier arrests, which never resulted in convictions, leading up to his most recent one, which finally did. It was a series of weapons charges, attempted murder, the whole nine yards, all stemming from his attack on the V.E.N.U.S. compound in Mount Washington about six months before, which was half a year after I left town. He'd leaned on Mina to give up my location, and instead, she fed him to Uzi-armed V.E.N.U.S. guards. From the looks of things, the Feds were trying to tie a RICO case to the Whale, and thus bring down the Kosher Nostra in Los Angeles. Fine by me. Seemed like Vassily was spending most of his time in San Quentin, getting shuttled back and forth for a series of interrogations. Near as I could tell, he hadn't eaten anyone yet.

This didn't absolve Vassily of what was going on. He had the kind of reach to get things done from inside prison. I set his file aside and opened up Mina's.

This one was far more focused, since Mina didn't have a criminal record to begin with. In copspeak, she was a citizen. There was her mug shot, and by the set of her jaw, I could tell she wanted to cry but wouldn't give anyone the satisfaction. She was trying to stare the camera down. I touched the picture briefly, then put my hand away, blushing and hoping Lara hadn't noticed.

"That's your girlfriend?" Lara asked. Her voice was softer now.

I nodded.

"Pretty. How'd you do that?"

"I have no earthly idea." I looked up from the page. "Why Lara, anyway?"

"*Dr. Zhivago.*"

I laughed. "I can't believe you tricked me into watching that. You said it was about cannibalism."

"Come on, if I had told you it was the lyrical examination of the troubled history of Russia, would you have Netflixed it?"

"No, but—"

"But nothing. I expanded your narrow-ass horizons."

I paged through the file and immediately regretted it. Neil's corpse lay on the floor of a living room, his head practically gone from a shotgun blast.

"Your girlfriend knows how to get it done."

"She didn't do this."

Lara was silent for a moment. "All right, she didn't do this. But believe me when I say it sure as hell looks like she did. I've seen a lot of files, Bobby, but this is one of the few honest-to-goddess slam dunks."

She was right.

That was Neil. I mean, I didn't quite recognize him, what with him being facedown and all. And missing his face. But he was the right size, the right shade, and I knew that green polo shirt that had turned Christmas-y from the flecks of blood blown across it. I wished Neil had gone through a biker phase or gotten a tramp stamp or something, just so there'd be more identifying features on him. But this was Neil Greene we were talking about. He spent his whole life as one of the gray men of the Underground. He didn't want to be noticed, so no tattoos, no tribal gauges in his ears, no festive penile piercings. Well, none that could be seen through pants, anyway.

Something bugged me about that picture. I couldn't put my finger on it, but it was like a tiny piece of glass in my palm, too small to cut but big enough to itch. Like I said, I've never killed anybody, but since I turned into the go-to gofer for the Information Underground, I've been around a lot of death. Hits, assassinations, frame-ups, and even your occasional accidental autoerotic mishap. Wasn't even the first friendly I'd seen lain out flat, or even the worst condition. But something was wrong.

Neil was found dead Friday night after neighbors reported a single gunshot. Police arrived to find the scene as the picture showed in horrifying detail. Neil Greene, late bureaucrat, was found in his living room, his head pretty much blown off. He'd been shot once in the back of the head at close range by a .12-gauge pump-action shotgun. The weapon was found on the scene, wiped down for prints. Of course, that didn't matter, because the gun was purchased by credit card online by Mina Duplessis. Unfortunately, my testimony that Mina would rather hump a polar bear than own a gun probably wouldn't carry much water, especially when I gave a false name under oath.

To make matters worse, the cops found a ton of emails between Neil and Mina, painting a picture that they were involved in some kind of tortured love affair. As the emails progressed, Neil was trying to break it off and Mina was becoming more and more unhinged. In the final one, Neil dumped her.

Let me pause here for a second.

There was no way Neil and Mina were dating. This isn't the ego of a jilted man talking. I mean, I know Mina has suspect taste in men because she's seeing me. But Neil? He made me look like a more considerate version of Don Draper. Still, even if she saw something in the guy, it wasn't in her to cheat. I'd like to say there was a little wheedling voice in my head reminding me not to be a sap, but there wasn't. I knew Mina. I trusted Mina. That wasn't her.

Still, the evidence piled up. There was a parking ticket for Mina's car outside Neil's place. When they arrested Mina, she had a key to Neil's place in her belongings, and she had no alibi. That last part was my fault: her alibi was that she was having a lovely relaxing weekend with me, someone whose existence couldn't be revealed. Mina even used some tail-losing protocols when she drove up north just to make sure she wasn't followed.

It was perfect. It was clean. It led to one place, and one place only. Mina Duplessis had murdered Neil Greene, and now all that remained was fitting her for an eight by ten concrete room.

I put the paper down and muttered, "Goddamn it."

"Looks pretty bad from where I'm sitting," Lara said. She had the decency to sound apologetic.

"Sure does."

"Means if it *is* bullshit, someone went through a lot of trouble to frame her."

"That's exactly what I'm thinking."

"Someone with a lot of influence, more power, and some kind of vicious beef. You best watch out for her, Bobby, or she's fucked."

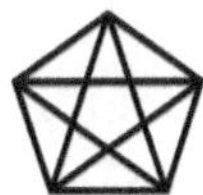

THEY SAY FRIENDS HELP YOU MOVE, BUT REAL friends help you move a body. If that's the case, then I became real friends with the Kosher Nostra two years into my old life. It was the first time I'd ever been accessory to murder, so if there's some kind of baked good associated with celebrating an anniversary that dark, mark me down for two. I had no idea I'd entered the trust circle with them, either. I'd just been dispatched on one of my errands: they handed me a bag with a sandwich and some potato salad. That hid the note, greasy now from the french dip, which listed an address and two words: "CLEAN UP."

When I got there, I saw why. The entire room looked like it had been hosed down with blood, and there were pieces, human and animal, scattered about.

It's impossible to throw up with any sense of aplomb, but I tried it anyway. I emptied my guts out right there on the floor. Hell, the place was going to be cleaned up anyway. Wasn't changing anything.

The two Russian goons already present were wearing

trash bags over their limbs. One was collecting the larger chunks while the other one wheeled in one of those wetvacs. They both impassively watched me empty my guts out over the carpet. I finally stood up straight and wiped the corner of my mouth, and one of them said something in a thick Russian accent that only got funny in retrospect.

"Bear got in."

I found out later that "bear got in" to the home of Tony Piazza, some low-level associate in the Cosa Nostra. Fortunately, he was the only one home at the time, and by the time me, Kolya, and Boris were done with the cleanup, you never have known that it used to look like a set from *Dexter*. I never knew what beef the Kosher Nostra had with Piazza—they trusted me enough to move a body, not to tell me why it had to be moved. I only knew they had killed Piazza. A lot.

I thought about that as I went out into the LA night with the wind kicking leaves and trash down the street. The air was sharp and I took a deep breath, trying to clear my head. Off in the direction of the Valley, a pillar of greasy smoke stretched into the sky, reaching outward as though to grab the wind. Helicopters thwacked through the air, circling the smoke. Because human beings are solipsists if you don't watch them carefully, I instantly drew a connection. I was back in my city, and she was burning because we were both in crappy shape.

"You and me both," I said to the smoke.

This thing was resolutely pointing me in one direction, something my subconscious was cheerfully reminding me of with "bear got in": Vassily the Whale. The fat fuck was down in Quentin, but his *organizatsiya* was out there making trouble, and I knew just where to find them. The question was, did I have the dangly parts to walk into a Russian mafia gambling den sniffing around after the recently incarcerated boss?

No, not really. Not if I had another play, but as much as I wanted one, I didn't see it. At least I wouldn't have to tangle with the Whale.

I took the Harbor Freeway toward the docks, planning my next move. The trick was to look around without attracting suspicion from men who were suspicious professionally. I checked my bandage in the rearview mirror. It was a little dirtier than it had been, but it hid my face well enough. At least, that's what I told myself, because fear-pooping would be a sure way to tell the Kosher Nostra that I didn't belong.

On the stereo: "Undestructable" by Gogol Bordello.

I couldn't even think of what it was about except for Vassily. Seriously, all I could think about was that gigantic monster, and every time I thought about him, he got bigger, shinier, scarier. Pretty soon he was the size of an actual whale, emerging from the briny deep to chow down on a couple cargo ships, longshoremen falling from his zeuglodonic jaws like screaming crumbs.

I pulled up near the Barbary Coast, which is a nice way of describing the docks. I parked a ways away and started toward the shore. Past the chainlink fence, the Port of LA stretched out in both directions on a little southern-facing spit of land. Industrial cranes loomed overhead, ships the size of city blocks floating beneath them in the oily water. The smell was an industrial stench, sort of tough to pin down into discrete scents, but strong enough to knock you on your ass. Diesel, dead fish, and something else apocalyptic tying it into Upton Sinclair's nightmare. Longshoremen drove forklifts and guided cargo to neat stacks. Even at night, the port was busy.

I ignored it all. Wasn't what I was after. I headed toward a section of the port crammed up against the side of the freeway, about as out of the way as anything could be in one of the busiest ports in the world. If you didn't know what you were looking for, you might miss it. It looked like a stack of shipping containers, and the two giants outside smoking could have been there loitering.

They were dressed awful nice, though. And I had spent enough time around people with guns to be able to know when someone was packing a Desert Eagle under his armpit because some hooker laughed at his junk one time. These guys would tell you to fuck off unless you knew the password, which I did. Problem is, I also knew them. Sasha Feldman and Mike "the Microwave" Mikhailovich. They knew me as Nicky Z, and if they recognized me, they might just decide to do Vassily Zhukovsky a little favor and drop my body in the bay.

I kept my head down a little, so both guys would be looking mostly at the haircut and the gauze duckbill. "Horrorshow," I mumbled at them. The password was a corruption of the Russian word for "good" courtesy of Anthony "Don't Call Me Tony" Burgess, though I doubted that when Vassily thought it up he'd had British literature in mind.

Sasha waved me past because I lacked a vagina and thus was not something Sasha wanted to waste his time with. I took a step forward.

Microwave looked at me, running a thumb over wiry stubble he probably had to trim with gardening shears. "Wait a minute."

Crap. I stopped.

"I know you, yes?" Microwave said.

"Don't think so," I said, putting a little more nose into my voice.

"No, I know you. Where do I know you?"

I had a little hope here. See, the human mind is three things. First and foremost, it's a miracle of evolution. A biological computer capable of astounding feats of cognition, like painting the Mona Lisa, putting a man on the moon, or writing those ID cards that used to come on the backs of G.I. Joes. The problem is, doing all this stuff takes a lot of space, and the human brain needs to be small enough at one time to pass through a pelvis without breaking literally everything, which accounts for the other two qualities of the human brain: it is stupid and lazy.

In order to do all those amazing things, the brain is filled with ridiculous shortcuts and workarounds. So while you occasionally get something incredible like *The Wire* or the pastrami burger, you also have fun little hacks to exploit when things get dicey. I learned every one of them in my years working as gofer for the Information Underground, for situations exactly like these.

Memories can be made up on the spot. The brain hates to feel like an idiot, so if it can't actually summon what it needs, you can supply it with anything plausible and it'll fill in the blanks.

"You watch a lot of Comedy Central?" I knew for a fact Microwave did. He was always quoting someone he'd seen and inevitably screwed up the punchlines. I watched him turn a harmless and hilarious Patton Oswalt bit about *Star Wars* into a shockingly racist polemic.

"Yeah...?" he said hopefully.

"I was on *Standup Showcase* last week. Albert Hall."

He snapped his fingers at me, "Albert Hall! You had that joke about..."

"Clowns lining up outside a party store like day laborers outside Home Depot."

Microwave laughed. "I knew I knew you! Why you here, Al?"

"I play cards. A friend of mine referred me."

"Oh, okay. You want to see the show later, you come find me. I get you in."

The show he was talking about was the dog fights. The psychos around here liked that sort of thing, but because they were insane, it wasn't always dogs fighting each other. They liked to catch the giant rats that lived under the city and pit those against each other or some other poor animal. I gave him a smile I hoped he thought was even slightly sincere.

"Have a good night," Microwave said, waving me through. As I opened the door, I heard him say to Sasha, "Can you believe it? Albert Hall. Here!"

"I know of no such person."

Microwave had a rejoinder prepared, but it got swallowed in the hubbub of conversation, the snap of cards, the clinking of glass, and the rushing of easy liquor. The place was nicer than I had remembered; apparently they had fixed things up in the year I had been gone. I wasn't sure what that said exactly, except maybe the Kosher Nostra wasn't missing their white whale as much as he might have hoped.

The rug was probably acquired wholesale from the Vegas collection, mostly deep red but with persistent and swooping patterns that would hide spills well. Spaced around the room were tables where people played cards, shot craps, spun roulette wheels, and did pretty much any organized activity where they could give their money to the Russian Mob without feeling like they were just handing it over. The lights were the same kinds of faux antiques you'd find in an ice cream parlor. They were tough to see under a haze of blue-gray cigarette smoke.

A bar ran along one wall, home to a couple sad sacks drinking off a losing streak and a few bros trying their luck with women who had to have day jobs working some kind of pole. Waitresses circulated through the crowd, trying not to look as tired as they obviously felt. The clientele ranged from Willy Lomans in rumpled suits to gym rats in Affliction shirts.

The women were mostly just model/actress/waitresses, the kinds of LA hopefuls that were thick on the ground.

Except one. I tried not to react, but seeing her made me flinch. Carmelita Donella, an auditor for the Knights of Malta. Italian accents can go one of two ways. Either someone talks like Super Mario and it's the most adorable thing ever, or they talk like Don Corleone and it's terrifying. Don Corleone wishes he were as scary as Carmelita. And even though you might mistake her for your standard cougar in a nice blue evening gown, it would be tough to miss the look she was giving the money as she glided between tables. She was like a shark, and that was what Malta needed her for. See, once upon a time they had been the banking arm of the Knights Templar, and these days, they were trying to recover all that Templar gold the Vatican had looted in the 14th century. The problem was, all that money had been invested for the past seven hundred years, and according to the Maltese, it was all theirs.

I didn't know what Carmelita was doing in a Kosher Nostra gambling den, but it was fair to say it was bad news for them.

If she saw me, she'd call me Chris, short for Cristobal Huerta, an enterprising young former CPA who had been drummed out after blowing the whistle on the wrong people. She had used me for any number of dirty tricks, mostly involving repossession of some kind or another. The most bizarre was probably an Oscar—a goddamn Academy Award, no shit—for Costume Design on that movie about Hitler's girlfriend. I can't remember exactly how Carmelita traced its origin to Templar lucre, but it had something to do with Eva Braun's earrings. I really wish I were making that up.

The reason I didn't want to be seen was not necessarily that she was more dangerous than the Russian Mob foot soldiers outside—she was, for the record, but for different reasons—but that I didn't want my finances completely destroyed because one of my ancestors once took a bribe from a hedge knight. She might have overlooked that in the past, but probably not after I'd vanished for a year. I knew that as good as I made Cristobal's finances look, they wouldn't survive a Donella audit. Nothing could.

I slunk to the corner of the bar and ordered a Coke. He offered Pepsi and I narrowly avoided asking for a cheeseburger and chips.

The door to the back, where the "show" happened, opened. A young couple dressed for a night on the town came out, and a mystery solved itself. I had wondered who was handling the day-to-day with Vassily cooling his heels in Quentin, and there was my answer. It didn't make me feel much better beyond the momentary endorphin rush of my brain rewarding me for terror.

The reason was because the couple was the Brangelina of the sociopath set: Arkady Lazarev and Tatiana Renko. Arkady was an old-school mobster out of Moscow who had a thing about dressing the part of a gangster. He looked it, too, almost like someone had reincarnated Bugsy Siegel but decided to crazy him up a little more. See, Arkady loved pain, but unlike most mobsters, he liked being on the other end. That's why he was always walking with a new limp, wincing at broken ribs, or adjusting bandages poking out of his sleeve.

The usual author of said pain was his girlfriend Tatiana, who had come over to the States from Kiev with her father Anatoly. If you don't know the name, he was one of the big bosses in the Russian Mob before getting taken down on an extortion scheme involving the Blue Man Group. Tatiana looked like a model in a catalogue that catered exclusively to damned souls in hell. With her ivory complexion and black hair, she almost looked like a mannequin. She was also guaranteed to be carrying six or seven knives somewhere in that body-hugging gown.

I didn't need trouble with them, either, but fortunately they weren't my immediate contacts. Sure, we'd met a couple times and I might have shared some caviar with Arkady once. But I didn't think they'd recognize me as Nicky Zorotovich... except that at the jail, a couple cops I had never met had done just that.

I circulated through the tables, keeping away from Carmelita, Arkady, and Tatiana. At a pai gow poker table near the back, where the real gamblers were getting their fix, I found one more contact. Vinnie Cha, degenerate poker player and a mid-ranking member of the Rosicrusophists, a Rosicrucian splinter group turned trendy Hollywood cult, was sitting there chain-smoking and winning. He walked around in a haze of cigarette smoke like a carcinogenic Pig Pen most of the time, but here in the gambling den, he was scaling new heights. He looked like he was trying to recreate the atmosphere of Dickensian London with little more than a cigarette and a can-do attitude. Vinnie was a decent source of information and unlike the other three people in the room I recognized, probably wouldn't do anything horrible to me.

I waited at the edge of the table, ready to catch Vinnie's eyes between hands, but the guy never looked up. He was so keyed into the game, the world around him—a world filled with armed psychopaths—had ceased to exist. I knew the man had a problem when I walked in, but I was beginning to think he might need a twelve-step program.

I waited until the douchebag across the table from Vinnie went bust and got up in a swirl of cursing and Drakkar Noir. I sat down at the table, watching Vinnie light a cigarette off the glowing stub of the last one.

I bought in. Vinnie never once looked up as the dealer turned my bills into chips. I wished the different denominations had Russian mobsters on them like the world's most insanely violent mint, but they were pretty generic. Decent quality, but nothing special. The dealer gave us each seven cards and I stared at what I had, trying to figure out how I was going to say what needed to be said.

The irony was that I got the joker, and so could build four of a kind with sevens for my bottom hand, and the king of hearts didn't make a terrible front hand. Problem was, that didn't say what I needed to say. So I was going to have to settle for a pair of sevens up top and a pair of fours on the bottom. As long as I was willing to look like a total schmuck, I could fold with my cards face up, so at least I wouldn't have to lose too much cash. Which is what I ended up doing.

Vinnie blinked when he saw the fold, finally looking up at me. He'd read the message in the cards: *Hi, Vinnie. How are you?*

He didn't nod; he was too much of a poker player for that. I caught the glimmer of recognition in his eye after he looked past the duckbill and haircut and knew he would respond in the cards. The conversation was slow, spaced out over several hands.

Go see Regina, he said to me with a bottom flush. The ace high up top added, *Now.* He meant Regina del Monaco, the local Knight of the Rose Croix, 18th Degree Practitioner, Enlightened Sage of the Ages, and Bursar of the Los Angeles Temple. My old boss. Well, one of them, anyway. I wondered why she wanted to see me all of a sudden, if that's what this was. Good timing. Or extremely bad timing, depending on your perspective.

Why?

Ask her.

The trouble with communicating like this is that you had to wait for the right cards to say what you wanted to say. To solve that problem, I was cheating. I have good hands. Seriously, it's one of my better traits. I pick up magic tricks pretty easily and I can hide a card without trying very hard, especially if I'm not cheating to actually win.

I have some questions, I said, with a pair of twos and a queen high.

Gorilla pants fish hammer.

Of course, if one side of the conversation is a degenerate gambler, you're going to get some misunderstandings from time to time. I don't even know why we bothered to include words like—oh, right. The fish hammer job. That had been fun.

Have you heard of any hits? I asked.

Of course.

Any on redheads or gymnasts?

Fortune favors the bald.

Goddamn it. Focus.

No hits on redheads or gymnasts.

How about frame jobs?

Hungry for floor wax.

I swear I will hurt you, Vinnie.

No frame jobs.

Tell me why Regina needs me.

She has something needs doing.

I had been playing pai gow poker with Vinnie for about an hour, and it was only because of my judicious cheating that I hadn't lost all of my money. I didn't like that Regina needed me for something, and it was a minor miracle that none of the other sharks in the room had recognized me. I held up a hand to cash out and got ready to get the hell out of there to hunt for leads elsewhere.

That's when a hand as big and smooth as a flipper came crashing down on my shoulder, making my bones grind together. "If it isn't Nicky Z," said Vassily the Whale.

☥

FUCKING *JURASSIC PARK*. WE'VE ALL SEEN that movie, and chances are, we all like it at least a little bit. Sure, we'd have liked it more had the dinosaurs gotten to eat those obnoxious kids, but it was a Spielberg film. He wasn't going to let kids get eaten unless that taught someone a very important lesson about fatherhood.

Anyway, the first time the T-rex shows up to wreck shop, right around when Jeff Goldblum is in the process of sleazing all over Laura Dern, the cup of water sitting on the dashboard starts wobbling. The monster is so big that her steps cause tremors in the goddamn earth. The thing is a walking earthquake. And to top it off, she can't walk two steps without unleashing an unholy roar designed to make everything within earshot lose control of its bowels. Yet at the end of the movie, she swoops out of nowhere to mess up the raptors going after our heroes with nary a thump. All of a sudden she's a stubby-armed ninja.

So, what, was the T-rex tiptoeing around? The alpha land predator of the entire history of the planet suddenly decided she needed to be sneaky? And really, for whose benefit? The audience, sure, but does that mean that the T-rex alone knew she was in a movie and behaved accordingly?

That always annoyed me. I couldn't get the image out of my head of a T-rex on tippy-toes, watching a glass of water for ripples and wincing whenever she took a wrong step. "I gotta save Alan Grant and the kids silently because dinosaurs nature-finds-a-way frog DNA."

Only it had just happened to me in real life.

Vassily "the Whale" Zhukovsky is the largest man I have ever met. I think there's something in the human genome to prevent us from getting bigger, or else Vassily himself is some kind of throwback to the days of the giant ground sloth. Actually, his mother being a *Megatherium* would clear a few things up. Anyway, the guy is gigantic, coming by his nickname in the most honest way possible: by looking like someone pulled a beluga whale out of the Arctic, put him in a shiny gangster suit, and taught him to talk like a Bond villain.

Vassily didn't cause earthquakes when he walked. That would have been silly, even in LA. But his footsteps weren't what you'd call quiet, either. Anytime he was indoors, the floor was usually squealing in agony with every thudding step. Plus, there was the whisper wake, in which everyone around would see the massive gangster coming and whisper general affirmations about how big, scary, or dreamed-up-in-the-mind-of-a-vengeful-God Vassily looked.

And yet I missed it. The first indication Vassily was there was his hand on me, already feeling like he was trying to mash me up into a thin paste. It was not a friendly grip.

"Hi there, Vassily," I said, affecting a little bravado in the hopes that it might confuse him.

He spun me in my chair, which fell to the ground. He was now holding me off the ground with that one hand.

"So, you're out of prison," I said.

He was dressed in a silver suit that looked like it might actually be made of silver. Everything on the man shone, from his shaved head to the jewelry dripping off him to the Bruno Maglis on his feet. "I am. Do you know why I was in there?"

"Poor career choices?"

Vassily hit me. Not hard. Well, not for him, anyway. He popped me right in the gut and dropped me in the same motion, causing me to hit the pai gow table and crumple in a soggy heap on the floor. Fortunately, I didn't have to stay there long; Vassily plucked me up by my collar.

"Your girlfriend. Bitch sent me into ambush."

"The way I heard it, you were going to kill me and her."

Vassily shrugged. "I don't see relevance."

"No, you don't."

Vassily smiled. He even had big teeth. Giant, prehistoric, and professionally whitened. Flat, the teeth of an herbivore. Bull elephants were herbivores, too, and it didn't improve their disposition.

"It's nice to see that you're out," I said.

"Thank you. I had to do some things, you know?"

"So you weren't paroled."

Vassily laughed. The room, which had been dead silent other than our conversation, broke out in guffaws, but it was only the Kosher Nostra joining in. I glanced around and realized that Carmelita Donella was watching the scene with interest. Goddamn it. "No, I am released on my own reconnaissance."

I didn't correct him. "Let me buy you a drink. We can catch up."

"No, no, Nicky. Did your girlfriend tell you why I was coming to see you?"

"She said something about the Publisher's Clearing House

sweepstakes."

"It is because of..." and then I saw an emotion on Vassily's face I had never seen before: embarrassment. Normally that would be a welcome sight, the terrifying mobster brought down to size and rendered suddenly human and vulnerable. Yet Vassily made embarrassment even more frightening, although I suspect it was because I knew what he would do not to feel that way. Which is to say anything at all. "We can discuss later. Come with me."

It wasn't a request. He dragged me out of the club like a kid with a teddy bear. As we went out the front, Microwave nudged Sasha and said, "What did Albert do to Vassily?"

Sasha had no idea, and frankly could not be more bored by the prospect of my impending murder. Thanks a lot, Sasha.

Vassily dragged me a hundred feet to a black Rolls, opened the trunk, threw me inside, and slammed it shut. A moment later, the car started and rolled out.

It wasn't my first time being tossed in a trunk, though I had the distinct feeling it would be my last. There was something about having it done by the originators of the trick—the mob—that gave it a classic, yet inevitable feel. My brain was working a mile a minute, and although my gut was pretty sore in a giant-fist-shaped way, I could move around pretty easily. Fortunately for me, murderers always bought cars with an eye toward how many corpses could be stuffed in the trunk.

From the sound of things, Vassily never dipped below fifty miles an hour, and no matter what the movies say, you can't walk away from a tumble at that speed. That was assuming I could spring the trunk from the inside, which would take some doing. My best bet would be to knock out one of his taillights and hope the cops pulled him over. Better to be arrested than killed, I reflected, disabling one of them.

The road started winding around, and my sore stomach

was now threatening to empty itself all over Vassily's trunk. Wouldn't really hurt my chances of survival, although I didn't want to be in a puke-smelling coffin. There's something to be said for quiet dignity.

This had gone well. I came into town and wandered into and out of a police ambush, only to get whacked by the mob. I should teach a class. Goddamn it, Mina was depending on me. There had to be a way out of this. Some way. I'd find it. I just had to stay calm and clear and I could work it out.

I got the clearest picture of Neil, lying headless on his floor, the stuff that had been him leaking out like a river delta. And naturally, my thoughts turned to Lebanon.

There are celebrities in the Information Underground. Well, not really celebrities, since that would be missing the entire point of being a clandestine operative of a group that can't officially exist. But yeah, there were guys who people told stories about, and who knew if they were true? The sure-fire way to be a rockstar was to be connected with one of the big conspiracies. Even people at home, never heard of anything know the big ones: the Moon Landing, the Fluoridators, Jonestown, Jim Morrison, and so forth into the black depths of paranoia.

Lebanon was involved in the biggest one of all: Kennedy. Supposedly, he was one of the grassy knoll shooters, though he never said one way or the other. I met him right after Castro died. Oh yeah, Castro died. Surprise! Anyway, I was working for Scorpio, this double-black cell in the CIA whose purpose seems to be ensuring that anyone who wins an election in Central America gets a free bullet with it. They called me in and paired me up with Lebanon, who by this time had shriveled into this pruny mass of elbow skin. We were going on a trip through the Southland, hitting every local playhouse, dinner theater, and concert hall we could find. Lebanon spent the first few days doing nothing more than grunting at me, and I figured I was in for a long haul of a whole lot of nothing, until day three when we saw an especially terrible version of *Our Town* out in this one-horse called Tulare, and he demanded to be taken to a bar.

Long story short, Lebanon got drunk. And not normal drunk. This guy was from the age when you could put whiskey on Cheerios. He got 1960s *Mad Men* drunk. And pretty soon he got to ranting. See, what was eating Lebanon was that back in the '60s, he had done his level best to kill Castro, and nothing worked. He ran it down, from top to bottom, and it started to sound like he was under the mistaken impression that Castro was actually the Roadrunner. He tried exploding conch shells, a poison pen with a spring-loaded needle, smearing Castro's scuba gear with LSD, camera guns... each one got progressively more ridiculous, and seriously, you can look these up, they're a matter of public record now. What really chapped Lebanon's ass was he had gone through all this time and money, and wouldn't you know it, Castro gets whacked by the North Koreans using one of the CIA's old plans: LSD-dosed monkeys released in his bedroom. A dead Castro wasn't much use, but a Castro in the CIA's pocket was much more useful, and that's how we installed Arnold Shapiro as dictator of Cuba.

Lebanon showed me some of the photos of Castro's bedroom after the North Korean hit. Not much of Castro left, not even so much as you'd know it was him. Just bananas, some gobbets of flesh, and monkey shit everywhere. I imagined the CIA shrugging and saying, "bear got in."

No monkey shit in Neil's place. Or bananas. And I could tell it was him, for the most part. But the sense that the scene was wrong somehow kept scratching at my head. I felt the thing that would break it, just out of reach. I groped for it, caught it...

...and the car stopped. Any rational thought was gone, replaced by the cold fear of the prehistoric monster now lumbering toward the trunk. No time to escape. The trunk opened and Vassily hauled me out with one hand, tossing me into the dirt. We were by the side of an access road and from the looks of things, somewhere in the Santa Monica Mountains. Below, the city glittered outward toward the black of the Pacific. Even farther, I could see the winking lights of oil derricks. This was as secluded a spot as you'd get in LA. The only illumination up here came from Vassily's headlights and a little slice of waning moon.

"I don't suppose the fact that I'm retired matters?"

"You're not retired, Nicky. Dead yes, retired no."

Vassily opened up the back door of his car and removed a shovel, tossing it to me.

I looked at it. "You just drive around with a shovel in your car?"

He grinned. "I have couple errands to run tonight."

"You mind sharing what those are?"

He laughed. "Oh no, Nicky. I am not some comic book bad guy who tells you his secret plan before he kills you."

"You look a lot like the Kingpin."

Vassily looked momentarily puzzled, although with the harsh shadows pooling on the underside of his face from the car's headlights, it mostly just ended up making him look more evil. "Dig," he said, nodding to the ground.

I dug. Because of the proximity to the ocean, the soil was fairly soft. That might be the saddest silver lining ever: the dirt was loose enough to make digging my own grave fairly easy.

"So you broke out of prison and you're going to settle some scores today, huh?" I asked between huffs and grunts, and for a moment even regretting not being in better shape before I remembered that would have just enabled me to dig my own grave quicker. I didn't bother to wait for any confirmation to my question. "So why do I get the position of honor?"

"Because you are stupid man, Nicky. You walk into my club and think you would walk out again?"

"In my defense, I thought you were in prison."

"You thought prison could hold me? You are *very* stupid man."

It was hard to argue with that sentiment in my predicament. "And you're sure there's really nothing we can do to settle this that doesn't involve the words 'shallow' and 'grave?'"

Vassily passed a flipper-hand over his shaved head. I half-hoped it would make a sound like someone rubbing a balloon, but that was wishful thinking. "You betray me, Nicky. Not once. Not twice. Three times."

"Three times? Really? That doesn't sound right at all."

I hit some rocks in my grave. Had I been as stupid as Vassily seemed to think I was, I might have thrown them at him. Sure, he hadn't pulled the pistol out of his jacket, but it wasn't like that was enough time to attack a guy who—and I can't emphasize this enough—is supposed to have beaten the shit out of a bear with his bare hands.

"First time, you are feeding information to other groups. Freemasons, V.E.N.U.S., and the Feds. Should kill you for last one alone."

"I never actually gave anything up on you guys," I said, knowing he wouldn't believe it. It was like admitting infidelity, but denying there had been any cuddling afterwards.

"Sure you didn't. Lots of money there, and you just turn up your nose? Not Nicky Z. You are gambler, loan shark, bookie... your whole life is money."

No, you psycho, the fake ID I made up to impress you is obsessed with money. While this probably wasn't the first case of someone's creativity conspiring to murder them, it was certainly the one that concerned me the most.

"What was the second time?"

"Chain, Nicky, remember? You knew where Chain of Heretic Martyr was. You and me were going to sell it. Earn your stripes, remember?"

I did remember. I even had a little flashback to the bunker in San Pedro where I'd been taped to a chair while Vassily proposed that particular business arrangement. It probably would be cold comfort to the Whale if I explained that a) I live by a simple code: do unto others before they do unto you, and I wasn't going to sit around and let him stab me in the back for the Chain, since in his case it would involve literal stabbing; and b) I still had the Chain, it was sitting in my trunk not a mile from his club, and it was currently bolted to another artifact many people would pay in the high millions for.

"I never found the Chain," I lied.

"Don't lie to me, Nicky. It hurts my feelings."

"You have feelings?"

Vassily shrugged.

"All right, what was the third time?" I asked.

He was silent, staring down at me in the steadily deepening hole. It was not a good position, because with every shovelful of dirt, I was making Vassily loom ever larger in the blue-black sky. He was starting to look like a planet with shitty taste in clothes. "The... probing."

"Oh. Yeah. I actually do feel a little bad about that one."

I had used Vassily as a very large, very loud, very Russian distraction during my rescue of Mina from the Little Green Men. Vassily wasn't going to win that fight, and honestly, just walking away from it was impressive. Sure, he was walking a little funny, but I wasn't going to make that joke.

"You feel bad? *You* feel bad?!" Vassily looked poised to jump into the hole with me, and that didn't bode well. Getting shot I could handle. Getting eaten by a man-mountain, not so much. "They melt my cars. They capture me and my boys. They take us up in ship and... and..."

Look, I can't say for certain. I mean, I was terrified. I thought Vassily was going to lose his shit at any second and beat me into something like uncooked Chicken McNugget slurry. I was trying very hard to keep things light. But I swear I saw the headlights of his car glint off a single tear shimmering on that titanic white cheek.

Vassily never finished the sentence, though I had a pretty good idea of what had happened on the ship.

He looked down at me and said with finality, "That is why you are dying tonight."

I swallowed. Things were getting a little dark. I still had no idea how I was going to get out of this situation. I didn't accept that there was no way out, but with every shovelful of dirt deposited at the lip of the hole, it was looking more and more like an actual grave. And graves aren't like pancakes; you can't just put a strawberry-and-bacon happy face on it and call it a day.

"Right, so... can't help but wonder about my girlfriend?"

"She dies, too."

"Already put that in motion?" I asked.

He stared at me. Finally: "All right, Nicky, all right. She is not hard to find, I think. When I do, maybe I bring her up here, have her dig you up. You'd like that? Be together forever?"

"Personally, I'd like you to let us go. Maybe some gift certificates to a nice restaurant or something."

"No nice restaurants, Nicky."

"So, what, like Olive Garden?"

"Very funny. You are making me think maybe I should kill you now."

"You sure you can track her down, huh?"

"She is model. I found her once, I can find her again."

"I see."

Vassily inspected the hole. It was about three feet deep. "I think that's big enough." He pulled a gold-plated Desert Eagle from his jacket.

"Vassily, look. We can talk about this, can't we? I have information. Lots of information!"

"Sorry, Nicky. This is the end of road for you. Goodbye."

He leveled the giant gold pistol at my head. The barrel got bigger and bigger until it was a black moon in a golden sky. The bullet would be so big my whole body would vanish into a little bit of pork-smelling confetti. I barely saw the giant man and his huge, fat, mitten hands enveloping the grip. He'd turned into a shadow behind the monster weapon that was ready to rocket me from my time on earth. I tried to think. There had to be a way out of this I just wasn't seeing. But all I could think of was the barrel of the gun positioned right between my eyes.

The gunshot was a rapid *pop-pop-pop*, and the sound was like someone punching ham. I didn't think I'd hear it. You're supposed to not hear a thing: you're there, and then you're not. It's over, lights out, time to go home.

There was another gunshot, this one an ear-shattering *choom* as loud as a Godzilla fart. The stench of cordite settled over me and my ears rang. I fell to the soft earth of my grave. The gun *choomed* twice more.

I opened my eyes, wondering why I wasn't feeling the sensation of having several new holes punched through my body. My hands crept over my chest and, in a stupid moment I wasn't planning to admit to anyone later, my forehead. I was unshot. Above me, over the ringing of my eardrums, I heard more gunfire, some close, some far. Flashes accompanied it. One of the headlights shattered and the world was a little darker.

I peeked up over the side of the grave. Vassily was crawling away, swearing in Russian, his Desert Eagle pointed off into the brush. By the light of his remaining headlight, I could see multiple bullet wounds across his massive chest. In the undergrowth, where Vassily was shooting, I saw a sustained flash and heard *pop-pop-pop* again. Dirt kicked up around him. Another bullet buried itself in his gut. I don't think the Whale noticed.

I thought briefly about waving to my rescuer but decided against it. After all, just because someone wanted Vassily dead didn't mean they wanted me alive.

Vassily looked over at me. "You stay!" he shouted.

I hit the ground as he fired, dirt raining down on the back of my neck.

The chatter of the gun brought a fresh round of cursing from Vassily, and this time his answering gunshots didn't throw more dirt on me. I waited until I could hear the clacking sounds that said Vassily was reloading. I poked my head up to make sure, just as he was ramming home another clip into the butt of his gun. I pulled myself up over the side, stumbled once, nearly fell, and bolted for the edge. The turn-off fell into a deep slope, dotted with California walnut trees and chaparral.

"Nicky! You stay!"

I felt like I should have said something pithy to Vassily, but I just jumped over the side. The *choom* followed me a second later, but I was already eating dirt and sliding down the hill on my ass, then on hands and knees as I tried to get to my feet. The gunfire and Russian cursing continued. Finally, I was able to stand, forearms, knees, and palms burning from where the hill had probably skinned them, and started down again as fast as I could. Finding the right mix of speed and caution wasn't easy, but I had good motivation. On one hand,

I had a Russian mobster at the top who was quite clear in his desire to murder me. On the other, this hill was fairly steep, and I didn't fancy sliding down it on my face.

"Nicky! You get back here!" Both guns fired again, getting quieter as I descended, hopping and running at turns, the stones in my shoes biting back with each step.

I hit the first stand of oaks and breathed a sigh of relief. Something between me and Vassily. I still wasn't sure Vassily wouldn't remember who he was and get up, ignoring the machine-gun fire in order to eat both the phantom gunman and me. Still, having some trees as shelter went a long way to restoring my peace of mind.

I glanced back up to where Vassily's remaining headlight still speared off into the darkness. There was a single shot from the Whale's pistol and the light winked out, almost like the bastard knew I was looking. More shots fired and pretty soon, the chattering stopped.

The shots from the pistol continued for a few more volleys and then they stopped, too. I swore. Would Vassily follow? Could he? How the hell many times had that guy been shot?

I turned back into the darkness and plunged into the trees. The branches scratched at my face and hands, but I kept moving through them as fast as I could and tried not to take a header into one of the trunks. I couldn't hear much over the sound of my blood or the persistent ringing in my ears from the gunshots. For all I knew, Vassily was following me like the boulder in the beginning of *Raiders of the Lost Ark*.

The trees were growing denser, multiplying as I got closer to flat ground. I pressed through them, not even trying to be quiet.

I smelled it first. Like a skunk, although not quite as powerful. Less of a diesel stink and more rotten milk. It might have been a coyote, but that was a lot of stench for one canid.

Then I heard other sounds. Heavy footfalls. Cracking branches from something very large moving through the same terrain I was. The deep huffing of something powerful sucking in great gusts of air. And that's when I knew for certain that I was not alone in those trees.

Bigfoot was there with me.

Supposed "experts" like to call him
"sasquatch," probably because it sounds more formal than
"Bigfoot." It's a derivative of a word in some Native American
language that roughly translates to "hoax that will cost the
white man millions in tourist dollars." Daniel Boone called
the big ape-like mammal he shot a "Yahoo," but there was
no way that would stick, not even after Bigfoot founded that
company. Every place he shows up, he gets another name:
skunk ape, yeti, alma, Momo. He doesn't really give a crap
what you call him, so I'm sticking with Bigfoot. Anyway, that
name showed up in the '50s, when people started finding his
footprints around. It's not the most creative name, sure, but
let's be honest: the guy has some seriously big feet.

On the West Coast, he keeps to the forested areas. He
wouldn't have come this far south had Los Angeles not been
such a Mecca for people like us. He spends most of his time
in Northern California, in the forested corridor between the
5 and 101 freeways that makes up the Trinity, Klamath, and
Redwood National Parks. When he's in LA, he usually sticks

to the San Gabriels or Griffith Park. If he has a meeting in town, I mean.

Bigfoot pops up in a surprising amount of conspiracies, and it's a testament to the guy that even *I'm* not sure of all of his exact ties. He's mostly featured in Little Green Men stories, though he has cameos in the weird Himalayan Buddhist groups, too. As near as I can figure, he collects cash from a couple different secret societies, though I have exactly zero idea how he spends any of it. Or on what.

To the public at large, the conception of what he looks like is the famous 1967 Patterson-Gimlin film. It shows a pretty convincing sequence of a large primate striding along some rocky terrain. The movements are relatively inhuman and in line with the differences in physiology you'd see in an ape that size and with that posture. It's been analyzed over and over again by experts around the world and not a single one has ever seen the zipper.

Sad thing is, that *is* a costume. Sorry. I wasn't part of the group that faked it. I wasn't even alive in '67, no matter what a couple of my more outlandish IDs might say. But I've met a few of the hoaxers and I've worn the suit, which really is a marvel of engineering. I mean, it was hot in there and smelled like a mile of wet dog ass, but I sort of felt like Bigfoot, even though I was looking through concealed eyeholes in his nipples. No, sorry, the Patterson-Gimlin film does not show Bigfoot.

Oddly enough, it was *filmed* by Bigfoot. So you see the confusion.

Anyway, I was panicked enough that it took me a moment to realize it wasn't Vassily following me. In my defense, they have some similarities. Like a lot of severely overweight guys, Vassily smells like a combination of baby powder, cologne, deodorant, and flatulence. And because it's Vassily, I swear the guy has a touch of a pretty distinctive fish smell to him. I like to think of it as krill.

Bigfoot has a wilder scent. He smells a little like a homeless man's dreadlocks.

Bigfoot and Vassily are of comparable size. The living fossil is taller, but the Russian is wider.

"Hey, Bob," Bigfoot said. The voice came from the darkness. I could only see a large shadow moving through the trees with impressive speed and grace.

"Hey," I said back. "You don't have a giant Russian with you, by any chance?"

"Nope. Saw one a ways back."

"Let's leave him where he is."

I never stopped. Bigfoot was skittish, even with people he knew fairly well. He hated being looked at and would only talk to me as long as we kept moving. He huffed a few times, and even though I knew him, it was hard not to get nervous at animal breathing that deep and loud.

"I thought you were retired," he said.

"I am. Or was. I don't really know. Someone framed Mina for murder, so I'm down here clearing that up." I paused, picking my way over a dangerous section of ground. "It's not going well."

"I'm sorry to hear that," Bigfoot said. He always liked Mina, ever since I'd introduced them last May. "Is that what that was all about?" I heard the gesture in his voice, catching only some movement in his big silhouette out of the corner of my eye.

"Kind of. Side effect of being back in town."

"That was Vassily Zhukovsky, wasn't it?"

"Sure was."

"Heard he was in prison."

"He was."

"Oh." Bigfoot considered that tidbit while I tried to figure out if the Russian Mob had any deals concerning sasquatch. "You don't think he framed Mina, do you?"

"He was the most logical suspect. He hates the both of us and he has the kind of resources to get it done, but he didn't seem to know Mina was in jail. I think he wants us both dead and decided to take the opportunity."

"I'm sorry to hear that, Bob."

"Me too."

"I hope Mina's all right," Bigfoot said. "Give her my love, okay?"

"I'll do that."

"Keep going the way you're going. You should get to a game trail in a little while, and you can follow that down to PCH."

"Thanks, big guy."

"Good luck, Bob." And just like that, he Batmanned me. You know, when Commissioner Gordon is mid-sentence, and he turns around and Batman is gone? Same thing. Only instead of a guy basically dressed like night, this was eight feet of stinking shag carpeting. It's one of the more impressive abilities I've seen in the Information Underground, and I've seen shit, to quote Winston Zeddemore, that would turn you white.

The tree cover broke, and down below I could see the strip of gray illuminated by the yellow lights of streetlamps and cars winding along the surface. I shivered in the wind coming off the Pacific. I was in short sleeves and it hadn't been day for a while now. The sky had begun to lighten, turning from the purple of the Los Angeles night into a softer blue. I started to see the ground in front of my feet and followed the game path Bigfoot had mentioned. Rabbits, deer, coyote, and maybe even the occasional mountain lion had built me a nice and relatively safe groove to make my way to flat ground.

I made it to PCH right as the sun was rising over my back

on Wednesday. Almost a full day and no real progress made, except for eliminating Vassily as a suspect. Maybe. I didn't like cutting him right out of hand. The Whale had to be involved in this somehow; the timing of his escape was much too convenient. I sat down by the side of the road and took off my dusty shoes, shaking out the yellow rocks and dirt that had accumulated in them.

I listened to the waves crashing against the rocks below as I pulled out my phone and called a cab. Normally I would have taken the metrorail back to my car, but that didn't exist on the west side. I'd like to blame the Rosicrucians or the Freemasons for that, but it was actually just some rich assholes who didn't want the riffraff coming into Beverly Hills. Money talks, as they say, so for the time being I was walking.

The cab picked me up twenty minutes later and I dozed in the backseat on the expensive ride back to my car. It wasn't restful, but it was a damn sight better than being in a trunk. Once I had been returned to the docks, I paid the nice man who smelled like exotic tobacco and got out of his cab.

I stood by my car for a long moment, trying to blink away my fatigue into the steadily brightening day. I was thinking I didn't have much in the way of leads when my attention turned back to the Barbary Coast. Things were picking up, the huge cargo cranes unloading long, drab boxes filled with poisonous junk from China. Vinnie Cha said Regina del Monaco wanted to see me. Chances were he already told her I had been at Vassily's club, and might have mentioned the brouhaha with the Whale. If I was on her radar, I should probably find out what was going on.

Hell, it might even relate.

On the stereo: "Missing the Moon" by the Field Mice.

Normal love song, right? Wrong. Look at the title. Now look at the lyrics. When we landed on the moon, the Little

Green Men were there waiting for us. They hovered over the Sea of Tranquility in UFOs the size of towns. Just ask Neil Armstrong. It was a warning. That's why we have yet to go back. So the song was a taunting message from the Little Green Men to us. Thanks, guys. We needed that.

The Rosicrusophists were based out of a mansion in Westwood. Sometimes I wondered why they weren't closer to their powerbase, which was Hollywood, considering how many starlets and It Boys were seen with the rose pins on their lapels. Wearing one of those said this person was a spiritual being who was being separated from their money through a combination of brainwashing and guile. It also said that talking to this person was likely to get you a forceful handshake and some lingering eye contact. It was a useful visual shorthand.

The cult had come out of the electric typewriter of one Ubiquitous Lothar Fitz-Chang. He becomes more recognizable by his Writer's Guild-approved penname of Frank Wood. He wrote a chunk of the third season of *Bonanza* and created that weird show about anorexic cops, *The Extremely Thin Blue Line,* after an ill-timed flirtation with the Guardian Servitors of the Anorectic Praxis. Unfortunately for Lothar, the failure of his show and the spate of lawsuits that followed effectively bankrupted him and ensured he'd never work in Hollywood again. It marked the first time in history anyone had ever lost a job by making actresses too thin.

With the bills piling up and his first and third wives (there was some bigamy happening) threatening to divorce him and take him for everything he owned (which at the time was an electric typewriter, a fifth of Wild Turkey, a rathole apartment on the east end of Hollywood, and six bottles of trucker uppers), Wood knew he had to do something. His solution was to down the whiskey and chew through the drugs in an ironic parallel to how his actresses had claimed to lose the weight during the filming of *The Extremely Thin Blue Line*, and write a tract. It was a self-help book called *Meet Your Face*, which made about as much sense as the title.

It was a massive hit.

With the money, Wood could finally afford some real drugs, and subsequent writings both expanded the scope of the original book, cleaned up a few of the odder ramblings (including an extended rant against drinking orange juice in the mornings, which, like a lot of his teachings, had something to do with the bowels), and added some more esoteric stuff.

It was around this time that one of the many Rosicrucian splinter groups got their claws into the guy, and his writing started adding elements of their mysticism into it. Before long, they supplanted him and had created the cult that we all know and love, lest their fleet of lawyers sue us back into the Stone Age.

I worked for the Rosicrusophists in many different capacities. They knew me as Jim Dawson, former agent. That's agent in the actorly sense and not the double sense, which was sort of ironic since, due to my possession of a conscience, I was much closer to the latter. To make certain they'd want me, I included a lot of self-sabotage in the bio. I made sure it looked like I was a guy who was not living up to his potential. Toss in some close calls with success, a couple of later stars who had only succeeded after firing Jim Dawson, and a problem with alcohol, and I was all set. And do you know what? The teachings of Frank Wood were just the thing to put me on the right path. That's some luck, right?

I had to take some of their classes to prove my bona fides. They were mostly harmless, but I could see how they might grab someone who wasn't quite so bored. It's not that I have a lot of willpower; I just have a keen bullshit detector and a lack of desire to improve myself. It's a potent combination. The real irony was that they *did* teach me something, just not what they'd wanted to: watching their techniques helped me identify the weak points in the brain, which helped me deceive people on a regular basis.

I pulled up at the gate at the mansion. "Jim Dawson here to see Regina."

The speaker barely crackled. They had tons of money, the Rosicrusophists, and weren't shy about spending it.

After a moment, the carefully emotionless voice on the other end of the intercom said, "Miss del Monaco invites you to join her on the veranda."

The gate opened with nary a creak and I drove up the semicircular flagstone driveway in front of the mansion. It was self-consciously English, with ivy climbing brick walls and cozy rooms stuffed with antiques and pretension.

I left my car out front and headed inside. The house was beautiful, with a few careful modern touches here and there. A flatscreen TV in a living room played the news to an audience of no one. A closed laptop sat on a desk looking out over an impossibly green garden. I could hear people lurking in the house, probably servants, but I didn't see a single person.

I went through a set of large French doors leading out onto a stone patio. There I saw Regina del Monaco at her wire-framed breakfast table, eating like a bird. Initially, I mostly saw the huge hat and sunglasses she used to keep out of the sun. I swear, it was shit like that that made half the Information Underground think vampires were real.

She smiled when she saw me come outside, but it was a brittle, artificial thing. I didn't take that personally. Rosicrusophists always came off a little phony. It was the fault of their obsessive need to control social situations: they lost the ability to be spontaneous.

Regina was an attractive woman, and had paid a great deal of other people's money to stay that way. She employed several personal trainers, a cook, a dietitian, and an army of surgeons. Thirty years ago, she had been legitimately gorgeous, a freckly fresh-faced beauty with the perfect black Irish complexion. Now her skin was a uniform shade of ivory, stretched tight and crepe-thin. Her body had not a single bit of softness, and with her muscles, I was pretty certain she could kick my ass without really trying. Her hair was dyed an unnatural black, lacking the subtle auburn highlights of her youth. Her green eyes, behind the shades, were in delicate pits. Her lips were the only plump things on her.

I stopped at the edge of her table. She was eating egg whites and spinach, with a little melon and blueberry on the side. She was drinking something thick and green. Swamp Thing's snot, from the smell of it.

She looked me over. "What on earth happened to you?"

I looked pretty bad. Other than my obviously broken nose, I was coated in yellow dust from the Santa Monicas, and abrasions covered my forearms and the heels of my hands. I had a few cuts on my face from brambles and some developing blisters from digging my own grave.

"Things got a little out of hand at the Bieber concert."

She clucked her tongue. "Mr. Dawson, how do you expect to ever rise in degrees if you persist in lying?"

"Nepotism and intrigue."

Regina didn't bother to dignify that. "Would you like some breakfast?"

"Actually, yeah. I'm starving."

"Finally, the truth."

No idea where the guy came from. Maybe Regina employed breakfast ninjas, trained to slink from the bougainvillea and provide eggs to hungry people in the mornings.

"Get Mr. Dawson a plate, please." When she spoke, she always met the other person's eyes. Though hers were practically invisible through her owl-glasses, I could feel them whenever they settled on me. She had the kind of palpable attention usually reserved for grade-school teachers and creepy uncles.

The man, dressed rather nattily in a stylized Salvation Army uniform—the Rosicrusophists had a thing about the Salvation Army—nodded and left. Regina gestured at the chair, which looked like it was made out of metal vines, across from her. "Please, sit."

I obeyed, settling down on the cold metal.

"Where have you been, James?" she asked.

"Here and there. You know, working on my spirit self. That kind of thing."

"You disappear for a full year, and that is what you have to say for yourself?"

"I'm here now."

"Indeed you are. I heard you were in the city last night. I also heard you had a rather... unfortunate encounter with a rough element." She was filling every word with distaste, trying to make it sound like anyone in the organization would be sullying their path toward enlightenment by frequenting such a place. But the fact was, she heard from a high-level operator who *lived* in places like that. And the Rosicrusophists didn't have a single leg to stand on when it came to worshiping the Almighty Dollar.

"Yeah. Little misunderstanding. He thought I was dating his sister, and I reminded him he doesn't have one."

"Your lies should be a little more convincing if you want me to believe them."

"Small debt. It's worked out now."

"Much better." She speared a blueberry. "I don't need to remind you that I still hold your contract."

No, you hold the contract for Jim Dawson, who is a figment of my imagination and still has a Blockbuster card because he has trouble letting go of the past. And you'll hold that contract for another trillion years, since the terms outlast my existence in corporeal form.

"You do."

A plate slid in front of me. It was—I hesitate to call it an omelet, but that appeared to be the intent—an egg white omelet shot through with slimy strands of spinach and smaller objects I later determined to be capers. Artfully arranged slices of fruit gave me a splash of color contrasting with the lump of bran muffin on the side.

"Make certain you eat the muffin, James. Your bowels could use the assistance."

"Good to know." I wanted to turn my nose up at the whole thing, but the fact was I hadn't eaten since Dan's office. I horked down the contents of my plate while Regina pretended not to notice.

"As I said, you disappeared quite suddenly and with no explanation, leaving me holding the proverbial bag."

I had the feeling she was trying to make me feel guilty. I played along. "I'm really sorry about that, and believe me, it will not happen again." *After this next time, as soon as Mina's out of jail and I never have to look at the creepy way your skin bunches up under your jaw when you chew.*

She smiled, beginning to resemble a really well-preserved iguana. "Fortunately, you have a way to make it up to me."

"I do?" I tried to sound more hopeful than I felt. Which shouldn't have been hard, considering that how little hope I was presently feeling could be found only with the assistance of very advanced electron microscopes. Regina was a powerful woman, and turning her down was a bad idea. She needed to be handled, and quickly, so I could get back to my real job without her looking over my shoulder.

Regina raised a bare arm that looked like it was made from white chocolate jerky. I heard the French doors opening and turned my head.

I recognized the woman striding through them, but I couldn't remember from where. I started running through secret societies in my head. She was in her late twenties and very pretty in a way that only the very deluded would call "Girl Next Door." Her coloring was all California: golden tan, sunbleached blonde hair tumbling over her shoulders, and big brown eyes I could see from across the room. She was dressed casually but stylishly—I'd hung around with Mina long enough to recognize expensive style when I saw it. It was killing me that I couldn't place her, and I realized I was staring. Instantly, I turned back to my food, not wanting the woman to mistake my brainfart for romantic interest.

"James, this is Heather Marie Tooms, 16th Degree. Heather, this is James Anthony Dawson, 3rd Degree."

"Pleased to meet you," Heather said with a sunny smile that showed off a mouthful of flawless, gleaming white teeth.

And just like that I knew where I knew her from. "Uh, hi! Nice to meet you. I'm a big fan."

Heather Marie Tooms, written in Papyrus across a dark screen while this same woman, five years younger and playing five years younger than that, was fighting demons with the rest of her all-girl band. Yeah, I knew her, but it was as Summer Frye, the lead singer of the Demon Eyez. Surfer girl cruelly turned into a vampire, she had used her powers to fight all the creatures of darkness. The girl who played the punky drummer had been nominated for an Oscar last year for playing George Clooney's age-inappropriate love interest, and the Asian keyboardist had her own TV show where she was a computer programmer who solved crimes with the internet or something. I don't remember Heather Tooms being in anything after the CW cancelled *Demon Eyez*.

"It's always nice to meet a fan," she chirped, although I swear there was a flash of rage in her eyes.

"I didn't know you were a Rosic... uh, one of us," I said, trying to regain my equilibrium after coming face to face with someone who would no doubt feature prominently in a "Remember the Early Aughts?" piece on Buzzfeed soon.

"Oh yes. Rosicrusophy helped me turn my life around."

I nodded eagerly, not voicing what I desperately wanted to: *Yeah, weren't you a successful actress before you joined?*

"I'm so glad you two are getting along," Regina said, though there was no sign of any actual gladness in her voice. "James, your assignment is to drive Heather wherever she wishes to go."

I blinked. That wasn't going to work. I had a girlfriend to clear of murder charges and some unknown person to stick those charges to. Not that I could say any of this. I settled on a guttural noise of abject confusion.

"I can't wait to work with you, James," Heather said to me, her relentless eye contact going far beyond intense into serial murderer and door-to-door evangelist territory.

"What are we doing now?" I managed, my perfectly engineered breakfast moshing in my innards.

"Whatever Heather needs you to do. Beyond that, I can't get into specifics with someone of your rank. Perhaps if you work on purging your negative eidolons and harnessing our technosis, you will be privy to more details later."

"Come on, James!" Heather grabbed my hand, pulling me up and out of my seat. "Can I call you Jim?" she asked, her hand settling into a far more romantic position, like we were strolling through a park together. I was acutely uncomfortable.

Heather towed me through the house. I stopped in front

of the television, where the news was showing a helicopter shot looking down at a section of the Golden State Freeway. A smallish bus with barred windows was on its side, a huge hole almost cracking it in half, with smoke billowing from the cab. Other cars had plowed into it and several were burning with the greasy smoke of oil fires.

"This was the scene yesterday in Burbank," the anchor said. "Vassily Zhukovsky, alleged head of a criminal conspiracy..."

Vassily's mugshot popped up on the screen, and the anchor kept jabbering on about the man's resume, of which he had less than half. Turned out Vassily escaped shortly after I arrived in town. *Thanks, K-PLOT,* I thought at the TV. *Could have used this information* before *that same maniac put me in his trunk. Good job.*

"Who's he?" Heather asked, abruptly noticing my interest.

"Some gangster, I guess."

"Looks scary to me." She flashed me a smile. "Stay here, okay?"

She scampered off, returning quickly with an overnight bag, which she handed to me without thinking twice about it. I was getting even more nervous. "Let's go!" She led the way outside, the smile pasted across her face never wavering once. "Which one is yours?" she asked, gesturing to the luxury cars and single dusty hybrid like she couldn't tell.

Just to mess with her, I pointed at a Rolls. "That one."

She put her hands on her hips, giving me the scolding schoolteacher pose. "Regina said I'd have to watch you."

"Yeah, I'm a stinker."

I led the way to my little car and nearly put her bag in my trunk before remembering if I did that, there would be moonrock growing over it and I'd have to explain why I had two ridiculously important artifacts in my trunk. I put the bag in the back seat instead. She got in on her side and we drove through the gate onto the street. "All right, where to?" I asked.

She rattled off an address on the Avenue of Stars in Century City. As it happened, it was an address I knew quite well. It was the local office for Quackenbush Security, a truly terrifying group of ex-spooks, soldiers, and general murderers. It was also a group I had recently pissed off when I led one of their top guys, an operative named Burt Shaw, to his death. Well, technically, I wasn't positive he was dead, but I was pretty sure. Regardless, he wasn't coming back from wherever he was.

If there was one group in the Information Underground you didn't want to piss off, it was Quackenbush Security. These were the guys the CIA called in when things got too dicey. And now we were wandering into their headquarters. Can't say I liked the timing.

"Do you know where that is?"

Sure. I had been there a couple times as Erick Levitt, a local burnout with a far-right-wing blog and glowing transcripts from high school. He even had a haircut like his hero Ronald Reagan.

"Nope," I said.

"Oh!" She rattled off directions that, as a practicing Rosicrusophist, I was expected to remember perfectly.

On the stereo: "Virginia Plain" by Roxy Music.

Sort of ironic, considering this one was about a group of Civil War-era mystics who attempted to bring both Union and Confederacy together under the obscure Roman god Glycon. Things did not go well. It reminded me a bit of Quackenbush, which was yet another group trying to create a consensus out of some bizarre belief.

Heather grinned vacantly, watching the street alertly. It was an odd combination, but you get used to it. She didn't have anything to say to the help, not once the directions had been relayed, and for the time being I was okay with that.

We pulled up in front of the glass and steel office building. My breakfast was desperately trying to escape again. Since Rosicrusophists believe any physical ailment is an expression of inner evil, doing that would convince Heather I wasn't to be trusted. Which, of course, I wasn't. Might also blow my cover at Quackenbush, which was much more dangerous that simply digging a grave at the behest of a Russian gangster.

We went into the lobby, and I hoped the guards couldn't hear my heart pounding. I don't know how they didn't. It sounded like the beginning of the *Hawaii Five-O* theme. A receptionist smiled at us and I was positive she saw right through the duckbill.

The elevator dinged right as we stopped in front of it, a bit of convenience that was probably meant to be nice but came off as creepy.

Heather stepped inside and as I made to follow her, she held up a hand. "You wait down here, Jim. I'll see you soon."

"Oh, yeah, no problem."

So I wouldn't know they'd seen me until the elevators dinged again and a bunch of Navy SEALs boiled out, ready to turn me into a hood ornament. Fun. I wandered back near the entrance, flashed an uncomfortable smile at the receptionist, and commenced to pacing.

The wait was not pleasant. I tried unsuccessfully to block out the fear. Of all the places she had to want to go, it had to be this place. A place not only able to tag me, but one that probably actively wanted me dead. Erick Levitt had called Burt Shaw to a meeting, and it was a meeting Shaw never returned from. The fact I hadn't physically, personally killed him was unlikely to hold much water with a group who thought the Tonton Macoute were too soft.

The elevator dinged and I did my best not to run. I held my breath as the door opened, certain I'd be looking into the scarred and craggy face of a man who knew how to kill me with my own ears.

Heather Marie Tooms smiled brightly at me and stepped out of the elevator, holding a manila folder. As she got closer, the smile froze on her face ever so slightly. Her eyes hardened. She was searching my face, examining my eyes, my hairline, what she could see of my mouth and chin. I tried not to notice.

She stopped in front of me, the smile completely congealed on her face now. For once, there wasn't any eye contact, because she was looking through me. I knew for certain, right then, what was in the envelope in her hands. It was a picture of Erick Levitt.

Me.

AFTER FIVE OR SIX YEARS, HEATHER'S FACE brightened, her eyes met mine, and she chirped, "Okay, let's go!"

Relief didn't flood into me so much as it was mainlined into my aorta like an Epipen filled with PCP. I couldn't quite talk for a moment and my legs felt like they were made of hot rubber.

I followed her to my car. "Where to now?" I asked, my tongue regaining some feeling.

"The Ritz-Carlton downtown. Do you know it?"

I nodded. Of course I did. It was the hotel that looked like a giant dick, at least from the side, which was the view from the freeway. In an act of stunning architectural wishful thinking, it even included balls. I started toward the hotel, settling in for another uncomfortably silent ride with my new charge, wondering how the hell I was going to get out of this and back to what was really important here: Mina.

I went through a couple plans in my head, dismissing each one as progressively more insane, until Heather, still sitting ramrod straight, staring out over the city, bubbled, "It's so thrilling, you know?"

"What is?" I asked, terrified that she might tell me.

"All of it. I mean, we're saving the world! One person at a time, sure. But when you get a chance like we're getting now, you have to just bask in it. You know? Just bask!"

"I'm basking. I'm not really sure in what, exactly."

She turned to me, and even though I was presently navigating the Santa Monica Freeway, I chanced a look at her. Little tears glittered in the corners of her big doe eyes. "You know I can't tell you. But you should know you're part of something really important, Jim. We're saving the world."

"Oh, good." I tried a smile, and against every instinct screaming at me to concentrate on the real danger sitting shotgun, I turned back to watch where I was driving. Good thing too; I hit the brakes to avoid a sudden slow-down.

"We're very lucky, you and I." She was quiet for a moment and, stupidly, I thought she might be done. Nope. "Regina tells me you're not as focused on your studies as you should be."

"Uh, no. No, I could be doing more. I just want to... you know how almost all of the world's ills come from misunderstandings?"

"Of course," she said, nodding. She didn't mention that the rest of the world's ills were caused by malevolent people secretly organized against the cult or by demonic ghosts from another planet called eidolons. It would have been gauche.

"I want to make sure I have the material really understood. So when I rise along the ladder of total bliss, I'm really *getting* it."

Heather nodded. "That's smart. That's really smart. I wish more acolytes were like you. What happened to your nose?"

"Nose eidolon."

"If you want, I have some time and I'm certified. We could try some technosis to spur healing and relieve pain."

"Really? That would be an honor!" And a colossal waste of time, to boot. "Maybe when we're done with this mission we're on. Save the world first, then save my nose."

"You're so good. There should be more like you." She put her hand on my shoulder and I tried not to flinch. Was she actually hitting on me, or was this some weird culty thing to put a wavering devotee in a car with a hot girl and see what happened? Did it really matter when all she was succeeding in doing was creeping me right the fuck out? "I'll bet you understand more of Dr. Wood's teachings than you think."

Rosicrusophists either called him Dr. Wood, despite the fact that his doctorate was honorary, or ULF, despite their staunch denial that he had another name.

"That means a lot coming from someone so high on the ladder."

I turned off the freeway and pulled up to the Ritz. "I need you to come up to my room briefly," Heather said. I dropped the car off with the valet, grabbed her bag, and ran after her with nary a shred of dignity. If I was lucky, she would give me my marching orders in the privacy of her room. If I was unlucky, she'd try some cult nonsense. And if I was *really* unlucky, she'd take another look at the photo I was sure was in the envelope and subtract a little hair, add a bandage... Nope, didn't bear thinking about. She checked in and we rode the elevator up to the 23rd floor. She had insisted on that floor. Conspiracies and that number. It's like a tic, I swear.

She let herself into her room and I put her bag on the bed.

She turned and, still smiling and staring right into my eyes, she said, with the clipped tone of a mother giving her unruly child a list of chores, "I need you to get me a Dragunov SVDS variant, a Heckler and Koch USP Compact, and a clean driver's license. Get some identification for yourself as well. Do you understand?"

I nodded. She wanted a sniper rifle, a small semi-automatic pistol, and fresh papers. She was, in all probability, sending me out to illegally acquire my own murder weapons. Wouldn't be the first time.

She looked me over. "I also want you to get a change of clothes. Shower and shave, please. If you like, you can do that here."

"No, I'm good. I have a place."

"All right," she said, without any kind of inflection to tell me what she thought of that. "If you could do that now? I need you back here by two-thirty at the latest."

"Right! Um, I need a picture." I quickly stripped the white sheet off her bed and hung it up on one of the walls. She stood with her back to it and put on a sour DMV face. I clicked a few photos with my phone. "I'll get on it." I left her to do whatever it was she was going to do in that hotel room. It wouldn't be normal, I knew that much.

This wouldn't end well. The thought rattled around in my head as I retrieved my car from the valet. She had given me several hours to get my errands done—more time than I needed, truth be told—so that left me with a lot of time to worry about my immediate future. I missed Vassily the Whale. At least the danger *he* represented was immediately obvious.

On the stereo: "Star Sign" by Teenage Fanclub.

Never one to miss irony, my iPod chose to blare a cheery anthem about the imminent return of a powerful species of alien whose very presence could drive people hopelessly insane.

My first stop was MacArthur Park, to see my ID guy. I parked at a meter and went into his newsstand, ignoring the sleeping guy at the front. I realized that, to my knowledge, the man had never been awake in his life. I passed him, pushing through the door marked "Employees Only," down a creepy hallway, and into a men's room marked "Out of Order."

Javier dos Santos slouched over his drafting table, working on IDs beneath the enervating fluorescents. He blinked at me as I entered, rubbing a hand over the few strands of graying hair bravely clinging to the other side of his head in the last exhausted vestige of a combover. "John? Been awhile."

"Sure has. I need an ID."

"When?"

"Rush job. Couple hours."

"How complicated?"

"Nothing fancy."

He nodded. "Picture?"

I handed him the phone. He hooked it up to his computer and grabbed a few. "What name do you want?"

"Ivana Balzac," I said without hesitation. I'm not proud of my sense of humor, but it had to be done.

He nodded. "Normal rates."

I almost walked out before remembering something. "Javier... do you remember that girl I came in here with last time? Short? You made a fake ID crack?"

Javier gave me an impressive poker face. I couldn't tell what he remembered or didn't. Granted, it had been a year since I had brought Oana Constantinescu into his shop while on another errand for another ID. Still, she was pretty distinctive, what with being four feet of solid muscle who walked like a show pony and wore glitter with a curious lack of irony.

I went on. "She probably came back to you for new papers after that day. I'm not asking for her name or anything, but you have to know a way to get in touch with her, especially if she wanted top-notch work." I grabbed a pen and a piece of scratch paper off his desk and scrawled my number down. "Give her that and tell her Jonah Bailey wants to talk to her." I put the scrap of paper on his table, knowing he'd never give any admission he knew what I was talking about by taking it.

My next two stops were in Silver Lake. I probably should have gotten real business done, but I had technically been ordered to do this, so it *was* all business. I could keep telling myself that all day. Truth was, I wanted a connection to her.

Mina lived in a Spanish-style bungalow on a hilly street in the hipster neighborhood of Silver Lake. The living room, which I could see through the large window in the front, was dark. I let myself in with my key.

The place smelled like her, or rather the range of scents that I thought of as belonging to her, even though the bulk were manufactured by shampoo, soap, cosmetics, and perfume companies. She combined them into something brand new, like a fruit salad but sexier.

I wasn't prepared for it, though, and I had this sense if I just went around one more corner, went into another room, I'd find her there. She'd be a little confused, but happy to see me, and we could have a nice afternoon of doing dumb couple things together.

I was pretty tired from going without sleep and running around digging my own damn grave, so I went into her kitchen and put on a pot of coffee so strong it would have the consistency of paste and be legally considered meth. Mina had made me coffee the first time I had ever been here, when I was also exhausted from something like this. I'd passed out on her couch, and she hadn't killed me. That lack of murder was the most romantic thing I'd experienced in my life to that point.

There was only a single picture of me in her apartment, and it was attached to the fridge in one of those plastic frames with a magnet on the back. It was a sunny day out in Santa Barbara and we had been walking up and down the pier and Shoreline Drive. Mina, with her ghostly complexion, never went near the beach without a layer of sunscreen, a hat, sunglasses, and a scarf. She looked like a movie star doing a really bad job of being incognito and I had been cracking up. She snapped a picture of me and I had my hand up, partially blocking the lens. I had spent a decade being paranoid about getting my picture taken and habits like that die hard. She loved the picture, even though all you could see was a shadowy head and hand, the sun blazing through outstretched fingers. She said it was very me.

Mina looked at the camera in another shot, giving the camera the smile I had nicknamed the "I've Got a Secret." She used it whenever she was hired for a traditionally male-oriented product. Made her look like she had something she wanted to tell you and only you. In that case, she had. I had taken the picture, and because of that, she considered it to be of us as a couple. Only I wasn't technically in it, unless you were Agent Cooper and somehow picked out my face in her eyes. I kissed my fingers and touched her face, almost immediately feeling like an idiot.

I took a shower. Mina was a big believer in baths and, as such, had managed that uniquely female trait of not owning any actual soap. I cleaned up with something I hoped was soaplike—despite being a thin liquid that smelled like coconut and looked like, well, I'm not going to say what it looked like because I'm a gentleman—and used Mina's deodorant. I went into her closet and grabbed a change of clothes. I didn't come here often, what with my LA paranoia, but I had an outfit or two readily available anyway. I cleaned up my various cuts and refreshed the bandages on my nose in time to enjoy the coffee. I drank it in her living room, staring at her vintage noir movie posters.

With a silent goodbye, I locked Mina's place up and went to my next stop. Conveniently, it was also in Silver Lake, not even a mile away. Farther up in the hills, it was a beautifully maintained mid-century modern home perched amongst a bunch of eucalyptus trees. I knocked on the spotless white door.

The man who answered probably wouldn't have been singled out from amongst Silver Lake's large gay population. He was fit and clean-shaven, his silver hair in a conservative, almost military cut. He was in his sixties, still in good outdoorsman shape. "Can I help you?" he asked.

"Hank. It's me."

His clear blue eyes narrowed, looking past the duckbill and to my face. "Dave?"

I nodded.

"What happened to your nose?"

"Tried to spite my face."

"I take it you're here for a purchase? Well, come on in. Rey's downstairs."

I followed Hank inside. The whole place was clean, spare, and elegant. Every single thing, just a few clocks, paintings, and knickknacks, made the place look like something out of an article on how to tastefully decorate a house. Even the photos—Hank in his fatigues, posing with fellow grunts on the shore of the Mekong, Rey with his extended family down in El Salvador—gave it exactly enough of a personal touch to keep it from being forbidding.

"It's been a long time," Hank said.

"How've you been?"

He led me down a set of wooden stairs. The walls were that kind of white that never stopped smelling faintly of paint, maybe because Hank repainted as soon as they got the slightest blemish. I knew that the stairs were leading into the earth of the hill, into the house's basement. Basements were rare in California. Hank had dug this one himself.

"I've been better." I heard the eyeroll in his voice. "Big Brother sent another audit. I swear, it's like they never learn."

"Well, maybe if you paid like, one tax. Once."

"Oh, don't you start. Taxes are theft. I maintain my property. Hell, I maintain the neighborhood. I fixed a goddamn crack in the reservoir and killed a couple coyotes that were eating neighborhood cats. The government should be paying *me*."

"You should tell them that."

"Don't think I didn't."

The door set into the wall was like a vault. No idea where Hank got it, or how he got it into his basement. He twirled his finger to indicate that I should turn around, which I did. He punched in the code, and with the sound of a whale taking a breath, the massive vault door swung open.

The room was covered in guns. It was like stepping into the loading program of the Matrix. Racks of weapons, sleek black murder machines hanging on the wall, tables of them, and cases under that packed with more. The central table was a workstation where Rey sat, oiling the manifold parts of an extremely illegal People's Liberation squad weapon. He was thirty years younger than Hank, and because he had long ago lost the ability to give a fuck, was wearing a hot pink tank top, tied up to show off some impressive washboard abs. Gun oil streaked both the shirt and cheekbones that could cut diamonds. He topped it off with Errol Flynn's mustache and Desi Arnaz's hair. Hank and Rey weren't connected to the Information Underground. They were just your garden-variety arms dealers with impeccable taste.

"Rey, look who's here. It's Dave." Hank added the last probably because of the bandage.

Rey looked up, a smile exploding across his face, quickly replaced by theatrical horror. "Honey, what happened to your nose?"

I waved it off, not having the energy to make up another response so quickly. "I'm fine."

"Well, come here," he said, getting up. He was wearing

a pair of cutoffs that Tobias Funke would have loved. Rey brought me in for a hug. We weren't close or anything; as near as I could tell, Rey had only two settings: hugging, and shooting you in the face for trampling on his Constitutional rights. He pulled back to look me over. "Somebody's getting laid."

"Wait, what?"

"You've lost weight, you're dressing better, and you don't smell like fried ass."

"I have a girlfriend, yes."

Rey let me go. "She's good for you, clearly."

"Did she make you cut the hair? I liked your hair," Hank said.

Of course Hank liked the Reagan hair. "Yeah," I said.

"I barely recognized you without it. You should grow it back."

"Not gonna happen. She's a registered Democrat."

"Sorry to hear it. So what can we get you?"

"Dragunov with a folding stock and an H&K USP Compact."
Hank clucked his tongue.

Rey said, "What do you want that Russkie Euro shit for? We've got some lovely Colts. Nobody ever went wrong with a classic 1911 .45 and I think we just got a shipment of M24 SMS. Honey, check the box by your right leg."

I stopped Hank before he looked. "It's not for me. It's for..." I wasn't going to say who, because who would believe me if I said "a washed-up teen starlet who's apparently now a hitter for a cult."

Hank cut me off with a raised hand. "None of my business who gets the weapon. Soon as we monitor that, Uncle Sam could get their hands on it, and then we're in a police state."

Rey nodded sagely, showing off his wedding band. The matching one was on Hank's finger. "First they come for your marriage, then they come for your guns."

I love Libertarians. They're adorable in their childlike belief that once you do away with government, absolutely nothing bad will fill the void.

"I'm still single," I said.

"Not for long, sweetie. Not if you're smart."

Hank tapped the air, counting through his merchandise. "Here we go. And here." He said this as he produced a foam case with the disassembled rifle inside, then found the pistol in a rack along the wall. "Baby, could you get a box of .357 SIGs and 762s?"

Rey went under the table and a moment later put two down with a thunk. I paid the guys and thanked them. Rey gave me another hug and returned to his machine gun.

"Don't be a stranger," Hank said as he walked me out.

"Have a good one."

I put Heather's guns in the trunk, careful to keep them away from the Genesis Flail. They wouldn't be in there long enough to grow any moonrock, but there was no reason to take a chance. I checked my watch and found I had some time to do what I'd come down to: solve Neil's murder to solve and get Mina out of jail. I didn't want her spending a second longer inside than she had to. That meant talking to someone who might know what was going on and a trip to the Masonic Temple in Burbank.

The temple was a nondescript building in the midst of a bunch of nondescript buildings, because this was Burbank, and character was against the Burbank town charter and nearly all of their zoning laws. I went inside, where a security guy stood up, ready to bounce me right back out onto Olive Ave.

"It's me. Colin Reznick."

The guard looked me over and muttered something into his wrist. "Stay here," he said. I nodded.

The antechamber of the Masonic Temple was the perfect match to the fading glory of the Freemasons. There was a time when these guys put together an apocalyptic plan involving a moon landing, a presidential assassination, and a nuclear bomb. These days, they were lucky if they could put together money for a beer run. The floor was scuffed linoleum and the bulletin board plastered with local flyers and a few coded want ads made it feel like a community center.

After a moment, the black curtain leading into the temple itself parted and Stan Brizendine stepped out into the antechamber. The guy had not changed a bit. He still had the perfect gray coif, the Ron Swanson mustache, and the unmistakable air of an off-duty cop.

"Brother Reznick?" he asked, plainly unsure.

"It's me, sir."

The head of the local Freemasons, Stan was the kind of person who thought he had more power than he actually did, mostly because the people who came before him did. He was slow to react to changing situations, including the internet and women wearing pants. I don't think he even noticed the bandage on my face except as an impediment to recognizing me.

"I didn't expect to see you after the business with the Genesis Stone."

I had exposed the Genesis Stone that had been in his vault as a solid gold fake. Long story.

"Yeah. I needed a little time off. I heard about Neil. I wanted to check in."

Stan nodded sadly. "A tragedy. It speaks well of you that you're still concerned about him. Considering what happened."

"How do you mean?"

"The rude woman you brought here. Her dropping you for Neil. I can't imagine that was good for the old ego."

I kept a poker face. Vinnie Cha would have been proud. "No, sir, it wasn't."

Stan nodded. "Speaks well of you." He considered what he was going to say next for at least three seconds, which for Stan might have been a record. "It's fortunate that you came by."

"Oh?"

"Neil was a member in good standing, and a vital part of our group." *And a turncoat funneling information to the Satanists, but you apparently don't know that.* "That woman murdered him. We can't let that stand."

"And you want me to do something?"

"I thought you would jump at the chance. She *did* betray you with another man. Now you have a chance to get your revenge."

"Good. I was hoping you'd say that." So Stan knew precisely nothing and had so little power he would send an absentee member to assassinate someone in custody. I listened to his pitch, nodded, smiled, and pretty much did everything I could to get out of there in a hurry.

I drove back to Javier. He handed over Heather's new ID. "Don't suppose you'll tell me if you gave my message to Oana."

Javier didn't dignify that with a response.

"Okay, good."

It was creeping up on two-thirty. I grabbed a burrito from a food truck, ate it while driving, and headed over to the hotel and possibly my immediate murder. Normally—and it worries me that this is a normal thing for me—if I get my hands on a gun I'm worried will be turned on me, I take out the firing pin. Why not the clip? The weight can be noticeable to the kind of nutbag who habitually points guns at people, which includes most hitters. A missing firing pin, on the other hand, isn't going to be noticed by anyone who doesn't take the weapon apart.

Problem is, any hitter worth their weight who has the time takes a gun apart and puts it back together before using it. To them, it's like greeting a new pet, only with creepy un-dertones that made me hope Heather never owned a cat. So when she took the gun apart and saw I had monkeyed with it, the best-case scenario was she'd think I'm incompetent and I get in even more trouble with Regina.

The firing pins would have to stay.

This all probably makes me sound like a gun nut. I'm not. I've absorbed the information by being around a lot of truly scary individuals who not only believe the old chestnut "guns don't kill people, people kill people," but really want to be the ones doing all that killing.

I'd gotten the email at the end of a long day doing all those weird errands I used to do. It was from the Brother-hood of the Magic Bullet, and all told, it was pretty straight-forward stuff: go to a location, pick up the car that would be waiting there, drive it to a place where it would be crushed into a ten-by-ten metal cube. The only indication that any-thing was off was a single line that I was to empty the trunk into a shed that would be on the property. I picked up the car, which was a nightmarish forest green Chevy Malibu, and drove that boat all the way out into the deep Valley where this guy had a junkyard set up that looked almost exactly like the oil refinery base in *Road Warrior*. He seemed to be expect-ing me, pointing me toward a shack that looked to be held up solely by wishful thinking. I opened up the trunk and had to stare, amazed, at what I found.

Guns.

All the guns.

I was younger then, and not quite as world-weary as I would later become. It seemed like every gun in existence, all in the trunk of that Malibu. Sure, the back end had dragged a little, but I figured (naive, remember) that it was loaded with books or bricks or something. There were pistols, submachine guns, assault rifles, and even one of those four-barreled rocket launchers that seemed to only exist in '80s action movies. I stared for a good five or ten minutes before beginning the task of lugging all of it into the shed. Which, other than a presently empty rat's nest, was bare. By the end, I was hot and miserable, but I was finished.

Wasn't until later I figured out what had happened, when they brought in the lone assassin of Assistant District Attorney Eduardo Guerra. Seems this guy, some empty-eyed nobody named Francis Michael Harden, decided to kill Guerra—and this was the official motive ascribed to the killing, so don't laugh—because he wanted to be on *American Idol*. Needless to say, this did not help his chances.

Anyway, I figured out the connection because Harden had supposedly shot Guerra two hundred and sixty-nine times with small arms before hitting his house with the rocket. All by his lonesome. And in less than two minutes from the beginning of the attack to the ending. Now, I could probably have found out who Guerra pissed off just by checking his caseload, but this was back before I stuck my nose where it didn't belong. You know, before I retired.

That was my first encounter with guns. And since, I've gotten a lot more experience, and none of it has been pleasant.

I parked the car, removing the case with the sniper rifle with one hand and sticking the pistol, ammunition, and new driver's license in a canvas bag I used for groceries. I had delivered enough weapons in my day not to feel too nervous as I walked through the lobby, but the odd look still got to me. I pushed through it, hit the button for 23, and hoped Heather wasn't about to kill me.

I knocked on her door.

Heather answered it. Her blonde hair was done up in a professional bun and her makeup made her look like the hottest lawyer in the office. She wore a suit, although the skirt seemed a tad short for strict professionalism. I looked at her face to avoid speculating on what the tops of her stockings looked like and how they were secured to her undergarments. Her smile widened slightly, like she could read my mind, happy she was finally eliciting the reaction she wanted. The really weird thing was her eyes were red and she was sniffling a little, like she'd been crying, but the smile was still plastered right where it had been.

"I got your things."

"And you cleaned up. Very nice! Come on in." Her voice was as chipper as ever.

She padded back in. She wasn't wearing shoes. The bathroom door was open and the swirl of scents she had used to craft her personal one was wafting out.

"Put them on the bed," she said.

I did, sitting down at the table by the window with my crumpled-up bag. Outside, late-afternoon LA sparkled under clear blue skies. Heather picked up the ID first, nodded, and put it back down. She picked up the pistol next, ejected the clip, checked the pipe, and reloaded it. I had a crystal clear vision of her leveling the pistol at me and putting two in my chest and one in my head. I tried not to look like I was expecting it, because that would mean on some level I thought I deserved it.

Then, with clockwork motions, she took the thing apart. Everything was present and accounted for, oiled and perfectly maintained because Rey took pride in his work. She put the pistol back together and laid it down. The rifle came next, and pretty soon it was back together, then in a few pieces and in its case. Finally, she seemed to remember I was in the room. "Good job, Jim! This is exactly what I asked for."

"I aim to please."

She smiled, putting the ID in a new leather wallet, which then went into a professional-looking purse along with the pistol. "Let's get going."

"Where are we going, exactly?"

"The courthouse," she said.

I really hoped no one would recognize me there. Guess it depended on how much they knew about Nicky Z. I was planning to use my Scorpio ID, since that one had the best combination of government faith and no apparent connection to what was going on. The name on it, Caleb Merrill, had no criminal record, and large swaths of his fictional past had been wiped away, leaving a southern gothic tragedy that would have made a good bio for an Olympian.

I drove past the parking structure where I always had to park when one of my many aliases got jury duty and I couldn't postpone or get out of it in some way. You want an unglamorous life, there it is, right there. I've served jury duties for literally dozens of people, and it's not like I could get out of it by saying crazy stuff. Not unless the alias was crazy, like good old Brandon MacGruder, stooge for the Little Green Men. I loved that guy. Anyway, no. I tried to build a presence, a reality, for all my names. So law and order guys like Erick Levitt and Colin Reznick had to show up and back hard-ass penalties. Touchy-feely types like Jonah Bailey and Jim Dawson had to insist on not-guilty verdicts and hope for rehabilitation.

I had the feeling we were going to need to get away a little quicker, so I found a spot about a block away and fed the meter. "How long will we be here?"

"Hopefully not more than two hours," Heather said, referencing the sign that told me when my car would be towed. I maxed out the meter while Heather left her weapons in the car. I made sure I wasn't carrying anything too incriminating and followed her down the steep hill of 1st to the courthouse entrance on Hill. Waiting in line to pass through the metal detectors, I tried not to show what I was feeling. Only yesterday I had been in a similar situation, and this time, if things went badly, I had an emotionally unstable hitter right next to me. I kept my head down but not too far down; I was pleasant but not nice. I was doing my best to impersonate a shadow, to be one of those gray people nobody looked twice at.

Which is a challenge when you've got a big white thing on your nose.

They were all staring at me. Or maybe I imagined it. I was working on no sleep, jittery from the sludge I'd made at Mina's place, and it's not like I was making this paranoia up from whole cloth. I put my wallet, keys, phone, and pack of gum in the little tray, moved through the detector, let them pass a patriot wand over my anatomy, and didn't make eye contact while trying to look like I wasn't trying not to make eye contact. Having Heather that close helped. Pretty blonde with a face just famous enough to seem familiar without the kind of baggage actual celebrity carried with it: she had the perfect combination to get through instantly. Add in her bizarrely chipper manner and she was a smokescreen in heels.

The guards were so apathetic, they didn't even wave us through. They merely turned their attention to the next poor bastards in line, the lawyers, jurors, relatives of defendants, the bored and curious.

The Stanley Mosk Courthouse existed perpetually on the edge of antique and old. Used enough to become rundown, there was still a certain quiet dignity to the vaulted halls. The people in them might have changed, started dressing differently, started wearing earbuds or futzing with phones, but it was pretty easy to feel like I had stepped into a time machine.

Heather confidently led the way, her heels clicking on the old floors. We went up a level and around a few corners, until finally she found a doorway that looked exactly like all the other doorways. She never stopped, never consulted anything to see if she was in the right place. She went exactly where she intended.

The courtroom, despite its high ceilings, was claustrophobic. There were no windows, because it was shoulder-to-shoulder with other courtrooms, like a single theater in a multiplex. The walls were beige; the pews were scratched wood. It had the feeling of a high school classroom right after lunch when everyone was nodding off, only stiffer punishments than detention were on the table.

The audience was full of humanity. I barely looked as Heather picked a bench near the back and slid in. I kept my eyes front, reminding myself that she'd left the guns in the car and there was no way we were here to kill a judge.

Oh god, I really hope we're not here to kill a judge.

I stole a peek at Heather, but she had retreated to her happy Buddha pose: totally still except for her gleaming sunny smile.

The door opened behind us and I reflexively glanced back. It took a ton of willpower not to snap my head back around, yelp, or tackle something.

Because the guy who walked in was the Archbishop of the First Church of the Antichrist.

He didn't walk in alone. Guys of his stature—pardon the pun, which you'll get in a second—never do. He had his standard entourage with him: a couple of heavies in dark suits with blood-red ties, three attractive-if-tired-looking bottle redheads, and a grinning jackass majordomo I'd once delivered goat's blood to. In the middle of all this, easy to miss if your eyes didn't go that far down, was Paul Tallutto, one of the Satanist bigwigs in the City of Angels.

Well, smallwigs. Paul was a primordial dwarf, meaning

the guy was seriously tiny. Around two foot seven if the rumors were to be believed. The Armani he was wearing was tailored perfectly, and I was willing to believe his crimson pocket square cost more than my entire outfit. His miniature skull was shaved and shiny, his goatee dyed a deep Baroness black. I turned around, hoping he hadn't seen me, and tried to remember how to breathe. As he entered, Heather glanced as well, and inhaled just sharply enough to let me know she recognized him.

Paul thought I was the Antichrist, or had at one time. Sadly, that meant he wanted to sacrifice rather than worship me.

That answered that: we had to be there for the littlest devil worshiper. I heard Paul and his entourage sliding into the pew behind Heather and me. The back of my neck felt like someone was running a French tickler over it. The few thumps coming from behind me said they were setting up Paul's little cushioned high chair. That's right when my whole body decided now was the perfect time to laugh.

Ever see chimpanzees laugh on a nature show? They do. And it's not just at Charlton Heston. See, a chimp sees a stick it thinks is a snake, finds out it's not, and laughs as a way to defuse tension. That's what the laugh is for: when your whole body is filling up with steam, the laugh lets a little of it out so you don't explode. Problem is, in really tense situations, your body will decide it's in the middle of a Louis C.K. set and there's not a thing you can do about it, except bite your cheeks, slump down, and hope for the best.

Which is what I was doing. I briefly wondered if Heather had noticed my mini-seizure and the thought touched off a fresh wave of hilarity. What would they put on my tombstone? "Killed by forgotten teen starlet"? Hell, what *name* would they use?

"All rise," said the bailiff. I got up and somehow avoided

doubling over.

The judge came in and for a single moment, I thought it was Lance Ito. That stuck me with another gale, and when I realized I was literally surrounded by murderers who'd probably get off after killing someone in Judge Ito's presence, well, that didn't help much either.

They ran through the opening procedure while I tried to think of the least funny things I could. I ran through the usual: genocide, human trafficking, sex crimes, season eight of *The Office*. Nothing worked. Not until they brought in the defendants.

I really should not have been surprised.

She stuck out, even in prison orange, cuffed hand and foot. I have no idea how she managed to look gorgeous, either. Despite what I learned about women's prison from Roger Corman, I highly doubted there was enough time for beauty regimens, pillow fights, and exploring one's sexuality. Her hair was hanging lank around her shoulders, but it was still that pretty shade of copper. She looked tired, her shoulders were slumped, and she was peering around the gallery like a hunted animal. My girlfriend, Mina Duplessis, recently accused of murder.

Her eyes met mine and widened ever so slightly. I tried to send her a psychic message: *Don't recognize me. Whatever you do, you don't know me.* I flicked my eyes to the side and she figured what I was doing instantly, looking over my shoulder. She knew Paul Tallutto, knew who he was, and knew how dangerous. She looked away then, like she had no idea who I was.

I kept still, hoping nothing showed on my face, knowing with my luck, something had. The best I could hope for was that Heather wasn't looking.

Paul Tallutto had a thing for redheads. Because Satan

supposedly preferred women with red hair and green eyes, Paul thought sleeping with them gave him occult powers. He was more stuck on the hair than the eye color and was just fine with dye jobs, which made me suspect it wasn't really about magic. In any case, it hadn't made him any taller. I was fairly certain he knew Mina—he'd popped up at one of her fashion shows, and he saw her when she saved me from a Black Mass that was about to go very badly. Even if his motives were pure—well, if "pure" meant "adding Mina to his harem"—I didn't like having Paul there.

Then again, Neil had been a Satanist. Maybe they were there for the same reason Stan Brizendine had sent me. A little payback. That didn't make it any better.

I scanned the gallery as well as I could without turning my head. I saw the back of Dan Onanian, the lawyer I'd hired for Mina, rising like a mound made of cologne. I hadn't noticed him earlier because I'd been too focused on the Satanists behind me.

I waited, watching Mina sitting on the bench with the other prisoners. Different parts of the gallery watched as well, picking whichever was the friend or the family member, communicating with little gestures and expressions. I wanted to do the same for Mina, if only to show her that I was thinking of her. Let her know she wasn't alone. I couldn't. And more than anything, that bothered me.

The court was arraigning a series of people busted for violent crimes. Every one of them had been booked on assault or murder. I didn't know if any of them were innocent, and I'd wager at least one of them was some poor lady who finally gave an abusing asshole what he had been begging for, but it was pretty clear Mina did not belong with any of them. Despite her size, she looked delicate. Scared.

Mina doesn't scare easy.

It was finally Mina's turn, dead last, and Dan stood up to represent her. They were reconsidering bail. The prosecutor started listing a litany of arrests on Mina's record: drugs, assaults, you name it, painting her as some kind of queenpin in the LA underworld. I had seen Mina's record, or lack thereof, just yesterday. Which meant all of this had been added very recently, and all of it was a lie. None of the actors present, other than Mina, seemed to know that for certain. This frame job was *thorough*.

Paul and his entourage were up as soon as the gavel fell, denying Mina bail. The judge dismissed everyone right after and Heather murmured, "We have to go. We're following the midget."

Duh.

I glanced at Mina as she went through the door, shuffling along with her ankles cuffed together. It was that look that doomed me. My eyes slid off her and met Dan's. I turned, hoping he hadn't had time to recognize me. I sped up, almost pushing Heather up the central aisle toward the back of the courtroom. Maybe Dan hadn't placed me. Maybe I'd get out of this.

Paul's people were at the door, ready to make it out into the hall.

Then I heard Dan, behind me. "Bob! Hey, Bob!"

Paul's people—the grinning asshole who knew me and the two monsters who probably got their jobs by strangling inspirational cancer survivors—innocently turned. Forcing me to turn around, right into Dan's face.

His grin got bigger. "Hey, Bob. It *is* you."

I WANTED TO SWEAR OUT LOUD. **D**AN LOOKED about ready to say something else that might doom me with any number of killers who were within arm's reach. I stuffed my hand into my pocket, pulling a stick of gum out of the pack and unwrapping it one-handed. I started walking back towards Dan, and when I had the gum unwrapped, I stooped and scraped the wrapper along the floor. "Sorry about that, sir," I said, holding out the wrapper to him.

Getting closer, I growled, "Take the goddamn wrapper and you do not know me." I smiled, handed him the wrapper, and headed back to Heather, who was watching me in confusion.

"What was that about?"

"He dropped his parking stub," I said.

"But he said 'Bob.'"

"Did he? Sounded like 'stub' to me."

The tiniest crease formed between her eyes, which was probably the equivalent of a serious frown on anyone else.

"The midget is getting away," I said.

"Mmm-hmm."

Paul's people were halfway down the hall, so we both picked up the pace. We spotted him by the massive wall of his goons, the redheads fluttering and bobbing around the perimeter. Paul would be in the middle of them, looking as pleased with himself as it was possible to look. With her targets in sight, Heather slowed down a bit.

"Hey, where do you think you're going?"

We both turned. The grinning asshole I'd delivered goat's blood to was leaning against the wall next to the john, smirking like he'd just pulled off a coup. Paul's majordomo, who thought that having the same shaved-head-and-goatee combination would lead to Satanic favor. Or possibly some kind of intergalactic royal title. He pushed off, ready to confront us while his boss got away.

Without hesitation, Heather shoved him through the bathroom door and followed him in. I didn't hear anything for the approximately three seconds they were in there together. Then Heather emerged, fixing her hair and flashing her brilliant smile at me. "All right, let's go."

"Yes. Let's." I glanced back at the bathroom, wondering what the hell had just happened, and realized, more than anything, I did not want to know. My overactive imagination supplied a scene from an Alexandre Aja movie, which was a dick move by it.

We followed Paul's group out onto the street where, naturally, the little bastard had a limo waiting. He took his sweet time loading the entourage, and I hoped it would be long enough.

We walked quickly to the corner and were reduced to sprinting up 1st Street. It wasn't entirely vertical, but it sure felt like it. My legs and lungs were both burning and I kind of wanted to throw up at the top, but didn't even have time for that. I jumped into the car, Heather following, and turned back down 1st and then onto Hill. I knew where Paul's route would probably take him: the Hollywood Freeway, only a couple blocks from the courthouse. I gunned the engine, driving a little recklessly, knowing I had to put Paul's brake lights in my sightline if I wanted to tail him.

I had an idea of where he was going, of course, but I couldn't exactly reveal to the killer next to me that I knew where the Satanist temple was in Malibu. That would definitely provoke an awkward conversation.

On the stereo: "Kundalini Express" by Love and Rockets.

Come on. Do I really need to walk you through that one?

I trailed him to the Santa Monica Freeway and from there to PCH, where I had been that morning after walking out of the wilderness with Bigfoot. If I paid attention, I could have probably pinpointed the exact spot where I came out of the undergrowth to stumble along the gravelly shoulder. But I had more important things to worry about, like the carload of Satanists in front of me.

"You planning to tell me what we're doing?" I asked her.

"I'm afraid you don't have the eido—"

"Oh, cut the bullshit. You killed that guy back at the courthouse, and now we're following the midget, and I want to know what's going on."

She stared out the windshield, not at Tallutto's car, but right through it. Finally, she whispered something.

"What?" I asked.

"Primordial dwarf."

"What?"

"He's not a midget. He has Meier-Gorlin Syndrome… it's a form of primordial dwarfism. It means, among other things, that he doesn't have kneecaps."

"How does he walk?"

"He has prosthetics."

I let that sink in. "Okay, I knew that. Not the formal diagnosis, or the kneecap thing, obviously, but the point stands. Why are we following the world's smallest galactic overlord?"

She finally turned to me, and her big brown eyes had gone all scrunched and parenthetical. She was about ready to have The Talk with me. I'd had The Talk, most recently with the woman I was presently trying to free from incarceration. See, in the Information Underground, your relative age is determined not in years, but in secrets. The more you know, the older you are, and by that kind of reckoning I am Gandalf. Problem is, they're called secrets for a reason. No one really knows how much anyone else knows, and generally assumes that they know more than everyone else because this big movie called Life is their story. They're the protagonist, so they're older. And thus, everyone else is a thirteen-year-old who just learned that his wang gets hard when he watches Jennifer Connelly ride the mechanical horse in *Career Opportunities*. Life in the Information Underground is like being constantly surrounded by parental figures who want to explain your changing body in the most condescending way possible.

Heather Marie Tooms, star of the late, unlamented *Demon Eyez*, was about to have The Talk with me. She had her Sincere Face on, concern radiating from every pore, trying to make sure she didn't shatter my fragile mind while I was winding along the highway.

"There are other groups out there, Jim."

I had to play along, too. That's the part that made me feel bad for both of us. "What? No!" God, I sounded like an asshole.

She nodded solemnly. "And none of them are as committed to raising the spiritual consciousness of all mankind as we are."

You mean not all of them will do literally anything for a buck, officially making you less discriminating than every prostitute in Los Angeles. I didn't say that. "But why not?"

"They're Misguided." In Rosicrusophy, "Misguided" was capitalized at all times, mostly because it had more of a sinister connotation than in normal society. If you were truly Misguided, you had a subconscious desire, rooted in past-life evil, to keep doing bad things. It was also a convenient club to beat members with. Fail on a task? Must be Misguided! Don't tithe properly? Misguided! Steal from the Temple? Misguided!

I mean, in their defense, I *was* Misguided. "Oh," I said. "Who are they?"

"Many different ones. All kinds, many rooted in the kind of occult nonsense Dr. Wood tried so hard to eradicate from modern thought." Sometimes their lack of self-awareness was a tad grating.

"No, I mean, who are *they*?" I pointed at the brake lights of the limo.

Heather took a deep breath. "They're devil worshipers."

I ignored that this was technically inaccurate and tried instead to think of what a normal—and I use the term loosely—Rosicrusophist would say when confronted with this new information. "That does sound Misguided." Then, because I could not stop myself, "Why would they worship the devil? If there's a devil, there's a God, and they're choosing to be condemned!"

I knew the answer—"they're idiots" is the short version—but I had to know what Heather thought.

"It's as I said. Their eidolons are stuck at a lower harmonic and can't shed the trauma of the exobirth. This causes them to idealize the immoral."

That was Rosicrusophist for "they're idiots."

"So they're Misguided. I'm thrilled that we're doing good

work here in trying to snap them out of their lower harmonic states. But what are we *actually* doing here? If this was a hit on the little guy, you would have waited outside the courthouse, probably on the roof of the LA Law Library right across the street. You would have had that Dragunov sniper rifle I got for you, and as soon as you saw his shiny little dome, you would have put a very large bullet through it. So I know for a fact we're not trying to kill the leader of this group of very dangerous Misguided."

A silence filled the car that was so goddamn pregnant I could feel its twins kicking. Finally, Heather quietly said, "I never said he was the leader."

I knew if I sputtered during my response, I was a dead man. "Give me a little credit. I *have* taken the course on Social Engineering in Negative Environments."

She watched me while I watched the limo two cars up the road. The sun was setting over my left shoulder as we drove north. Probably took her some willpower to stare directly at me with the sun shining in her face, but if there was one thing Rosicrusophists were good at, it was staring. "How did you do?"

"I passed."

"Good." Her tone was noncommittal. "He is the leader of all the Satanists in the city."

In point of fact, he's the leader of one sect of Asmodeans, but now was not the time to be pedantic.

"What are we doing?" I repeated, this time harder.

"We're looking for someone."

"What, one of them?"

"A Satanist, yes. He murdered a security consultant, and now he's being hidden away by his fellow travelers. We're going to get him back."

I started feeling sick to my stomach, but I had to know if

my fears were about to be confirmed. "Does he have a name?"

Heather was silent, deciding whether or not to tell me. "Erick Levitt," she said.

Yep. Although there were a couple problems with her version. One, Shaw was not a security consultant. He was an old-school spook responsible for enough deaths to put him squarely in war criminal territory. Two, I didn't even kill the guy; Mothman took care of that. I could see why everyone thought that, though. As a story, it tracked remarkably well. Pretty much confirmed whose picture was in the envelope.

I swallowed. "This Levitt is a Satanist?"

"Of course," she said. "Why does that matter?"

"It doesn't! Just curious. It's a lot to process." And incorrect. The First Reformed Church of the Antichrist, whose leadership I was tailing, knew me as Sam Smiley.

"This is precisely why I didn't want to tell you. You have not climbed the ladder far enough to really understand the darker aspects of the world around us. You're susceptible to insanity and even death right now."

"I know! I'm so glad I have a certified technotist here or I'd be scared."

I expected a little laugh, maybe a squeeze on my shoulder. What I got instead was silence I chose to interpret as stony. With the sunset and the traffic, I didn't want to look over at her to see what was going to happen next. The mystery was solved when I started to hear sobs coming from her side of the car.

I glanced over; she was sitting ramrod straight as always, her face in locked in a grinning rictus. Tears poured from her eyes in rivers. The sobs were coming from the involuntary movements in her throat as she tried to swallow each one.

"Heather? Are you okay?"

"I'm just so happy!"

She didn't look happy. She looked like Harley Quinn at the Joker's funeral.

"Are you sure?"

"Sometimes I cry a little. It's okay. Nothing to be worried about. It's the technosis working, resolving the eidolons to my harmonic."

"Uh-huh."

"You know that sensation of crushing sadness, where nothing matters and nothing makes sense, and you feel utterly insignificant and unloved?"

"No."

"You will when you're higher up the ladder."

"Oh, good."

"When you feel that way, you have to concentrate on your smile. That helps resolve it, tamping down those feelings in the negaverse where they belong and you can resume being perfectly happy and steadily going upward on your path."

"I see."

Heather continued sobbing and smiling and freaking me out. We passed the turnoff where the old Church of the Antichrist had been. I was glad I'd followed the limo instead of just driving there, another case of my knowledge being a year out of date.

Paul's limo broke off to the right, winding up into the cliffs of Malibu. I wasn't surprised: Satanists love beachfront property. It's one of the odder facts I've found to be true during my time in my former life.

Traffic lightened up. I sagged off the tail a little, trusting my ability to find the limo even if we lost him for a turn or two. It wouldn't do to get caught now. The sun was almost all the way gone, plunging us back into the LA night, which was never fully dark. A whole day without sleep. Fun. This really was just like the old days. Goddamn it, I was supposed to be retired.

The limo moved farther and farther into the cliffs, and now we were in the part of Malibu that was the exclusive purview of actors, athletes, corporate raiders, and the odd devil worshiper. Paul Tallutto was moving up in the world, it seemed. I guess when you find the Antichrist, that adds a little something to the faith.

Finally, the limo pulled off onto a street that led to a single property perched on the very edge of one of the cliffs. A self-consciously gothic building, the place practically screamed evil. If I went up and knocked, I'd be disappointed when Lurch didn't answer. I parked on the closest street and turned off my car.

"What now?" I asked, not really wanting an answer.

"We're going in. Erick Levitt is in there somewhere, and we're bringing him out."

Actually, Erick Levitt isn't in there yet.

Heather grabbed her pistol, loaded it, checked the pipe, and put it in the pocket of her jacket.

"Are you sure about this?"

"We have to do it. The psychic well-being of the world is at stake."

"Well, when you put it that way."

The salt wind bit into me and I shivered despite myself. The gothic castle on the beach cliff really should have had a full moon behind it, but there was only the tiniest slice of moon left in the sky. The place had a large oblong parking lot, like something outside a rec center, only the asphalt was baby-smooth and had not a single line of paint. As such, the cars were parked somewhat haphazardly. I took a moment to picture the graceful Dance of the Luxury Sedan it would take to get out of this place. And that's when I noticed the behemoth that would chew up the other cars under tires as merciless as the Northridge Quake of '94. It was bright yellow, but that apparently had not been enough peacocking for the owner. Purple and blue flames billowed up the front and sides, and for a moment, I was overwhelmed with the urge to set it on fire. It was a Hummer of some kind, but some kind of heretofore-unseen special model, one for a buyer whose penis was so small so as to become an innie, and needed a steel cock of such power and girth that none might doubt his manhood. Just looking at it, I could imagine the geological sound of its engine turning over, smell the factory effluvium belching from the ass end, and the sensation of wonder that such a thing could be driven by someone other than a warlord.

"Jim?"

"Sorry. That's a big car, is all," I said, snapping out of it.

"I've seen it before," Heather said.

"Where?"

She shook her head helplessly and tears glittered in the corners of her eyes. "I can't remember. But I took Memory and the Enlightened Mind!"

That was a class where they would show you a picture of a house, then make you draw it from memory. This was repeated until you could reproduce it perfectly, and if you were bad at art, well, sucks to be you. It was supposed to expand the temporal lobe of the brain and enable race memory. In practice, it just made you unable to ever forget that stupid house. When I took that class, I swapped out the picture of the house with one of an abandoned Rally's down in Norwalk. My instructor was ready to call it a failure until I showed him the picture he allegedly showed me. He ended up thinking he was the crazy one and I passed the class with flying colors.

"Don't worry about it," I told Heather. "It'll come to you. Just stop thinking about it."

"You must think I'm a fraud."

"I don't think that." *I think you're a crazy person, but*

you're totally sincere.

She broke into a false and gleaming smile. "You are far more enlightened than your advancement would indicate. You have this way about you."

"Thank you?"

"No, Jim." And she got right up into my personal bubble, where really only Mina is allowed on a regular basis, and put a slender arm around me. "Thank you."

"Don't we have a Satanist to kidnap?"

"And we won't fail with your can-do attitude!"

I extricated myself from her curiously strong grip and crept toward the gothic castle, reflecting that I was probably the only person who would regard a Satanist Temple as preferable to the possibly amorous intentions of a fallen starlet.

The front had a heavy double door currently shut against the windy evening. There was a side door, which would have been a terrible design flaw had this castle any intention of repelling Norman invaders. It was perfect for us, though, and even though it was locked, I was through in seconds. I have good hands.

"Regina said you had useful skills." Heather sounded a little impressed and a little suspicious all at the same time.

"And the sense to only employ them on the Misguided."

The side door opened up into a kitchen. It was pretty big, roomy enough to prepare food for the entire congregation. I wondered how many pancake breakfasts the Satanists typically held per month. The whole thing was gleaming and new, the appliances still smelling of the packaging. The floors and counters weren't just polished, they were unused. Other than Heather and me, the kitchen was empty.

We heard voices, turned muddy by distance and barriers, somewhere in the direction of the front door. I wanted to go first, since I had a lot of experience breaking and entering—

and yes, I realize this doesn't make me sound like a very good person, but there you go. But I didn't want to tip that hand too much to Heather, and I also wasn't sure how much I wanted her lurking behind me.

She drew her pistol.

I let her go first.

She went to the door to the kitchen, pushing it open a crack, waiting, then pushing it open all the way. The door led into a small hallway, probably the kind of thing intended for servants. The voices grew louder, but didn't resolve into anything intelligible. Heather and I went out into the hallway and turned toward the front. We went through another door, finding a hallway that finally looked fit for a real Satanist. Coal-black walls and a thick crimson carpet made for a solid base to lay evil down on top of. Gold-framed portraits of some Satanic luminaries, including Aleister Crowley, Gilles de Rais, and Colonel Harlan Sanders, provided some accents. There was even an end table with some black roses, which honestly, was a touch too far.

Of all the conspiracies out there, the First Reformed Church of the Antichrist was the most *nouveau riche*. I wish they'd had a fraction of the aesthetics of the Order of the Morning Star. Those guys at least had decent taste in art. That picture of Colonel Sanders looked like Genghis Khan.

Wait. It *was* Genghis Khan.

Heather pushed open the door at the end of the hall and the voices finally resolved themselves. Two speakers, one with the helium pitch dripping with lust and avarice that could only be Paul Tallutto.

"...the Temple is brand new, constructed entirely by the donations of members in good standing. It is the largest edifice dedicated to his Satanic Majesty on the West Coast."

"Bitchin' wainscoting." That voice sounded familiar as

hell. I knew I had heard it before, and shouting for some reason. Deeply pitched but rusty, probably from all that shouting, and definitely male. It had the rounded vowels of a dedicated resident of the San Fernando Valley and the sleepy cadence of a surfer.

Heather moved away from the crack in the doorway.

"We have a guy," Paul said, explaining the bitchin' origins of the wainscoting. "We have every amenity you could want. Cells, of course, in the spires, although you would be in the Archdemon Suite. Outdoor pool and hot tub, should you want a change from the ocean."

I took Heather's place and while maybe I should have been surprised, I made a little "uh-huh" noise in my throat when I saw the second speaker.

"I swim in the nude. Exclusively," he said. "Except when I'm wearing my hat."

Rodrick Rand, who you remember from, oh, every action movie ever. At least in the past couple years. Let's see, he was the blind gunfighter in *The Last Day*, he was Apocalypse Jackson in *Apocalypse Jackson*, and the cop on the edge with nothing to lose in *Killing Time*, *Loaded for Bear*, and *Standing Fast*. He has jumped away in slow motion from more explosions than most people will ever see in their lives. He has killed more German terrorists than Mossad and crashed more cars than Dominic Toretto. Supposedly, his commitment to method made him a nightmare on set, and got him kicked off of *Inglourious Basterds* because he wanted to research the role by beating a Nazi to death with a baseball bat. While I'm fine with this in principle, supposedly "German" was close enough to "Nazi" for Rand's purposes, and no one wanted *that* lawsuit.

Rand was on the wrong side of forty and getting closer to fifty than he or his publicist were willing to admit. What hair he had on the top of his head was there entirely due to will-power and positive thinking. His hangdog face was craggy and ugly, making him a sex symbol only out of the stubbornness of studio executives. In his defense, he fought the inevitable march of time well, considering how much lean muscle he had packed onto his five-and-a-half-foot frame.

Paul's goons lurked at a respectful distance from the two small men.

"That is no trouble at all," Paul was saying. "As long as you don't mind the odd paparazzo."

"I *love* those guys! *Wooo!* You know, otherwise you gotta pay someone to look at your junk."

I shut the door gently and turned to Heather. Her eye was twitching.

"Something wrong?" I whispered.

"I know him."

"So does, like, all of America."

"No, I *know* him. We did a movie together."

"You did a movie?"

She did not find that amusing. "We should just shoot them both and dangle Paul out a window until he gives Levitt up."

I didn't want her doing anything to Paul until I knew why he was at Mina's arraignment. "Or," I said, holding a finger up, "we could take this as a great opportunity to search the place while Paul is otherwise occupied."

Heather considered. "Okay."

I let out a breath I hadn't realize I was holding and we crept back towards the center of the house. It took some time, since the place was laid out like a maze, but we found our way to a spiral staircase. This led upwards into what I assumed were the spires. The staircase leveled out every floor, revealing a short hallway lined with doors. The doors opened to small, single rooms. They were nice enough, and large enough to avoid being called "cramped," but they were less than comfortable. Each had a single window, which was by far the best feature. Malibu stretched out below, the glittering lights stopping at the beach, the delicate wash of the waves at once the cheapest and most expensive lullaby in town.

With each open door, Heather grew crisper in her actions. She was fighting the negative emotions, because that's what her cult taught her to do. She was getting that tautness unique to mothers who are one tantrum away from murdering their offspring, but know that's not really an option. "He's not here!" she snapped at the last room.

"We still have three more of these. And something called the Archdemon Suite."

She ejected a frustrated sigh. "That's where Rand is staying."

"Maybe there's some overlap," I said, trying to cheer her up. "Don't Satanists love orgies?"

"Yes," she said, and the little quirk fighting to move her lip looked almost genuine.

"Let's check those other spires, then keep your fingers crossed."

We went back down the spiral staircase to the ground floor. We turned into the hall to come face to face with Paul, Rodrick Rand, and the two goons.

"Sam Smiley," Paul said. "What a pleasant surprise."

THE GOONS WERE HUGE, AND JUDGING BY HOW quickly they had Heather disarmed and both of us in painful jiu-jitsu holds, I'm not sure they understood mass and acceleration very well. They had my arm jacked up high behind my back, and out of the corner of my eye, I saw they had done the same to Heather, who was stubbornly swallowing her fear and anger. Her gun had fallen to the floor, where Rand scooped it up and gazed at it goggle-eyed.

"Sam? Who's Sam?" I asked.

"I'll admit, with the haircut and that thing on your face, you're almost unrecognizable. Almost," Paul said.

"All right!" Rand crowed. "Let's take 'em out back and I'll shoot 'em both. No, wait. Let's let them go, and then I'll hunt them. Most dangerous fuckin' game! Yeah! That's what we're doing. Frodo, Yolo," he said to the goons, "Take them out back. No! Wait, put them in like... bikinis! Banana hammock for the guy, bikini for the chick!"

"We're not hunting them," Paul snapped.

"Why the hell not? I want to hunt a person!"

"And we'll find someone at a soup kitchen for you. But this man is very important. This is Sam Smiley, or, as you might know him better, the Antichrist."

"Whoa," Rand said.

Heather's head snapped around. Well, that got her attention.

"So we're not hunting him, we're sacrificing him."

"Can I hunt the girl, then?"

"Maybe," Paul allowed. "But if I remember correctly, our Mr. Smiley has the devil's charm and a weak spot for the ladies. Keeping her around will ensure he doesn't use his infernal powers against us. Won't it, Sam?"

"I don't know what you're talking about."

"Another lie. You're a chip off the old block, aren't you, Sam? Barnabas, Jeremy, take these two to the dungeon and secure them." This last was directed at Frodo and Yolo, and was probably their real names, but after Rand christened them, there was no way I was going back.

"I'm going with!" Rand exclaimed.

"The tour was going to the dungeon eventually," Paul said. "Might as well head there now."

With one meaty hand clamped on my wrist and the other one encircling the back of my neck, Frodo gave me the bum's rush. He practically carried me down a flight of carpeted stairs, then a flight of stone ones, each step giving my shoulder a little twinge. The whole time, Paul kept up the tour for Rand, who responded with distinctly Californian noises of amazement.

"Normally, I would show you the first sublevel before getting to the dungeon. I'm certain you'll find the sex arena and the spawning range to be to your satisfaction. The dungeon can store a combination of willing and unwilling guests, with no need for any alteration in basic accommodations."

He wasn't kidding, either. The dungeon was exactly that. It

had authentic-looking stone walls with steel rings bolted into them, some equipped with chains and manacles. The lights were electric, the kinds of fake lanterns usually intended for outside use. Not really dungeon-appropriate, but they probably didn't want to deal with open flame, no matter how much ambience it might have added. The devices scattered throughout the room were decidedly not period-accurate, though. Made the whole place look like David Cronenberg's gym.

"And this is the largest sex dungeon on the West Coast."

I didn't give him a derisive snort, since Frodo still had my favorite neck in a vise. But in point of fact, the Vatican had a much larger one in Santa Clarita. Supposedly disused, they kept it around to "test" themselves. I should know, I spent the bulk of one summer picking up sex toys from this giant warehouse store in Sun Valley and taking them to the dungeon. It was a long, hot, extremely uncomfortable summer in which I did my best not to look at anyone directly.

Still, this was easily second place and nothing I could think of touched either one. Not that anything would want to. Not without all the hand sanitizer in the universe.

"It's pretty big," Rand allowed. "And I can work out down here whenever I want?"

Paul scratched his goatee and, in a slightly frightened voice, asked, "You know this isn't a gymnasium, correct?"

"I stay in shape with tantric calisthenics and penile stretches."

It was the first time I had ever seen Paul creeped out by anything. I wanted to applaud, but Frodo wasn't having that. "Uh... well, we are fully equipped for anything you might wish to do sexually."

"Paula Deen!"

"I meant hypothetically."

"Oh."

Paul sighed. "Secure them."

Yolo slammed Heather against a stone wall, clapping manacles over her wrists and ankles. "You can violate my body, but my soul has advanced far beyond your understanding," she said. There were no takers.

Frodo picked me up and stuck me onto a leather saddle, strapping me into place with a series of belts and cuffs. I quickly determined that moving too much would get me probed a little more than I generally like.

"And you... I expected more of you," Heather sneered at Rand.

"Baby, I give a hundred and fifty percent of myself at all times. On screen. In reality. To..." he reached out and pointed at her face in a manner that suggested Elvis Presley after a debilitating stroke. "You."

"You weren't always like this! Remember when you bought the whole crew massages after we had that long day on *Adrenaline*?"

Rand's face was blank. "Are you a hairdresser?"

"No! I was your co-star!"

Rand laughed. "No, you weren't."

"I was!"

"I'd remember that. My co-star on that picture was... was... Kate Winslet?"

"Me!"

"No, wait. I wasn't in that one."

"Yes, you were! I was there! Don't you remember? The director was an assh... taskmaster. Taskmaster! And he drove us all crazy?"

"Baby, I'm the sanest johnny in this place. Now, you want to get out of here and get some grounds for a paternity suit?"

"We're not letting them out," Paul said wearily.

"Hi, I'm Rodrick Rand," Rand said, reaching out to Heather.

"*The* Rodrick Rand."

She reflexively tried to extend a hand, causing her chains to angrily clink.

"Come on, Rodrick. Let's show you the rest of the place," Paul said tenderly, almost as though he were talking to a child. A child who had apparently switched his anti-psychotic meds for cocaine.

"All right."

The Satanists abandoned us in the dungeon, though they left the lights on. It wasn't out of concern for us; it was because the First Reformed Church of the Antichrist was so obsessed with evil, they did things like leaving the light on and pulling the little tabs off of the lids of gallons of milk.

Heather was fuming in her chains. "Doesn't remember me? Doesn't *remember* me? I was his co-star!"

Adrenaline was a flop, and not one of those *Joe Versus the Volcano* kinds of flops where a good movie gets buried by an indifferent audience. No, *Adrenaline* was as crappy as its nearly nonexistent reputation suggested, and generally only got brought up as the answer to the trivia question, "What's the only Rodrick Rand movie to lose money in every country except Moldavia?" And to be perfectly honest, I had totally forgotten Heather was in it.

"He seems like he might do a lot of drugs, and then there looks to be about a mountain of crazy on top of that," I suggested.

"Still. I'm an *actress*, Jim. That's how I earn a living... and now not even the co-star of my biggest movie remembers me."

I didn't want to press, since I was pretty certain she hadn't worked since that film. Nowadays, my guess was all her money came from doing nasty errands for the Rosicrusophists.

"I'm saying it has nothing to do with you. It's not that you're unmemorable or anything. I mean, I fully plan to tell my girlfriend I met you... if I had a girlfriend, that is. I don't have one of those." Crap. Didn't need another total psycho knowing about Mina.

"Yeah?"

"Yes, definitely. This is a very big day for me. I mean, back when I was..." Shit. What did Jim Dawson do? When his nethers weren't being lightly tapped by threatening latex? That's right: "Agenting. Being an agent. When I was doing that, I'd have given my left arm for a client with half your talent."

"Really?"

"Oh, sure."

"That's sweet to say."

"We can talk about it later. Now we should probably focus on maybe figuring a way out of here."

Heather quieted down, swallowing the tears that had been threatening to explode out of her. "Why do they keep calling you Sam?"

"Maybe we focus on getting me off the... penis rodeo thing?"

"Sam. The way he said it... he was so sure. He knows you. As Sam."

"It's like I said. Lots of drugs and some crazy."

"Rand, sure. But he wasn't the one calling you Sam. Paul Tallutto, who you said you had never met before tonight, called you Sam and acted like he knew you."

"I don't think I ever said that. You might have implied or inferred it. I always get those two confused, don't you?"

"You implied it. Answer the question."

"Well, you know Satanists..."

"Do you?"

"Well enough to get strapped to a sex toy, apparently."

Heather watched me without blinking. I promptly withered under that gaze. "You're changing the subject, *Sam*. Tell me how they know you."

I had to think fast. Granted, there was no way for Heather to murder me right at that moment, but I had plans, plans that involved not dying that night. Meant I didn't want to burn any bridge I didn't absolutely have to. And also, there was a part of me that believed she would find some way to kill me from ten feet away.

Sam Smiley's actual bio wouldn't help me much. I created him while trying to get in with a group that actually looks at evil as something fun and desirable. They have the moral compass of a Silver Age comic villain. These idiots self-identify as evil, which is something supposedly no one does. In Hans Gruber's mind, he's just a good thief. Darth Vader was the thin black line between order and chaos. Sauron was like the Dude: he just wanted his stuff back. Sam Smiley, on the other hand, was a bad guy who would call himself such. Proudly.

I couldn't give him a criminal record, since I was relatively young at the time, and too much time inside wouldn't have been believable. So I started with a sealed juvie record. I created a string of residences, never staying at any one address for more than six months. I then seeded fake stories to follow me around: vandalism, malicious mischief, animal-related sex crimes, that kind of thing. When I applied for the job, I could point to that stuff and say, "See, I'm as evil as you guys. Now let me get you lunch." The things I did for that job. Another reason I tried to leave it all behind.

Anyway, I couldn't use Sam's history. Had to come up with something on the spot. "Well, you know how I used to be an agent, and I wasn't doing all that well? I had this one guy who could fit six chipmunks in his mouth at once, but that's good for what, two bookings tops? I mean, once you do Letterman, that's it. So like any agent in that situation, I turned to Satan. Turns out, Satan has a bit of a 'physician heal thy-self' attitude when it comes to his favorite occupations. So I thought maybe the Rosicrusophists could help me out, seeing as there's so many stars of your caliber involved in the group. I thought I could get some clients, but instead I found a great new way to live my life. I didn't mention my prior affiliation because I didn't want you to think I'm Misguided."

"This is a pretty bad Omission," Heather said. Omission was capitalized. Since technically Rosicrusophists never lie (except to Misguided and then it doesn't count), any deception was considered an Omission. "But it doesn't answer my question. Why do they think your name is Sam?"

"You think I would join a Satanist group and give them my real name?"

"That makes sense."

It should; for once, it was even the truth.

She thought about it some more.

"And why do they think you're the Antichrist?"

"You'd have to ask them. That's new."

Heather appeared to consider it.

"Is that it?" I asked her. "Can we get to breaking out of here?"

We tried and we failed. I couldn't do much more than twitch, the way I was wrapped up. They had even left my phone on me, but there was no way to get to it. Heather had a little more freedom of movement, and I knew for a fact I could crack her cuffs in a couple seconds if I got my hands on them. Problem was, both hands were strapped to something moist and latex and I didn't really want to think about it. Af-ter a solid hour of both of us struggling, we both sagged back.

"Come on, Jim! Stay positive. We just need some way to apply Dr. Wood's teachings to the situation and we'll be out!"

"I think when Dr. Wood said we were all prisoners, he

didn't mean it quite so literally." I yawned. "Look, they're not killing us yet, so I'm thinking we take this opportunity to get some sleep."

"You're going to sleep?"

"That's sort of what I meant by that, yes."

"How can you sleep at a time like this?"

"Use the technosis, Heather," I yawned. "You'll..."

I might have finished the sentence, or I might not have. It didn't really matter, since I was going on something like thirty-six hours with no sleep. In my dream I was camping, which should have tipped me off I was dreaming, because screw camping, and I was wrapped up in a sleeping bag so tight I couldn't move. I kept hearing things off in the woods, outside of the comforting firelight. And that's when something behind me started prodding my butt. As I tried to move away, it got more insistent, and this worried me, to put it mildly.

"Wake up," something growled.

I opened my eyes. The thing was still poking at my butt. "Oh, it's just the dildo," I sighed with relief.

Frodo loomed over me and for a moment, he frowned, trying to process what I'd said. He settled on, "Wake up."

"I'm awake, Frodo." I yawned in his face. "Sorry about that. Haven't brushed my teeth in... yeah, let's not go pulling that thread."

He pulled me off of the machine and put me on my feet. I had spiders going through my whole body, so I nearly collapsed before Frodo kept me upright with one of the fingered hams he called hands.

"Jim!" Heather said.

"Yeah?"

"No, I was calling your name. They're taking you out, and when that happens, you call the person's name."

"Right. Heather!"

"What?"

"Now I'm doing it."

"Move," Frodo said, shoving me in the back, sending me stumbling forward to my knees while the blood was finally getting around to inflating my legs.

"You know, I *am* the Antichrist," I pointed out, getting slowly to my feet and wincing with the fresh spiders greeting every flex.

"Then do something." Frodo hauled me to my feet and shoved me again. I was able to keep upright that time.

"See. Didn't fall. Devil magic."

"Shut up and move." Frodo punctuated that with another shove, because he lacked imagination. When we got to the stairs, he hauled me up in the bum's rush hold. I got feeling back in my arms for this? I wasn't going to give the guy the satisfaction of making a sound, even though my freshly revived limbs felt the twisting much more acutely than they had before.

Frodo hustled me along to the ground floor. I started to hear voices, much louder than what had been waiting in the Temple when Heather and I had come in originally. This time the words were rhythmic and repetitive. There's a name for that: chanting. And nothing good has ever come of chanting. Frodo pushed a door open with my face—I turned to take it on the cheek rather than my broken nose, but it still twinged the barely healed wound—and we were in a hallway just behind the Sanctuary. Yolo waited back here as well, draped in a black holocaust cloak.

"What took so long?" Yolo asked.

"This guy won't shut up," Frodo said.

"Don't listen. He's the Antichrist. He'll take over your mind."

"Fair point, Yolo," I said. "Listen, how about you let me go, and I'll give you a truly non-fattening alternative to ice cream?"

They looked at each other, and I wondered if they were considering it or just baffled that I was still smarting off even with a Black Mass in the next room. "Here," Yolo finally said, tossing some black cloth to Frodo.

Frodo shoved me again and Yolo caught me, spinning me back into the same unpleasant hold. Frodo wriggled into the robe Yolo had tossed him.

"The Dwead Piwate Wobutts leaves no surwivors!" I said.

"Huh?"

"Oh, never mind."

Frodo approached and each man grabbed an armpit. I giggled a little, because it tickled, and I'm only human. They lifted me about an inch off the ground and carried me into the Sanctuary.

Yeah, it was definitely a Black Mass. I hate these things. They combine all the worst parts of religion and heavy metal, two things with precious few positive aspects. The worshipers stood in rows, all of them draped in black robes. Chances are they were totally naked under there, and considering that most Satanists had the same workout habits as your standard suburban swinger, this was not an appealing thought. They clutched black candles and chanted their silly gibberish.

Up on the pulpit, a black altar awaited. There were more manacles and chains for whatever poor bastard got picked as the sacrifice, and at this point, I was sure that meant me. More black candles burned in gold candelabras, while stained-glass windows depicting the anti-saints gazed down on us from their rapes and murders. Paul Tallutto stood by the altar; as I got closer, I saw he was standing on a box. They had draped some black cloth over it, but I was pretty sure if I pulled that away, it would be an apple crate or something equally ridiculous. He wore robes, accented with a silver inverted pentagram hanging around his neck by a thick chain. He carried a serrated dagger that was practically a broadsword in his tiny hand.

Paul's harem surrounded him, and I don't know what they were going for with those outfits, but they looked like Buck Rogers's dominatrices. Really, bikinis should never have giant bladed collars. Nor do boots need talons, and no one should ever have heels higher than their own fibulas. It really was a shame Jim Lee wasn't there to draw them.

The last person waiting at the pulpit was Rodrick Rand. The light of every candle seemed to find its way into his eyes and glittered off his giant, too-even teeth. He chanted, putting his own little spin on things, throwing in extra gibberish every now and then, the expression on his face one of pure glee.

Frodo and Yolo hoisted me onto the altar and the harem secured my wrists and ankles in the manacles. I was having trouble looking at anything other than the knife in Paul's hand. These manacles would be child's play if I had a single goddamn thing to pick them with. Things were beginning to look extremely bad for me.

"Hey, Paul. It's my turn!" Rand said.

"We're not taking turns. I found the Antichrist and I get to sacrifice him!" Paul hissed back.

"I've always wanted to kill a demon," Rand said wistfully.

"I know where you can find shit tons of demons," I said to Rand. "You just have to let me go."

"Sorry. Not falling for that one again," Rand said. "Stick him, Paul! What are you waiting for?"

"The Mass needs to reach the proper pitch. And we're still waiting on one person who absolutely insisted on being here."

"Fuck that. We got him now! You know how many evil plots get wrecked by waiting?" Rand grabbed Paul and hurled him to the edge of the pulpit, snatching the knife away. The assembled congregation stopped chanting to gasp as one. Rand let out an exultant "Woo!" and kicked away the box Paul had been standing on.

"Wait, you fool!" Paul shouted from the floor.

"No more waiting!" Rand shouted back, holding the knife up high over my chest. "I've got a need! A need to bleed!" And the knife came down.

THE KNIFE STREAKED A QUICKSILVER PATH
right to my heart. Gutted by an insane and drug-addled movie
star in service to a dark god. I mean, I always knew I'd go out
like this, but I'd hoped for a little more time on this spinning
ball of dirt and failure. I think my life actually tried to flash
before my eyes, but I ended up mostly regretting not getting
to see how *Game of Thrones* turned out.

The weirdest thing was the booming sound my heart made
when the knife plunged through it. I'd always figured on more
of a wet pop. Maybe a splooshing sound like throwing a bowling ball into a kiddie pool full of clay. And to be honest, I never
expected my heart to speak with a Russian accent.

"You don't kill him yet!"

I opened my eyes. The dagger was poised less than an
inch over my chest, like I was Mia Wallace and Vincent was
hopelessly confused about proper resuscitation techniques.
I followed the path up the blade, to the upsettingly vascular
hand of Rodrick Rand, to the sleeve of his black Armani suit,
to his open-collared shiny red shirt, all the way to his face. No

longer looking down at me with a crazed gleam in both eyes and teeth, his attention was on the front door. I turned away from my imminent death to have a look.

Oh, Vassily the Whale. Of course.

The Whale stood at the threshold. I don't think he had changed clothes since I saw him last, though the day had nothing to dim the mirror-like sheen on that suit of his. Bullet holes were torn in sleeves, chest, and legs. His tie was gone, his shirt unbuttoned halfway down his enormous gut. His chest, the skin tone of which was more suited to something that lived deep in the ocean where the sun would never see it, was covered in a variety of bandages, some of which were weeping with fresh blood. Not that Vassily noticed his injuries. He was too busy brandishing a pair of gold-plated submachine guns at a room full of Satanists.

"Not without guest of honor," Vassily said.

"Wait, I know you," Paul said, standing up. He snapped his tiny fingers. "You're the gangster. Vlad the Whale!"

"Vassily," he said. And he pulled the triggers. Paul disappeared in a spray of blood. "Vlad is other guy."

A moment of silence followed. Not out of respect to Paul, but because no one could believe he was dead. In the back of everyone's head—including the superstitious part of mine I wasn't the biggest fan of—there was the sense that should Paul ever die, His Satanic Majesty would do something about it. This thought had legs despite the fact that I'd seen multiple Satanists get taken to that farm upstate where they could run and play all day long, and not a single one ever got a last-second reprieve.

That's when the screaming started. I will admit to a certain amount of *schadenfreude* there, as much as I was capable of while still chained to an altar. But watching a bunch of people who until five seconds before had thought of them-

selves as the black-clad army of the apocalypse start screaming like terrified kids and flinging themselves under pews to
hide is *hilarious*. The pulpit was no exception; Rand dove behind the altar and Paul's harem hit the deck. Frodo and Yolo
went for their guns, but Vassily gently explained that error to
them with approximately five pounds of lead apiece.

I could feel Rand huddled against my right arm. He was
blubbering something, but I couldn't make it out.

Vassily began his glacial advance up the center aisle, gesturing at the cowering Satanists with his ostentatious guns.
"Now? Now are we all finished shooting?"

"Psst! Hey! Rand! Hear me?" I whispered.

He kept up the blubbering. Vassily fired his guns a few
times, bullets chattering up pews, shredding the tops into raw
wood. "Nicky! So good to see you alive and well. For now." He
was calling to me, but the lion's share of his attention was on
whatever he was shooting at the time.

I ignored him, focusing on Rand. I softened my tone like
I was talking to a dog or child. "Hey, buddy, you okay down
there?"

Rand whispered something. Then he said it again, and
this time I could actually make it out: "He shot Paul."

"Don't worry about that now. He's in Hell, where he's a
lot happier. I need you to unlock me, though."

"We're sacrificing you," he whined.

"I think that plan went out the window when your archbishop got the hard goodbye, wouldn't you say?"

He didn't have a good response to that one. It didn't help
that Vassily was accompanying his shooting with a steady
stream of trash-talk. Half of it was directed at me, generally
insults to my integrity and intelligence, and half was at the Satanists, who he compared to portions of a stripper's anatomy.

I decided to switch tracks, knowing I didn't have time to

do this again if I crashed and burned. There was one thing I knew about actors, and it was a universal thing, learned over a lifetime spent in the entertainment capital of the world. "I don't know if I mentioned this earlier, when you wanted to hunt me, but I'm a really big fan."

His voice, hopeful, floated up from below. "You are?"

"Oh yeah. *Killing Time* is my favorite movie of all time. Fuck *Die Hard*." That was practically blasphemy, but I forced myself to say it, knowing I could make it up to *Die Hard* later if I made it out of this.

"I always thought *Die Hard* was better."

"Oh, come on. John McClane could barely kill one terrorist at a time," I said, continuing to spew awful nonsense. It became abundantly clear to me that I would say anything to stay alive. I hoped Mina would still respect me afterwards.

"I killed whole rooms of guys."

"With karate." God, that scene was so dumb. "That scene was amazing."

"Yeah," he said, warming to the thought.

"Nicky! I think this is irony, no? You go from dead in the hills to dead in some slightly different hills?" Gunfire choked off Vassily's laugh, and I didn't have time to explain irony to him.

"So, Rodrick... can I call you Rodrick? Good. If you could just get me the key to these manacles, you'd not only be saving the Antichrist, you'd be saving a really big fan."

"The Antichrist likes me?"

"You are the Antichrist's favorite actor." I felt like that, at least, was the truth.

I think he heard the sincerity in my voice, because he went to Paul's tiny corpse and rummaged through what was left of the pockets.

"Hey! I know you," Vassily said, gesturing with the submachine gun. "You are guy from *Adrenaline!*"

"Yeah, I..."

Vassily sprayed the front of the pulpit with gunfire, sending Rand to kiss the carpet. I tried to roll away, but I didn't have much freedom of motion. Bits of wood and carpet fibers flew upward to hit me in the face.

"Is nice to meet you!"

"Rodrick, please tell me you got the key," I said, spitting out a little red carpet.

"Right here."

"I can't look over and see it. Just unlock me, please?"

"Sorry, man. Keep watching."

He mashed the key into my hand and sprinted for the exit.

"I love *Adrenaline!*" Vassily yelled, chasing Rand out of the church with bullets. "Is best movie ever!"

I have really good hands. On a normal day, these manacles would already have been open and I'd be following a coked-up movie star at high speeds. This wasn't a normal day. As he lumbered forward like a constipated bear, Vassily kept hosing the front of the altar down between my left wrist and ankle.

"Aim for the chains!" I shouted at him.

He laughed. "Oh, Nicky. I will miss you little bit when you're in the ground!"

In my right hand, shielded from Vassily by the altar, I worked the key around into the lock at my wrist. "Why miss me? We were partners once!"

"Partners? *Partners*? You were employee!" He punctuated that with a solid wall of lead that ripped into curtains, cut candles in half, and probably ruined that wainscoting Rand had been admiring. A member of the harem screamed.

The key was right at the lock, but I couldn't get it to slide in. Sorry about the imagery there, but it's literally impossible to describe opening a lock without sounding like you're losing your virginity to a robot.

"A good employee! I backed you against Markov!"

"Did you kill anybody? Did you beat anybody?"

"I gave you information!"

"I have internet, Nicky. So until you also give me naked girls, you are useless."

The key slid home and the lock cracked open. I leaned over, opening the lock on my left wrist in one motion.

"Nicky?" Vassily asked, momentarily stunned.

I wanted to say something cool, but I really didn't want to be shot. Or grabbed. Or shot and grabbed. Vassily might be toying with me now, but he wasn't known for his patience or restraint. I did a sit-up and had the shackle undone on my left ankle.

"Nicky, stop!"

Right ankle. I heard the gun and hoped he was still shooting to warn. Bullets chewed the front of the altar, spitting out broken bits of wood. I jumped off it, hit the carpet, and ran. The gun barked again and the carpet directly in front of me disappeared into blackened holes.

"Nowhere to go, Nicky!"

I skidded to a stop, every fast-twitch muscle in my body trying to hurl me forward. He fired again, and if there had been a guy in front of me, or at the door Rand had gone through, he would have been *so* dead. Vassily wanted to prove this point so badly, he kept firing, turning the floor into a mass of bullet holes.

Then: *click-click-click*.

Vassily cursed in Russian and I sprinted for the door. I hit it and turned the corner. Bullets followed me through into the hall, shredding the portrait of either Genghis Khan or Colonel Sanders, then slamming into the closing door behind me. Vassily was calling after me, switching back and forth between

English and Russian before settling on something in between that had never before been used outside of a Kubrick film.

I plunged into the labyrinth of the First Reformed Church of the Antichrist. I could get to the kitchen quickly, and from there get to my car. Losing Vassily in the city would be child's play. Escape. If I wanted it, I could take it.

Heather was in the dungeon.

Goddamn it. She was a deranged killer, sure. She was hunting me as freelance work for a monstrous super-conspiracy. But I had the ability to get her out of there, and she hadn't yet attacked me. God, I was a sap. I was going to do this, wasn't I?

I was annoyed to realize that my feet had already made the decision. I found the stairs down just as I heard a crashing sound from one hall over. "Nicky! Where are you going?" It was muffled, but not muffled enough. Had Vassily just burst through a wall like the Kool-Aid Man? Probably.

I ran downstairs, sprinting along a hallway and down the flight of stone steps into the dungeon. Heather was still where I had left her, chained to the wall. "Jim?" she asked.

"Yep. We're leaving now."

Above us, I heard Vassily crashing around. I called him a T-rex before, but that's not fair. He was King Kong, Godzilla, and the Cloverfield Monster all rolled into one. Sometimes it was smashing sounds, other times the guns were chattering death. He was coming, and I had annoyed him enough to change his mission from detain to delimb.

I picked Heather's cuffs with the buckle of a leather restraint. "Come on."

"What's that sound?"

"I guess you could call it *deus ex mafia.*"

"What?"

"The Russian Mob showed up."

"The reds?"

"They're actually capitalists. A communist mob would make zero sense."

"Oh Niiiiiiicky..." Somehow his voice was closer. How the hell did he keep finding me? Did he have some kind of me-sense or was he just getting lucky? I should ask him. I ran deeper into the sex dungeon and tried not to see what was all around me.

"Nicky, Nicky. You down here?" His voice was coming from the top of the stairs.

The dungeon kept on going. I would have been impressed by its sheer size, had that not been the thing now trying to kill me.

"Where are we going?" Heather whispered.

I wasn't sure. All I could think of, apart from how stupid it was to come back for Heather, was Oana's slick. The tunnel from her kitchen to her hidden garage, the one thing that kept her alive. I couldn't get the image out of my head. Any smart conspiracy would have something like that in their headquarters. Of course, the First Reformed Church of the Antichrist weren't exactly smart.

Still, this was a freaking gothic castle in LA. It wasn't authentic; it was more about what a bunch of Ren Faire people thought looked cool. Secret doors would be practically required. In the corner of the dungeon, I found a cell. It appeared to be a real cell, someplace to lock someone away as opposed to something dedicated to carnal bliss. It was locked, but I picked the door with a small needle-like thing I really hoped hadn't previously been inserted into anyone.

"Wow. You sure know how to pick a place, Nicky," Vassily called. "I should bring girls here."

"Why is he calling you Nicky?" Heather whispered.

"Do you really want to have this conversation now?" I

hissed back.

I went into the cell and touched the walls. Cool stone. They had carved some things into the walls, mostly Satanic prayers and Metallica lyrics, but someone had put a little— well, I hesitate to call it a poem, but:

I was here
Here I was
Was I here
Yes I was.

I stared at it. It was right at the foot of the little cot. In the sea of self-conscious evil of the late teenage years, it was out of place. It was almost cute in its way, and Satanists were many things, but cute wasn't one of them. I traced the words with my finger.

"Oh, Nicky...?"

"We need to go! That monster is almost here and I don't have my gun!" Heather whispered.

Crouching by the words, I poked the brick. With a masticating grind, the brick moved. "Huh," I said.

And fell through the floor.

IT WAS A PIPE, WET AND SLIMY, CANTED AT about a 45-degree angle. I couldn't be sure exactly: I had left my level in my other pants, and I was screaming. Later, if I ever spoke about this again, I would have to amend that to bellowing, yawping, or some other, more manly vocalization. But let's face it, I was screaming. That's what happens when you're suddenly zooming through the wet, throatlike darkness, hurtling toward an unknown that's practically guaranteed to be unpleasant.

The nice part was this chute was way too small for Vassily, and I couldn't even hear his voice over the sound of my screaming and the rapidly increasing distance between us. The pipe slowly leveled out and I lost a little bit of speed, and then it opened up and I went sliding across a slick concrete surface, coming to a stop... somewhere in the pitch dark. All I know was my ass made little echoing sounds when it zoomed across the wet floor.

A hiss followed me, getting louder and louder. I tried not to have a heart attack as I went for my phone. I hit a couple buttons and a light shone from one end. I pointed it in the direction of the hiss in time to see Heather shoot out from the pipe about thirty feet away and slide across the floor on her butt. She bumped into me, most of her momentum gone by that time. Only then did she open her eyes.

"Jim?"

"Yep."

"Where are we?"

I shined the light around the room. The phone's glow was brighter than might be expected, but a real flashlight would beat the pants off it any day of the week. We were in a large concrete room. The fishy aroma of algae permeated pretty much everything, and I knew I would have to air myself out afterwards to be remotely presentable. An open doorway led out, though not to anywhere I'd want to go on a normal day. Things skittered away from the beam of the flashlight. For the time being, I planned to ignore them. I got to my feet and helped Heather to hers.

"Storm sewers, by the looks of things."

"What was that?" she asked, nodding into the dark in the vague direction of the waterslide.

"Escape hatch. Means there's probably a way out of here that won't kill us."

"Probably?"

"Satanists, remember?"

Dimly, I heard the echo of crashes and pops above. The geologic sounds of Vassily having a tantrum in the sex dungeon, filtering down through the slick to our ears. I had a hard time feeling much sympathy for anyone topside. I moved gingerly across the floor, trying not to slide my feet at all. Heather slipped on a patch of algae, windmilled her arms, and I caught her without thinking.

"Thank you," she said, holding onto my arm.

I smiled to myself. I remembered meeting Mina a year ago; I had been convinced that there was no way someone that hot wasn't out to get me. I had been braced for the inevitable betrayal the whole time, ignoring the fact that Mina took a little while to warm up to me, if I want to put it mildly. Had she actually been out to get me, she'd have thrown "do me" vibes at me the whole time. Like Heather was doing right at that moment, holding on even though she had long since gotten her balance back. Heather was a killer, probably her cult's favorite one, and she had done that Satanist back at the courthouse with her bare hands. Or possibly the sink, or the paper towel dispenser, or the handle of the flush toilet. I hate my imagination sometimes, but it was doing a good job reminding me that I wasn't holding some ingénue with a few crow's feet.

I let go of her and shined the light at the doorway. In the darkness ahead, something crawled over an uneven surface and flopped into water. I cursed.

"What?" Heather asked.

"I hate the undercity."

"Why?"

"Seriously? Look around."

"Oh, I thought there was more to it than that."

"There is. The best parts smell like dead fish and the worst parts, well... let's move fast."

I was worried about a persistent legend in Los Angeles known as the Lost City of the Lizard People. No, seriously. It's a real thing and you can google it if you don't believe me. Like most things in California, it had all started with gold. Specifically, a deposit said to be located under Fort Moore Hill, downtown. In 1934, local lunatic G. Warren Shufelt (The G was for "God, are you kidding?") claimed a wise old Indian had told him about the underground city of the lizard people, and because he didn't seem to understand that such a thing, if real, should be avoided at all costs, promptly sunk mineshafts to find it. He *did* find it, stretching from Broadway downtown all the way to the Southwest Museum (which, for conspiracy buffs, is less than a mile from the former headquarters of V.E.N.U.S.). Shufelt went into the city and was either crowned prince of the lizard people or eaten (accounts vary), and the *LA Times* claimed the whole thing was a hoax.

It isn't.

Oh, God, I wish it were.

When I said I worked for every conspiracy, cult, or secret society, that's not entirely true. I never worked for the lizard people.

Because they are fucking *crazy*.

And here I was, in their domain. Granted, we were west of their city, but in getting away from our present predicament, we'd be going toward it. I was going into Moria knowing exactly what was waiting for me in the dark. No reason to panic Heather, though. I was panicking enough for the both of us.

I went to the doorway, a rushing sound growing louder and louder as I approached. I shined the light down, revealing a single slick step leading to a larger pipe. Concrete borders gave us a place to walk. In the middle was a sluggish six-foot river of black water turgidly plowing its way through the dark.

"That way," Heather said, pointing in the direction of the flow. "That will lead us out."

"Not necessarily. I mean, yeah, if we were aboveground. Down here, sometimes those dump into flood chambers, reroute into pipes. It's a goddamn maze."

"I hate the undercity," she said.

"Damn right." I led her downstream anyway. My sense of direction has never been stellar, and down here, whatever

I had was completely scrambled. I kept my eyes peeled for markings on the wet concrete walls, either conspiracy symbols or something mundane added by a municipal employee. I didn't see anything, and that worried me. We were *theoretically* west of their city. Nothing said they hadn't branched out. Or separated into warring clans.

The water didn't look deep, but that was deceptive. It was completely opaque, with angry eddies periodically swirling up from the depths. It was either the slide down or the ambient filth, but all the little scratches I had received during my first escape from Vassily had started itching as my subconscious mind provided the feel of infection. I kept my back to the wall, inching along the side. Heather imitated me, probably thinking I had some secret way to move around down here. Ahead, the pipe opened up into a pool, which boasted two more pipes, going in opposite directions.

Jutting from the side of the pool was a short pier. A skiff was secured to the side with some greasy rope. "You gotta be fucking kidding me," I said.

"Whose boat is that?"

"I really hope it's not Zed's."

"Who's Zed?"

"We're not doing this."

"Doing what? Jim? Are you stealing that boat?"

"Yes."

"You can't... it's Mis... you need permiss..."

I wasn't getting permission from whatever lizard person or mutant owned this thing. Instead, I could hope they had some kind of subterranean ride-share program, and if they ever asked me to kick in a couple bucks or maybe some roadkill, I'd happily do it. I gingerly stepped out onto the dock, putting my weight carefully on one foot. The wood was waterlogged and filthy, but it looked mostly solid. I pressed down. It creaked a little, but held. I took another step, now completely on this odd little structure. The skiff was small, but it would fit two people as long as one was standing. It was entirely empty, except for a bit of dirty water collecting at the bottom.

"If I fall in, you'll save me, right?" I asked.

"You want me to jump in there?"

"It's not my first choice, no. But if this thing sinks, yes."

"Of course!" Heather said, the happy smile audible in her voice.

I had no idea how sincere she was. I put one foot in the skiff. It wobbled, but didn't seem like it was going to sink. I winced as I slowly transferred my weight into it. I took my foot off the dock, and now I was officially standing in a stinking skiff I found in the LA storm sewers. A long pole with grimy tape around one end was on hooks on the side of the dock. I picked it up.

"I think we're okay. Can you untie the boat?"

"You see, Jim? Positive thinking. You believed you could stand on that boat, and you did it."

"Is that what happened?"

She nodded, untying the ropes. She hopped in, and though she barely weighed over a hundred pounds, I winced again, sure the vessel would tip over, sink, or maybe even explode, because it had been that kind of day. When nothing of the sort happened, I handed her the phone flashlight. She lit what little of the gloom she could as I pushed off from the dock. The pole found purchase at the bottom of the pipe; judging from that, we were in about six feet of water. There were currents at the bottom moving a good deal faster than the stuff on top. Someone falling in would likely be sucked to the bottom, then get shunted along on a very drowny trip through the under-city to be spat out into the Pacific as fish food.

I moved us out into the center of the underground river. Then, remembering something Mothman had told me one time, picked the left tunnel and pushed us over there.

"Jim?"

"Yeah?"

"Why did that monster call you Nicky?"

"I owe him some money. He came in shooting."

"How did he know you were there?"

"That's a really good question." I thought about it, and short of Vassily tracking my phone, which seemed unlikely, it meant he was either watching the place or someone tipped him. Who? I had no idea. Vassily's full net of contacts was a mystery, and it's likely that through Neil he could have met any number of Satanists, both low- and high-ranking.

"Any ideas?"

"He was probably watching the place," I decided. Then, spinning it up with some lies, I said, "He probably has any number of debtors in there. Gambling evokes greed, envy, probably gluttony, so they're big fans. When I was there, they were always trying to get me into high-stakes poker."

"Is that how you built up your debt?"

"Yep."

"And you used a fake name? Why?"

"Would you tell a loan shark your real name?"

"I wouldn't deal with a loan shark."

"Well, yeah, that would obviously have been the better decision for me."

She was quiet. I could feel her staring at me, even though she kept the dim beam of light barely clearing the path ahead. When she spoke, it was resigned. "You're a complicated man."

"You could say that."

I pushed down the tunnels for hours. We were making good time, especially when I was able to make the current work with us. Of course, "making good time" was on a trip to

God-knew-where, so maybe speed didn't matter much. Along one of the tunnels, the light picked out a shape about the size of a terrier loping along one of the concrete walkways. It was moving towards us, eyes glowing red in the beam, totally fearless in its domain. And it should have been. It was a gray rat, huge and mangy. I almost muttered something about Rodents of Unusual Size, but I didn't want to annoy it.

I pushed us over to the far size of the stream. It paused, watching us float by. Soon, the darkness swallowed it back up, but the sound of its claws on wet concrete dogged us for several hundred feet.

"What was that?"

"Tijuana pet," I said. I knew that wasn't enough, so I elaborated. "It's an urban legend. Old lady goes down to TJ and she loses her glasses or something while she's down there. I don't know what an old lady would be doing in TJ, but that's the story. Anyway, she meets a street dog and it's starving, so she feeds the poor thing. It's one of those heartwarming tales about someone rescuing a stray, and they become best friends. She brings the dog back to the States, where she takes it to the vet. That's when the vet breaks the news to her: it's not a dog. It's a giant rat."

"And that was the same one?" Heather gasped.

"No, the story's bullshit. The truth is that rats can get big down here and they're dangerous as hell."

We drifted down more tunnels before emerging in a large chamber. A series of risers on either side made it look like a flooded Mesoamerican ballcourt, though that was probably not the intent. A large splash greeted us. The beam jumped as Heather tried to focus on what had caused it. Gold coins, apparently hovering an inch above the waterline, glittered back. They weren't coins; they were eyes.

"Is that...?"

"An alligator? Yes."

"What's it doing down here?"

"Floating."

Even though Rosicrusophists are never supposed to get annoyed, Heather's voice was shot through with it. Her nerves were probably pretty frayed after the night we'd had. "I meant why is it floating down here."

"Supposedly people flush them down toilets, but it's probably more likely they get put into storm drains."

"Sewer alligators? I thought those weren't real."

"They're not real in New York. Gets too cold there. Winter would wipe them out. Here, it's warm all year round."

She watched the gator watching us. It wasn't all that big, maybe six feet long from what I could see poking through the surface. Just like the rats, the gators could get very large. In any case, I gave it a wide berth and tried my best not to look like anything it would want to eat.

"Heather, I need you to point the light at where we're going."

"Okay," she said, and I heard her muttering a mantra over and over. Technosis to keep the gator away. I had no idea if it would work, but as long as she kept the light where I needed it, I didn't care. The gator stayed in its reptilian trance, waiting for something to happen by that it could snack on.

We traveled for another hour or two, every now and then passing another dock, sometimes with a similar boat tied to it. They weren't uniform, though, looking like whatever put them there had scavenged or built whatever it could and called it a day.

My phone beeped. "Low battery," Heather said.

"I was worried that this was getting too easy," I muttered.

I was exhausted. It had to be morning soon, if not already. That would make this Day Three on the investigation and no closer to finding who killed Neil and framed Mina. I was going to have to ditch Heather somehow, and do it in such a way so as not to be murdered in a men's room. Distracting her while conducting my investigation and making sure she didn't realize I was her quarry was turning out to be impossible. And that was before the sewer.

Although, since my only lead was Vassily Zhukovsky, it might be nice to have a killer along for the ride. Once I'd re-armed her, of course. Re-arming a bounty hunter on my ass. I guarantee Han Solo never had to do that. Han had it easy. Don't see me dumping my cargo at the first sign of Imperial cruisers, do you? Hell no.

We passed a large chamber, running parallel to our underground canal. Metallic hisses came from the inside and I really didn't want to know what else the undercity had in store for us. Heather didn't have my sense of resigned fatalism and directed the light into it.

Thousands of writhing tentacles dripped from the ceiling. Some were metal, others were bundles of cables with naked ports at the end. They curled around one another, reaching and grasping at nothing.

Heather swallowed a yelp.

I took it as good news.

"What's that?" she managed.

"Shub-Internet," I said.

"Are you sure?"

"Pretty sure."

Things were looking up, because the avatar of the god of the internet was underneath an abandoned building in downtown LA, a little to the southwest of a cluster of skyscrapers that made up the Los Angeles skyline. I ignored the fact that Shub-Internet had grown. Last I heard, it managed to incarnate the Four Horse_ebooks of the Apocalypse and started dating Alison Brie, so that was bound to make it feel like a big god.

I started looking for another dock, and shortly found one. It had a skiff on one side, so I angled for the other one. I hoped whoever owned it wasn't around and checked my weight on the little pier. Though it creaked, it held me. Heather held out her hand and I helped her onto the dock. She handed the phone back. I checked the battery. A sliver of red left.

I inched along the little walkway around my subterranean Venice, and after about fifty feet and one more yawning pipe, there was a door in the wall. I climbed up and peered in. My light sputtered as the phone used a little bit of its precious battery to beep at me. This looked like an access tunnel, leading somewhere that was slightly less wet. That was good enough for me.

I went up the stairs with Heather nervously following. The phone sputtered again. I picked up the pace. The beam picked up something ahead, shadows bobbing with every step. It was a fall of shattered concrete, probably shaken loose in one quake or another. As I got closer, I saw that the wall was entirely broken, creating a hole easily big enough to fit through. The blocks looked like they might have been moved to provide a passage, but the debris hadn't been cleaned up or the wall repaired, hinting that it wasn't municipal employees who'd done it.

A breeze, rank and metallic, wafted through the hole. *That'll do, pig,* I thought at the universe. I climbed the little hill of broken concrete, stooped under the irregular arch of the hole, and emerged in another tunnel. This one was much larger, with easily ten feet of head clearance. The breeze wasn't a phantom. I felt it, and knew which way it was coming from.

Heather came out of the hole and landed next to me. "We're almost out of here," I said.

I should not have said that. The shuffling started pretty

much instantly after, coming from deeper in the tunnel behind us. It sounded almost human, but not enough to make me comfortable with what was happening. Several somethings were all rushing through the darkness, loping over uneven ground to get at Heather and me.

"We should probably go," I said.

She didn't need to be told twice, and soon we were both running along the tunnel. Whatever it was moved quickly. We couldn't outrun it. Not for long.

I ran anyway, my burning lungs sucking up the air. The phone sputtered and died. Plunged into darkness, I was pretty certain this was it. At least I would vanish. No one would have to know I'd ended up as poop. But that would mean Mina in jail, busted on the fake murder charge. I wasn't just running for me. I was running for her, and that meant something. I dug in, feeding off the stitch in my side, the exhaustion in my body, and the ache in my limbs.

The tunnel wasn't quite as dark as it had been. I could barely make out walls. Each step brought the light up, brighter and brighter. And then it was clear. A doorway opened into a huge tunnel crossed with tracks. The metrorail. I even let myself grin a little. "Don't touch the third rail," Morgan Freeman said in my head, although to be honest, I had no idea if the third rail was even a thing. Good looking out, Mr. Freeman.

We came out into the rushing wind of the tunnel. The next car would be along soon, if not already bearing down on us. I spared a glance back at our pursuers and immediately wished I hadn't. The creatures moved like hillbillies in a Wes Craven movie, their eyes shining like that gator's had. There were little flashes: of teeth, of hands, and worst, of scales and forked tongues.

A platform was about twenty feet away. We ran for it as

the headlight of a train haloed us from up ahead. I wanted to wave the phone flashlight to stop the train, but the battery was out. I couldn't even spare the breath for a curse. I ran up the stair access and threw myself aside as the train slid into the station, effectively blocking the things following us.

I slumped against a wall, trying to catch my breath. Looked like we were below Union Station, giving this a certain amount of nostalgia: I had almost been killed here about a year ago. A few Angelenos standing on the platform gave Heather and I some looks, but all erred on the side of not getting involved with the two filthy subterranean joggers.

"What were those?" Heather asked. She was barely panting. Must be nice to be in shape like that.

"Lizard people."

"What?"

"Like people. But lizardy," I clarified.

"That... that's a thing?"

"You saw them."

She glanced backward superstitiously, trying to make that jibe with what she knew about the world. I put my head down and sucked in air.

That's why I didn't notice her grabbing me until her hands were already yanking me up by my shirt and slamming me face-first into a lit map of the LA metrorail.

"Now that we're safe, how about we go see Mr. Quackenbush?" she said.

Blood ran down the front of the map and
over my right eye. There was a scar there, picked up when
Ingrid Brady, a member of the Guardian Servitors of the
Anorectic Praxis, decided to turn my face into her personal
speedbag, and from the pain on my brow, I figured it had just
split like a seam. At least I'd managed to turn my face at the
last moment, which kept my nose from breaking again.

Heather held me there, and though she was small, she
had all the leverage in the world. I was off balance and, generally speaking, had fighting skills somewhere between "tod-
dler" and "dummy you teach mouth-to-mouth on."

"How many groups are you playing with, Erick?" she asked
me. The creepy thing was, her tone was still bright and happy
and even though I couldn't see it, I could *hear* her smile.

"I don't know what you're—"

She punched me in the ribs, digging up and under. I
dropped to my knees, trying to reinflate lungs that didn't
seem all that interested in breathing anymore.

"You shouldn't lie, but it's not like you're really one of Dr.

Wood's students. Gambling debts? Satanists? How much did you think I'd swallow?"

"Is that a trick question?" I gasped.

"Is your nose even broken?" She tore the bandage off my face. Last time I'd looked at my nose, it was a vibrant blue-black, and I had no reason to believe that had changed. "Oh, I guess so."

I heard her sniff, and I figured it was one of those cocky sniffs Bruce Lee would do back before he kicked all the asses in existence. I braced myself for another ruthless beating and reflected that I had spent a decent amount of time getting my ass handed to me by women. Cheryl Bartek of the ONI knocked me out with a headbutt on a floating casino that used to be out beyond Catalina, Mina beat me up right after we met, and then Ingrid Brady did this karate shit at the headquarters of the Guardian Servitors of the Anorectic Praxis. To be fair, I had my ass kicked by men a lot, too. Sometimes I thought I was the Information Underground's designated punching bag.

Yet another reason I tried to walk away from that life.

Something wet hit my cheek. And again. For a second, I wondered if the ceiling had sprouted a leak. Then Heather spoke, and her voice was thick with tears and snot. "How could you lie to me?"

I thought about a response to cut through everything like a lightsaber made out of pure logic. She would see the error of her ways, let me go, and decide to become my faithful sidekick on the quest to free my girlfriend from jail. I formulated it in my mind, got everything in the proper order, and said, "Huh?"

"This whole time! You pretended to be my friend!"

"I never actually pretended to be your friend. I was friendly, but that's less about deceit and more about mann—"

"You said you were one thing! And you were a totally other thing!" She mashed my face into the map, like she thought my cheek was a marker she was trying to use to color the whole thing in.

"You were going to kill me."

"I was going to take you to Quackenbush!" she sobbed.

"Do you know who Irving Quackenbush *is*? Name a dictator in Central or South America. Chances are that asshole got into power because Irving Quackenbush killed every single rival, intellectual, college professor, and anyone who even knew someone slightly left-wing to put him in power. What do you think he's going to do to me? Someone he thinks killed one of his people?"

"You lied to me!"

"You're not listening! You never even asked me if I killed that guy!"

"Did you?"

"Of course not! I've never killed anybody!" I'd just been a repeated accessory to murder, but I wasn't about to bring up that delicate distinction.

She seemed to be considering it. "You're a liar! How can I believe anything you say?"

"Oh, for the love of—"

"Let that man go, and put your hands up."

I blinked and looked over. Two transit cops had their weapons drawn and were pointing them at us. It was mostly at her, but they were LAPD: the only thing stopping them from shooting both of us was the paperwork.

"Officers! This man is a murderer!" Heather protested.

"Let him go, step away, put your hands up, and we'll sort this out." I don't think he wanted to sort this out. I think he wanted to shoot someone.

Out of the corner of my eye, I saw a couple people surreptitiously filming the whole thing on their phones. I tried to turn away from that, since the last thing I needed was my face on YouTube, but she had me pinned pretty good. "Get this crazy bitch off of me!" I howled. Normally, I'm not a big fan of the word "bitch," but when communicating with the law, it's usually best to go for lowest common denominator.

"Sir, be quiet!" one of them barked at me.

I was quiet.

"Miss, I need you to put that gentleman down."

I'd said "bitch" and instantly been upgraded to "gentleman." I briefly wondered if the top hat and monocle set threw the b-word around like rappers.

Heather finally obeyed and I dropped to my hands and knees. The blood on the left side of my face had begun to get tacky and my nose was throbbing.

"Sir, put your hands behind your head."

"I'm the victim here!"

"We'll be the judge of that."

"Can you at least shout 'I am the law'?"

"Don't smart off."

The younger cop was staring at Heather, clearly trying to place her. They weren't looking at me. I must have looked pretty bad, the purple bruising under my eyes now visible; the lumpy, barely healed nose; and the split eyebrow. To say nothing of the scratches on my face, arms, and hands. It's a shame I couldn't play noir anti-hero without a forcible rearrangement of my face.

"Both of you, hands on your heads, get down on your knees, and cross your ankles on the ground."

I sighed. Didn't have a play here. Not until I got a little closer. I obeyed immediately.

Heather said, "We were just having an argument, officers. There's no problem here."

"You just said he was a murderer."

"I'm mistaken, obviously." She giggled, and for a second, the laugh wormed its way into the heads of the cops and they dropped their guards slightly.

"Well, do what we said and we'll figure this out."

One of the cops spoke into the radio on his shoulder, calling us in.

The other one came closer. I stayed still.

"All right, who wants to go first?" he asked, stepping within arm's reach of me. I knew what I was going to do before I actually did it, and even though there was a part of me being Morgan Freeman, calmly reiterating that these were cops, and I should under no circumstances do this, there was another part, too. The id. The Jason Statham of the mind, the Kickpuncher, the Sterling Archer, who was going to do something because it was fucking awesome and end of story.

With one deft motion, I went for the cop's belt. He reflexively went for the holster of his gun, but I was going for the other side, and the split second it took for his brain to register that and recover was enough. I slid his mace from the holster and sprayed him right in the eyes. The other cop's eyes were widening and he was about to shout right as I got to my feet and maced him, too. I spun and gave Heather a hit as well.

"Goddamn it! Baez, you see him?"

"Fucker maced me!"

I glanced around and saw the gleaming lenses of several phones pointing in my direction. "Uh... stay in school," I said to them. And sprinted for the escalator.

"All units in the area! We have an assault on a police officer!"

People got the hell out of my way. One of the benefits of assaulting a police officer, I guess. Probably the only one. I hoped they only saw my injuries, rather than the face underneath. I could probably worry about that if I lasted through the next couple of minutes. I came out on the second level, where another escalator would lead to the ground floor. I ran for it, and this time the people were confused, which was a good sign. I emerged at the top and slowed to a walk. I passed a garbage can, wiped the can of mace, and dumped it, joining the crowd as we made our way into the vaulted central hall of Union Station.

This place is one of the architectural jewels of LA. It's right out of an old Hollywood movie, a Spanish-style building all done up in muted earth tones. It's the kind of place to meet Ava Gardner before she disappears forever with the money. The garish yellow Wetzel's Pretzels sign hurt the ambience slightly, but on the upside, the place smelled delicious.

This was right about where my luck would run out. Where, if this were a high school movie, the record player (why there's still a record player in this day and age is beside the point) would scratch and the cover of "What I Like About You" (a song about Shangri-La, if anyone is wondering) by the flavor-of-the-month pop band would stop while everyone looked at me awkwardly. Only instead of that, it was cops coming in, talking into their radios with stern eyes on the crowd. Fair to guess what the description was: white male, dark hair, six feet tall, medium build, face that lost a bet with a truck. And I fit that description. Every word.

Wasn't long before a pair of eyes locked on me and there was a cop talking into his radio and coming my way. Soon as our eyes met, it wasn't magic. Instead, he almost immediately called, "You in the gray shirt! Stay where you are!"

My shirt was powder blue, but that was before the trip through the storm sewer, so I could forgive the mistake. I didn't stay where I was. I turned and ran like a bastard.

Pretty soon I had whole trail of cops on my ass, yelling

and hollering. I ran through the confused crowd at its thickest for as long as I could, knowing that fear of a public shooting was the most reliable way to avoid getting shot myself. Had I been black or Hispanic, I'd probably already be mostly bullets. I glanced around, and the sea of angry cop-faces behind me would be etched in my nightmares for a long time.

I hit the front doors, knowing I was about to run into prowlers as far as the eye could see, flashing blue and red, while a hundred guns pointed at my face. For an instant, I was blind in the harsh white light of the clear morning. I kept running, knowing that the bullhorned cry of "Get down on your face!" could react on its own time.

There was nothing, and as my eyes went from blinded white to vein blue, I saw only the parking lot. Right as I was contemplating just how long I could sprint before my lungs actually exploded from my body, a shiny black Cadillac screamed around a corner on two wheels and screeched to a stop in a nauseating puff of burned rubber. It was a 1959 Eldorado hardtop with big fins in the back, but it was so new I could smell it from where I stood. The windows were tinted suicide black and the chrome gleamed silver in the sun. The passenger-side door opened with a sepulchral clunk.

The driver leaned over. He was in a black suit one size too small, a black fedora, and black '80s Ray-Bans. His skin was grayish and he grinned at me with teeth far too large for his head. All of his features were big, making him look like Tex Avery had decided to draw a government spook.

"Enter my conveyance if you wish to retain molecular consistency!"

That was Man in Black for, "Come with me if you want to live."

IF HE HAD OFFERED CANDY, **I** MIGHT HAVE hesitated. Instead, I dove into the car headfirst, and the door clunked shut behind me like one of those refrigerators that used to kill kids. It was saying, "You got to choose how you die! Isn't that fun?"

Acceleration from zero to warp speed plastered me against the seat. No earthly Caddy could do what this one did, and as though to prove it, the dash blinked and booped like the set of an Ed Wood movie. The most normal thing was the key in the ignition with the dyed green rabbit's foot on the chain, along with the fuzzy dice dangling from the rearview. I righted myself and immediately regretted it, as now I had the perfect view out the windshield of this huge boat of a car weaving in and out of traffic like a crotch rocket. I hoped the damn thing had airbags.

The driver's name or, more accurately, designation was Victor Charlie. He was an associate of the Little Green Men, one of their Men in Black. I don't know what he was original-ly, but smart odds landed on bargain-rate clone brainwashed one too many times. It was tough to tell with these guys. Some people thought they were your standard government agents, trained to act weird so that anyone describing them would come off sounding like a lunatic. Others thought they were aliens. And then there was the clone hypothesis. Really, they were all true to a greater or lesser degree, since there were a ton of organizations that used them. It's not like everyone had a meeting beforehand to decide how they would bizarrely mess with history.

Victor Charlie would have been a standard MiB if not for his association with a group of other figures I called the Gang of Five, who abducted and then set me free one time last year while inadvertently demonstrating the dangers of poor communication. Those other figures: my vanished friend Oana Constantinescu, the obese menace of Vassily "the Whale" Zhukovsky, Quackenbush-spook/Guardian Servitor monk Ingrid Brady, and my murdered ally Neil Greene. These last two days had been hammering home the importance of the Gang, and now here was the fourth member to rear his extremely ugly head.

"Hubba hubba," VC said. "Missed ocular notification in a dog's half-life."

"What the hell are you doing here?"

"You were about to get the dirt nap, Temporary Buckaroo."

"Temporary... what?"

"LAM's designation for the collection of lenses, baby." He let out a hideous giggle that sent chilled fingers up and down my spine. LAM was VC's name for the head, or possibly the ruling council, of the Little Green Men. I always called the guy Zeta Prime. It probably didn't really matter. The more disturbing part was that I apparently merited a designation now, rather than my former alias of Brandon MacGruder, which had served so well for so long.

Brandon was perfect. I invented the platonic ideal of the

X-Files nerd. Pretty easy, since I was basically already that guy and had the comic book collection to prove it. I took what was there and added a UFO blog, a description of some sightings, and a few stories to really make the point that I desperately wanted to be abducted and have probes put into some part of my anatomy. I talked about how the all-knowing Visitors—that's what I called them—were here to usher in a new golden age of peace, prosperity, and mutilated cattle all over the world. The identity was so effective, I woke up a week later with some metal implanted under the skin of my left forearm, and so I went to work for the Little Green Men. It's still there, and it's the reason why sometimes I hear a tinny voice counting in Mandarin.

Zeta Prime knew I wasn't Brandon MacGruder. VC knew the other names: Nicky Zorotovich, Jonah Bailey, David Antonucci, and Colin Reznick at the bare minimum. Other names floated outward in an ever-expanding web, one or two known to other members of the Gang of Five. If there was any conspiracy that might be expected to know more than it should, it was the Little Green Men. And now, I was Temporary Buckaroo. Why wasn't I Perpetual?

"Did LAM send you to rescue me?"

"Negative, Buckaroo. LAM's concerns do not intersect. This unit detected a threat to immediate molecular dissolution."

"Someone's trying to kill you?"

"Prognostications are hazy, please ask again." I puzzled that out, eventually figuring that was how he said maybe.

"Why do you think someone is trying to kill you?"

"Neil Greene and Vassily Zhukovsky have suffered dissolution. Oana Constantinescu and First-Name-Unknown Brady are not available. Probability of dissolution is high. This unit is left."

"Fair point. Wait, Vassily the Whale is dead?"

"Affirmative. His vessel was located on landform adjacent to shoreline. Cause of dissolution: organ failure hastened by small, lead-based projectiles."

"Sounds about right." The Satanists had gotten their revenge for Vassily's murder of Paul Tallutto. That whole thing still bugged me. It made no sense on the face of it, but I knew that was just because I hadn't found the key. Everything, even insanity, made perfect sense once that key was found. Vassily did what he did for a reason. For the time being, I didn't know what that that was. Might have been crazy, but it would have made sense to him.

VC hummed a clear, high note, which sounded like his version of clearing his throat to speak. "Temporary Buckaroo is this unit's favored comrade."

"That's the saddest thing I've ever heard."

"Zigzag, baby."

VC's souped-up space Caddy fishtailed, throwing up a solid wall of white smoke, and he gunned it onto the freeway. He slowed, merging with the sluggish traffic on the 110, heading toward Pasadena.

"How did you find me?" I asked him.

He jerked a misshapen grayish thumb toward the backseat. "You bear the signs. Extra electrons sing like a canary. Harmonic convergence pulled magnetically to the wheelman. Once matched, this unit followed."

I looked into the back seat and found a machine that looked like a very large coffeemaker designed by a German Expressionist. Sitting in the place where the pot should go was the Genesis Stone, the Chain of the Heretic Martyr snaking out of it to drip from the seat onto the floor. The stone glowed silver and the machine faintly hummed.

"Locate the prime matter, locate the Buckaroo," VC said with a giggle.

"Great. So should I be looking forward to an abduction in the near future?"

"Future? Past. Buckaroo can assist this unit in remaining in a singular state. Information, not from LAM, but from associated cell. Designation: Ordo Templi Orientis."

That explained why we were heading to Pasadena. The Ordo Templi Orientis were big shits back in the '40s after Hitler had been shown the door and America wanted to get back to business. A magical cabal, they had links to both old-school Satanists and postmodern UFO cults. At their core, they were hermeticists, but like any good wizards, they really liked sex. The place was supposedly like a key party back in the day. A ton of big names came out of there: Aleister Crowley, Jack Parsons, L. Ron Hubbard, Flash Gordon. They were a who's who of the Information Underground in 1948. These days, they'd fallen on hard times, and, like a lot of the older conspiracies, were floating along on past glories.

The OTO knew me as Lester Pruitt, a stage magician on the quest for a perfect illusion. Like I said, I have good hands, so stage magic is second nature to me. I can find your card no problem, and if you want me to fish it out of your shoe, I can do that too, even while you're looking right at me. Anyway, Pruitt figured there was more to magic than what he learned from Penn and Teller or whoever and wanted to find a way into the true power he knew was out there. I had to fake a couple gigs and I even hit a few open mic nights for some credence. Built a cheap website, too. I had a gimmick as a masked magician to keep other people from recognizing me and to put it in the OTO's head that anyone who would wear a mask like a Venetian hooker might be into orgies.

"You know the OTO, huh?"

"Affirmative."

I pulled my phone from my pocket. It was totally dead.

"You mind if I charge this?"

VC took his hands off the wheel, snatched the phone, and plugged it in. He unplugged it immediately and handed it back. I was pretty sure we were going to go rocketing into the twenty-foot culvert that paralleled the freeway, but the car seemed to know where we were going and stayed locked into its lane.

My phone beeped, fully charged. Gotta love Little Green Men technology. I unlocked the screen, saw I had a voicemail, and checked it.

"Jonah, I got your message." It sounded like a little-girl version of Dracula. I smiled. Oana Constantinescu. She was alive, or was when she had called, which was in the middle of my sewer crawl. "Don't call back. This phone goes in the garbage when I hang up. I'm alive and safe, but I'm hurt. Four bastards came into my house with guns. It was a hit. You probably know Mina Duplessis is in jail, and you probably know as well as I do that she is innocent. Free her and I bet you will find who tried to kill me. And then I owe *you* one."

The message ended. I definitely could have used her, but at least she was all right. That helped a little. I saved the message because I'm a sentimental soul. "Oana is still alive."

"There is verification of that unit's continued existence?"

"She called last night."

"Interrogation on the subject of dirt naps?"

"She's in hiding, VC, and I don't think she knows any more than we do. It seems to bear out the theory that someone's after the five of you, though. I figured it was the Whale."

"Cetaceans are seldom a danger to LAM."

"No, I meant Vassily Zhu... wait, does that mean whales are *sometimes* a danger?"

"Vassily Zhukovsky has suffered dissolution."

"Yeah, I know that now. There were others who knew

about you, weren't there?" I thought of what Neil had said, that Stan Brizendine knew I had infiltrated those groups in the Gang of Five and had admired my initiative. If Neil had told his boss about it, there was a chance the others had as well, a group that included Russian mobsters, space aliens, and black ops killers.

I rattled the suspects through my head, but a combination of lack of sleep and various aches and pains from the last two days kept the thinking from bearing any fruit.

On the stereo: loud static with muddy voices mumbling underneath.

I turned to look at VC. He tapped the wheel and bobbed his head like he was listening to music. I could only shrug.

"Hey, you think you could get me something to wear?"

"Affirmative. Suitable togs await beside the prime matter."

I leaned back between the seats. Sitting next to the coffee-maker and the Genesis Flail, and camouflaged by being the same color as the jet-black upholstery, was a black disc that I would have described as looking like a record album if that hadn't made me feel incredibly old. I climbed into the back, emptied my pockets onto the seat, then stripped out of my filthy shirt and pants. There wasn't much modesty to be had when dealing with the Men in Black. VC's bosses had seen my colon, so what was the point?

The disc was covered in something almost like shrink wrap, but when I drew a finger across it, the stuff split down the path I traced and fell off; when I looked for it later, it had vanished. The disc proved to be layer upon layer of mashed-down clothing. First was the black suit jacket. I peeled it off the top and shook it out into something approaching a gar-ment. Then came the pressed white shirt, the skinny black tie, and the black slacks. The next layer straightened out with a pop. Wingtips. I cast those aside. If Mina couldn't get me to abandon Chuck Taylor, there was no way Victor Charlie could. Lastly, the black fedora snapped into shape, disgorging a pair of black shades.

I pulled on the MiB uniform. It was a smidge too small, making me look like a hipster government agent, or maybe a Reservoir Dog who had gained a little weight recently. I checked myself in the mirror. Between the hat, the shades, and the black-and-blue nose, I was still pretty unrecognizable. It would have to do.

I scooted back into the front seat.

"You can burn those clothes," I said.

"Affirmative."

"No, wait, I was jok—"

The back seat burst into blue-white flame for a split second. When it was gone, so were my clothes. The coffeemaker and the Genesis Flail sat there, unharmed.

"What was that, Chekov's Flamethrower?"

"The inquiry does not match existing parameters. Abort, retry, fail?"

"What's the difference between abort and fail? Other than one making a certain kind of person cringe?"

"The inquiry does not match existing parameters. Abort, retry, fail?"

"You're a blast, VC."

"Stone cold, Daddy-O."

The Caddy pulled off the freeway onto Orange Grove, a scenic street connecting the cities of Pasadena and South Pasadena. The section we were on was almost perfectly straight, lined on either side by mansions and apartment buildings. These days it was chiefly famous for housing the headquarters of the Rose Parade, and don't get me started on how the goddamn Templar keep that thing going.

The Templar, there was another one. That would be the

Knights Templar, who claim to trace their origins back to the same group of Crusaders who used to protect pilgrims on the way to the holy land. Whether or not the line is unbroken is immaterial; the important part is that they believe it is, so they've kept up the various grudges for which the Templar are infamous.

With all of these enmities, it's not uncommon that the Templar sometimes feel the need to eliminate someone. Templar hitters could never use guns, though. I swear, they were like the hipster assassins of the Information Underground. No, if they were going to take someone out, it was going to be with a broadsword. You know, like great great great great (etc.) grandpa would've wanted.

Remember in *Godfather*, when Michael is going to take out Sollozzo and McClusky? He goes into the can to get a pistol that Clemenza planted for him earlier. I've never been Michael, but I've been Clemenza a ton of times. This was one of those times.

I knew what I was there to do even without them telling me in so many words. When Richard Colby, the local cheese of the Knights Templar, ordered me to hide a broadsword in the bathroom of the Bonaventure Hotel lobby, I didn't think he was trying some new terrifying alternative to toilet paper. I knew that these crazy medieval fetishists were going to hack someone up—although I never conclusively found out who. Harbor Patrol pulled an oil drum out of the drink that was stuffed with a dismembered corpse, but there are so many murders in the City of Angels, it's impossible to know if that was the one.

In any case, I smuggled the blade into the hotel in a guitar case and had to wait in one of the stalls for a good thirty minutes before the bathroom emptied out. Only then did I tuck the sword into the ceiling panels. I never pointed out to Richard that a pistol would have been easier. I could have taped it right behind the toilet tank just like in *The Godfather*, even, which would have been both sensible and classic. No, even then I knew the Templar were maniacs.

VC turned down a side street and pulled over in front of a craftsman mansion. This was Agapé Lodge, headquarters of the Ordo Templi Orientis in LA. It had been a while.

An iron gate and high wall separated the house from the street. As we walked up, a flock of wild parrots flew overhead, screaming like madmen. VC touched the callbox. "Victor Charlie to see Lord Hezebolus."

The gate buzzed and creaked open. I climbed up the concrete staircase leading to the large porch overlooking green Pasadena. VC followed, shutting the gate behind him.

The porch was a comfortable place to spend an afternoon. Concrete, but decorated with wicker chairs and big cushions, it was clearly a place where people did a great deal of reading. The OTO loved books. It was their best feature. The door was a dark piece of oak, surrounded by a few windows looking into a spacious foyer equipped with a sturdy staircase heading up. I knew what was going to be happening inside, so I steeled myself.

I was about to knock when VC opened the door and wandered in. I followed. The rooms in the front were empty, though the one on the right had a half-finished canvas drying in the corner. The painting depicted Dora the Explorer in such a way that might lead to litigation or, at the very least, a watch list of some kind.

VC kept walking, ignoring the stairway and going down a hallway leading into the back. Doors opened up on either side. I tried not to look. Really I did.

Three people were having acrobatic sex without touching. They had been suspended around the room like Cirque du Soleil really dropped the ball on that one and were sort of moaning and thrashing. They were all in their mid-forties and soft for it.

In another room, a group played Arkham Horror. Okay, that actually looked like fun.

In the next room, there was a seminar on the proper goat-sacrifice procedure. While the instructor, a man who looked almost exactly like Stanley Kubrick, gestured to the obviously frightened goat, a student raised his hand like this was elementary school. It probably was, basically.

In another room, people were smoking out and listening to Phish. I hate Phish.

We emerged into a large back room, where big glass doors looked out onto a wooden patio and an overgrown backyard. VC and I ignored the people having sex back there and stepped outside.

"What now?" I asked my guide.

He was motionless, like someone had hit his switch. I sighed and waited.

A moment later, a rotund man came around the side of the house. He wore a silk robe, gold and embroidered with black roses, a helmet with a pair of real ram's horns curving around his head, and a pair of flip-flops. Other than that, he was nude. His chest hair was thick and mostly black, covering an impressive gut but failing to hide the gold rings in his nipples. Though there was literally no way he could see his penis—it had long since been relegated to the status of legend for him—I could see it flapping around like a dead duck in the window of a Chinese market during an earthquake. This was Hezebolus, the present Caliph of the OTO and one of my many employers.

"Victor Charlie," he said in a curiously high-pitched, sing-song voice. "You're here. Thank the gods." Bolus paused, hands on his hips, standing like Superman if the sun's yellow rays had turned to pork fat.

"The unit you have requested is present. Temporary Buckaroo awaits the download."

Bolus looked me over. "Lester?" he ventured.

I thought I might as well play along with VC. It gave me a plausible reason for my duplicity and, besides, I'd played one of these guys in the past. "Affirmative. This unit has multiple designations."

Bolus nodded. "I had no idea you were so close to the spirit guides before now. I'm impressed."

"Hubba hubba, Daddy-O."

"Uh, right. Can I offer you fellows something? Lunch? Wanda?" He raised his voice. "Wanda, guests!"

One of the people having sex in the other room poked her head up. She looked like someone's aunt. She got up, playfully smacking a chubby hand from her drawn-out body.

"Negative," I said, trying not to show any fear. "This unit requires information, not herpes simplex."

Bolus frowned, watching me closely. "Wanda, you can get back to it."

She dove back in. I figured from the looks of everyone involved, they'd have to stop soon, if only to pick someone up from soccer practice.

"Victor Charlie assured me that you are the... uh... unit to handle this situation."

"Need more detailed parameters regarding this situation."

"The information I have. I need to sit down." Bolus waddled over to a wicker chair and sat. I couldn't help but imagine what his ass was going to look like when he got up: a giant hairy waffle. I sat down across from him, grateful his gut had swallowed his genitals. He tasted the air like a reptile and said, "There are several groups of Satanists in the southland.

For a long time, there were two, the First Reformed Church of the Antichrist and the Order of the Morning Star. The Church worshiped the devil as an expression of ultimate evil. Bad is good, and so on. In the beginning, there was a good theological reason for this, namely that without evil, there can be no good, but they have degenerated into people who do horrible things for no real reason."

He wasn't saying anything I didn't know. In the parlance of the illuminated, this kind of Satanist was known as an Asmodean because of the name they gave to their god.

"The Order of the Morning Star," Bolus went on, "sees the devil as the real good in the universe. They're almost Gnostic in a way, recognizing the Old Testament God as the true source of evil. Lucifer rebelled in an attempt to create a better world and was cast out and punished." Considering the stuff in the Old Testament, it was a little hard to see Yahweh as anything other than a bipolar bully. Didn't mean I was eager to sign up with the opposition. Well, technically I had signed up to both sides, but with my usual amount of loyalty. Anyway, these kinds of Satanists were known as Luciferians. Always helps to have your terminology correct.

Bolus continued. "For a long time, these two groups existed in relative harmony. Oh, they had their little spats, but it was stable." You know, like most holy wars. Idiot. I had been on both sides of those "little spats" and there was nothing stable about them. And for all the Luciferian rhetoric about goodness and light, they were just as bad as the Asmodeans. Worse, actually, because at least the Asmodeans were honest about being dicks.

"Until recently," Bolus sighed. "Now there is a third group, the Sons of the Crimson Gaze. They're new. I'm not certain where they came from, exactly, but they're stealing converts from both the Church and the Order at an alarming rate.

They've even stolen a few from us. I reached out to the spirit guides for assistance, and they sent Victor Charlie to me."

It was a huge amount of information. It didn't necessarily explain everything I had seen with Paul's people, but it all seemed to fit. The heightened security, the ostentatious new digs, the desperation for new power and converts.

"When did the new conglomeration first become apparent?" I asked.

"Three months ago? So around December, I suppose." Bolus sighed wearily. "There is even worse news. My contacts informed me that the archbishop of the Church was assassinated last night."

I tried not to react, even though I wanted to correct him or at least make a hobbit joke. "Understood. And the Sons of the Crimson Gaze are responsible for said dissolution?"

"Disso... oh, yes. I believe so. Who else would do it?"

Who else would kill the leader of the Asmodeans? Let's see, the Inquisition, the Knights Templar, the Assassins... shit, I would probably have an easier time listing people who *wouldn't* want Paul Tallutto dead. Who actually did it might be significant or it might not. After all, Vassily got his start as an enforcer and had been known to perform the odd contract killing whenever it suited him. He was versatile like that.

"This unit has no present list of suspects. Who leads this new conglomeration?"

"I don't know. They're so new they haven't reached out to any established groups. They only take from us. I know there is a man named Hollis Nguyen, a former deacon with the Order of the Morning Star who is now with the Sons. I don't think he is the leader, though."

I nodded. If these Sons of the Crimson Gaze were stealing people from the Satanists and Neil caught them at it, that gave me a motive. They would have every reason to destabilize the Church by hiring Vassily to kill Paul. Getting rid of Oana made decent sense, considering her connection to Neil. I couldn't link them to Mina, and it was the one conspiracy in the world I couldn't link to myself. It wasn't quite adding up yet, thought it felt like Bolus had just handed me a big piece of the puzzle.

"We convey gratitude," I said, standing up.

"You'll look into it?"

"We already are," I said, and fought a smile as Bolus looked the tiniest bit scared.

"Lester... uh, Templar Buckaroo, I had no idea you were, that is, if I ever offended you or made you do menial tasks, I apologize."

"Sing sing said the bluebird."

Bolus found a nice place between confused and frightened. VC and I left him in it, returning to the Caddy while keeping our eyes to ourselves. The Eldorado rumbled to life and smoothly moved into the street.

"Input destination," VC said.

"Our Lady of Eternal Disappointment in Boyle Heights."

VC hit the gas and returned to the freeway. If I needed background information on the Order of the Morning Star and I couldn't go to the First Reformed Church of the Antichrist, there was one place to go. Only one group hated the Order as much as the Asmodeans, and that was the Inquisition.

They knew me as Michael Hagen, devout Catholic out of Boston. Mike had wanted to be a priest, but lacked the moral fiber and incisive mind to understand scripture. He was also plainly only into adult women, but I'd have to be pretty cynical to think that had anything to do with his failure. Anyway, though he had the lifelong loyalty drilled into him by Catholic school (and no, not like *that*), he didn't find anything wrong with dirty tricks and shady errands, making him the perfect person to do little things. The Inquisition threw in confession so poor Michael Hagen's soul would still get its eternal reward, and it was fine.

Even if I lived in constant fear someone would find out I was circumcised.

VC drove into South LA, making for the decaying inner-city neighborhood of Boyle Heights. The church was in better shape than most of the neighborhood, though the Vatican was smart to repress their crippling vanity enough to let the building be a little shabby.

VC pulled over by a crumbling section of curb, somehow maneuvering his giant boat of a car into a space that barely seemed big enough for a compact. The church was behind us now, visible through the dark tint on the Caddy's windows, looking even dingier for it. VC went for the door handle, but I stopped him with a hand on his arm. His flesh felt unnatural, like gel with a thin rubber coating. "Hang on."

VC obeyed, grabbing the wheel, his grayish knuckles turning white. I didn't bother to correct him.

I was trying to decide how to play this. VC and I could go full Men in Black. Throughout history, the Vatican had dealings with black-clad strangers, showing up and acting weird. Most of those were before the powdered wig days, though. Somehow, the Church had managed to get even less tolerant of weirdos in that time.

I checked myself in the mirror again. I wished I still had the bandage. Look past the uniform and it was pretty obvious who I was. The trick would be to keep anyone from looking past it. Maybe I could play the actual government card. Claim to be from one of the alphabet agencies, flash something almost like a badge—assuming I had one—and get what I needed. Last I heard, Father Liam had retired to San Diego, so there might not even be anyone who would recognize me.

"Okay, here's what we're doing. When we go in, I'm going to say we're Feds. You flash a badge… you have a badge, right?"

VC nodded and removed a wallet from his coat. "Hubba hubba." He opened it up, and the badge, though it had no clearly identifiable shape as coming from a specific agency, nonetheless hit that part of the human brain that craved authority in the form of little hunks of metal.

"All right, I'm going to identify us, you flash that, and under no circumstances are you to speak. You stand there and don't do anything. Got it?"

VC shot me a curt nod that made me think he was almost normal.

"Okay. Let's do this." I opened up the door. Even this far inland, with big buildings and palm trees shielding us, the wind slapped us around a little. I clamped the fedora down on my head, while VC strolled toward the church without a care in the world. Was his hat surgically attached or something? That was a line of thought I didn't want to pursue, but it kept poking at me, like a kid kicking the back of my seat on a plane.

I composed myself at the door of the church, straightening the tie, checking the collar, brushing out the sleeves on the jacket. With a final nod to VC, I opened the door and stepped through the vestibule and into the sanctuary.

I saw the guns first. A whole bunch: little silvery pistols, big fat shotguns, an anorexic carbine, a few stubby assault rifles, boxy submachine guns, and all pointed at each other, like the finale of a John Woo movie.

In the sanctuary, seeded through the pews, two groups were stuck in a Mexican standoff.

On my right, agents of the Inquisition. I recognized a couple of them, and the priest collars solved that little mystery for those I didn't. Beyond the collars, some looked like a typical priest in his casual suit, others wore the traditional robes, and I swear to God, one was the "vaya con dios" guy from *King of the Hill*.

On my left were the Knights of the Sacred Chao. And yes, that's pronounced "cow," and it means a single unit of chaos, which is the best way to describe their leader, Dame Ladysmith. She was not there, in my one stroke of luck. These guys looked like an escaped gang of carnies, old French whores, and Batman villains. Fitting, since they were a Discordian splinter group described by the other Discordian splinter groups as "the weird one." That's a hell of a thing when you worship the Greek goddess of chaos.

A few glanced over at the new arrivals. One by one, they became aware of the two men in black suits standing just inside the sanctuary, looking confused in one case and poker-faced in the other.

"Uh... well, you're obviously all very busy, and this has nothing to do with my thing, so we'll see each other out."

"Steve?" asked Happy Hobart.

"Mike?" asked Father Liam.

All the guns turned to me.

My hands shot up toward the ceiling. "Goddamnit!"

The Inquisitors cocked their weapons.

"I mean, gosh darn it?"

The weapons didn't lower. Instead, Happy Hobart—so named because he wore a mask like those bright yellow Have a Nice Day buttons, stared at me. His eyes completely vanished in the shadows of the rubber mask, turning into little black pits. "What the hell are you doing here, Steve?"

Steve, that's Steve Holt, and yes, that was intentional. To fit in with the Chaoists, you need to have an entertaining handle, and I lacked for creativity. So I took one that was already out there, and perfectly pitched to shout jubilantly while pumping one's fists into the air. It had the desired effect, of course, since there isn't a single Chaoist who hasn't seen *Arrested Development*, and if you think its cancellation wasn't a New World Order plot, you're insane. I geared the bio toward the kind of low-level anarchy the Chaoists seemed to love. Lots of warnings, fines, and community service for petty acts of mildly amusing vandalism. My crowning achievement was a fake press release about the creation of euthanasia shelters for the city's homeless.

"Mike? Why is he calling you Steve?" asked Father Liam.

Liam Fratelli had been my handler for my years of employment with the Inquisition. He was an all right sort, as members of the Inquisition went. I don't think he was responsible for any heretic deaths, at least. Besides, they outsourced most of that these days. Guess he hadn't retired after all. Seemed like a lot of that going around lately.

Happy Hobart, naturally, had been my handler for the Chaoists. Hell of a coincidence there, if you ask me..

"Well..." I started, trying to gather my thoughts into some kind of coherent lie. I glanced at VC to find he was doing exactly what I had asked him to do. He stood motionless and silent, acting like he had no idea an entire NRA convention's worth of guns were pointing at us.

I carefully removed my shades, since they were doing nothing, folded them up and stuck them in the breast pocket of my shirt. I figured acting like it didn't bother me was probably the best move, a turkey curse to get them into a less shooty mood.

"Am I really the problem here?" I asked. "I'm unarmed and I don't really care why you two are pointing guns at each other. I stopped in for a little information, but I can wait until you're done. If you want, I can even call 911 so you'll have ambulances standing by."

Happy Hobart didn't sound very happy. "Why did he call you..."

"I think it's more important to remember why all of you are pointing guns at one another. I'm sure it's an excellent reason. Remember? You guys were just about ready to kill each other."

The guns stayed right where they were.

"So, what were you all so mad about until I showed up?"

"Grilled cheese," Happy Hobart growled.

I smiled and nearly laughed, since when an armed man makes a joke, it's best to let him think it landed. No one else was laughing, and a couple of the priests on the other side of the room nodded grimly.

"Wait, what?"

"The Virgin Mary Grilled Cheese," Gabe said.

"You're kidding, right?" I asked, the last bit of hope I was capable of feeling in the intelligence of humanity dying by the side of the railroad tracks.

"Nope," Happy Hobart said, jerking his head in the direction of the pulpit.

Right in front of the little lectern was a ceramic plate with a red napkin. On top was a wedge of grilled cheese sandwich with a bite taken out. If I got closer, I'd see a reasonably recognizable depiction of the face of an attractive woman in the burn patterns on the bread. Though the person who originally grilled this particular cheese took it to be a picture of Mary, a woman who, if real, was decidedly Middle Eastern in appearance, the woman on the bread looked distinctly Caucasian and pretty in a very 1940s way. I always thought she looked like Donna Reed. But no matter how much you love *It's a Wonderful Life*, the Donna Reed Grilled Cheese wasn't going to get credited with any miracles.

"And what do you want to do with it?"

"These psychopaths want to eat a holy relic!" Father Liam shouted, punctuating this by turning his pistol back on the Chaoists. The other Inquisitors followed suit.

"These wholly relics want to lock it up in some lucite," Happy Hobart shouted back. I heard the pun, mostly because he threw a little emphasis on it, and Discordians really loved their word play. They also loved pointing guns at the Inquisition.

"This isn't some kind of elaborate prank, is it? You aren't messing with me?"

The two sides shook their heads and I nearly laughed. I had to admit, if they *were* messing with me, it was really good.

"Okay, so both of you want the Grilled Cheese. Seeing as we're in a church and all, have you thought about cutting it in half?"

The guns swung back to point at me.

"Or not."

The guns pointed to the other side.

I thought about what I was going to say very carefully. I thought about not saying anything at all and just trying to slink out like this was the tail end of a Michael Richards stand-up set. I thought about trying to solve this little dilemma. In my old job, I probably would have been the guy they called to get the Grilled Cheese to this place. And the guy who sold that secret to the other side, but only after they had asked me to find out and I spent a day or so farting around pretending to look. While it might have been tempting to angst that this was all my fault for leaving, the truth was that these dipshits could cut themselves on safety scissors.

"I need to ask everyone a few things, and it's going to sound a little weird. Don't freak out, okay?"

There were a few general noises of assent and nobody shot me.

"This little situation right here... I don't suppose anyone saw a giant Russian mobster around? He didn't set this up?"

The frowns and nonplussed murmurs said no.

"Let's see. Romanian gymnast?"

It was a longshot, but I am a suspicious soul. I was pleased to see the answer was no.

"Satanists?"

"You mean other than them?" one of the priests said.

"We're not Satanists, you babyfucker," a ballerina unicorn shot back.

"How about we stay away from religious differences for the duration, hmm?" I said. "I mean real Satanists? Especially from some new group called the Sons of the Crimson Gaze?"

More murmurs, more shaken heads. Although I thought I saw a glimmer of recognition flicker across the faces of the Inquisition.

"Order of the Morning Star?"

The Inquisition exchanged some angry muttering, but didn't pin this on the Order.

"How about Feds? Especially a skinny blond guy with a mustache?"

More baffled shakes of the head.

"All right. Best of luck to everyone here. I would like to remind everyone you're fighting over a sandwich, and there's literally no way Mary looked like she was in *From Here to Eternity.*"

I started backing away, putting a hand on VC's arm. He backed off with me, never breaking character.

"Mike, wait!"

I stopped. It was Liam, his pistol trained on Happy Hobart. The priest winced in frustration, doing the peepee dance as he tried to decide whether to stick with the Mexican standoff or come over and talk to me. He ended up splitting the difference, jogging awkwardly over while keeping the gun on Happy.

"This Steve business has me concerned, Mike. You disappear for a year and a bunch of," his voice dropped to a stage whisper, "nutjobs—"

"We heard that!" the ballerina unicorn shouted.

Father Liam glanced over his shoulder, where the gun was still pointed.

"It doesn't matter. You clearly want to tell me something. What is it?"

"You mentioned the Order of the Morning Star? They're almost gone. Barely any of them left."

"Congratulations."

"No, it wasn't us." He glanced around, lowering his voice even farther. "They're in the middle of a doctrinal schism. The old guard has the normal take on things. Lucifer cast from Heaven, rules in Hell still. The other side says Lucifer is here, now."

"What, on earth?"

He nodded. "Closer than that. Los Angeles."

"It's either here or Vegas."

"This side says Lucifer has incarnated a physical form and is preparing for Judgment Day."

"Anything to that?"

"Of course not. Lucifer is mostly metaphorical."

"What the hell does 'mostly' mean?"

"Mike! This is still a church and you are still a child of God!"

"Sorry, Father."

"Two Hail Marys should do it."

I abruptly thought of a dirty joke and turned my snort of laughter into a cough. "And this new side... the Sons of the Crimson Gaze, I take it."

"What are you doing with them?"

"Against them. Don't worry. There might be a little confusion about my name, but not where I stand." I looked him in the eye because that's the best way to lie to a priest. "I just need to know where they are."

"They have a theater on Hillhurst, near Franklin. Do you

know Los Feliz?"

I had lived there for about seven years. "A little."

"One thing. Who's he?" Father Liam nodded to VC, standing impassively at the door to the vestibule like a statue covered in flop sweat.

"He's a friend. We're really into the Blues Brothers right now."

"That... movie?"

"There's a movie?"

He narrowed his eyes, trying to see if I was joking, finally deciding he was most comfortable with clerical sincerity. "Godspeed, Mike. Whatever you're doing, see me later. I could use more information on this new enemy."

I nodded. "And, you know, good luck with getting that sandwich. I think this should turn out really well for everyone."

Father Liam broke into a sunny smile and returned to his side of the standoff, gun once again pointing right at Happy Hobart. Have a nice day.

"Goodbye, everyone. I hope the sandwich is miraculous or delicious, depending on your affiliation." Only the ballerina unicorn waved happily at me, momentarily disrupting the aim on her AR-15.

I pulled VC out of there. As we walked across the street, the gunfire started. With the thick walls, it was mostly muffled popping. I hunched over and ran across the street anyway and ducked behind the Caddy. There were no bullets flying this way, but I felt safer with something made of literally space age materials. VC strolled along behind, casually opening the car up.

He plopped down and silently stared through the windshield.

"You can talk now."

"23 skiddoo."

"Right. Did you hear what Father Liam... what that priest said?"

"Negative. This unit collated data from unconscious emissions."

"I don't want to know what that means, do I? No, don't answer. We're going to Los Feliz."

"Affirmative."

He turned the key and the car's engine rumbled and hummed. It swerved out into traffic to the sound of popping and chattering from the gunfight in the church. In my head, everyone was jumping around in slow motion, doves fluttering artfully in the foreground. Unfortunately, real gunfights are seldom so much fun, even for a spectator like me. There's a lot of screaming and blood and loud noises, and really you just want to find somewhere to throw up. At least Liam Fratelli would die the way he lived: protecting something meaningless for no real reason.

We went north, through downtown proper. I reflected that I'd been there less than twenty-four hours ago at Mina's arraignment. A lot had changed since then, but not enough to really matter. I was maybe a few inches closer to figuring out who framed Mina and murdered Neil, but I had dug a couple feet into shit. It felt like a net loss.

As VC drove up Hillhurst, one of those very uniquely Angeleno streets that split the difference between urban thoroughfare and suburban main street lined with brilliant green trees all dancing in the wind, a solid wave of nostalgia knocked me over. This was the old neighborhood. Not for one of my many aliases, but for me. *I* lived here, not a figment of my imagination. Sure, I'd rented my place under a fake name, but this was where I laid my head. It was also the place I spent my first night with Mina.

That part was much better.

No, we didn't have sex. I couldn't fathom her actually being attracted to me, since she is basically a redheaded Marilyn Monroe. I didn't know at the time that she's also intelligent and really sweet, which is good, since I would have been convinced I had no shot, even if I hadn't also been convinced she was setting me up to be killed. Besides, we had just met. As things turned out, there were a lot of steps between meeting and Greco-Roman wrestling.

VC and I passed Ambrose Ave, where my old apartment was located. I looked away. I didn't need nostalgia now.

I had the vague recollection of a theater around here. I had passed it a lot but never paid it much mind. It wasn't part of my weird life and so it never really registered as a place to remember. I watched the street go past and almost missed it. "Right here."

We were a block or two south of Franklin, so Father Liam hadn't been far off. VC turned the Caddy down the block, and the businesses of the main thoroughfare instantly turned into wide craftsman homes on either side of the street. Parking was hell, especially for the boat VC was driving. He found a spot a few blocks down and parked with machine precision. The street was enclosed by corpulent cedar trees, making me feel like I was indoors.

We got out and I put the shades back on as we walked toward the theater. It was a low black building, apparently one story, but I would bet money there was at least one subterranean level. Two displays stood on either side of the doors with a section overhanging to protect theatergoers from the nonexistent Los Angeles rain. Some street art had been sprayed on the walls, a collection of symbols meaningless to most, but legible to me: mostly Luciferian rambling. Blah blah original rebel blah blah true good blah. According to the advertisements, they were performing an original piece written by "local artist" Hollis Nguyen, called *Salvation from Space*. Well, that sounded like a piece of shit, but I held out hopes for a Wiseauian level of incompetence. A man can dream.

VC and I strolled into the lobby. A small box office was on the left, with a few flyers and band postcards waiting for whoever wanted them. They had a concession stand with theater candy, pretzels, and a beer tap. The place's liquor license was framed on the wall behind it. There was no one out front, and that made me nervous. Places that didn't care whether you broke in were often much more dangerous and unsettling than those that did.

I went around the side of the concession stand and opened the door into the theater proper. It was fairly large, with easily twenty or thirty rows of seats. Three people sat dead center watching the action onstage.

One thing about LA is that we have great theater, at least from an attractive-actor standpoint. The reason being, we have an unlimited amount of actors, the vast majority of whom are extremely good-looking, and there is a limited amount of work. To stay busy, they do theater.

The people onstage looked like the cast of a CW show. The actual acting wasn't great, but they were all chiseled from really sexy marble. So sexy it took me a second to actually hear what they were saying.

Guy With Ridiculous Abs: "The world is dying. Rape, child molestation, genocide. Who will save us?"

Girl With Inflatable Chest: "We need a savior!"

Guy With Blue Eyes To Die For: "Look to the sky!"

"No, no! You sound like robots!" the director shouted. He had a bit of an Asian accent of some kind, but I'm lousy at identifying those. I could guess he was Hollis Nguyen until something changed that.

"The savior exists in a vibrational state," VC said to me.

"That's great. Come on, I want to find a way backstage to look around." I headed back into the lobby. A door near the box office opened up and an attractive young woman exited. I knew her. Brenda something. She looked up at me and I could see the wheels turning. She knew me, too, and I could see she was right on the edge of fighting past the suit and nose to recognize me. Play it where it lies.

"Hey, Brenda! How are you?" I enthused.

"I'm good... Eli?"

"Yeah!"

Elijah G. Simms, member of the Order of the Morning Star. Discipline problems in elementary school, leading to more pronounced rebellion in junior high and high school. Way cooler than me, in point of fact. Smarter, too; Eli Simms scored at the top of most standardized tests. If he really buckled down and applied himself, there's nothing he couldn't do. But Eli was too much of a rebel. Sure, he was into his poetry and even had a few published in some zines and online, but he would never spend too long on one thing. He was all potential, attitude, and cool. Perfect for the Order.

We hugged. She had grown out her hair into a loose afro. It looked good on her. "I can't believe you joined up. I heard you'd disappeared."

"You know, I was upset with the direction the Order was taking, you know. So I kind of freaked out and went my own way. Then I heard about the Sons and I thought I'd check it out."

"I'm so happy you said that!" She flashed very white teeth. I think Brenda was an actress or something, when she wasn't worshiping the devil. "Who is this?"

"This? This is my cousin, Victor."

"Hello, Victor." She reached out to him.

He took her hand, wrapping her healthy brown skin in sickly gray. It was dim in here, but VC still had the shades on.

That was good, because his bulgy eyes were not his best feature. He didn't have a best feature. "Hubba hubba. The savior is harmonically sound and vibrationally varied."

"Uh... thanks?" She pulled her hand away from his a little too fast and turned a wince into an almost-convincing smile. "So, Eli, can I show you and Victor around?"

"We'd love that."

"We have to be quiet. The play is rehearsing—we open in two weeks and nobody is off book yet. Hollis is losing his mind."

"Isn't that always the way?"

"You've done plays?"

"Never, but I'm from here."

"You know, Eli, you're like the only man in LA who isn't an actor."

I laughed at that, since there was no other sane reaction. Brenda took that in stride, smiling along like she got the joke.

"Come on," she said. "Remember, be quiet when we go through the theater."

"Got it."

She pushed the door open and VC and I followed. The action onstage had proceeded as unfortunately as it began. The actors weren't worthy of the embarrassing words they were being compelled to say. I immediately knew there was an NBC show in their futures.

I turned my attention to the man in the center of the seats, the director who had been shouting. He was a small man. Tough to tell how tall when he was seated, but I guessed he might be a hair over five-and-a-half feet. Impressive hair, too. Streaked with silver, it was done up into a perfect Elvis pompadour glistening with oil. His angular face was a mask of concentration, and his neat van dyke made him look a bit like a swashbuckler. Despite his periodic rants directed at the actors, I wasn't getting a bossman vibe from him. Besides, I didn't remember him from my association with the Order, meaning either he rose quick or he was from outside. There was someone else. Had to be. Or this guy had fallen ass backwards into a hell of a gig.

"That's Hollis Nguyen?" I whispered.

Brenda nodded and put her finger to her lips. We went up a short wooden staircase, through a dusty curtain, and we were backstage.

"Where did you find him? Was he in the Order?" I asked her.

"Yes, but he was one of the first to come over to the side of the savior."

"Lot of talk about the savior."

"He walks among us," Brenda said with the terrifying joy of the true believer.

"What, here?"

Brenda favored me with an *Oh, aren't you cute* laugh. "No, He is not in the theater. The play we're doing is all about His arrival, although Hollis wanted to cloak everything in a layer of metaphor. You know, to make the critics happy."

"I think they should be pleased." Pleased at getting to come up with new synonyms for "trainwreck."

Brenda led me through the backstage, mostly a maze of pulleys where we were. I reflected that if my mysterious enemy was here and even the slightest bit respectful of proper conventions, he'd at least try to drop a sandbag or stage light on me. I superstitiously peered up to the catwalks over the stage. There was not a single living thing up there.

Near the back wall and off to the left, the scuffed wooden floor opened up into a stairway down. "Dressing rooms and so on. I really want to show you something."

That line was enough to make me feel like I was getting

tickled by a ghost. If someone ever offered to "show me something," it was either a kid wanting me to check out some roadkill or it was someone about to show me my future murder weapon. I shrugged. I pretty much collected those now.

The hallway was cramped down here, and painted the same Bohemian black as the theater proper. It looked like whoever had taken over had done a few repairs, given the place a coat of paint, and called it refurbished. There were doors on the either side of the hallway and Brenda headed unerringly toward a specific one. Second door on the right.

She opened it up, revealing a dressing room. One side had two tables with lighted mirrors, where someone would put on stage makeup. A bench bolted to the floor, like in a locker room, stood on the other side. Large closets were just beyond, and a couple full-length mirrors leaned against a third wall.

"You're going to love this," she said.

I tensed for a fight. Not that I can fight. I pretty much have one move, and since Brenda lacked testicles, that meant I was down to zero.

She rummaged through the nearest closet. I heard a soft clink. *Here we go.* VC might be with me, he might not. I would be committed.

"Behold, the Savior!"

She whirled around, and I might have flinched. She brandished a gray costume with big wings and a terrifying face topped with two huge red eyes. It was a face I'd seen before.

That thing had killed Burt Shaw.

ALLOW ME TO DIGRESS TO 1961 IN A SMALL
town called Point Pleasant. It's on the West Virginia side of
the Ohio border, with the Silver Bridge spanning the river.
Things were going fine until one night when a couple was
driving home and saw what looked like a man crouching in
the middle of the road. Only when he stood up, stared at them
with giant glowing red eyes, and unfolded a pair of wings did
they start to suspect he wasn't a man at all. The monster, who
would later become known as Mothman, took to the skies,
following the car as it reached speeds of a hundred miles an
hour. And the monster never once flapped its wings.

Mothman popped up from time to time after that, getting
variously ID'ed as an angel, a crane, a butterfly, and once as
Batman. Things kicked into high gear in '66, when Mothman
was sighted first at a private residence (carrying off a dog in
the process) and later at a local abandoned munitions complex (where it was eating a dog). Mothman was described in
roughly the same way every time: manlike legs, no real head,
hypnotic red eyes seemingly growing right from its chest, and

a pair of giant wings. It moved around in a stiff shuffle, or flew at dizzying speeds and not at all like an organic creature. It shrieked or squeaked at times, and mesmerized people with its gaze.

Mothman continued to bother folks in the Point Pleasant area, generally acting like a curious drifter. Its presence, other than being unnerving, made electronic devices go haywire. Televisions tumbled into zigzag static while radios played a speeded-up voice muttering gibberish.

This is when Mothman got his name. It started out as "the Bird," but that didn't really carry the necessary mystique for a cryptid as unique as that. Then they went with "Big Bird," but since there was no accompanying Snuffleupagus, that had to be jettisoned as well. Finally (and partly due to the Batman incident), they went with Mothman.

Only one person ever got a clean look at his face, and she described it in the most unhelpful terms: "Like something out of a horror movie." She also suffered Klieg Conjunctivitis, sort of an eye sunburn commonly afflicting people who see UFOs too close. Unsurprising, since Point Pleasant was in the middle of a serious UFO flap, with accompanying cattle mutilations, poltergeists, and Men in Black. This has associated Mothman with the Little Green Men, but that's not really accurate, at least from what I know.

Anyway, at a certain point during the paranormal chaos in Point Pleasant, people started getting phone calls from something identifying itself as a UFO entity. It warned that on December 15, 1967, the Silver Bridge would collapse. Other people hypnotized during Mothman sightings reported reoccurring dreams of Christmas presents floating in the Ohio River.

Sure enough, at 5:05 p.m. on December 15, 1967, the Silver Bridge did indeed collapse, dumping Christmas shoppers into the frigid water. Forty-six people died. Mothman prompt-ly vanished.

Some people claimed he was harmless, that he just want-ed to communicate. Chances are, they were right. The poor guy was too alien to make himself understood or just didn't get that he was scaring people. Although the dog thing was still weird.

Granted, my own encounter with Mothman wasn't so gran-diose, but the big guy saved my life. Not once, but three times, including once when he appeared in person, dragging Burt Shaw, high-ranking member of Quackenbush Security, into the sky and possibly another reality. Thanks to Heather, I found out I had gotten the blame for this, but better that than what Shaw had planned, which was to put a bullet in my head.

And now these dime-store Satanists had a Mothman costume.

"This is the savior?" I asked.

She grinned. "He is risen! Lucifer Himself walks the earth!"

"This is Lucifer?" I rephrased. "Somehow I imagined some-thing more... shining Greek god. Less Guillermo del Toro."

"Lucifer is an angel. Read the Bible. Angels don't look as we picture them. That's a construct of artistic tradition. They were much more inhuman than we imagine."

"I see." According to the Bible, angels looked like rings with eyes on them, or else like four-faced monsters. Then again, if I expected everyone who said "read the Bible" to ac-tually have read the Bible, I'd probably go insane.

"And He's here! Makes sense, right? It's the City of Angels, after all."

Fighting the creep-me-out vibes Brenda was throwing my way, I said, "So how about we go back topside?"

She rehung the Mothman suit, tossed another smile at me, and led the way back into the main theater. Emerging from backstage, I first noticed how many more people were in the theater. Other than the director, his two companions, and the actors onstage, the seats were now peppered with other people. They were pretending to watch the rehearsal, but as we came out into the muted lights, I felt eyes on me. Phones came out, some dialing, others texting.

"So, what did you think?" Brenda whispered.

"Just fantastic," I said, picking up the pace for the door.

"I'm so happy you're joining us, Eli," she whispered, quickening her own steps.

I glanced around. Some of the audience had gotten up. They were openly staring now, speaking into their phones quietly so as not to disturb the rehearsal of the terrible play. "I'm thrilled, too." *You might be changing your mind soonish, though.* I hit the door, glad this room was empty. VC came abreast of me, using an admirable g-man quick-walk. He would have looked good closing in on John Dillinger at the Biograph Theater.

"Do you have to go?" Brenda asked.

Her phone buzzed with a text.

"Yeah, I think I should go."

"Well, okay. It was great seeing you." Brenda pulled out her phone to look at it. I was through the door and on the street when she shouted after me, "Eli, hang on!"

I broke into a run and VC did the same. The Sons didn't come boiling out of the theater like I thought they might. We made it to the black Caddy a block over and VC pulled into traffic on Hillhurst.

"Input destination."

"I'm hungry. Are you hungry?" I desperately needed some calories to run my brain, try to navigate this maze I'd found myself in.

"This unit requires five hundred calories per day to

function."

"That's a yes. Wait, five hundred? That's it?"

"Affirmative. This unit has an efficient metabolism."

"Well, this unit doesn't. Go to Chinatown."

I'll admit it. I was morbidly curious to see VC eat. There were so many stories of Men in Black being baffled by everyday objects, including food. If any food were already a little weird, it was dim sum, so I figured it was worth paying for a dim sum brunch over at the Empress Pavilion to find out.

VC pulled into the parking garage, where there were only a handful of cars, and we walked down the stairs into the odd, one-building outdoor mall housing the restaurant. The parking garage surrounded the few storefronts on the three-level building. Tables were set up along one walkway, selling knickknacks, and in the store that sold bamboo arrangements, there was a guy who would tell you how you'd die if you bought a jade Buddha from him. As I came up on the restaurant, I saw a Closed sign on the glass doors. Peering through them, it looked like the restaurant had been completely abandoned, along with every other shop in the shopping center. A year is apparently a longer time than I thought. Long enough for your favorite dim sum place to close with nary a word. Depressed, I led VC back to the car and we went a block down to a little place situated inside a ground-level courtyard.

Since it was a weekday, we got a table easily (although I strongly suspect it was partly because the mostly immigrant staff believed us to be from the government). Unlike the Empress Pavilion, which had picture windows overlooking Hill Street, this place was as dark as a tomb, most of the light coming from a fish tank stuffed with lazy koi. As the carts stopped in front of our table bearing a variety of Chinese pastries and dumplings, I picked my favorites and ate in silence, watching

VC the whole time.

"This unit eats a thick paste made from peanuts and fish oil."

"Then you should be thrilled for a change. Try one of the big white fluffy ones. There's pork inside."

Seeing him insert the chopsticks in his ears and eat the dumplings with his fingers was strangely calming, like tuning into a public access show in the middle of the night to get to sleep. My mind wandered as I shoveled food into my mouth. Empress Pavilion was closed. That's what happens when you leave town for a little while: your favorite brunch place in the whole city closes. I had eaten there so much, I was almost offended they hadn't sent me a condolence card.

I initially found Empress Pavilion after a job. It wasn't much of anything, really. INT-13 had me in an empty brick apartment building overlooking the 101 freeway. I had to stay up, keep the door locked, and at five in the a.m. the next day, I had to let the guy in who knew the password (I still remember it because it made me laugh: "Rear Admiral." Yes, I'm in the fifth grade). Anyway, that was the entire job. I mean, I worked out what I was actually doing there pretty quickly, because despite all the blows to the head I've suffered, I've miraculously escaped any permanent brain damage. I was keeping the place clear as a sniper's nest. It was an empty apartment building, and I brought something to read, and that's how I spent the night, hunkered against one freshly painted wall, reading old issues of *Tales From the Crypt* by flashlight like some kid.

Come morning, I got the knock, heard the password, tried not to snicker, and let in a woman who looked like she had been freshly dug up just for this purpose. The bag with the rifle in it wasn't fooling anyone, but there was no way I was going to mention it. Not to someone who looked like they quit sleeping sometime in the '80s.

I left her to it and went to find some breakfast, ending up in Chinatown. Later, I looked into it, just out of curiosity you understand, and found out that someone had been shot on the 101. Here's the weird part: that person had no apparent connection to anyone. A citizen. But they somehow needed to be rubbed out by INT-13, which is one of the nicer conspiracies out there. And, like most of hits, they weren't happy until the killee had been rendered extremely dead.

Empress Pavilion closed. End of an era.

On the other side of the table, VC had expertly dissected several shu mai, creating a remarkably detailed map of the Earth as seen from space. There were a couple extra continents, but he was just trying to be accurate.

Woolgathering had apparently freed my subconscious to do the real work of deduction, because the answer hit me square between the eyes then and I felt a little dumb for not seeing it sooner. There was someone out there who knew both the names Nicky Zorotovich and Erick Levitt. Someone who hated Mina and Oana. Someone who absolutely despised me. And who at least knew people who'd witnessed Burt Shaw's departure from this reality.

Ingrid Brady.

If I had a reflection (in one of those skinny carnival mirrors, but still), it would be Ingrid Brady. A member in good standing in at least two shadow groups, she had connections to a half-dozen more. She was the nominal leader of the Gang of Five and did the whole trick in drag, complete with a little blond mustache. They didn't even know her first name, let alone her gender. She'd contracted Vassily for a hit on Mina on behalf of the Guardian Servitors of the Anorectic Praxis and she had tried to kill me at the Ana Temple when Mothman intervened. She'd also worked for Burt Shaw and might be a wee bit upset about the whole "feeding him to a monster" thing.

Confronting Brady would be a trick. She was formidable in her own right, and had the resources of her pseudo-government contacts to fall back on. VC and I wouldn't have a prayer of subduing her, so we'd need backup. I rattled through my mental list of the Information Underground, trying to figure out who I could depend on. When that list came up blank, I tried to figure out who I could bargain with. The answer came quickly, and I might not like it, but it would have to do.

"So, Victor Charlie, how did you arrange meetings with your little group?"

"The inquiry does not match existing parameters. Abort, retry, fail?"

"Your group. Brady, Oana, Vassily, that group."

"Affirmative. Smoke signals, hobo signs, vibrational asides."

"And these are things you can do?"

"Affirmative."

"Can you contact a specific member of the group?"

"Affirmative. Signals harmonized to alpha waves. Zing zing."

"Great. We're contacting Brady."

"Negative, negative. Brady is not available. Probability of dissolution is high."

"She's alive, and responsible for all this."

"Gender parameters have been altered. Brady is male."

"We can debate this later. In the meantime, I'm going to get us some backup."

"In anticipation of violence?"

"Oh, yes."

I wrapped up a few of the non-seafood leftovers in a Chinese takeout box and we returned to the car. "The U.S. Bank Tower."

I named the tallest skyscraper on the Los Angeles skyline.

A multi-tiered building, it even had a crown of lights at the top, which would be red and green at Christmastime. There was only one group arrogant enough to put their headquarters on the top floor of a place like that. And now I had to deal with them.

I overpaid for parking downtown and VC and I swapped the dirty and noisy street for the cathedral-like lobby. "Stay quiet," I told VC. "If I need you to go into the whole MiB schtick, I'll nudge you."

"Affirmative, Temporary Buckaroo. This unit's pleasure centers are humming."

"I... uh... are you trying to say you're having a good time?"

"Affirmative."

"Oh, good." He had said I was his best friend.

Our shoes clicked on the hard floors of the lobby, VC's space-age wingtips much louder than my Chucks. We had to go through a metal detector, which momentarily worried me, because who the hell knew what was inside VC, but the check was perfunctory at best. I didn't even have to show them my Illuminati ID, which was good, since it was in the trunk of my car. We were waved to the elevator, where I used the ID with the concealed magnetic strip on the keycard reader. I hit the up button on the elevator and waited for the ding. The doors opened, giving us a mirrored box.

I pressed the buttons for floors 5, 17, 23, and 76. Then I leaned over into the call box and said in a clear voice, "This is Kenneth. 23 megahertz." The elevator doors shut and the panel displaying a digital readout of floors started cycling through hieroglyphics. The mirrors shifted and turned into computer screens, showing off my identity.

Daniel Isringhausen, a failed mortician from Redondo Beach. Fired during a minor scandal in which he used various putties, appliances, and makeup to alter the appearance of one corpse into another when the original bodies were too damaged by death. Was discovered when a shark attack victim suddenly had a head, despite that head's present location in the tummy of a fish. His prodigious skills now on the wrong side of the law, it was rumored he was involved in corpse smuggling. I painted a picture of a man who wanted power, but was a much better tool for those who already had it. And was hired.

On VC's side of the elevator, personal information popped up, but it was garbled. A driver's license for an Encino man named Dong Ha. A marriage license in the name of Jake and Fran Rosenblum. Court records on an attempted carjacking in the name of Caleb Cates. These flickered, switching with other documents, all in a dizzying array of names, only to be replaced by redacted forms, flashing question marks, and blurred faces.

I grinned inwardly. Them not knowing VC gave me a bit of power, something I'd need in these negotiations. Never go to the Illuminati with your balls in your hands.

That's where I was, the headquarters of the Ancient Illuminated Seers of Bavaria. These guys were the conspiracy's conspiracy. Everyone modeled themselves on the Illuminati, and if even half the stories were true, they were to be feared. Supposedly, they founded the U.S. of A. as an elaborate experiment to free the world from the grips of inbreeding, going so far as to replace George Washington with a doppelganger named Adam Weishaupt. There are so many Illuminati references on our money that if you show one of them a dollar bill they collapse in hysterics.

They have one motive: power. They don't really want it *for* anything. It's not like other organizations that look to information or money or sex as a road to power, and usually a road back. No, with the Illuminati, they just want raw power and are willing to use it as a cudgel. And unlike most of the older organizations, they're more than willing to roll with the times. They don't do it compulsively like the Discordians, but take the parts from other groups that work in order to ensure the entire future is a pyramid with an eyeball at the top.

The elevator dinged and the hieroglyphics had changed to that eyed pyramid. I shot it the finger and walked out onto the penthouse floor.

I'll say this for Bavaria, they had taste. A nice mixture of old and new, the decor was, in a word, elegant. Dark wood-paneled hallways led off in spokes, doors separated by alcoves boasting impressive-looking *objets d'art*. Ceremonial Baalish daggers, Atlantean pottery, a golden crown from El Dorado, and I had no doubt it was all authentic. I immediately wondered if they'd placed the crown there as a reference to the car I'd arrived in. Paranoia, it's a blast.

"Mr. Isringhausen," said a voice from thin air. "Wait in Room Four."

I didn't like the sound of that. Four was bad luck, and it was possible they were threatening me. Or maybe Four was just the room they had open. I was probably reading too much into things. I went down the hall, where floor-to-ceiling windows gave a dizzying view of LA. I could see all the way to the ocean on one side and the mountains on the other. The wind had scoured the sky, and for a moment, I was struck by the beauty of my city. Apparently she wanted me back bad enough to try to kill me.

I turned the corner and found Room Four between a shining broadsword that just might be Excalibur and a chunk of wood that could possibly be from the original cross. I opened the door, coming into a spacious office setup. The desk was almost bare except for a few completely mundane touches: a computer, a blotter, and some expensive pens in a holder.

There was no nameplate. Two chairs faced the desk, and those who sat down would have their backs to the door. A huge pitcher plant grew in a lighted alcove. An old man in a dark suit, his skin hanging in lank folds, juggled bright red balls in one corner, apparently oblivious to us.

Two could play at that, old man.

I sat down and pretended the old man didn't exist. He continued to juggle. He was pretty good at it. VC sat in the other chair and we both waited in silence, neither one of us removing hats or sunglasses.

It was around fifteen minutes later the door opened. It took a lot of willpower not to turn around, but to do so would have been an admission of weakness. That wasn't happening as long as I was here.

Diane Shah stepped around the desk holding two plates in her hand. She set them down on the far side of the desk, near us, and took a seat behind the desk. The plates held one slice of sweet tea pie each. I took mine without a word and ate it. Then I ate VC's, mostly because I didn't think we needed to watch him mash it into his ears, and he hadn't reached for it anyway. The whole time Diane remained perfectly silent, watching us expressionlessly. Her eyes, so dark brown as to be almost black, were empty.

Diane was severe-looking, pretty like a stylized drawing of an Indian princess. Her brown skin was flawless, her long black hair glossy. Her arms, shown off in a sleeveless blouse, were lean and muscled. She looked like she spent at least two hours a day in a gym, and I knew she would be multi-tasking the whole time. She was a genius, and I mean that literally. Her IQ wasn't quite off the charts, but it was close to the edge. She had won the goddamn National Spelling Bee when she was ten and supposedly had multiple post-graduate degrees. She was also the highest-ranking Illuminatus in LA.

Yeah, she was better than me in nearly every measurable way, but there was no way in hell she was going to beat me in this game of social chicken. In the corner, the juggler switched to one hand.

"What are you doing back, Daniel?" she asked finally.

I grinned at her. "I need to borrow your golem."

THE GOLEM, THE ORIGINAL ONE, WAS CREATED
in Prague by Judah Loew ben Bezalel back in the late 1700s.
The Rabbi created this clay man to defend his people from
various pogroms, which were the main hobby for most gentiles back then. Turns out gentiles were dicks. Anyway, the
Rabbi, also known as the Maharal because he was basically a
superhero, made a golem called Josef. This thing was essentially the Thing from the Fantastic Four, only he could turn
invisible, summon the spirits of the dead, and had to get shut
down every Saturday because what's a Golden Age hero without some ridiculous weakness? Josef was destroyed when the
Maharal accidentally left him running on a Saturday.

The secret was not lost, though, and the Illuminati weren't
going to ignore the chance of having powerful clay men serving them. A couple groups still have golems, but as far as I
knew there were only two in LA. I'd rather deal with the Illuminati in this case, since the other one belonged to a Rosicrucian splinter group and the last thing I needed was another
potential run-in with Heather Marie Tooms.

To her credit, Diane didn't flinch. "What happened to your nose?" she asked. If you could box the perfect accent, where every letter is enunciated and the meaning of every word conveyed exactly while being sprinkled with just enough aristocratic distain to know who was in charge, it would sound like Diane Shah.

"Is he here? Or should I wait?"

It was a stupid game we were playing. Trying to get the upper hand by dictating the terms of the conversation. On a normal day, I would put up a token resistance and then give in, because Daniel Isringhausen was an underling. Not today. If I negotiated from a position of weakness, there was no telling what she was going to get out of me.

"Does it have something to do with your disappearance? A year ago, you suddenly vanish. And then, just as suddenly, you return, dressed like that, injured, and demanding my golem."

"To be fair, it was a request."

She smiled in that Diane way of hers, managing to display neither warmth nor humor. In the corner, the juggler bounced the balls off the ceiling and caught them behind his back.

"Is this to get revenge on whoever broke your nose?"

"Oh, the guy who did this died thirteen hundred years ago."

Diane didn't react. I was being honest, which might have had something to do with it. "Why do you want my golem?"

"I need muscle."

"What about him?"

I glanced at VC. "He's mostly gel-based."

VC nodded in agreement. "Hubba hubba, Miss Kitty."

Diane's eyes widened slightly. I'd never seen her react so strongly to anything. "Elias is a lot of muscle."

"Why do you think I'm here? If I wanted to lay my hands on flesh-and-blood goons, I'd go elsewhere."

"The Russian Mob, maybe?"

I kept my poker face, but inside I was cursing. Why had she said Russians? Did she know about my connection to Vassily the Whale, or was she fishing? "There's a lot of choices out there. It's a buyer's market."

"That it is. Any bounty you get with Elias is split seventy-thirty in my favor."

"Noted." Seventy percent of zero was zero, so I was fine with that. All I needed the golem for was to catch bullets and eat Brady's kicks. Maybe hold onto her while we... I don't know. I wasn't going to beat anything out of her. Reasoning with Brady had proven to be a lost cause in the past. I trusted myself to come up with something once we had her. No reason to start planning stuff now.

"And any prisoners are to be kept at our facility."

"Nope."

"Ah, so you're collecting a prisoner. And there's no bounty."

I cursed myself and then Diane Shah and her giant brain. "I'm catching a murderer, Diane."

"The police do that."

"Oh, come on. If you were that naïve, you wouldn't be sitting there."

She liked that one. I could tell by the slight crinkling of her eyes. "I had never known you to be so civic-minded, Daniel."

"Somebody has to be."

If I didn't know Diane, I might not have seen the subtle change in her expression. It flickered over her face in a wave, a subtle widening of the eye, a twitch at the corner of her mouth. She was surprised. She was reassessing me. The juggler threw the balls from between his legs.

"Elias is yours. You have thirteen hours."

I checked my watch. Until one in the morning. It would

have to do. "Thank you."

"This isn't a gift, Daniel. You owe me one favor to be named later. You *did* abandon your duties for a full year, and I am letting you off very easily."

"Old rules are still in effect."

"I know about your squeamishness. No killing. It will be something more suited to your revealed talents." She paused, and when she spoke again, it was to the air. "Send Elias in."

A moment later, the door opened, and a man stooped to get in. He wore a double-breasted suit, a trenchcoat, gloves on his hands, a scarf over his face, and a hat pulled down low. Gold eyes peered outward, and when you got close enough, the distinct clay smell of his wet reddish skin was apparent.

"Elias, this is Daniel. You are his for the next thirteen hours. Do what he says, then return here."

"Ma'am," Elias said. His voice carried an abrasive hiss under the rumbling words.

"Good luck, Daniel. I hope you catch your killer."

"I always have in the past." Technically it wasn't a lie. It was just that there was only that one time and the whole thing had been a misunderstanding.

The juggler added two more balls from somewhere.

VC and I left the room with Elias lumbering along behind. We returned to the car, and when the golem sat down in the middle of the back seat, the car lurched before correcting for the weight. I thought about VC's back-seat flamethrower and briefly wondered if that would fire Elias into a nice clay pot. That had to be sacrilegious somehow.

"Okay, Victor Charlie, let's do this protocol."

"23 skiddoo, Daddy-O." He punched a few keys on the dashboard and a screen emerged like a CD being ejected, pivoting up so that we could view it. Google.

"Wait, Google? Seriously?"

"Affirmative. Proper vibrations dip south into the mass consciousness."

He drew his finger upward on the screen, causing a virtual keypad to appear. He then tapped in "scarface cocaine" and clicked on image search. The first image was Al Pacino at his desk with a mountain of booger sugar. VC pulled it up and clicked print. The dashboard spit a good reproduction out.

He gunned the engine and drove out to Palos Verdes. An upscale neighborhood along the coast, it was next to working-class San Pedro. He drove down the Harbor Freeway, turning off on PCH to climb the shoreline. Eventually he pulled off and into the parking lot of a Subway.

"I just had pie," I said.

"Affirmative." VC leaned over and opened up the glovebox, retrieving a roll of Scotch tape. I got a look into the compartment; there was a lot of paper in there. No guns, which was nice. Was the car's registration in there? Was this car even registered?

"Wait here," I said to Elias.

VC and I went into the Subway. He headed right to the soda fountain and taped the picture of Scarface and his Columbian creamer over the Coke logo on the first spigot. Then he went to the first hapless employee and flashed a badge. "I am part of your Federal Food and Drug Administration. No disease claims more human lives per year than *Escherichia coli*, known to your scientists by the colloquial term 'food poisoning.' It has come to the attention of this agency of comestibles that your entire shipment of sliced pickled cucumbers might have been contaminated with the bacteria called *Escherichia coli*. You will provide 453.592 grams of sliced pickled cucumbers to test for the presence of this bacteria."

"F-f-four hundred..." stammered the baffled sandwich artist.

"Converted to your king's measurements, that is one pound."

"One pound?" The poor kid, who could not have been more than sixteen years old, looked around helplessly but the other employees had vanished at the sight of two black-suited FDA spooks.

"This sample will be provided in a timely manner." VC leaned over the sneeze guard. "The Federal Food and Drug Administration shall not be trifled with."

I had to admit, the guy was pretty intimidating when he wanted to be.

The kid turned around and opened the fridge behind him, removing a metal container of pickles with plastic wrap over it. "I... uh... I don't know if this is exactly a pound or however many, uh, grams..."

"This will do," VC said, snatching it out of the kid's hand. "May your day be nice."

The two of us left, climbing back into the Caddy and screeching out into traffic. I held the pickles in my lap. "*E. coli*?"

"This unit is immune to any number of bacterial infections."

"Not really what I was asking, but good to know."

VC rode the gas pedal, driving inland. He stopped in Gardena, a neighborhood south of downtown in that section of LA really only distinctive for how much crime it had relative to others. He found a nondescript intersection with a four-way stop in a residential neighborhood. The houses were old LA, and most of them had seen better days. Leaning over, he removed a small white rectangle from the glovebox and got out of the car. He went over to one of the stop signs and slapped what turned out to be a sticker beneath the STOP. Now, in white lettering, in the same font, were the words "collaborate and listen."

He got back in the car and pushed the thing to sixty. The posted limit was thirty-five. "You ever wonder where you made the wrong turn in your life?"

"Negative. This unit needed to make a left and did so."

"I was born from the unliving clay, given life in the Word of the Almighty," rumbled Elias.

"Right. Forgot my audience here."

It was afternoon by the time VC made it to Hollywood Boulevard. Even though it was a Thursday, the street was far from deserted. People trudged up and down the dingy walk of fame, disappearing into the low-rent boutiques, or else headed for the massive new Babylon on Hollywood and Highland. There was probably something deeply symbolic about a homeless guy farting on Montgomery Clift's star, but I didn't care. VC pulled over by a meter, leaned over, and took a can of spray paint from the glovebox. I was beginning to think that thing was some kind of half-assed Bag of Holding.

"Now what?"

"To be seen from the sky, a larger signal is needed." He nodded at a billboard. A skinny model gazed listlessly back at me, a bottle of perfume next to her. Although, judging by her skeletal physique and hooded eyes, it could have been heroin.

"We're vandalizing a billboard?"

"Affirmative."

"In broad daylight?"

"The wavelengths have not..."

"Don't do a literal joke. It cheapens this for both of us."

I got out of the car. The billboard was mounted on the roof of an apartment building with stores on the ground level. I knew once we got up there, there would be a cage of razorwire to stop us from doing exactly the thing we were going to do.

VC led the way into the storefront on the ground floor. It sold lingerie, and not the high-quality kind. It was the kind that I'd buy for Mina if I ever wanted her to dump me. The clerks were a mixture of teenagers earning a paycheck and older creeps trapped in a life without choices. I don't know what they thought of the three of us. Probably the weirdest gay threesome they had seen in a long time.

We went through the racks of rubber, and I thought about how Paul had probably loved this place. I could swear I saw a few of the outfits the harem was wearing on hangers here. Our shoes squeaked on the dirty linoleum as we went back to the door marked "Employees Only." If the clerks saw, they either didn't care or they thought we were too scary to bother with. I had to admit, that last option was sort of cool.

The storage area for the store included racks of leather, lace, and lust in shredded plastic that looked like old cobwebs. Shelves held sagging cardboard boxes and the chipped concrete floor was covered in discarded and dirty labels. VC went right through, opening up an unmarked door at the back to reveal a metal staircase. We went up it and emerged on the windy roof. The billboard sprouted from the east side, letting the wan girlchild stare sullenly out over Hollywood.

A ladder, enclosed in chainlink and razorwire and blocked by a horizontal gate, prohibited access to the billboard. I picked the lock in a second and all three of us were through.

"Now what?"

"Messages emanate from one to another," VC said, shaking the can of spray paint. He walked right to the golem and climbed the guy without saying another word. Elias scarcely reacted, and when VC stood up on the golem's shoulder, Elias clamped his meathooks on the Man in Black's ankles. The can hissed, and VC seemed to steer Elias not with words, but by shifting his weight, forcing the golem to react by moving under him. I watched the street, waiting for the wail of sirens. None came, and really only a few people even looked up. Apathy has always been the Information Underground's best asset.

A clank sounded, and I saw that VC had dismounted Elias. "The task is finished. One more step remains." He had drawn black sunglasses and a fedora on the model. The weird thing was, using only black, he had managed to add accents and shades. The sunglasses gave the impression of a reflection and the fedora had contours. I might be biased, but VC had improved that billboard in every conceivable way.

We left the store and drove south into Hancock Park, a rich neighborhood smooshed between grungy Hollywood, hipster Melrose, and the unwashed masses of Koreatown. The Wilshire Country Club was a section of rolling green hills hidden on all sides by fences, hedges, and gates. The rich folks must have decided it was best not to taunt others with what they could never have, and so these idyllic fields were only visible in the places where the acidic LA haze had eaten into the screen of plants. VC pulled over on Rosewood, a residential street bordering the country club.

I climbed the fence, VC following me over. We landed in a gap of the privacy hedge, and I was barely scraped at all. It was a nice change from my steadily increasing litany of injuries.

I looked back at Elias standing on the street, who projected a forlorn sense of being the last kid picked for kickball. "Uh... you can wait here, if you..." The golem wrapped his gloved paw around the underside of the fence and pulled upward. With a rattle and groan, the fence bent upward. He waddled underneath, then pulled the fence back down. The gaps in the chainlink were hopelessly deformed, but it wasn't terrible. "Or, you know, you could just perform a terrifying feat of strength."

"My strength is terrible only to the evildoer."

"Wait. Did you really just say that? Because that is awesome."

VC led us across the verdant field, the trees whipping and undulating in the wind. The last time I had been on a golf course was with Mina. The woman loved to golf, and I didn't mind being outdoors. Granted, she had to slather SPF a million over her arms and face and she wore this silly green visor like she was dealing blackjack, but it was all worth it for her. And, frankly, for me, too. There was the conversation on one hand and Mina in capris in the other, satisfying both the Goofus and Gallant in my psyche. It was a good reminder of why I was dipping back into the madness of my old life.

"I speak only the truth," Elias rumbled.

It's tempting to chalk most cryptids up to hoaxes, and oftentimes you'll be right. People love faking them because, even to experienced agents, they're scary as hell. But real cryptids will bust something out and you'll remember, "Oh right, this is a space alien/refugee out of time/clay monster man."

"Have you ever given any thought to fighting crime?"

"I fight threats to the Creators."

"Right, yeah, but have you ever thought about how that includes common street crime?"

Elias was silent. I was a little worried I might have broken the little scroll of prayers that amounted to his celestial punch card when he spoke. "Explain, please."

"Okay, so you people get made to protect a small group from the depredations of a larger class. The group you were created to protect is a small group with enemies, sure. But they're also the most powerful group out there. In the never-ending struggle for power in which we're basically pawns—okay, you're a rook, but still—they're on top and they're remaining there. They're there partly because of the culture and society as a whole. The prevailing social order is what keeps them on top. So the problem becomes when something destabilizes that social order, whether it's a banker crashing the world economy or some gang shooting a kid on the way to school. Maybe imperceptibly, that damages the underlying social order that the Illuminati uses to maintain control on the world at large. Not a lot of damage, sure, just a little crack. But enough cracks can break a dam, bring down a building, or destroy a secret society."

Elias walked next to me, leaving footprints in the grass. "You speak the truth," he rumbled after a while.

"Every now and then, yeah."

We arrived at the pro shop, ignoring the confused looks from the two caddies who drew the short straw and had to work on Thursday afternoon. One look at Elias and they realized they might have something important to do inside and promptly vanished. VC reached into his coat and slapped something on the bottom corner of the paned window in the front. It was a little UFO sticker.

We returned to the car. "Where is the meeting?" I asked him. "Someplace out of the way?"

"Affirmative. Latitude 34.120—"

"Not coordinates. Names."

"Roosevelt Municipal Golf Course."

I knew the spot. It was in Griffith Park, not far from Mina's place, and one of her favorite courses. It hosted a more working-class clientele and she appreciated the appealing lack of snobbery. It also helped that Griffith Park is legitimately pretty for someone who has never spent an evening catering one of the many bizarre rituals conducted within the Park's boundaries. It's easy to forget, but Griffith Park, the eastern part of the Santa Monica foothills, is the tenth-largest urban park in the nation. It's bigger and wilder than Central Park, and even hosts the odd and extremely lost mountain lion.

There's also a golf course, pressed right up against the southeastern edge of the park. With the trees and greens, and the purple San Gabriels on the horizon, it almost doesn't look like Los Angeles. But one glance at the faux-Spanish municipal buildings and there was nowhere else it could be.

VC guided the car up the winding roads into Griffith Park. The place got progressively wilder the deeper and higher you went in. Down here, there were still maintained lawns, and barely any daytime coyotes. It was practically cosmopolitan. VC parked in a small lot overlooking the combination pro shop, bar, and grill that served the course. I thought about getting something to eat, but that would have meant moving and I wasn't certain I really wanted to do that. So instead I ate the leftover dim sum and wished there were more.

I cracked the window, getting the clean rosemary scent of the LA foothills into the car and scooted low on my seat. "Wake me up if anyone starts shooting."

"Affirmative."

And, this might seem insane, but I dropped off to sleep in a car with a couple cryptids. I have no idea what I dreamed about, either. The next thing I knew, I felt some rubbery fingers on my shoulder, shaking me. I opened my eyes, and it took me a second to realize the black was my MiB hat over my eyes. I took that away and groggily blinked.

Night had fallen. The course was dark, because no matter how cloudless the sky might be, the ambient light of the city made sure the sky was an almost unblemished blanket. The moon was only a rumor. The few lights came from the pro shop, set up along the corner.

"What time is it?" I asked, my voice thicker than Turkish coffee.

"Twenty-three hundred hours."

"You're right, that was a dumb question."

We got out of the car. A concrete staircase led down to the grass. Unlike the clean, uniform green of Wilshire, Roosevelt had small patches of yellow. The wind rushed over us, staggering VC and me for a few gusts; Elias didn't notice. We walked out onto the green and waited. A few copses of trees about thirty feet away rustled in the breeze.

Killing time in the dark, I practiced the summing up of the case in my mind. That was how this thing was done. When Ingrid Brady showed, I'd explain to her how she did it even though she was the one person in the world who knew exactly how she did it. After all, she was there.

Then I'd have Elias nab her, disarm her, and I'd call one of the intelligence groups I was on decent terms with, probably Scorpio or INT-13, and turn Brady over with the caveat that Mina goes free and my file is scrubbed. Hell, I could turn Brady over to Stan Brizendine at the Freemasons; he'd probably have enough juice to do what I needed. As long as Neil's death got avenged in some way, he'd be happy as a clam. I had options. Assuming I could grab a trained spook with semi-mystical powers gained through denial of pizza.

As I was thinking about it, they materialized at the far side of the green. At first, they were hard to see, since they were so slight, they looked like they should blow away. There were three of them, all with the same model's build. Tall, willowy, cadaverous. They were dressed like VC and me, if we'd had any style. Their suits looked like Hugo Boss—thanks, Mina— and were tailored to hide the weapons I was positive were on them. All three looked like men, but I was pretty sure that was drag. These were Anas, followers of the fashion and anorexia goddess Anamadim, pretending to be government spooks.

I knew for a fact the person in the lead was a woman. The conservative wig and the wispy blond mustache didn't fool me. Though to be fair, they had the first time I saw her in that getup. She stopped about twenty feet away, calling out to us. She hadn't recognized me yet, but it was dark, and she seemed focused on VC. "What's with the backup, Victor Charlie? Don't trust me?

"Negative. Accompaniment appears in proportional measure."

"You'll forgive me. With Greene and Zhukovsky murdered and Constantinescu almost, I had to take precautions."

"Oh, that's rich," I said. Brady's head snapped around. I could see it on her face, trying to place me from the voice. The costume wasn't helping her recall, nor was the busted nose, or the backlight from the pro shop.

That wouldn't stop someone like Ingrid Brady. She and her two companions pulled pistols. "You?" Brady said. I know I didn't imagine the edge of hysterical fear cutting the word in two. "How?" *Yeah, bet you never expected me to make it this far.*

"That could take awhile." Movement in the trees beyond Brady caught my eye. Something metallic glinting off the diffuse light from the pro shop. "Brought more backup?"

Brady glanced around and screamed, "Ambush!" Her gun barked and I dove behind Elias. I don't think she hit anything. The golem lumbered forward; Brady was running for the pro shop, firing into the trees that had once been behind her. I scrambled to my feet and pursued, even if I had no idea what I was doing. Lights flashed along the treeline, kicking up clods of dirt around my feet. I could hear bullets slamming into the giant wad of clay that was Elias. Ahead of me, one of Brady's two companions caught a bullet and went spinning grotesquely to the ground. I didn't stop to look at her and just hoped she hadn't even known what hit her.

I put my back against the cool stucco wall of the pro shop,

breath burning in my lungs. I could still see Elias out on the green, striding toward the first gunfire, but VC had vanished. Good for him. I hoped he would stay low.

I tried the glass door into the pro shop, becoming abundantly aware I was chasing not just Brady, but also her friend who was probably merely a lesser version still extremely capable of handing me my ass. I went through the door as quietly as I could and found myself in a little foyer of a faux-hacienda. A glass case had pictures of various golfers brightened up by a stand of fake bamboo. The burgundy rug, worn thin by thousands of golf shoes, did nothing to hide my footsteps as I crept to the archway leading inward.

In this second room, a staircase on the left went upward to a landing, then switched back and disappeared to a second floor. A small bar, almost entirely lost in deep gloom, was next to the staircase. On the right was the pro shop, although it looked like most of the equipment was for rent rather than sale. The largest space, straight ahead, was a dining room. Circular tables were scattered about and the northeastern corner was mostly plate glass. I could see flashes outside on the course, but they were farther away, deeper into the trees. Elias was gone, and the only evidence of anything happening was the shredded turf and the crumpled body of Brady's friend.

I ducked back into the pro shop and grabbed a golf club, listening for footsteps. While it was a little tough to hear over the sounds my heart made whenever the guns went off, it seemed like I was alone in here. If Brady had been here, she was probably gone now. I went back to the door, now armed, if bringing sporting equipment to a gunfight constituted armed.

Exiting out into the stiff wind, I saw VC's car waiting in the lot. I took two steps toward it when the wailing of sirens stopped me. Two cop cars, lights flashing the colors of an Icee machine, were zooming up the road. A moment later, three more appeared at the first bend in the road. Guess someone reported gunfire. Seemed like an awful fast response time. Those cars would block me from getting out even if I made it to VC's Caddy. Tack on time to hotwire it if the Man in Black had gone another way through the golf course. I ran back down the stairs onto the lawn, sprinting for the trees as far from the intermittent gunfire as I could manage.

Passing Brady's friend, who was mercifully both still and silent, I made it to the thicker trees just as the cops were getting out of their cars. Silhouetted on the little hill by their lights, they had drawn guns and were proceeding cautiously onto the lawn. I knew if I headed east, I'd eventually hit the Golden State Freeway and I could get the hell out of here relatively safely. I briefly considered calling for a cab to meet me, but the cold blanket of paranoia wrapped around me. They were listening. They had to be. Don't know who "they" were, exactly. Brady's little cabal, now dedicated to the sole purpose of getting me. Seemed cold-blooded, even for her, to sacrifice her ally like that. But hey, for all I knew, that was a traitor getting what Brady had intended all along.

I reached the trees. On the other side of the open green, shapes had emerged from the treeline. I couldn't see them clearly, not in the dim light, but I could be fairly certain those were Brady's guns, ready to sweep in. The police were on the other side of the pro shop, spreading out into the woods on my side and heading toward finding Brady's friend's body.

I plunged through the trees, hoping I was basically aiming east since what I was taking to be the hiss of traffic on the freeway could very well be the wind whipping through pine branches. I could see more movement ahead, coming around from the far side of the green to encircle me. With Brady's guns to the north and east and the cops to the west and south, I was getting caught in a very nasty zipper. I picked up the pace, grateful for the groundskeeping that kept the terrain relatively level and the trees from raking my face with every step.

Until a shape loomed up out of the dark. I skidded to a stop. It was obviously a man, leaning against one of the trees, back to me. He looked like he was dressed in a black suit, but it was tough to tell. Pretty much everything looked like various shades of black. It wasn't until I saw the outline of a fedora, almost eaten up by the tree the man was hiding behind, that I knew. I raised the golf club.

"VC?" I whispered. "Victor Charlie?"

He didn't react one way or the other. I poked him with the club and I knew it was going to happen about a second before it did. VC slumped off the tree and fell bonelessly to the ground. I could barely see anything, but I saw the bullet hole in the center of his forehead. I cursed. VC had been a weird creep, but he had been *my* weird creep. He was the best ally I had since this thing began. I couldn't help but feel like I had gotten him killed, even though I knew rationally it was Brady. She had killed the other two and tried it with Oana. She succeeded in this case.

Footsteps were getting closer, thumping on the grass. I added the name Victor Charlie to the list of people I was doing this for, even if he wasn't really a person. I rummaged through his pockets, his body already growing foamy, then found his keys and sprinted away. A gunshot tore into a tree nearby. Nobody had a prayer of hitting me, not as long as I stayed in motion and in the trees.

I ran east. A few gunshots chased me, and once I felt the sting of bark kicked up and burning across my still-injured face. A stitch dug into my side and my lungs were on fire in a distressingly short period of time. I tried not to let that bother me, and made yet another promise to myself to get in better shape. I tried to pretend I was a kid again, since back then I could run all day and not care. Make a game of it. Those lunatics with guns weren't trying to kill me. They were actually clowns!

No, wait, that's worse.

Turns out I didn't have the hang of optimism, either. Not even when I burst through a line of trees and found the edge of the golf course. Green nets, each one around fifty feet high, kept golf balls from beaning commuters. I dropped the golf club where it wouldn't be immediately obvious it was connected to the shootout and turned right, following the line of the freeway, knowing I'd get to an access road soon. I snaked between some short pines and there it was, a parking lot. Shielded from the freeway by thick greenery, a stretch of broken asphalt held a couple cars, even this late at night.

I almost ran down into it, but something stopped me. I took VC's keys out of my pocket and put them in the crotch of a couple tree branches. If someone was really looking, they might find them, but otherwise, the keys were basically invisible.

I stepped out into the parking lot and the light hit me in the face like a right cross.

"Hold it right there!"

Rough hands grabbed me, practically carried me, and slammed me onto the hood of a car. In the dim light, I hadn't noticed that one of the parked cars, the farthest one, screened behind a van with a very virile-looking wizard painted on the side, was an LAPD prowler.

"You're under arrest," the cop said.

I WAS QUIET IN THE BACK OF THE CAR, SITTING
with my cuffed hands pressed into the seat. I tried not to let
anything show, but this was what I had been worried about
since the close call at County. The two patrolmen, who were
the primal fear of every guy like me—giant, muscled badass-
es with shaved heads and unchained ids—weren't what you'd
call gentle. I was a one hundred and eighty-pound bag of dog
food to be swung, carried, and slammed as was convenient.
They hadn't even advised me of my rights, but I was savvy
enough to know that would happen before interrogation, if
at all. Wasn't like they were above claiming they had Miran-
dized me if it meant a conviction.

Not that I knew what I was being charged with or even
who was behind the arrest. I mean, it was probably Brady,
but it didn't really feel like her style.

The car wound its way out of Griffith Park. Periodically,
the red and blue flashed through breaks in the trees. The silhouettes of cops moving through the area had a dreamlike
quality. I was driven to Wilshire Division, but instead of book-

ing me, the cops put me in an interrogation room and hand-cuffed me to the bar on the table. I was grateful it wasn't Hollywood Division, considering someone might recognize me as Detective Saroyan, though slightly worried since the place of my arrest should have taken me right there.

Then they left me alone.

I could have panicked, but that wasn't going to do me any good. Besides, they didn't seem to recognize me as the guy who had maced two cops at Union Station and fled. I pieced that together when my arresting officers didn't put more than a few perfunctory bruises on me. Granted, it had only been one day, but I had made a career of being a chameleon, and it was really paying dividends in the "not getting totally racked by a pair of 'roided up cop meatheads" department. If they knew who I was, I probably would have been booked for Nicky's alleged crimes, either before or after being introduced to the wall a few times. I was going to play this as cool as I could and hope for the best.

That resolution was tested when I had to wait for what felt like several hours. It's the waiting that gets to me sometimes, especially knowing that every minute I was cooling my heels was a minute I wasn't trying to get Mina out of stir. Being in an interrogation room didn't help my cheery mood either, pushing me right back to the time I had almost been caught, and I mean *really* caught. It was a disposal job. Folks at Quackenbush Security wanted me to deliver some very full garbage bags to a chemist out in Lancaster. I knew what was in them when I picked them up. I mean, you know a dismembered body even if you've never actually seen one in greasy black plastic before. It's in the genome, I guess. The mistake I made was in peeking.

I knew the face looking back at me. It was my old pal Lebanon, he of the Castro replacement. Someone had gotten fed up with the old spook and hacked him up, and now Quackenbush was getting rid of the body. It might have even been an internal beef, since all those old-school right-wingers had some kind of tie to Irving Quackenbush. At least until it was time for him to bump them off. And Lebanon's time was up.

So I stuck the garbage bags in the trunk. I was pretty shaken up, since, like I said, I knew the guy. We weren't friends or anything, but we'd had some good times. He was fun, kind of a racist old horndog grandpa. I knew his body was going to be dissolved in acid, Heisenberg-style, and that would be it. No body, no funeral... hell, no name. Like he never existed.

So it took me awhile, but I finally pulled into the apartment complex. Abandoned, and not the friendly kind of abandoned. It looked like if someone moved in and started cooking meth, it might actually raise the property value. I pulled my car over, opened the trunk, took out a bag full of Lebanon, and bam. Lights.

The prowler had pulled in right behind me, and I guess my mind had wandered, and there I was. Haloed. The cops.

So I'm panicking. I almost think I should just run. Take my chances. That's when I realized if I did that, I'd have to burn everything involved with the alias that owned this car, which included my apartment at the time. So instead, I decided to stand pat and answer questions. Just as we were about to get to the fun stuff, gunshots echoed around the complex and one cop's radio clicked. Never been so relieved for random street crime.

My contact was very impressed with me, and he even offered to let me hang out and watch him dissolve the body in acid.

I passed.

In the interrogation room, I yawned. It was definitely morning. Meant it was officially Friday. Hell of a week.

Finally, the door opened. I didn't turn around, letting the guy loom behind me and showing I didn't really care. He closed the door after a few seconds and sat down opposite me. He had the g-man look down pat. His suit was cheap, and his tie clip even cheaper. He had a haircut that, if he paid more than ten bucks for, should have come with a coupon. The horn-rimmed glasses made me think he was a classicist. His face was scarred, but it was from acne, so I didn't have to concern myself with some ex-Special Forces badass trying to waterboard a confession out of me. Worst thing this guy was going to tell me was about the time he had to take his cousin to prom.

"You're in a lot of trouble," he said, in a very comforting yet moist '50s TV host voice.

"Am I?"

The g-man fidgeted on the other end of the table, the sleeves of his jacket riding up to reveal a cheap watch and the edge of a tattoo. Well, that was at least interesting. "Oh, I should think so."

"I hadn't realized walking around a park was a federal crime."

"Who said anything about federal?"

"Your haircut. If a barber had done that to an LA cop, his ruthless beating would have been on the news."

The g-man flushed. "You know you were doing more than walking around a park, and that's what's got you in trouble."

"Was I?"

"There was a shootout in the park right around where you were."

"So it's an open-and-shut case. I was within hearing distance of a shooting in Los Angeles. I have to be the only person in history."

"You were involved."

"Where's my gun, then? When I was arrested, I was carrying a phone, not an assault rifle. Unless there's an app for that, too?"

"And no one in history has ever dumped a gun."

"Do a GSR test," I said, holding up my fingers. "Not a bit of residue. I haven't fired a gun tonight or any other night." The last time I'd fired a gun was about a year ago up at the Griffith Observatory, and in my defense, it had sort of gone off accidentally and I still felt bad about it.

"Gloves can be ditched, too," the g-man said.

"Look, I'm really scared about this trespassing beef you have me on. Of course, that doesn't explain why I wasn't booked or advised. I can't help but wonder if I need to request a lawyer."

He raised thick eyebrows. "You're saying you need one?"

"To get one over on you? Probably not."

"What do you have to get over on me?"

"The truth. That you're trying to stick some kind of gun charge on a trespasser that said trespasser is going to beat and make you look like an idiot. Sorry, *more* of an idiot."

The g-man leaned back, a reptilian smile creeping over his face. "We both know it's much more than that."

"News to me. Hey, I realize this is probably a silly request, but can I see some identification?"

"You're smart, or so you keep trying to tell me. You tell me who I am."

"A proud alumnus of the University of Phoenix?"

He ignored the dig. "Something brought you to Griffith Park last night. Someone walking around a park usually does so without a shirt and tie."

"I like to feel fancy."

"And usually does it in the daytime."

"I work days."

"And what do you do for a living?"

"I'm an airline pilot for Pan Am."

"That airline has been closed for almost two decades."

"That explains the lack of calls."

He sighed. "You were there for a purpose. Another suit was found, almost identical to yours. Empty, but covered in green goo. Care to explain?"

"The man in it melted?"

"You're not going to tell the truth, are you?"

I shrugged. I thought I *had* just told the truth.

He reached down and put a briefcase on the table between us. With a click, he opened it up and removed a file, then closed the case and set it down by his side again. "Normally, I might believe you're just some nattily dressed wiseass caught in the wrong place at the wrong time."

"You think I'm natty?" I blushed.

"But if that's the case, you have some very interesting luck."

"Call me Zelig."

"You've been around, for lack of a better term." He removed a picture from the file, a nice eight-by-ten, showing Vassily and me going to the Whale's car. From the angle, the gun in Vassily's giant flipper hand was invisible. Our facial expressions were hard to read, mine because of the bandage, and Vassily's because he was a sociopath who didn't really have feelings. Vassily's mugshot was paperclipped to the file. They had to use two pictures to get his whole head.

"That is Vassily Zhukovsky, a.k.a. 'the Whale.' The boss of the local Russian Mob."

"That's not Bob Hoskins after exposure to gamma rays?"

"Escaped during transit from San Quentin to Los Angeles for his testimony Tuesday afternoon. Here he is Tuesday night, with you."

"I'm not seeing me."

"Then a shootout at the headquarters of a cult, and here is your car. Registered to a false name, of course." He produced another picture of my car. The interior belched flames, the engine block was spewing a cloud of smoke, and all four tires were melted. *Goddamnit. I had it paid off and everything.* I kept the poker face because I'd be damned if I'd admit that car was mine. "I am, of course, assuming Jim Kata is not your real name."

"It is not. And that's not my car. I drive a stretch Hummer for a limo company because of my hatred of breathable air."

"I thought you were an airline pilot."

"Somali pirate," I enunciated. "Common mistake."

"Am I to understand you're confessing to piracy?"

"Yeah. I need a maritime lawyer. Is Chareth Cutestory available? I hear he's good."

"And lastly, someone matching your description assaulted two police officers and a former television star."

"That doesn't sound like me."

"So here you are, in the middle of cult activity, in the company of known organized crime figures, and at the assault of peace officers."

"And television stars," I pointed out.

"You're admitting it?"

"No, I wanted to make sure you have your bullshit story straight so you can hear how ridiculous it sounds before you tell it to a grand jury."

"You're Russian Mob, aren't you?"

"I'd need to check my date book."

He smiled then, like he'd just caught me in something. "See, I know exactly who you are and what you've done. I even know why. You see, I know things. I know you're Russian Mob, but not Jewish, for example."

"I'm as Jewish as fuckin' Castro," I said, bundling a *Leb-*

owski reference into a meta-gag no one would get except me and my old pal Lebanon, if he weren't soup.

"Whatever you say, Mr. Zorotovich." The smile grew. He really thought he had something here.

"Okay, let's pretend for a second I *am* this Zoroaster guy."

"Zorotovich."

"Right, him. Still doesn't explain why I wasn't booked or why I'm being interrogated by a government stooge who doesn't even have a badge."

"Racketeering, loansharking, and now links to a couple assaults and murders? You're moving up in the world, Nick."

"You've got nothing and you know it," I said, for the first time taking the guy in, trying to figure who he was really working for, and why he was bothering me. "Now why don't you tell me what you want? This isn't about putting me away or you'd give what you got to the boys in blue. No, you want a favor like everyone else, and you're going to lean on me until you get it."

"You're a disruptive influence here."

"I'm minding my own business."

"How much were you paid for the golf course hit?"

"To my knowledge, there was no golf course hit." This was true, but I didn't expect him to believe it. Brady's people tried to off me because that was her plan all along. I don't think she got paid for it.

"And to kill Vassily the Whale? Who hired you to do that?"

"Whaling is illegal in the US. I looked it up. Maritime law and all that." While I kept my face relaxed and mocking, my brain was whirring. He knew some, but not all. And he actually sounded confused and maybe even upset over Vassily's death and the gunfight at the golf course. He didn't look like Russian Mob to me, and he sure wasn't an Ana. If he had a connection to Brady through the government, he would have brought her up. Someone else, then.

"Lot of work for a hitman in Los Angeles."

"Is there? Maybe I'm in the wrong field. Is there like a class you take, or is it more a weekend seminar thing?"

"Who's your next target?"

"I'm not a hitman."

He slammed a palm into the table. "Who's your next target?" he repeated, shouting this time.

"Settle down, or those cops you convinced to let you in here are going to check on us."

He glanced over at the door, and I used that moment to slip the paperclip off Vassily's mugshot and palm it.

"Answer me," he growled, trying to be scary.

"Worried that another hit is going to destabilize this nice little thing everyone has going here? You worried about all-out war?"

"And if I am?" He seemed too straightlaced to be with Xanadu or the Harmonic Convergence. I'd guess INT-13 if I wasn't one hundred percent certain the guy got seasick if he even *looked* at a boat. New World Order, maybe? He had that stink on him. They weren't peace lovers, but their one-world government schtick made them a little more peaceful than the really scary spooks.

"I'd remind you that it's in no one's interests to start anything too big. The reason this whole thing works is because we all want it to. The minute someone steps out of line, they tend to get smacked back into it by the status quo."

"What game are you playing with here, Zorotovich?"

"Would you really believe me if I told you? Here's some truth for you: I didn't kill Vassily, I didn't fire a gun at the golf course or anywhere else, and I've never seen that car before in my life. You're wasting your time with me." I paused for a fraction of a second, tempted to give up Brady's name. Do that, and I would lose any little leverage I had. And then Mina might rot in prison. They didn't care about her. "You're aiming a little low."

"Do you know who killed Zhukovsky?"

That cinched it. He was NWO, and they were in the dark about what was happening. They hated being in the dark, since their whole gimmick was being an Orwellian gateway to a dystopian future. I'm serious. It's on all their internal marketing.

The NWO knew me as Dwayne van Owen, amateur snoop. It's possible this guy didn't recognize me. There's a lot of internal bureaucracy with that order, and a low-level schmuck like me could have fallen through the cracks . He might actually have believed I was Nick Zorotovich.

"I don't know who pulled the trigger, no."

"Who made the call, then?"

"Can't tell you that."

"Then I'll give you to the police. Even if they can't pin that on you, there *is* a warrant for your arrest. Were I to tell them who they have, that would be the end of things for you."

"And for you, too. Put me away and I clam up. You get nothing else."

"I'm getting nothing."

"You're getting nothing *now.* That might change if you, say, brought me breakfast. It's got to be, what..."

"Five in the morning."

"Seriously? Did I doze off before you came in? There's a Jack in the Box not far from here. Why don't you get us a couple artery-cloggers and some coffee and maybe I'll fill you in on everything that's happening."

He stared at me, his eyebrows knitting into an admirably stern expression. He really was trying to get me to feel like I was talking to Dad. It might have worked on someone who had one of those. I smiled at him.

"Very well," he said. "I'll return as soon as possible. You stay here." Now he smiled like he'd made a joke. The file went back into his briefcase and he left the room.

I had no intention of sticking around. I gave him five minutes, then straightened the paperclip and popped the cuffs. I stood up and stretched my back out, massaged the cuffed wrist, and generally tried to alleviate the stress of spending the last couple hours in the same awkward position. I placed my improvised lockpick on the center of the table because I'm a dick and cracked open the door.

Outside, the police station ran like nothing strange was going on. Uniforms brought in suspects, did paperwork, or milled around and bitched. A few suspects cursed; most were sullenly silent. A young woman sobbed somewhere. Everyone looked strung out and exhausted. Perfect atmosphere for a guy like me. Fatigue reproduces many of the same symptoms as alcohol, and I had just been handed a way to get out of a station full of, essentially, drunks.

I straightened the tie and brushed off the suit, trying to look a little more respectable, and walked out into the station. The key to looking like you belong is twofold. The first is confidence. Act like you're supposed to be there and your chances of getting hassled fall like a stone. Dress the part and your chances fall even further. I probably could have used my badge, if only to flash it when needed, but that had been confiscated back at County.

I squared my shoulders and strode for the front door. No one really looked my way, and I didn't go out of my way looking for anyone else.

Except for that crying. It wheedled into the part of my brain that was still a social primate out in the Kenyan Rift Valley and had to keep the group in good spirits so we wouldn't all get eaten by lions. I turned around, and the waterworks choked off right as I saw who it was, since the sobber had seen me too. The tear-streaked face belonged to Heather Marie Tooms. She was sitting right by a detective's desk, probably in the middle of giving some statement or another. Safe bet it was about me.

She stood up, and the actress in her put a look of happy hope all over face. I swallowed a curse and turned around, hunting for a side exit. Right as I did, the front door to the police station opened and a group, led by Brenda the Satanist, walked in. I recognized some of *those* faces as the pod people at the Crimson Gaze theater. And here they were to finish whatever creepy-ass thing they were planning to do to me yesterday. This was entirely too many people who wanted me dead.

I briskly headed for another end of the station. I stopped at an empty desk and made a phone call. The voice on the other end was muzzy; I'd woken her up. "Hey, I need a ride."

"Who is this?"

"It's Bob."

"Bob?"

"You know, Jack?"

The recognition flooded into her voice, though she was only barely more awake. "Bob? Do you know what time it is?"

"The g-man said around five in the morning? Look, I'm really sorry, but I need a ride and my car was torched."

"Your car was what?"

"I'm at Wilshire Station, and if you could step on it, I'd really appreciate it." I hung up and quickly called an all-night pizza place in the right neighborhood and ordered sixty pizzas. They were used to that kind of thing and just quoted a price. I told them I had cash.

I hung up, then turned around to get my bearings.

Right into Heather. She grabbed me and planted a kiss on my surprised mouth. "Oh, there you are, Jim! I was so worried!"

"WHAT THE F... MMMPH?" SHE CUT ME OFF with another kiss and I got my mouth shut in time. I didn't need this crap.

She pulled back just a bit, wrapping an arm around my elbow and calling across the station. "Detective Wahl! I found him!"

A confused detective, walking in from the breakroom with two coffees, gave her a puzzled nod, then looked the two drinks with the disappointment of a man who had just lost out on coffee with a pretty woman.

"Goddamnit, Heather, do you have any idea of the danger we're in?"

"Oh, you are such a negative aspect. I was hoping you had turned over a new leaf."

"In one day?"

"The ladder to spiritual perfection can sometimes seem like an elevator!"

"Oh, Jesus. Look, there are, like, twenty Satanists here, and they're not too happy with me."

"About what happened at the Church?"

"Different Satanists."

"How many different kinds are there?"

"In LA? Three and a half."

I tugged her toward the side of the station, pretty much where I was going before, only this time with a crazy person who might or might not want me dead. The Sons fanned out across the station. Some were intercepted by cops, but there were so many of them they slipped through the cracks in the social defense. They acted lost, confused, never forming an overt threat.

"What do they want you for?"

"Sacrifice, probably. And they won't be overly picky about you, either. You're with me, you die too."

"We're in a police station. Why not wait them out?"

"Uh... I'm sort of arrested right now. If I stick around, the guy who knows that will come back and my life gets so much worse."

"I really think your dishonesty is impeding your enlightenment."

"You're probably right about that."

"If you only applied Dr. Wood's technosis properly, you'd live a much simpler, more honest, and less violent life."

"You should have quit while you were ahead."

I passed a bare desk, and sitting right next to it was the NWO man's briefcase. Of course. He had claimed a desk in the bullpen. I grabbed the briefcase and kept moving.

"Is that yours?"

"Yes, Heather. I had them hold onto it for me."

A hallway led out into the parking lot. Outside, the blue of dawn was giving way to the light of the day. I was a little disappointed when I hadn't passed any pink boxes full of donuts on our way through the station, but oh well. Escaping custody was more important than the gnawing in my belly.

I turned. A single Son had made it into the hall behind us and he was closing fast. The nearest cop was out in the bullpen, so I said, "Heather?" and pointed.

He lunged, and she grabbed him and used his momentum to introduce his head to the wall. We were out the door a second later. Heather grabbed my arm again, her posture saying this was a romantic gesture, but her freaky grip strength saying this was *her* arm now and I was only renting.

She dragged me out to the busy street and I hoped my ride would beat the g-man back. "What are we waiting for? My car's..."

"Not getting into your car. Try to pull me over there and I'll take my chances with the Satanists."

Heather didn't call my bluff. We watched the traffic on Venice Boulevard and the few people out there early on that Friday morning probably thought we were a cute couple. Heather had changed into a skirt, tights, and long sleeves. That alongside my *Reservoir Dogs* suit and we were a cool pair after a night that went on longer than either of us had planned. Under the swaying palm trees, it was practically a postcard.

The green Prius pulled to a stop on the corner. I glanced through the windshield and saw Lara mouthing, "Get in the goddamn car."

I got in shotgun and Heather dove into the back.

Lara looked like hell. Her hair was all over the place and she didn't have a bit of makeup on. She hadn't even had her coffee, and if memory served, that meant we were all in danger of being beaten with the nearest unsecured object.

She pulled away from the curb and I saw the NWO g-man driving through the intersection, eyes glued on the police station. I slumped down in the seat.

"Okay, you best explain what's happening right now."

"I got into some trouble with the law. It's not my fault."

"You know I could lose my job if they saw me helping you."

"Thank you?"

"Goddamn right, thank you." Lara glanced in the rearview mirror at Heather. "Hi, I'm Lara."

"Heather. I'm so happy to meet you!" She snaked a hand into the front seat that Lara took uncertainly.

"What have you been saying about me?" Lara asked out of the corner of her mouth.

"Nothing. She's... she's like that."

"Ah. Where are we going?"

I punched an address into her GPS. The Cylon voice set a route out snaking into the nearby Hollywood Hills.

Lara looked into the rearview mirror for long enough to establish who she was talking to and said, "I've heard a lot about you. You're a model?"

"Actress, actually," Heather said brightly. "I did some modeling when I was younger, though."

"I thought you had red hair."

"I've dyed it red for parts!"

"Wait," I said, finally realizing what was happening. "This is not my girlfriend."

"Then who is she?"

"She's an assassin who was trying to feed me to some ur-right-wing assholes."

"Then what the fuck is she doing in my fucking car?" Lara screeched.

"Really enjoying the company," Heather said brightly.

"She was trying to take me in back there and there hasn't been time to ditch her." I mouthed "yet" even though I was certain Lara knew that was implied.

"I don't know what passes for a brain inside that head,

but you have a plan, right?"

"Kind of. I'm sort of making it up as I go."

She sighed. "Where *exactly* are we going?"

"The temple of the Guardian Servitors of the Anorectic Praxis."

"Who?"

"Anorexia worshipers."

"And why are we doing that?"

"Because they want to kill me. I've found in my long experience of being the city's whipping boy that when multiple groups want to kill you, it's best to let them fight it out."

"Or get them together to kill you even deader," Lara muttered.

"I kind of want to kill you," Heather piped up from the backseat.

"You barely know me," I said. "Besides, you technically want to take me to people who will then kill me. It's totally different."

"Bitch, you touch a hair on his head and I will *break* you." Lara had mastered the Mom Voice and both Heather and I instinctively sat up and quieted down.

"Thanks, Lara," I said.

"Don't 'thanks, Lara' me. You put a crazy woman in my car."

"I'm not crazy," Heather said. "I know all of Dr. Wood's teachings by heart."

"Sorry about that," I said.

The GPS voice directed us into the Hills, getting snippy the one time Lara missed a right turn. I wondered how long until Shub-Internet got its digital tentacles into these things, or if that had already happened. Maybe if the thing flickered green or started chanting I'd know for sure.

On the stereo: "Far Away" by Nickelback.

What, seriously? It was bad enough that I had to give

voice to that thought.

"What?"

"Are you actually listening to Nickelback?"

"What's wrong with Nickelback?"

"Jesus, Lara, if you have to ask..."

"Goddamnit, don't make fun of my music. I rescued you from the fucking cops at the ass-crack of dawn."

"Yeah, but had I known about the Nickelback, I might have surrendered."

She smacked my arm and turned it up. I silently waited for the hackneyed lyrics, grunting vocals, and what I can only describe as the sounds guitars make when they beg for death, to do what they had obviously been designed to do. I closed my eyes and fought to retain my sanity in the face of raw douchebaggery, wondering if I would still be the same person when I emerged on the other side. Probably not. That man was dead now.

To attempt to distract myself, I opened up the briefcase. There's a trick you can use to break into a combo-locked brief-case. Input whatever combination you like. I prefer "666" be-cause I've seen *Pulp Fiction* too many times. Then push the clasps inward. That resets the combination from whatever the original owner used. Then you push the clasps outward. Bam. Open sez me.

The case contained the file the g-man had tried to intimi-date me with. The pictures were in there, as was a copy of Nicky Zorotovich's warrant. I looked it over, but it told me nothing other than the fact that it looked totally legit. Brady either faked it really well or she used her contacts to actually put out an arrest warrant on a figment of my imagination. I was mildly relieved to see there wasn't any picture attached, just a comfortably vague physical description, known associ-ates (including people like Vassily the Whale), and a list of places to find me. I folded that stuff up and put it in my jacket. He had a file on Vassily as well, along with ones on Vinnie Cha and Carmelita Donella, hinting that he had been staking out Kosher Nostra hangouts and I had gotten unlucky.

He had a few business cards identifying him as Leonard Rice, and one reasonably fancy pen. I closed the case.

After a hundred thousand years in hell, the car stopped and the stereo silenced. I thought it might be bad form to weep for joy, but when I looked into the back seat, I saw that Heather was already doing that. Or suffering one of the numerous crying jags that came courtesy of her command of all of Dr. Wood's technosis.

We were at the crest of the hill, where the street dead-ended into a gate. Beyond was the Temple of Anamadim. It looked like the lair of a *Miami Vice* villain crossed with a game of Tetris played by someone with a grudge against Pythagoras. Gleaming white geometric blocks were stacked on top of one another, with the occasional window peeking out from shadow. I wondered if the architect had suffered a crippling head injury right before designing the building.

In there I was known as Ivan Cohen, which was one of the odder aliases I put together. The difficult part was understanding an alien mindset, and I mean that as someone who has dealt with actual aliens on many occasions and can even understand them a little. Cohen's bio started as a fashion designer, but I had to make sure he failed, like most of my aliases. He was making clothing too small for even the walking sticks they call runway models to fit into. I posted a few rants about the increasingly large women in the fashion industry in relevant comment threads and created a blog of my tiny designs. I did shockingly little research to play a fashion reject, and generally just thought of the most horrible thing to say and then said it. I fit right in.

Outside the gates, three hatchbacks waited, the little shining dorsal fins advertising for "La Pizza Nostra." In the back, hot bags were stacked high, keeping pizzas toasty warm that would tragically never be eaten. At that thought, my stomach gurgled, and I briefly considered attempting to bribe one of pizza guys for a slice or eight. No, I had to focus on the task at hand: breaking into the temple.

"There a party in there or something?" Lara asked.

"I ordered the pizza. I needed a distraction. You should get out of here. The last thing you want is a bunch of Anas on your ass."

Heather and I got out of the car.

"Are you sure? You said she wants to kill you."

"Don't worry, I'll be safe. Well, as safe as I get."

"You forgot your briefcase."

"It's not mine. I'd appreciate it if you destroyed it."

"All right. Good luck, Bob."

"Thanks. I'll let you know how this all turns out." I patted the roof of the car. Lara put it into reverse, three-pointed, and was back down the hill. I stared at the Ana compound, already bright even before the full light of day. Behind us, the city stretched out all the way to the ocean.

A long driveway led back from the gate. The grounds were set around a circle and a cross, with a fountain in the middle of the cross and lawns in the slices. The figure at the center of the fountain could only be Anamadim, since there was no way anything else could possibly be that thin. She looked ready to snap apart in the first insistent gust, but she had remained intact. Most disturbing was the water, dripping from her mouth and slashes in her wrists to splash into the clean pool below. The grass was bermuda, possessing some of the thinnest blades there were. I knew from experience those sections of lawn were as soft as a bed.

The hill rose up a little more on our left, paralleled by the Anas' high iron fence. Unlike the artificial landscaping inside the compound, the slope was the uniform dusty brown of the LA hills, a few shrubs tenaciously clinging on and fluttering in the wind. I climbed up onto this, following the land at a quick trot. I turned to find Heather easing her way up the path behind me.

"You might want to pick up the pace," I said. "The Anas will be out any second. I basically just committed a hate crime on their lawn."

She moved faster, the wheels turning in her head.

"Before you think about grabbing me, remember you have no ride, and you're surrounded by your mortal enemies." I paused. "Well, you will be. Give it a minute."

"So I should grab you now?"

The front door to the temple opened and some of the monks wandered out into the sun. They did everything with a dazed expression, blinking a lot in the bright light. Their skin had paled with starvation, making the darker-skinned members look grayish, while the Caucasians turned almost translucent. The Anas were dressed in flowing white robes, their skeletal faces, hands, and bare feet the only flesh visible. Their hair was falling out in clumps, a badge they wore with pride. After all, they had defeated the human need to eat.

"Too late," I said with a smirk.

They shuffled toward the gate slowly, clearly fighting the horror of being confronted by carbs.

"We have sixty pizzas? Thirty pepperoni, thirty sausage and mushroom?" asked one of the drivers, a baffled-looking teenager who must have thought he was about to be the protagonist of a Romero film.

I swear one of the Anas hissed like a vampire seeing the sun. This is how rumors get started, people.

With the attention of the Anas in the yard, and likely the entire compound to boot, focused on the pizza delivery boys out front, I turned to the fence. It was formed from thin steel rods, pointed at the top, and painted white. Two horizontal bands of metal ran about a foot above the bottom and a foot below the top to connect the whole thing. It would be a rough climb any way I sliced it. The funny part was, back in school, I was the one who couldn't scale the rope. Actually, at my school it was a steel pole, but I still couldn't do it. I didn't get used to climbing anything until I started this bizarre life and every other job took place behind a fence, on the second floor of a locked building, or on a rooftop of a CHUD-infested warehouse. I grabbed the posts of the fence and leaned back, trying to let my weight stick me onto the bars. For about the millionth time since I was five years old, I wished I were Spider-Man.

Heather might have actually *been* Spider-Man, because she was up that fence in a second. I hauled myself up and over, promptly lost my balance, and thumped heavily to the earth on the other side.

"Ow," I said philosophically.

Heather landed gracefully next to me. "What now?"

I got up to find that a good bit of my black suit was now covered in yellow-brown hill dust. At the gate, the Anas were telling the pizza guys to get out of here in voices that sounded like they were trapped at the bottom of wells and asking for help. The pizza guys, probably at the end of their graveyard shift and now comfortable they weren't dealing with the risen dead, angrily demanded payment.

"Back entrance. Stay away from the central temple. You're thin, but to them you might as well be Vassily Zhukovsky," I told Heather.

"Who?"

"The monster at the Satanist Church."

"His life is ruled by anger."

"Hard to argue with that."

We circled into the backyard, where a free-standing garage was pressed into the corner of the property. Like everything else, it was painted a bright white and somehow managed to look like it actively repelled dirt.

I popped the lock on the back door effortlessly. This place had probably been a mansion at one point, bought and repurposed by the starvation goblin the Anas referred to as the Reverend Mother. As such, the room I had found myself in was most likely intended to be the kitchen. Kitchens, as any devotee of Anamadim would know, are blasphemous. The cupboards had been taken out of the walls, leaving bare patches decorated with very spare, very modern, art. The stove was gone and the gas lines had been carefully hidden with an end table featuring a fluted vase and a single slender orchid. The refrigerator was still there, and morbid curiosity caused me to open it.

Water. Bottles and bottles of it. All of the same brand too, Shining Spring, which was an Ana front. I'd done deliveries for them, and had once driven the tanker truck from the Hollywood Reservoir, where they stole the water, down to the bottling plant in Wilmington. Public water the Anas stole, later sold for a buck forty-nine a pop. Pretty good business model, that.

"What is this place?" Heather whispered.

"It's hard and disturbing to explain. Come on."

We went into a hallway. The left side was open, columns marking the border between a combination living room/ place to sit silently and starve. Being extremely hungry myself, I thought the space was a restful place to feel this way. Very open, very airy, and nothing to remind one of food. Other than some shouting from the gate, the place was quiet.

I crept to one of the windows facing the front and peeked through. Three more Anas had joined the others and they were holding hands in a semicircle around the gate, singing a wispy incantation against hunger. The pizza guys were backing off, frightened. Less of the freaks behind the gate, and more because several sedans had pulled up to box the pizza delivery cars in. Large men in dark suits, their slicked hair shining in the sun, had gotten out. They were the ones shouting.

Satanists? If so, these weren't the Sons, shadowing me from Wilshire Station. These guys were big and scary, with the sharp suits of paid assassins and the complicated goatees of Tony Stark. They really did look evil.

"What is it?" Heather whispered.

"New guests."

"Who?"

"I don't know." I wasn't a fan of those three words, and considering the dues I'd paid, I shouldn't have to say it about any group. Yet here I was doing exactly that. A year was a long time. Enough to get a whole city to turn on you, apparently. "Come on, the living quarters are this way."

I led her over to the north wing of the mansion, where a staircase led up into a mirrored hall. A year ago, I'd seen a good length of this hallway shattered into a million pieces and I had only been able to escape because I had remembered that shoes were a thing. My assailant, the woman I was now hunting in her own home, had not. I couldn't duplicate the glass-shattering trick—that had come courtesy of Mothman—but I had brought a killer of my own. Hopefully it would even out.

Everything in the hall, including the doors, was mirrored, and the damage from my previous visit had been repaired, like it never happened. Getting to the doorknobs was a little difficult, but I managed, even if I looked like a one-eyed man trying to give the T-1000 a handjob. I had no idea which cell Brady was in. Odds were good she was here, though, since in this place she was safe while she took out her former comrades one by one. I had to take the doors as they came, opening, peeking in, and closing one after the next. Most of the cells, bare rooms equipped with a cot and a few fashion magazines, were empty of people. Some held an Ana sleeping through her hunger pangs.

I was halfway down the hall when a door opened and Ingrid Brady stepped out. She was dressed in her g-man disguise, complete with wig and mustache. Her pale blue eyes widened when she saw me.

I advanced, Heather right behind me. "Hello there, Ingrid."

Ingrid Brady recoiled, and in a frightened voice asked, "Why are you trying to kill me?"

IT WAS SO FAR FROM WHAT I EXPECTED BRADY to say when she slapped eyes on me, my brain was left groping for a response like a blind guy at an orgy.

Brady, regaining her equilibrium after only a moment of sheer horror, settled back into a kung fu pose, her hands quivering with—I hesitate to say fear, since I am only dangerous to things that have already been killed, properly seasoned, and lovingly cooked. Heather moved up next to me, watching Brady with open curiosity. In the mirrored hall, I could see every side of everyone, from the small gap at the back of the neck where Brady's wig didn't reach to the tag sticking up out of Heather's skirt.

"You know, I was going to ask you the same thing," I said to Brady.

"After you fake a rendezvous with one of my people and ambush me?"

"First off, 'your people'? If VC was one of your people, why the fuck did you put a bullet in his head?"

"I never shot anyone except that ape of yours!"

Oh. Right. Elias. I wondered if he'd managed to get home. I wasn't looking forward to talking to the Illuminati next time. How do you tell someone you lost their golem? There probably wasn't a Hallmark card for that.

"He's sort of immune to bullets. Common sense, too."

"What do you want?"

"You killed Neil and Vassily." I realized that sounded wrong, so I continued: "I'm not really mad about that last one. But the first one, yeah."

"I never touched Greene. I only *tried* to kill Zhukovsky and then only after he came after Constantinescu. I knew I was next. I caught him up in the hills the other night while he was getting ready to execute someone. I put several clips into him, but that disgusting fat monstrosity wouldn't go down."

Oh. Ingrid Brady had saved my life. That was a weird thought to have.

"Then you didn't frame Mina Duplessis?"

"No!"

"Don't act shocked. You tried to have Vassily kill her."

"On orders from the Reverend Mother! I never wanted to make a martyr out of that cow."

I took an involuntary step forward, raising my arm. I'm not a violent guy, but calling Mina a cow made me want to hit Brady on so many levels it was irresistible. The problem is, I'm so unused to committing any kind of violence, I had no idea what sort of fist I should make, and ended up with this loose devil-horns kind of gesture. Here's the weird thing: she flinched. Brady *flinched*. This is the woman who, when we tussled in this very hallway last year, rolled me up with all the methodical brutality of Anderson Silva fighting Dennis Nedry. It was like a fight between Ryu and Frogger. She was Bruce Lee and I was every Chinese guy in 1972. I had been mercilessly beaten down and would probably have been killed had not Mothman bailed me out. And here Brady was, flinching.

"You're telling the truth? You didn't kill any of your old cronies? You haven't tried to kill me?" I asked.

She looked at the cocked hand and flinched again, like the devil horns were really intimidating. Maybe she wasn't a metal fan. "No! I swear! We can even call that first hit and your ambush of the handoff even."

"Ambush?"

"At the golf course."

"Those weren't my people. I thought those were your people."

She shook her head. "Then you aren't going to kill me?"

It was probably silly, but I had to know. "Why are you so afraid of me?"

"Because you're a wizard!"

Sometimes a sentence can hit with more force than the punch of a trained martial artist. I might even have staggered. I was caught somewhere between laughter and total bafflement. "I'm sorry, I don't think I heard you."

"I've seen what you can do. You shattered these mirrors with the force of your mind. Then Burt Shaw went after you—Burt Shaw, an agent with forty years of experience. Real Cold War experience. He went after you and just vanished. The agents who came back from that night told some weird stories. I know what you can do, and I promise if you just let me live, you'll never hear from me again."

"Uh... huh."

My mind was reeling from my latest hypothesis getting completely unwound in front of me. I tried to find another explanation of what the hell was going on and realized I had no hope of it in the high-stress situation I was in. I was going to have to talk to the woman who, until moments ago, I had thought of as my arch-enemy. My Magneto, my Joker, my Larry Bird.

"Listen, Ingrid, I have no interest in hurting you. Assuming you continue your policy of not killing Mina and Oana, that is. And you stop that Quackenbush bullshit with the fascist dictators down south."

"Agreed," she said quickly, nodding to emphasize just how important this was to her.

Right then, the distinctive pop of gunfire came from the front gate.

And then there was the click that came maybe an inch behind me. In the mirror, I saw Heather holding a pistol to my head. "All right," she said, beaming happily, "you talked to her. Now it's time for you to come with me."

"Would it help if I told you she technically works for Quackenbush Security?" I asked, pointing to Brady.

"Actually, I worked through Shaw. After you killed him, there was a purge. I barely survived."

"Seriously? You couldn't lie to the crazy woman with a gun for five minutes?"

Heather sniffed, the tears already beading in the corners of her eyes. "I really wish everyone would stop calling me crazy. I'm not crazy. I'm the sanest person you know! I've learned all of Dr. Wood's lessons! I've mastered his technosis! I've—"

She didn't get out the rest because Brady, in a blur of cheap cologne, was on her. She grabbed the wrist of Heather's gun hand. The pistol went off, deafening in the hallway, and we were showered with little bits of glass from the ceiling. That was the only shot she got. Brady twisted Heather's arm, sending the gun skittering away across the floor, where I picked it up. Brady popped an elbow into Heather's temple, tossed her over a hip into the floor, and slammed a fist into

Heather's jaw. The Rosicrusophist killer was out in under five seconds.

"Well, okay then," I said. "Shall we?"

Brady nodded.

Outside, the sounds of gunfire had multiplied. It sounded like a pitched battle.

I handed her the pistol. "You're going to need this."

"You're not worried about me having it?"

"Wizard, remember?" I waggled my fingers at her and she cringed a little.

"Come on. My car is in the garage."

She led me over Heather's unconscious body and back out through the kitchen to the garage with the roll-top doors. Brady touched a button on her keyring and the second garage door from the left opened. From the front of the house, I could hear the different kinds of guns: the light pop of pistols, the chatter of submachine guns, and the car backfire of a shotgun. Good to know there were a lot represented. I hoped Hank and Rey made a ton of money off that deal.

At a glance, I knew Brady's car was a thin white Porsche that could only have been more '80s if it had a Nagel print on the side and was blaring Flock of Seagulls. Nothing else in the place fit her quite as well. She jumped behind the wheel and I was next to her in an instant. The car had admirable pickup, and as she skidded around the turn for the straightaway to the gate, spraying up a wall of gravel and dust, I was fairly certain she'd already hit sixty. For my part, I was trying not to panic, mostly because I don't remember Gandalf ever panicking and I was going to give this wizard thing a try. My fingers had closed into a white rictus around the front of my seat, though.

On the lawn, a few white robes fluttered in the wind, the fallen Anas so thin as to be two-dimensional when lying flat.

Others had retreated to the nooks and crannies of the geometric house, firing weapons at the gate. Up ahead, two black sedans had formed a roadblock and the dark-suited men were peppering the Anas with gunfire. Where the bullets struck the house, little plumes of white were freed to wash into the windy blue.

The gate creaked open. Slowly. Much more slowly than Brady's Porsche.

"Uh, Brady?"

She hit the gas. I don't know if the stars in the windows turning into lines were actually there or if I imagined them. I knew Chewie had fixed the hyperdrive this time, and the world was about to spin into a barrel roll as we made the Kessel Run in less than twelve parsecs. The men at the gate had become aware of the low white car barreling at them with no regard to safety, physics, or object permanence.

"Hey, Brady?"

Maybe she had been conditioned so that every time someone said her name she had to go faster, because her foot came down harder on the gas. It had to be scraping the floor by now. I imagined the Grim Reaper was sitting in the back seat waiting calmly for us to plow into the roadblock. I prayed for airbags, knowing this car didn't have them, and even if it did, they would be likely to rebreak my nose as a best-case scenario. The gate opened at the same stately pace as always, used to reacting to the slowed synapses of an Ana acolyte, not to Ingrid Brady, a woman whose starvation had turned her into something almost superhuman.

"Bra—"

That's all that came out as the car streaked through the gap in the fence. I winced, cowered, and generally tried to retreat into the shell evolution had so cruelly denied me. I expected the scream of metal, maybe for a sideview mirror to get clipped off and go hurtling into the gravel, or just a cacophony like the sound of a hundred empty drums rolling into a quarry. Nothing. Nothing except the two sedans and all the guys with guns who were just figuring out it might be a swell idea to, you know, make us fail the next Ana weigh-in via the injection of lead into our bodies.

Brady pulled the parking brake and spun the car into a controlled skid, spraying up the best smokescreen of dust, gravel, and cancerous rubber smoke I'd ever see. She gunned the car, spinning around the back end of an enemy sedan. The guide rail was less than an inch from her car, but it never touched, and as soon as she saw open road, she hit the gas again and we were at warp speed. I think they got off all of one shot, and it never even came close.

She slalomed down the winding street, heading back into the city. She merged the Porsche into traffic on Franklin and instantly slowed, at once blending with the herd.

"What did you want to ask me?" she said finally.

"Does this car have a place to vomit?"

"Of course," she said, touching the glovebox. It opened, revealing a selection of airline barf bags. "Sometimes one of the sisters has a lapse and it must be corrected."

"I think I changed my mind."

"Suit yourself. They're in there if you need to. Or if you want to lose some of that disgusting flab around your middle."

"I think it gives me gravitas. Or possibly gravity. I forget which."

"What did you really want to ask me?"

"First, I need something to eat. Could you get me to someplace that serves breakfast? What's good around here? Right, dumb question."

"I am not going into a restaurant, wizard or not."

"Then take me to a place with takeout. I don't care where."

She sighed, taking me to a deli. It was an upscale place, used to serving the rich and famous of the Hollywood Hills. They made an egg sandwich and coffee, and frankly that's all I really cared about.

I got back into the car and Brady was scowling. "Open a window. It smells like a chicken's ass in here."

I rolled down the window.

"I can still smell it," she moaned.

"Take us somewhere where we can talk and you won't whine."

She sighed, peeling off from the traffic and gunning it back up into the hills. I barely paid any attention, instead savoring the aromas Brady found so horrifying. If you ever get to the point where bacon, eggs, and cheese smell bad, it might be time to reassess your life. That's all I'm trying to say.

Eventually, Brady pulled to a stop. A clean hillside looked out over Hollywood. It was actually very pleasant, even with Brady for company. I had a seat on the curb, watching the traffic on the 101 move through the Cahuenga Pass and into the Valley, and enjoyed my sandwich. After several bites, I felt the look. I turned, and sure enough, Brady was starting at me in rapt horror.

"Seriously?" I asked her.

"Do you know what that's going to do to you?"

"Stop my stomach from sounding like a Tibetan throat-singing choir?"

"Cholesterol. Building up in your tissues. Making you slow, sick, stupid. It's going to kill you."

"Does cholesterol kill wizards? Because Elminster never mentions it at our weekly meetings."

Now the look said she was trying to figure out if I was being serious or not. I took the time to polish off the sandwich and wipe the savory grease off my hands with a napkin.

"What do I call you?" Brady asked.

"Huh?"

"Erick Levitt? That's what they call you at Quackenbush Security. Or is it Nick Zorotovich? Jonah Bailey? David Antonucci? Brandon MacGruder?"

"The name's Blank."

"All right, Mr. Blank." She considered. "That sounds fake."

"Very much so."

"Ask me what you're going to ask. You've already made me watch that disgusting act with the heart disease time bomb, so you might as well talk."

"You mentioned a 'first hit' back there. Did someone try to kill you?"

"Sunday morning. You used Victor Charlie's protocol to contact me, so you know about the ways we arranged meetings."

"In broad strokes."

"Each member of the group had a different protocol to contact one another. The first step gets the attention, second says the kind of meeting, third verifies the sender, and the fourth selects the location. Anyway, I went to my usual dead drops. I wasn't expecting anyone, since after Shaw's disappearance, our group has been somewhat quiet. That morning, I saw Oana Constantinescu's protocol. I followed it, and she set the meeting at Forest Lawn Cemetery in Glendale. I never trusted Constantinescu. Not completely."

"Because she's V.E.N.U.S."

"Correct. Their devotion to an outmoded body form threatens not only the health of the present generation but of our daughters and our daughters' daughters. Constantinescu was only in the group because of Greene. He recruited her. Said she could be trusted. Of course, now Greene is dead."

"You knew about that?"

"By Sunday, of course. Even if I don't retain contact with

my group, I keep tabs on them. I knew when Zhukovsky was arrested at the V.E.N.U.S. compound, and I knew when Greene's body was found."

"Were you worried Oana was trying to set you up?"

"The thought crossed my mind. The Guardian Servitors expected V.E.N.U.S. to retaliate after the hit on Duplessis came to light, but they never did. Eventually, we figured they might not. Anyway, I decided to trust my former ally, but I took a pistol. Trust, but verify."

"That's actually the opposite of trust."

"It's a good thing I did, because a hit squad was waiting for me, one that looked like the men in front of the Temple of Anamadim," she paused to draw a finger over her mouth, in the Ana equivalent of a Catholic genuflecting, "today. Might be the same men for all I knew. I fought my way out and returned to the temple. I only left in disguise after that."

"Speaking of which, what's up with the drag? Is it for the mystical power or an identity dodge?"

"A little of both."

"Makes sense." I put what Brady told me with the rest of the information I had. The puzzle was beginning to take shape, and fit better than it had when I had thought she was behind it all. Fewer forced pieces, certainly.

"If you're not trying to kill me, then who is?" she asked.

"Okay," I said slowly. "I think it shakes out like this. About a year ago, I had a run-in with Burt Shaw at the Griffith Observatory. You probably don't know this, but Neil Greene was there as well, with a team of Satanists."

"What was Greene doing with Satanists?"

"He was one."

"I thought he was just a Freemason."

"And you're just an Ana."

"That's Guardian Servitor," she sniffed. "Ana is a pejorative term cooked up by those behemoths in V.E.N.U.S."

"Neil was a reasonably high-ranking member of the First Reformed Church of the Antichrist."

"How high-ranking?"

"I don't know, deacon? I never asked. I saw him at a party."

"You were at a Satanist party? That should not surprise me."

"It's a wizard thing. Anyway, Neil and any number of other Satanists witnessed what... uh... what happened to Shaw. Because of certain assumptions that had already been made..."

Brady cut me off. "What assumptions?"

"That I might be the Antichrist."

"Are you?"

"I don't know! How do you know something like that?"

Brady fell silent. "Did you know your father?" she asked finally.

"Well, no."

"Did you grow up with large, scary dogs?"

"Are you just running through what you know from *The Omen*? Because newsflash, not real." Everyone knew *Rosemary's Baby* was the docudrama, but I didn't want to throw gasoline on this particular fire.

"I've never dealt with devil worshipers extensively!" she snapped.

"Anyway, taking what they—and I cannot emphasize this enough—*thought* they knew about me, they assumed the creature, I, ah, I summoned, was Satan. And he took Shaw to Hell."

"What was it actually, and where did it take him?"

"How the hell should I know?"

She moved another butt-length away from me on the curb. Well, butt-length for me. It was like eight or nine for Brady.

"All right," I continued. "Neil takes this story back to the cult. They're thrilled. They've seen Satan in the flesh and he's in LA. They get ready for his coming. A group maybe takes things too far, thinks the heads of the two big cults in the city are doing things wrong, so they set up their own group, the Sons of the Crimson Gaze, and start stealing converts from the Church, the Order of the Morning Star, and even the OTO. Neil either joins and thinks they're going too far, or else he finds out about it after the fact. So they kill him. Neil had already brought in Vassily Zhukovsky as a convert, which is how they knew about you, Oana, and VC, and now they're killing everyone who knew about Neil's connection to other corners of the Information Underground. They framed Mina because she was convenient. They knew about her from the party, where she basically humiliated them by walking out with me."

Brady chewed it over, since it was the closest thing she would get to protein. "I'm not sure."

"Neither am I. But we'll find Neil's killer at the headquarters of the Sons."

"We?" Brady asked.

"Yeah. You're in this with me now. Someone tried to kill you, and that same someone offed my friend and framed my girlfriend. We both want the same thing. Conspiracies make strange bedfellows, Ingrid."

"Never, ever, imply that you and I are in bed together."

"I didn't say we were having sex. We could be watching *Project Runway* or something."

"Stop talking please."

I dusted myself off and looked out over the city. She was still beautiful, even if the last couple days had made it abundantly clear she was mad at me. And who could blame her, really? Walking out on her for a year, only to come back unexpectedly and start doing my whole roguish noir antihero thing and stirring shit up. Maybe coming back had been a bad idea. But as the wind brought me the clear salt smell of the Pacific and I closed my eyes and felt the sun on my face, I thought maybe I had rushed to judgment last year. Maybe the city wanted me back after all.

"You coming, Blank?"

"Yeah, yeah. Sorry. Monologuing." I tapped my temple and got into the car.

Brady gunned the engine, spinning the car around on the cul-de-sac and burning down the hill. "Where's this headquarters?" she asked.

"An old theater on Hillhurst. Los Feliz." I kind of wanted to talk to Brady about what had happened. It's not like we were friends or anything, but straightening a few things out would have been nice. After I McClaned her in that hallway last year, I had followed it up with the colossal dick move of sending her a pair of shoes. At the time I felt justified, but it really was unseemly. With all the lying and betrayal, we should have more of a collegial atmosphere. Yet I couldn't quite bring myself to broach the subject. It helped to remind myself that in the scheme of things, she had been involved with some pretty bad people over at Quackenbush Security.

Just like me.

On the stereo: some horrifying self-help stuff.

A woman who sounded maybe a thousand years old spoke in a frog's croak about the power of denial in the self. She ranted—in a soft, grandmotherly way, but still—about the tyranny of eating and how it was an artificial concept real humans could do without. I didn't mention it to Brady and she didn't comment, although occasionally she would make a little noise of agreement in her throat and nod ever so slightly.

The drive was a relatively short one. I directed her to park right around where VC and I had the previous day. It felt like a hundred years ago. I was going to start measuring everything in dog years just so it would make a lick of sense later when I tried to unpack the whole mess.

"That's the theater?" Brady asked.

"That's it. I'm thinking there should be a side entrance and we use that."

"What exactly are we looking for?"

"We'll know it when we see it." I put a lot of confidence in my voice. Maybe Brady was convinced. I sure wasn't.

I ducked down the narrow alley running between the theater and the dry cleaner next door. A gutter ran down the middle and a single Dumpster slumped against the side. The alley barely looked big enough for a single car. A fire door led inside, and the lock clunked open after a second of tinkering with a section of wire hanger I found under the Dumpster. Brady and I went into the warm dark of the theater.

We were in a small corridor, with three stairs leading to another door. This would be the side exit. I opened it a crack. I recognized the booming voice, even if I wished I didn't.

"Nobody expects me. Not even my family. I show up to Thanksgiving and it's like, bwah! Boom! Pow! And I have a headache, so it's time for some stuffing." The voice, with its Valley inflections and lazy vowels, belonged to Rodrick Rand, movie star and member in good standing of the First Reformed Church of the Antichrist.

"I am certainly pleased you're here, Mr. Rand." That voice belonged to Hollis Nguyen, who appeared to be the current leader of the Sons and former member of the Order of the Morning Star. "Our condolences in your time of mourning."

"When the little guy got blown away, it was amazing, like his life force just shot right into... have you ever had a Bangkok Balloon?"

"I'm sorry, a what?"

"It's where you get, like, a narrow hose and pump liquid

cocaine into your cock."

I supplied the confused frown in the pregnant pause that followed. "I can't say I have."

"It's fucking amazing. Stick with me and you'll get one. And a Backwards Cactus, Four-Fingered Push-Up, maybe a..."

"We can catalogue the various sex acts later, Mr. Rand."

"It's called a Balloon because it's like you're getting inflated. *With cocaine.*"

"I figured that out."

"When the midget died, his life force went right into my cock. And now it's like I have his soul in me, too. Only I ate it with my penis and now I am power."

"Right, yes. My condolences. And congratulations."

"Fuckin' ay."

"So, with you as the nominal head of the First Reformed Church of the Antichrist, we need to formalize your absorption into the Sons of the Crimson Gaze. This will of course begin with your ritualized rejection of your former heresy and an initiation..."

"And then you make me the leader."

"No, Mr. Rand. We already have a leader. You will be... well, think of yourself as a bishop, though we do not need titles. The important thing is making this world a welcoming place for our lord and to prepare as much of the population as possible to follow Him."

"By beating them in a cage match, one by one."

"No, to alter the culture and educate the masses."

"With face kicks."

"No." Nguyen sighed, going for a different tack. "I don't have to tell you how much informal power a celebrity of your stature holds in our culture." He paused, as though expecting Rand to say something insane.

"Go on," Rand said.

"Oh. I thought you were going to tell me about... doesn't matter. The point of this is, with your assistance, we can reach a wider audience than ever before, and our message, the true message, carries with it the weight of someone the listener already trusts. Has already invited into his or her home."

I opened the door a bit wider. Because of the way the door swung, I could only see into the audience, rather than what was transpiring onstage. There were a few people in the crowd I recognized, including Brenda. Some of the other faces were from the theater earlier, others from the Church. I trusted in a combination of religious rapture and my black suit against black walls to camouflage me. If there were answers, they would be backstage.

"Yeah. The midget wanted me for the same reason. I'm a hot commodity. On fire!"

I moved purposefully down the aisle, never once looking over to catch anyone's attention. I was up the stairs and behind the curtain in a few quick strides. Out of the corner of my eye, I saw that they had a table set up onstage, the house lights on Rand and Nguyen. A few others were onstage with them, all in costumes I remembered seeing in the dressing rooms downstairs.

"We were beginning with a little community theater, but with your connections... I have a screenplay. It's called *Son of Heaven*, and it would be perfect for you."

"Do I get to play Satan?"

"I was thinking the Antichrist, but really, the choice of roles would be up to you."

"Incredible. I'll take this to Mark, Tommy, Uwe, Zack... we'll get this thing made."

I was struck with a deep ambivalence. On one hand, I wanted to bring down the conspiracy and get Mina out of jail. On the other hand, that movie sounded so amazingly terrible

I couldn't help but want to midwife it into the world. I was in the kind of pickle that would normally be solved by Mina smacking me on the arm and telling me to focus. See, this is why I needed her around.

Safely out of sight from the Satanist conclave, I finally turned around and saw that Brady had followed me. "Was that Rodrick Rand?" she asked.

"Yeah."

"I remember when he won the Oscar."

"Right, yeah. For *Shining Tall*. He played the handicapped transgender Iraq War veteran." I thought about it. "That movie sucked."

"It did. And that woman who played his wife was far too fat to be in any Hollywood movies."

"She was hospitalized for anorexia."

"She's doing it wrong."

I realized then that arguing with Brady was a waste of both our time. I needed to ransack this place for anything that might help put this whole thing to bed. And while I hoped for a giant book titled *The Entirety of My Evil Plan* by Hollis Nguyen, I was unlikely to find something more damning than a couple receipts or an internet search history featuring some combination of "shaved," "tanned," and "bison."

I passed the dressing rooms and kept opening doors. I found a maintenance closet and a bathroom before I got to an office tucked way into the back. It held a single cluttered desk, a bulletin board so full it looked more like the plumage of a very flamboyant bird, and a computer that had probably served its original Cro-Magnon owners well. This was how these idiots were attempting a Satanist coup?

Not just attempting, but winning.

There was literally no way this was their headquarters, no matter what anyone was saying. This was the place we were supposed to *think* was their headquarters. The public façade, while someone else directed things from the shadows. Give their enemies a convenient place to focus hostilities.

"Well? Aren't you going to look for your clues?"

"There's nothing here. You're welcome to tear this place apart. It'll only take you six or seven years, and when you discover the theater isn't properly reporting its income, you can take that right to the IRS."

"What are we doing, then?"

"I want to take a quick look in the other rooms. You should go out and get the car. Last time I had to get out of this place, I had to move fast. After that and the adventure at the police station, they probably won't be so easy to give up."

"Police station?"

"Do you really want to talk about my record right now?"

Brady's fake mustache twitched, which was one of the funnier things I'd seen that day. She left. I gave the office a once-over to make sure my knee-jerk assessment had been accurate. There wouldn't be an address lying around, would there? Probably not. A look through the bulletin board and the desktop didn't yield anything of interest. At least not anything my brain could piece together. I needed Carrie Mathison to come in and pinch hit, but she'd probably just end up sleeping with Rand.

I poked my head into the dressing rooms. Empty. I went back upstairs, my next move still nebulous in my head. I felt like I had hit a dead end, forced to sit on my hands while the asshole in the shadows made his play. More time for Mina to be miserable in jail. More time to threaten me or Oana. Or Brady. She was sort of an ally.

I came upstairs and nearly jumped out of my skin. Mothman was right there, waiting for me. I was behind the second curtain, in the corner of the stage where they kept unused props, sets, and costumes for easy access. Someone had hung the Mothman costume up so that he was invisible when going downstairs, but would be the first thing you'd see when you came back up. I was impressed that Brady hadn't yelped. I almost did, and I kind of knew the guy.

As my heart started to get back into its normal rhythm, a plan started to form in the section of my brain that was between Jason Statham and Morgan Freeman. The kind that actually thought about incredibly stupid ideas, debugged them, and put them into practice with the assumption that everything would work like aces.

Which is why, a minute later, I was inside that sweaty, bulky monstrosity, waddling out onto the stage. "I am your lord!" I boomed from inside the Mothman outfit.

IT WASN'T THE FIRST TIME **I**'D IMPERSONATED a deity. Through the eyeholes, which were probably around where Mothman's mouth would have been if he'd had one of those, I could see Nguyen and Rand getting up. Nguyen stood smoothly, more confused than frightened. Rand jumped away in terror, his eyes huge, sending his chair thumping across the stage. He scrambled to his feet. The rest of the Satanists backed away to either side of the stage.

"Holy shit," Rand whispered.

"I don't know who—" Nguyen started.

I cut him off. I had to. The human brain, if allowed to work, naturally arrives at a distrusting place. If it continually gets interrupted, especially with things it already sort of believes, it can be strung along. "I am your lord!" I boomed again. "It is I, Lucifer, known as Asmodeus, come to save and also doom the world."

This is where I was going to have trouble with orthodoxy, and if that isn't a universal concern, I don't know what is. The problem was, in the room I had members of all three sects of

Satanist, and they had some widely varying views on what made a good Adversary. The Asmodeans would be expecting someone so ridiculously evil even Serpentor would tell him to tone it down a notch. The Luciferians were all about the misunderstood rebel thing, treating the devil like he was a combination of James Dean and Che Guevara. And to top it all off, I was in the nominal headquarters of the one goddamn cult in LA whose bullshit I didn't know backwards and forwards.

So I was going to have to wing it.

"You have called! I have answered!" Seemed nice and vague. "I have come to guide you to... the kingdom!"

At that moment, with a metallic thud, the house lights went dark. I could see, because the lights in the false eyes of the costume shone with a red glow, washing across the front of the audience and the two heads of the Satanist conspiracy presently onstage with me. I'm sure I looked much more impressive now, a looming shape in the dark with hypnotic eyes. A lot like the real Mothman. Ominous music, so quiet as to be almost subliminal, grew behind me.

Brady. She had gotten to the control booth and she was backing my play. Three cheers for teamwork.

"Ask! Ask your lord what you will of him!" I managed, needing a little assist.

"Lord? Are we working Your will?" Nguyen asked, now cowed a bit by my performance.

"That's a good question!" I yelled. "Remind me what that is again?"

"Lord?"

"I've been in Hell!" I glanced at the Asmodeans in the crowd. "Torturing the unjustly condemned!" And then the Luciferians. "Which includes me! So I've had a lot on my plate recently!"

"Well..." Nguyen said, chancing a look out of the corner

of his eye to see if anyone else was buying my act. Rand was weeping openly, so that answered his unspoken question. "Yes, well, we're uniting all the devoted under one roof, of course. And then we will begin spreading Your message far and wide."

"...which is?"

"Now that You are here, You can tell us."

"Right! Well, for one thing, no more eating high fructose corn syrup! It causes obesity and diabetes! Satan has spoken!"

"Yes, my lord."

"Also, you should shower every day! And really wash under your armpits! Deodorant is a supplement, not a substitute! Satan has spoken!"

"Of course. Should I be writing this down?"

"Every Friday shall henceforth be known as the Day of the Dance! You will dance everywhere! Walking is forbidden on Friday! Satan has spoken!"

"Someone get me a pad and paper!" Nguyen hissed. "It's unfortunate the prophet is not here to receive your teachings, Lord. He will be so disappointed."

"I, too, am disappointed! I hoped to meet my prophet in the flesh! Up until now, I could only speak to him through pictures of kittens wearing bonnets!"

The Asmodeans murmured angrily.

"...who are participating in ethnic cleansing!"

The Asmodeans calmed down. The Luciferians murmured now.

"...for really good reasons you'd find out if you just talked to them for a second!"

"Lord, if you can manifest whenever you choose..."

"You dare question Satan? I am here now!" Nguyen was trying not to cower. I was getting really good at this. "So, remember, lot on my plate lately, but could you remind me who the prophet is?"

"You don't know?" Nguyen asked.

"We do not deal in names! I know him as Swirly Plaid Aura Man! It is likely he has a different, more human name for use with trifling mortals!"

"Of course, Lord. We know him as Jonah Bailey."

"Wait, what?" Surprise made the question come in my normal voice.

"Lord?"

"Did you say Jonah Bailey?" I boomed.

"Yes, Lord."

Jonah Bailey was the name I used with V.E.N.U.S. I had never used it to start a Satanist cult. Never once, no matter how many times I had been tempted.

"Where is Jonah Bailey now?"

"He's making sure that traitor Sam Smiley gets what's coming to him."

Sam Smiley, the name the First Reformed Church of the Antichrist thought was mine. Now there was an eerie feeling: one of my aliases was trying to kill another one of my aliases. I did a quick mental calculation and determined there was absolutely no way I set all this in motion. No, this time Mr. Blank was real and he was out there trying to fuck me over.

"And how is Jonah Bailey going to do that?"

"He's getting..."

The opening chords of Boston's "Peace of Mind" rang out through the theater. First Nguyen, then everyone else in the theater was looking around in confusion. Only Rand was not. "The music! The infernal music!" he blubbered.

"Hold that thought," I said, snaking one arm out of Mothman's wing and fishing the phone from my pocket.

"Bob? It's Dan Onanian." Mina's lawyer.

"Not really a good time, Dan. Can I call you back?"

"Uh, sure, but this is..."

"Thanks." I ended the call. "All right, where were we?"

"It's just a costume! He's an impostor!" Nguyen screamed with the righteous hatred only the truly religious can muster.

"Blank! Hold still!" Brady's voice, from across the theater.

I obeyed, and was rewarded with gunshots popping from the back. Nguyen fell, a hole blooming in his shoulder. The other Satanists dove for cover. I unzipped the Mothman suit and threw the head at Rand, who screamed in terror.

"Satan has no head!"

I hopped out of the costume and ran for the side door. A moment later, Brady pounded down the aisle. The Satanists were beginning to get up, but Brady waved the pistol at them. "Stay down!"

From the stage, cradling his bloody shoulder, Nguyen pointed at us. "Get them! Any who fall will have rewards in Hell!"

Some of the Satanists charged immediately. Others, the ones who weren't a hundred percent into this whole "worshiping the devil" thing, were a little slower. But soon there was a room full of pissed-off religious fanatics coming at us, and though I wasn't sure how many bullets Brady had in that gun, there weren't enough. She came to the same conclusion after shooting a couple, following me to the door while the great mass surged after us. Brady and I burst out into the alley, with her white Porsche waiting at the mouth, nose out to the street.

The door popped open for a second, a sea of enraged faces on the other side. All of a sudden I was in a zombie movie, and me without a Louisville Slugger. Pushing my back against the door, bracing vainly against the tide of lunatics, I knew we had no shot to get to the car. I was going to get torn apart by Satanists.

"Brady! Help me hold this thing closed!"

"Hold on," she said, running to the Dumpster.

"What are you doing? That's way too—"

I was going to say "heavy," especially for someone who considered ninety pounds to be obese. I had forgotten that weird Ana monk strength of Brady's. She put her back into it, and with a deafening scrape like a giant running his fingernails over a blackboard, the Dumpster inched toward the door.

The door popped open, and for a heart-stopping second my feet were off the ground. I think it surprised the angry mob of true believers behind me, because they faltered, and when my feet hit asphalt, I leaned back and the door slammed into their howling faces.

The Dumpster, throwing out metallic grunts like an over-the-hill robot getting up from a recliner, inched over the doorframe. I stepped away. The door slammed open again, only to smack into the metal hide of the Dumpster. A deep clang echoed down the narrow alleyway, while the hands of pursuing Satanists, turned to claws by religious fervor, reached through the barely open door.

I kicked the Dumpster as a "fuck you" and got my karmic just desserts in the form of a stubbed toe. "Goddamnit!"

"Well, then," Brady said, dusting her hands off.

We hopped, me quite literally, into her car and she gunned it onto Hillhurst before the cultists realized there was another exit.

"So you got nothing from them," she said.

"Nothing worth mentioning."

"I'm beginning to think you don't know what you're doing."

"Only beginning? Listen, could you take me to Griffith Park before you throw me out of the car?"

She grunted what I took to be assent. I took my phone out and called Dan back.

"Dan Onanian, attorney at law."

"Dan, it's Bob."

"Bob! Hey, where were you just now? It sounded like you were in a tunnel."

"Giant monster costume. What's going on?"

He paused for a second, but decided to press on. "I was calling about your girlfriend's case. Something weird happened. All the charges were dropped. Apparently someone else confessed to the crime, produced evidence, knew the kind of things only the cops and the killer knew. The whole nine yards."

"They released her? Is she with you?"

"No, her cousin picked her up. Bob... she didn't mention any family in the city when I talked to her. This stinks."

"You're right about that. Let me ask you something. The killer, he have a shaved head and goatee?"

"Yeah. How'd you know that?"

"Lucky guess. Dan, you're off the hook. Thanks for the help, and if I need you, I'll call."

"No problem. We have to stick together against the Reptilians, right?"

"Oh yeah. Rule number one."

I hung up and turned to Brady.

"I've got good news for you. You're going to get that payback for the assassination attempt."

"You've said that before."

"Just trust me."

"You've said that, too."

"I need you to contact Vassily the Whale."

"Zhukovsky is dead."

"Is he?"

I EXPLAINED THE SITUATION TO BRADY. SHE was dubious, but listened anyway. I told her to set the meeting at Leo Carrillo Beach and she agreed. It was a hell of a situation I had found myself in. I couldn't trust my only ally, not really, and her powerbase had all but entirely eroded. She had lost her connection to Quackenbush Security, and the Anas would be dealing with the fallout of the attack on their temple. She was still a dangerous woman, especially in close quarters, who had once attempted to kill both me and Mina. A blast of paranoia shook me. Maybe she had been lying and really was behind the whole thing.

No. I'd put the pieces together again and they'd fit. In retrospect, it had been right in front of me the whole time, from the minute I looked at the crime scene photos. Something had been off, and now I knew what that was. I had thought the city was out to get me. I was partly right.

Brady dropped me off in the same parking lot I had been arrested in the night before, then spun her car in a redlined three-point turn and floored it like she had seen *Evil Dead* too many times and had developed a tree phobia. I went to the little dirt divider where the three pine trees grew. Beyond was a screen of greenery, and beyond that would be the driving range.

I approached the right tree and stood on my tiptoes, hunting around for the car keys I'd stashed there. I was hoping no one had spotted them, or even worse, some curious bird was now using them to line a nest in the vast wilderness of Griffith Park. There was nothing there. Panicking, I boosted myself up for a better look. Still nothing, except a line of ants marching down a branch. I cursed. I should have asked Brady to stick around until I had the keys in hand, or at least had another way to contact her. Had I just stranded myself in Griffith Park? And would I be a big enough asshole to get Lara stuck deeper in this thing?

I jumped down, still swearing, when something glinted at the corner of my eye. Oh. Wrong tree.

I grabbed the key with the green rabbit's foot and set off toward VC's car. The golf course was eerie after the previous day. It was Friday, and the rolling lawn was free of any golfers. There was no sign of the shootout that had happened either. I wish that kind of thing surprised me anymore, but it didn't. There were too many groups with a vested interest in keeping things quiet. Unless whoever controlled the cops these days had a specific mad-on for the cabals involved, there would likely only be the odd mention in News of the Weird or a story buried in the back of the *Times* saying nothing of import.

I reached the place where I was pretty sure VC had died. There was no sign. No suit, no goo, no bullet. It was as if he never existed, and according to most sources, he had not. The clearing, between several pine trees, had slightly fewer pine needles on the ground considering the wind that had been blowing all week. That was all I'd find. Rest in peace, Victor Charlie. You were memorable. I felt a little silly getting maudlin over a brainwashed mutant, but he had helped me out. I hoped I could at least bring the people responsible down.

I passed the place where Brady's companion had fallen. No outline, no blood. She was gone as well. If there was a story about her, it would probably be called something like, "FASHION MODEL DEAD OF LEAD POISONING" and the text would detail something that couldn't possibly be true. A young woman, found her in her apartment, shot. The police would call it a suicide, but the pistol in her apartment had never been fired and the bullet dug out of her was a large caliber only suitable for assault rifles. It was amazing how many murders got covered up as suicides, and yet the people in charge still left these colossal plot holes. There it was again, so obvious now that I stopped to think about it.

VC's Caddy was waiting right where we left it. The key crunched in the lock and I opened up the heavy door. The Genesis Flail was on the back seat, sitting in the harmonic converter. The engine turned over with a barbaric rumble. I hoped to borrow a little of that confidence for the evening.

My first stop was to my ID guy for a new set of papers. Javier regarded me impassively, his scalp shining between the stubborn strands of hair glued to the other side of his head, and quoted a price. While he worked up the documents, I ran a few errands getting the rest of what I needed: a couple stage lights, some cellophane, batteries, and a remote control. I picked up the ID a couple hours later and drove out to the meeting site.

Leo Carrillo State Beach is one of the more beautiful beaches on a stretch of coastline known for beautiful beaches. Bordered on the landward side by the rolling avocado-colored cliffs of Malibu, the beach seemed secluded even though the two-lane Pacific Coast Highway ran right by it. The beach was distinctive for the large lava rock formations rising from the sand like a craggy prehistoric creature emerging from the deep to mess up Tokyo. It's most famous for guest-starring in movies, and there might have been a tiny part of my id that picked this for its appearance in *The Usual Suspects* when the guys bury Benicio del Toro. Maybe I hoped Fenster's ghost would look after me and babble gibberish at the people who would shortly be arriving to kill me.

I pulled into the parking lot across PCH. Only one other car was there, a salt-scarred Range Rover with a surfboard rack on the roof. The guys were probably in the water, catching the last couple waves before the sun went down and the California Current turned the water into liquid nitrogen. The new papers went into my breast pocket and I took the bags of electrical equipment and the Genesis Flail from the car. An underpass led from the lot to the beach itself, the cars passing overhead on PCH surrounding me with an unearthly hum.

The two surfers passed me in the tunnel, their wetsuits peeled to the waist, their skin and hair fried from a day in the sun. We exchanged a nod, and I felt their eyes on me as I emerged from the tunnel. After all, I was dressed like a jazz musician and carrying what looked like grocery bags and a radioactive rock on a chain.

I sat the bags down in the sand and went to the closest of the rock formations. I placed the Flail next to the lava rock, winding the chain around it carefully. I judged that by sunset, the hungry tide would cover it up, and by the time my guests showed up, it should be totally hidden. It wasn't immediately obvious, even though the colors didn't match. The natural formations ranged from a sunburnt yellowish to a rich chocolate; the Genesis Stone was a glowing gray, the same color as a full moon in a clear sky. The texture matched almost perfectly, though.

I returned to the bags and assembled the lights. I placed them in pairs on three different rock formations and covered the ends in cellophane. I had to wade out into the surf for one. They would be easy to see in the clear light of day. At night, though, they should be invisible. After all, they were stage lights, designed to be unseen in the dark. I silently thanked Hollis Nguyen for that idea. From the oil-drum trashcan at the mouth of the underpass, a cartoon raccoon shot me Disney eyes, imploring me not to litter. I obeyed, stashing the bags in the trunk of VC's car. I didn't need my hand tipped. And last, I keyed the remote. After a few tests, I got the hang of it.

All that was left was the buzzing of nerves in my limbs. A hundred questions flitted through my head, all useless. Would Brady do what I asked her? Would she sell me out to Quackenbush to get back in their good graces? Was Mina still alive? Couldn't think about that. She was still alive. She was fine. And she'd be home soon.

A slender shape emerged from the tunnel, walking into the golden light of the falling sun. It was Brady, and with her aviator shades and her mustache slightly askew, she looked like a skinny blond Burt Reynolds. I was laughing a little when she stopped a few paces from me. My pants were soaking from the water, caked in salt and sand.

"What?" she snapped.

"I was thinking about something else. Not how you look like Burt Reynolds."

She sighed, clearly getting tired of our association. Couldn't blame her. Only one more thing, then I'm either dead or victorious and our association was at an end. "I sent the message. What now?"

"I need you to move your car. I don't want them seeing anything else in the parking lot. Then come back and stay on the other side of that underpass. If they try to make it out, I need you to stop them."

She stared at me, eyes invisible behind the black lenses. "You're sure this is going to work?"

"Wizard, remember?"

She nodded like I hadn't just made a joke. "Good luck, Blank."

"You too, Brady."

She trudged up the beach, the setting sun turning her back gold. The tunnel swallowed her up, and a moment later, her little white car was zipping up the road for the next parking lot. I really hoped she was going to be back in time. Whatever else I might feel, it was still nice to have a heavy hitter around. A sympathetic Quackenbush hit squad would have been better, assuming I wasn't the top target on their list, but Brady would do. Beggars, choosers, and all that. I sat, my back to the Pacific, the harsh wind ripping at my clothes like flags, and powered my phone up. The Ana Temple had made me think of Tetris and I had a couple hours to kill until the meeting time at the numerologically approved twenty-three hundred hours.

The sky turned pink right as a dark blue Mercedes pulled off the road and into the parking lot. I cursed inwardly. I wanted the beach deserted for this. There was going to be some crossfire, a little magic, and a whole lot of stagecraft.

But the car did not look like the vehicle someone would take to the beach. And who would be showing up so late?

I stood up, sand falling off me to be carried away in the wind, and squinted toward the parking lot.

Showtime?

Fuck.

I straightened up, knowing I didn't look nearly as tough as I hoped. The broken nose might help a little for that, but not enough. My legs were frozen to the knees by the gusty wind. I peered into the tunnel, hoping this wasn't what I knew in the pit of my stomach it was. They got the message. They got it early.

My plan wouldn't work in the daylight. I was a dead man.

Three silhouettes, almost entirely eaten by darkness, appeared in the tunnel, growing larger as they approached. Which was difficult in at least one case, since that silhouette was about as big as any human being could be while still be considered *Homo sapiens* and not something Jabba the Hutt might use to guard his basement. It was Vassily "the Whale" Zhukovsky, his shoulders rolling in that distinctive aquatic lumber of his. He loomed behind the other two smaller figures like the Hulk in an Avengers group shot.

The sun hit the other two figures, and if there was any doubt about one identity, it vanished. Mina's hair shone blood red in the dying light of day. She had pinned it down, but it looked like a rat's nest, probably not having been washed since her arrest. She wore the same thing she had when she drove from my place back to hers, an old Stone Roses shirt and a pair of ripped jeans. She was the most beautiful woman I'd ever seen, like always, and I wanted to do something horrible to Vassily, whose gold Desert Eagle flashed in the sun as he pointed it at her head.

The other figure was the smallest, though walking with the most confidence. His head was shaved, though there was a clear tan line where his hair had used to be. His dark goatee was mostly stubble, but it was growing in nicely. He wore a tailored black suit and a red tie, and was grinning at me like he'd just played the best joke ever on someone. The pistol in his hand was trained on my heart.

The group stopped about fifteen feet away from me. All three were squinting into the sun, which was a nice bonus, even if it was the sun that was going to kill me. I was Takezo at the end of *Duel at Ganryu Island*, ready to use geography against the other samurai. Yeah, right. In reality, I was just some lovesick schlub about to try a Hail Mary against a pair of multiple murderers.

In a scene like this, the woman is usually crying. Not Mina. She just looked angry, like she was waiting for Vassily to drop the gun so she could render him incapable of having children.

"Hello, Neil," I said.

"Hello," Neil Greene answered. "What do I call you? Colin? Jonah? Sam?"

"I get that question a lot. The name's Blank."

"Blank it is."

"I like the new look. Pretty evil."

"Thanks. You have to look the part if you're going to do what I do."

"I'll bet. You admit to your Satanist pals you own Care Bear PJs and you're a dead man."

"What is Care Bear?" Vassily asked.

"Hey, Whale. I heard you were dead."

"Heard same thing about him, too!" Vassily laughed.

"Nice trick. What'd you guys use for a corpse, a beluga whale?"

"Who needs a corpse?" Neil asked. "The only people reporting it were Satanists."

"Good point."

"What happened to your nose?"

"Stuck it where it didn't belong. So, what do you say you let Mina go? We three can have a nice talk, just like you intended."

"Sorry," Neil said. "The girl stays for now."

"Uh, Neil? You might not want to refer to her as 'the girl' or she might forget about the gun and turn your balls into a dugout canoe."

He flinched and looked up at Mina. She nodded. He stepped away. In a desperate attempt to regain control, he sneered, "So you figured it all out, huh? I thought you might. Hell, I counted on it."

"Let's see. You were there that night at the Observatory. You tried to save me from those other guys with guns."

"Don't be coy. I know they worked for Quackenbush Security."

"Sure, you do *now*. After it went down, using your contacts, you found out that was Burt Shaw, and who he worked for. You also saw... what you saw."

"Yes, I saw your father take Shaw into the sky at your behest."

"Right. That. Anyway, after that night, you pieced together what you could and guessed at the rest. I vanish along with a couple fairly big players and two powerful artifacts. You had to figure the Antichrist was gearing up for something pretty big."

Neil waggled those caterpillars he called eyebrows. He hadn't bothered to pluck them into anything more evil, which he really should have talked to his stylist about. "Oh yes."

"And you knew my names." Well, six or seven of them, but I wasn't going to give the guy the store. "You saw how much power I'd lucked into by walking between the conspiracies, and you knew I'd somehow gained a little bit of a rep. It was a rep you figured you could use. You know, once you eliminated everyone who knew differently. The first step was creating your new group. You knew what Satan really looked like, and that he was back, so it would make sense to form a cult. You started with disenfranchised members of the First Reformed Church, then widened the net to the other Satanist groups. Your big coup was snatching Hollis Nguyen from the Order of the Morning Star. I'm betting he brought a good chunk of membership your way."

I glanced at Mina. It took a lot of self-control not to just run to her. As strong as she was, she had spent a week in county lockup and the rest of the time with a Satanist and a gangster. She needed a hug. Hell, *I* needed a hug.

I kept talking instead. "You know when I finally realized it was you? When I thought about how it felt like the city itself was out to get me. But it wasn't the whole city. Just the one-seventeenth of it you controlled from your desk."

Neil grinned at that.

"It was bugging me the whole time, too. Ever since I saw the police report on your 'murder.' I've been around a lot of that in my time. More than I'd like. And the thing that every murder in the Underground has in common? Overkill. Nothing's ever normal. Nothing's ever neat. A man shot in the back of the head with a shotgun and everything pointing to a love-sick woman? No, sorry. Too neat. Too simple. Too sane. Not unless she's also an alien mind-controlled by the Templar."

"I wanted you," Neil said. "It had to be something only you would see. Took you long enough."

"I'm out of practice. So you needed to put me back in play, and you needed to deflect suspicion from yourself. You knew Mina from the Satanist party and you saw her again at the Observatory, so you figured she was important to me. You kill two birds with one stone by faking your death and framing Mina. I'm guessing you got some poor homeless guy and you switched his fingerprints with yours in city records."

"All correct so far."

"You knew the only person you could really trust in this thing was Vassily. Not because he's especially trustworthy, but because he's the kind of sociopath who would love to consolidate power in LA. No offense, Whale."

"None taken. I am sociopath. I took test."

"Along with the faked fingerprints, you created some

dummy parking tickets and forged emails. It would have been easy to steal Mina's credit card number. Seriously, sweetie, you need to buy a shredder."

She shot me a look telling me to get on with it. But I couldn't, because the sun had decided to become stately in its waning moments. It wouldn't sink below the waves until it was goddamn good and ready. If I tried my plan now, they might take enough time to laugh at me before the bullets dropped me and then her.

I continued. "You sent Satanist hit squads after two members of your little gang, and both bounced. It was blind luck that you managed to get Victor Charlie at the golf course. You were officially in scramble mode. You had Vassily kill Paul Tallutto to ensure you would be the last man standing in that particular cult. I imagine you planned to do the same to the leadership of the Order of the Morning Star and the OTO."

Neil shrugged. "If I was going to take over, I might as well make it a clean sweep."

"I don't suppose that if I promise you I'll get out of LA and stay gone, you'll let me go."

"Sorry, Blank. To become the Antichrist, you have to kill the Antichrist."

"You might be thinking of the Highlander."

"No more jokes."

"You know, Neil, during my trouble last year, right after the guy tried to open up my skull, you were the first person I talked to. You know why? I thought you were too much of a goober to betray anyone. Then I saw you at that party at Paul Tallutto's. I should have known you were a lot more cunning than I gave you credit for, but for whatever reason, my initial impression stayed in place. I actually came down here looking to bring your killer to justice. Can you believe that?"

"You made a shitty Antichrist."

I had run out of things to talk about. The sky had faded to dark blue above and pink behind. The plan was happening now whether I liked it or not. The long shot was going to be even longer than I'd hoped. "Tell me about it. All right. I'm surrendering." Mina's eyes got like big, angry saucers. I couldn't shoot her a calm-down look, either. Not without giving it to Vassily and Neil, too. "We're trading. You let Mina go, and each step she takes away, I take a step toward, got it? I'm unarmed and I'll go quietly."

Both guns pointed at me. The sun still glowed like a molten coin behind me. I'd found the end of the rope and it was time to swing. In my palm, the tiny remote was fairly soaked in sweat.

"Okay," Neil said. I knew their plan. Take me or just shoot me, and then shoot Mina. Not that I needed the exchange to function for my plan to succeed. That should be the first rule in any handoff: never construct a plan that depends on the trustworthiness of a Satanist or Russian gangster.

I took a step forward in the sand. Mina did the same. Her eyes were on mine, trying to employ couple telepathy.

I took another step forward. Mina did the same. I nodded to her. And I knew that look. The one saying, *Are you being a cocky bastard or do you actually have this?*

The sun dipped below the horizon. The residue of light rapidly dimmed. I shot her a look that said, *I have it now, I think, but just the same, you might have to run.*

I took a step forward. Mina did the same. We passed each other.

The sky turned from pink and gold to blue, falling into the vast dark of the new moon. Offshore, the lights of oil rigs began to twinkle on.

I took a final step forward. Mina did the same. In my dim understanding of things, she was far enough away to start the plan. I hit the button on the remote.

Neil's eyes got big as he looked over my head toward a rock formation out in the pounding surf.

I clicked the remote once, twice. Neil's eyes flicked off to my left, his mouth going slack. "Vassily," he muttered. "Look!"

The huge mobster furrowed his brow, peering off into the flamboyant Southern California sunset. "What? Is light."

"No. No, it's not. It's Him."

I clicked it again, taking a step forward. Once more. Neil's attention went even farther, Vassily's following with it.

"It's Him!" Neil shrieked ecstatically. "He's here! He approves!"

I started to run.

I reached into the frigid water, grabbed the chain, and with a salty splash, yanked the Genesis Flail out of the tidepool where I had hidden it. Vassily turned his head, his brow once again splitting into deep furrows as something else happened that he thought he'd never see. I swung the rock, connecting on an upward trajectory, smashing Vassily's jaw back into his temple. I don't care who you are: get hit there, especially with a moon rock, and you're counting sheep. Vassily fell with a continental thump, throwing up a plume of sand.

Neil turned, bringing up his pistol. I swung again, flinging off drops of seawater now glowing silver from the touch of the stone. The pistol went off, but the rock slammed into Neil's hand at the same moment. I heard a crunch and the gun flipped end over end, splashing into the churning surf.

Neil screamed and ran back up the beach toward the tunnel. Right into my trap. Assuming it was there, but I had more important things on my mind at that particular moment.

I turned to say something to Mina. She was apparently already in motion, grabbing me in the nicest hug I'd gotten in awhile. A moment later, she was pressing her lips to mine and it was pretty easy to forget, well, everything. She parted from me. "You don't smell so hot."

"Says the woman who smells like County."

"Thank you, Rabbit," she said, using her pet name for me. "For doing whatever you've been doing. The little guy said that's why I'm out."

"What, I was going to let the woman I love rot in... why are you looking at me like that?"

Her voice was small, rusty. "You love me, huh?"

"Well, yeah. I thought that was assumed."

She smacked my arm, and then she was kissing me again. She tasted like prison food and smelled like the inside of my high school gym locker, but it was the best kiss I've ever had. I wouldn't have minded it lasting a couple weeks. "Guess I love you, too," she murmured when we were finished. "Why are you dressed like you're in a ska band?"

"I had to borrow some clothes from a clone."

She shook her head, then nodded in the direction of the retreating Satanist. "What about him?"

"I have someone waiting in the tunnel for him, probably. It's fine. We can keep making out."

"Rabbit, no. He's not using the tunnel."

I looked. Sure enough, Neil was sprinting across PCH. "Goddamnit. Watch him," I said, pointing to the beached Whale. "I think his gun is..."

"I got it! Just go, before the little guy gets away!"

I ran up the beach, slipping in the sand, my legs burning with every step. I know most people would equate it to running in a dream, but I never had those particular dreams. Instead it felt like trying to run through snot. When I finally hit the asphalt, it was a relief. I climbed the little hill of hard-packed earth and jumped the railing. A car whizzed by on the other side and I dashed to the on-ramp for PCH. Neil was below, making for his car in the parking lot. Brady sprinted for him from the street, apparently having just arrived. She was firing her weapon, the bullets hitting everything except Neil.

He slammed the door shut and the car roared to life. Brady leapt away, but Neil had no designs on her. He streaked toward the on-ramp, and me. I was in the middle of the road, spinning the Genesis Flail, playing chicken without a car. The on-ramp was a half-spiral. Neil, at the base, looked up and saw me. His face went from fear to glee in less than a second. The car screamed around the turn. The headlights haloed me. I swung the Flail over my head like Wonder Woman gearing up for a good lassoing. The car bore down on me. To Neil, I wasn't Wonder Woman. I was a bug he was planning on splattering all over PCH.

In one motion, I threw the Flail and jumped. I sailed over the border at the side, hitting the slope down into the parking lot and rolling, throwing up dust and tweaking the hell out of my shoulder. Above, there was a deafening crash.

And then silence.

Brady was running toward me and I had a brief flash of terror. Was this a betrayal? I mean, it would be the right time for such a thing. "By the sculptor!" she breathed instead, gazing up at the ramp where I had been.

More footsteps, tapping up through the tunnel. It was Mina, running, Vassily's ridiculous gold-plated pistol looking like a giant toy in her hand. "Rabbit?"

I got up, stretching. "Did it work?"

Brady pointed. Mina stopped, relief flooding over her features. I climbed up the little hill and had a look.

The Genesis Flail was buried in Neil's bumper, right where I'd wanted it: on the collision sensor. Neil was slumped in the front seat, knocked out cold by the airbag. I yanked the chain, and with the protest of metal, the Genesis Flail came free. I pulled Neil's unconscious head back from the bag. He was safely in dreamland.

"Damn. Didn't break his nose," I said.

Brady snaked in and popped Neil. His nose squirted bright red blood all over the airbag and he slumped back down.

"It's broken now," she said.

"Uh... thanks. Listen, one last thing. Call the cops. Tell them you know where to find escaped Russian mobster Vassily Zhukovsky, and let them know they can also pick up Nicky Zorotovich at the same time."

"You're Nicky Zorotovich," she said, confused.

I took the papers out of my pocket and showed them to Brady. "Not according to those." Javier had done a great job with what I'd given him. I wiped my prints off them and tossed them into Neil's car.

"What are you going to do now?" Brady asked.

"I'm thinking nudity, adult content, sexual situations, that kind of thing."

"Ew."

"Stay cool, Ingrid," I said, heading down the slope.

"We... we're okay, right?"

I grinned at her. "I think so. Long as you keep up your end of the deal."

"I will." She nodded, taking out her phone and calling the police.

I joined Mina in the parking lot. "I don't know whether to kiss you or kill you for that insanity," she said, pointing to the car.

"Come on. That was awesome."

"Who's the stick?" she asked, looking up at Ingrid, who was speaking very intensely into her phone.

"Oh yeah. You never actually met her. It's a long story... I'll tell you tomorrow."

"Fair enough." She slid an arm around my waist as I walked her to VC's car. Well, my car now. "What's this?"

"Oh, Mina. You are not going to believe the week I had."

We skirted the wreck of Neil's car and rolled up PCH, Mina's head on my shoulder, my arm around her, and we were gone into the night.

On the stereo: Nah, let her get some rest. She'd had a rough couple days.

23

It was all over the news, what with the Whale's Bruckheimerian escape from custody. Neil barely merited a footnote in those reports, referred to, if at all, as "a low-ranking associate of Zhukovsky's." Of course, that wasn't Neil, not legally speaking. Neil Greene was dead. He'd done such a good job faking his death that now that he wanted to unfake it, he was screwed. And besides, all the papers said he was Nicky Zorotovich, and the one thing everyone who had run into Nicky over the past week remembered was that Nicky's nose was broken. Thank you, Ingrid Brady.

I followed the trials with a little interest. Vassily was returned to San Quentin with another twenty years tacked onto his sentence for the escape and the injured deputies involved. Neil was sentenced later, for the racketeering and loansharking he'd put on me, along with aiding a fugitive. Sorry, Neil. Sad part was, I'd done such a good job on the alias, the courts thought "Nick Zorotovich" had a real record.

Three months later and they're cellmates in San Quentin,

where Neil's main hobby is trying not to get eaten.

That's a little unfair, isn't it? Three months in the future without mentioning any of the sympathetic characters? You're probably worried about Oana. I know I was.

Mina and I spent the night at my place. It was already Friday night, and that's date night. The weird part is, she seemed to think the adventure on the beach was a good date. Apparently, she thinks the whole noir anti-hero thing is a turn on. It does finally explain what she's doing with me, at least. Anyway, as I was telling Mina the story and we got to Oana's part, Mina said she should really call her. And then she did. Had Oana's information the whole time. Yeah, that might have been handy.

Ingrid Brady still thinks I'm a wizard as far as I know. I stay out of her way, and I haven't seen her, so I'm going to assume she's staying out of mine. Hopefully seeing what happened to Neil will quash any ideas she has of trying the same bullshit later. If not, I guess I'll deal with that when it happens. At least I didn't send her any dickish presents this time.

I saw Heather Marie Tooms in a Lifetime movie called *Not Without My Uterus* about a woman who marries a Brazilian organ thief and has to later steal her babymaker back from the guy. It was not good. I found it on the DVR again and recorded it for Mina. She will not believe it.

On the other end, Rodrick Rand also went into television, playing the lead in a show called *Suck It* where he plays a heroic vampire. It's terrible, but people seem to like it. Sometimes I see him make the exact same face he had when he was about to sacrifice me, and I just shake my head. Method actors.

There have been a rash of reports of a man in a trenchcoat, scarf, hat, and gloves fighting street crime in LA. No word as to whether he smells faintly of clay. I blame myself.

The Sons of the Crimson Gaze seem to have mostly fallen apart, absorbed back into the same groups they originally poached from. Hollis Nguyen put on his play a few weeks after the whole thing wrapped up, and I went to opening night. Don't worry, I wore a mustache. Mina did, too, which was both adorable and hilarious. The play left me with the intense desire to somehow create a live theater version of a midnight movie. Mina and I spent the whole time eating Junior Mints and trying not to fire them out our noses with laugh-rockets.

I moved back home. Well, not home-home. Mina sold her place in Silver Lake and we held onto my place up north and rented it out for extra cash. I sold the bookstore to Khaali, who passed her citizenship test. She told me she just remembered what I'd taught her and answered the opposite. I was so proud.

Mina and I got a place in Venice together, so I'm trying the whole cohabitation thing. You know, with more than just salamanders. It's actually pretty nice. Everything smells good— other than the axolotl tank, because there is not enough potpourri in this dimension—which is a huge plus, and something I am not used to in the slightest. The axolotls spend most of the time on a faintly glowing rock with a rusted chain bolted to the side and they're seeming a little... glowier these days.

Mina's arrest had shown me I'd been stupid trying to run from LA. The city wasn't going to let me go. Not after everything I'd seen. Hell, without me, there was no one to tell the old girl's story. I knew the secrets like no one else.

Better to use it. I started placing coded ads in the same places I had once found jobs. Offering my services as a fixer, a freelancer, a detective. And wouldn't you know it? I get calls. Granted, a lot of them are for horrifying sexual favors, which I politely, yet firmly decline. But I get actual jobs, too.

Usually easy stuff. Well, easy for me. I can hear Mina: *Don't get cocky, Rabbit.* But I look in her eyes, that secret twinkle that's only for me, and I can see she kind of likes it when I do.

The money's decent, and I'm doing something I'm good at. You can see me tooling around the City of Angels in a 1959 Cadillac Eldorado that still smells new. The Little Green Men never repo'd VC's car, so it's mine now. Call it squatter's rights, or the execution of a nonexistent will. I was his best friend—he'd said it himself in that VC way of his—so I was going to keep his ride. I had it detailed and got it painted white and seafoam, because the black seemed a little too badass for me. I even had the guy paint a little pinup girl on the side. It's no coincidence she basically looks like Mina with green skin and antennae, posing in one of those old-style bathing suits Mina modeled for Hepcat's vintage line. The Caddy's the Roswell Belle, and she's starting to get known around town.

Along with Robert Blank, the magic man who fixes things.

If there's one thing I learned from the experience, it's this: you can't outrun your past, but you can kick it in the ass every once in a while.

And sometimes that's enough.

ACKNOWLEDGEMENTS

I have to thank my wife Lauri, without whom none of
this would be possible. She believes in me even when I don't.
She has supported me throughout this quixotic adventure
into being a novelist, so if you like anything I've done, it
couldn't have been managed without her.

I would also like to thank my friend and publisher Kate
Sullivan. I'm not going into the lavish praise I heaped upon
her previously just because I'm straying into restraining
order territory. She's still amazing and I still admire her.
I still count myself lucky to have entered her orbit.

And of course, I want to thank all of you out there who
have championed my books. If you've left a review, if you've
recommended it to a friend, if you've bought my stuff as a
gift, you have done so much to help me. Indie authors like
me live and die by ratings, reviews, and recommendations.
Thank you for your time, your effort, and your support.
Every time you do that, you help me write another book. You
make it all possible.

ABOUT THE AUTHOR

Much like film noir, Justin Robinson was born and raised
in Los Angeles. He splits his time between editing comic books,
writing prose and wondering what that disgusting smell is.
Degrees in Anthropology and History prepared him for
unemployment, but an obsession with horror fiction and
a laundry list of phobias provided a more attractive option.

FOLLOW THE AUTHOR ONLINE

www.captainsupermarket.com
Twitter: @JustinSRobinson
Facebook: http://on.fb.me/JustinRobinson

The ADVENTURE
CONTINUES ONLINE!

Visit the Candlemark & Gleam website to

Find out about new releases

Read free sample chapters

Catch up on the latest news
and author events

Buy books! All purchases on the
Candlemark & Gleam site are DRM-free
and paperbacks come with a free digital version!

Meet flying monkey-creatures
from beyond the stars!*

www.candlemarkandgleam.com

*Space monkeys may not be available in your area. Some restrictions may apply.
This offer is only available for a limited time and is in fact a complete lie.